BECOMING

Olive W.

S. LEE FISHER

THE WOMEN OF CAMPBELL COUNTY: FAMILY SAGA BOOK 1

Cover Design by 100 Covers
Formatting by Nola Li Barr

Print ISBN: 978-1-7367526-0-9
eBook ISBN: 978-1-7367526-1-6

This book is dedicated to my parents, Robert and Jean Fisher.
Their support and love are constant.

'TIL DEATH DO US PART

WESTERN PENNSYLVANIA, 1905

"*M*ama, Mama!"

Olive, a curly blonde-haired girl with pale blue eyes, climbed onto the bed and wrapped her arms around her mother's neck.

Polly Westchester coughed at the touch of her child. She lay motionless, waiting for the pain of her next contraction. Her children circled the iron bed, watching Polly struggle to breathe. Polly's pale face had assumed a shade of gray. Her eyes reflected the purple and yellow wallpaper deliberately darkened by drawn draperies. Shining on the ceiling, a single dot of light refracted from the daisy-filled crystal vase.

Ben, Olive's oldest brother, grabbed the child around the waist. "Come, sweetie. Leave Mama be."

After carrying her out of the bedroom, Ben deposited Olive in the corner landing of the back staircase, leading to the kitchen. Olive immediately began a backward descent on her hands and knees.

"Do not play on the steps alone, Olive," said Ben, gently. "Stay here and wait for me."

Olive sat on the plank floor, drawing circles with her finger in the sticky, warm, red liquid that covered her legs. A bitter taste filled her mouth as she sucked on her fingers. She gagged.

"Mama," the tiny voice repeated, sobbing.

Her father, Henderson, rushed in from the barn, pushing her aside on his way up the stairs.

"When did labor start? Why wasn't I called sooner? Levi, fetch the doctor. Hurry. Ride hard," Henderson barked at his third son as his calloused hands caressed his wife. "Polly, stay with me. You've done this seven times before. Look at me. Stay with me."

Henderson lowered his head to hear his wife speak. "Where's Olive?" A tear dropped onto her cheek.

"Don't worry about the child. You need to save your energy." Henderson squeezed Polly's hand. Knowing it would take at least ten minutes for Levi to gallop four miles into Campbellsville and another twenty minutes for the doctor's buggy to arrive, he asked anyway, "Where's the damn doctor?"

"Tell the children I love them. Henderson, I love..." As Henderson moved closer to Polly, he stepped in front of the gap in the drapery, blocking the sun's ray; the room went dark. With an expulsion of air, Polly's voice stopped.

"No. Don't. No! You mustn't leave me!" Henderson buried his head in the pillow. He commanded a muffled, "Everyone, leave the room now. I need to be alone with her."

The girls clutched each other while the older boys remained straight-faced and stoic. Salty tears dripped down Fred's face, Polly and Henderson's youngest boy. Reluctantly, all complied, leaving their father alone with their mother. Engrossed in their grief, no one saw Olive sneak past them and back into the bedroom.

The farmer stroked his wife's sweat-drenched, curly blonde hair, his fingers catching in the tangles. His face streaked with tears, absorbed in grief as he gently closed her eyelids. They were married twenty-six years. She bore him seven healthy children—Ben, the oldest, was already twenty-five. The thought caused Henderson to bolt upright. *The baby. What of the baby?*

The quilt under which Polly lay was drenched in blood. Henderson carefully lifted back the bed coverings. He was met with the stench of excrement. The foulness penetrated his nose and mouth. Polly seemed to float in a pool of dark red jelly, polluted with black globules. The expelled fetus lay, lifeless, a mangled blob of flesh and slime, the umbilical cord wrapped around its neck. Henderson grabbed for his mouth, nearly vomiting at the sight. The infant was a boy.

"Papa?"

Henderson, feeling a tug at his trouser, looked down to see two tiny, outstretched hands, pleading for attention. Olive was too small to see the horrors he was subject to. His reddened face twitched at the child. Olive was supposed to be another boy. Instead, the boy lay motionless on the bed.

"Matilda, come get your sister."

Nineteen-year-old Matilda wiped her nose on her sleeve before jumping at her father's order. The remaining Westchester siblings waited outside their mother's bedroom door, hugging, crying, and consoling each other.

"Yes, Father. Come, Olive, we have to leave." Hurrying into the room, she reached for the child's hand. Olive slapped at her sister, refusing to go.

"Papa, Mama!" Olive rubbed her eyes. Tears streaked her blood-stained face. She clutched at Henderson's leg. "Papa, please. Up." She begged with an urgency not understood by her young mind.

Henderson shook his leg in dismissal. Olive slid across the room in bewilderment. Stopping in the corner, she faded into the shadows and sobbed.

Ben's wife, Bessie, reentered Polly's bedroom and picked up Olive, smearing blood over her clean frock. Carrying Olive out into the hallway, she patted the girl's back. "Now, now, honey. You come stay with Ben and Bessie tonight. Your Papa is busy. You can play with Nellie and Benny."

Olive, kicking and wiggling, managed to escape from Bessie's

3

arms. Clomping forward, determined to reach her mother, she cried, "Mama!"

Her lip quivered as she ran toward the bedroom. Twelve-year-old brother Fred's quick reflex foiled her re-entry. Clutching the child by the pinafore, he managed to divert her attention.

"Come on, Olive." This time, she accepted Fred's hand. Looking up into her brother's face, she listened as he said, "Let's go pick some wildflowers. Mama needs them."

Shedding tears of his own, Fred led Olive down the flowing front staircase, across the expansive foyer, through the double doors, onto the porch, and outside to the flower garden.

"Freddy, why does Mama need flowers?" The tiny voice was barely audible.

Fred halted at the garden's edge. His knees buckled as he fell to the ground. Grabbing Olive around the waist, he held tightly. Fred swallowed to wet his throat, but the words still cracked.

"Mama is now a beautiful angel. We'll pick flowers for her to give to God as a present when she enters heaven."

ASHES TO ASHES

*O*live, holding a small bunch of black-eyed Susans, squirmed on the dining room chair, out of the way in the corner. She fussed with her blue silk dress, Sunday best, as family and neighbors streamed in and out of the house, paying their respects. Matching blue silk ribbons held her hair in curly pigtails.

"Olive, sit still. You'll rip the lace." Tildy grabbed unsuccessfully for Olive's arms.

"It scratches." Olive flung her arms away from Tildy's reach, then rubbed at her neck. The stiffly starched French lace caused a rash where it touched her skin.

Tildy scowled at her sister as her siblings greeted visitors. "You better behave yourself today."

Just then, Tommy and Alva Jamison entered the dining room. As Tommy glanced in Tildy's direction, she fluttered her eyes and smiled. Tommy turned away to face his mother. No smile was returned. Tildy bit her lip.

The Jamisons' farm was next to the Westchester acreage. Although a much smaller tract of land—one-tenth the annual yield of the Westchesters'—the Jamisons were also considered members of Campbellsville's elite. Placing various refreshments on a china plate,

Tommy offered food to his mother, trying to cover a conspicuous awkwardness. Tildy's green eyes never left the pair.

"Is he the one who made your belly big?" Olive's chin jutted out as she questioned her sister.

"You little brat. What are you talking about?" Tildy's face drained all color. She pulled at her dress to hide her belly, then looked away from the Jamisons.

"I know about these things. Mama's belly was big. Papa made it that way. Will you be an angel too?" When Tildy didn't respond, Olive added, "I won't miss *you* like I miss Mama."

Olive deliberately grabbed her collar again. Tildy pulled her hand down roughly as she choked on a sob.

"I said stop tugging at the lace! And don't mention my belly or I'll... " Tildy covered her face with her hands. "Oh Mother, how can you be gone when I need you the most?"

Olive jumped off the chair and thrust her hands on her hips, crinkling some of her flowers. "I don't have to listen to you. Only Papa and Mama. Now Mama is in heaven, so I only listen to Papa." She stomped her tiny foot.

Tildy whacked her sister across the face. "Don't you ever say such things to me!" Visitors, including the Jamisons, turned to look in the direction of the slapping noise.

Olive burst into tears. Weaving in and out of the throng of wake-goers, she ran across the foyer and to the back of the parlor, where a large, ornately carved casket sat in the corner between two windows. The afternoon sun cast a golden glow on the surrounding flowers and mementos. Olive stopped short at the sight of her mother.

Polly looked angelic. Her hair was pulled back in purple and yellow ribbons; she held a Bible in her hand. Daisies, lavender, hollyhocks, gladiolas, sweet Williams, and a few lingering roses created a room-sized corsage for the dearly departed. A small, closed, but equally decorated casket sat to the side, in front of the larger one. Instead of flowers, a delicate hand-embroidered blanket draped the tiny box.

"Mama, Mama."

The crowd parted as the child held out her bouquet. Standing on her tiptoes, Olive reached up to her mother. She tried to place the flowers inside, but the casket was too high. Her flowers landed on the parlor rug. Murmurs of *Poor little darling,* and, *Sweet thing,* rumbled throughout the mourners. Polly's sister, a woman strange to Olive, retrieved the flowers. Reaching down, she lifted Olive, enabling her to lay them in the casket beside the Bible. She hugged the child and handed her a cookie. Olive accepted her reward. Polly's sister spoke to Olive gently as she tickled her tummy, carrying her back to the dining room chair.

Olive giggled and kissed her cheek. "You look just like Mama," she said.

Tears welled in Polly's sister's eyes. "Darling, we both look like your mother. You are the spitting image of her when she was your age. I shall miss her dearly." Kissing Olive on the cheek again, she added, "You be a good girl and sit on the chair. Please?" Satisfied, Olive sat quietly, again watching the crowd.

Henderson, standing by the coffin, flashed his eyes at Tildy, who lagged behind Olive. "I asked you to do one thing. Now mind your sister, and keep her on that chair," he shouted over the din of the crowd.

Turning her head from side to side, Tildy searched for a place to hide from her embarrassment. All eyes had watched the incident unfold, including the Jamisons. Mrs. Jamison snickered. Tildy gasped when she saw Tommy drop his head—then, erupting into hysterical sobs, she ran out of the house.

"Tildy, what's wrong?" Ginny, the oldest Westchester daughter, slung her infant son on her hip and followed Tildy down the porch steps. She cupped Tildy's arm as they walked the path toward the front gate. The garden's aroma of lavender produced no calming effect. A cooling summer wind provided no relief.

"Oh, I wish Mother was still here. That wretched Olive, embarrassing me in front of Tommy Jamison." Unrelenting gasps for air choked Tildy. "And in front of his *mother*. She already disapproves. Now he'll never marry me. Adding a Westchester to your family is an honor. Why don't they realize that?"

"Oh, Tildy, dear. You silly goose. If Tommy intended to marry you, he would have done so by now." Ginny wrapped her arm around her sister's expanding waist. "We better face it; we are the Westchester black sheep. Neither one of us shall escape raising Olive. Father won't consider hiring a governess with us around. As much as I'd like to, I'm not going anywhere soon. She's our responsibility now, along with our own children. It's Father's frugal nature." Ginny sighed. "He *graciously* provides food and shelter for us, and expects us to be grateful for that, alone."

"Mother was the gracious Westchester, not Father," said Tildy as she buried her head in her sister's shoulder.

"You must keep a brave face, Tildy. So many visitors shall be pouring in and out during the wake."

Tildy surveyed the massive house and property, a mansion by the town's standards. An escape route from her captor was not evident. "Father has us imprisoned."

"That may be so, but we have no other recourse without husbands," Ginny said, resigning to her similar fate.

∞∞∞∞

Three days after the death, the wake over, Campbell county visited the Westchester estate en masse. Polly and baby boy Westchester were laid to rest in the family plot, on the top of a hill. A large grove of elms stood in the middle of the cemetery, providing eternal shade. Grand monuments marking the life and death of Westchester ancestors dating back to the Revolutionary War occupied the stone-walled graveyard.

Alone, Henderson stood over Polly's open grave. He clenched a clump of dirt in one hand and a single daisy in the other. His fingernails dug into his palms; a drop of blood dripped from his thumb.

Henderson had ignored the doctor's warning. At Olive's birth, Polly labored twenty-four hours. Far too long for a seventh child. There should not have been another pregnancy, but Henderson selfishly insisted they try for another boy, to be his namesake.

Refusing to toss the dirt onto her coffin, he stood staring, unable to imagine the task of either raising or providing for seven children, some with offspring of their own, by himself without her help. He loved his children, but he was a farmer. He understood agricultural management, not parenting; that was Polly's expertise. Henderson's parenting skills were nonexistent. *Ginny or Matilda can raise Olive in exchange for their keep, although both should be out on their own. The younger boys, Fred and Levi, can fend for themselves, but they are only adolescents. Damn you, Polly. I need you to keep this household organized, to keep us all in line. The boys I may be able to guide, but what am I to do with the girls?*

He relied on sons Ben and Clyde to help manage his lucrative farming enterprise. In addition to running the house and mothering the children, Polly helped with the farm paperwork and fulfilling orders. *Polly, you are the driving force behind my success. I need you to ground me, support me, to keep me whole. I'm half a person without you.* Henderson questioned his ability to maintain the same level of prosperity without her guidance.

Squinting in the late afternoon sun, he surveyed the yellow and white rolling hillsides. Polly loved the daisies that grew wild in most of the uncultivated fields. Several exotic varieties grew in her formal flower gardens that flanked the large, covered front porch.

A grand, luxurious work of Georgian architecture, the Westchester home dominated the stand of buildings. Ben and Bessie lived in the original cottage built by Henderson's great-grandfather, Colin, a Colonel in the Revolutionary War. Colin Westchester was granted one-thousand acres as payment for his war services. It was the new government's solution to populating the frontier while chasing out the native inhabitants. Henderson's father added a two-story, seven-room left wing, and Henderson built the two-story, seven-room right wing, resulting in a twenty-plus room mansion. Hedgerows of berries encased the sprawling lawn's enclave, which included two barns, a spring house, vegetable garden, cutting garden, and fruit orchards, in which the largest specimen, a pear tree twenty-five feet high (a gift to Henderson's father), produced juicy, succulent fruit. Many a child suffered their first broken limb while attempting to reap a reward from the pear tree. The complete complex was the envy of Campbell and Madison counties.

Ben interrupted Henderson's solitude. "Father, you have guests and dignitaries waiting at the house." Henderson jumped. Lost in his thoughts, he did not hear Ben approach. "It's time to go. The field hands need to close over the graves."

Henderson didn't move. A gentle breeze tousled the green, silk tufts of the northern cornfields. Soon, the landscape would be filled with a golden sway, extending to the horizon.

Ben studied the rolling Pennsylvania hills, admiring their labors. He took a deep breath. Thick hazy air, ripe with heat, warmed his lungs. "It won't be long before harvest."

Henderson smiled, unclutched his hand, and tossed. Ben followed suit—bending over, he scooped a handful of dirt and threw it over the coffin. Henderson placed his arm around his son's shoulder.

"Rest in peace, dearest Mother," Ben said.

"Ben…" Henderson paused, cleared his throat, then added softly, "Thank you for all your help."

Ben's eyes widened. Water pooled. Before a tear could drop, Henderson's humor changed.

"Enough. Let's go," Henderson said, slinking his arm off Ben's shoulders. "The sooner we get these bastards out of my house, the better. I'm in no mood for company."

Father and son walked down the knoll in silence. People spilled out of the house, onto the porch, and into the front yard. Every chair, bench, step, and stump supported a Campbellsville body. Spotting Henderson's approach, the Presbyterian pastor scurried through the front gate. His gangly frame tried to prohibit Henderson's passage.

"Henderson, I do hope to see you at Sunday services. Polly was a key parishioner." The demure pastor yielded before the bold Westchester man. "Her smiling face and the faces of your children certainly brighten our congregation."

"Lots of good your sermons do my girls. Don't worry, pastor; I'll continue to tithe, however, do not expect us to attend." Henderson sneered; Ben winced. "When it comes to my eldest daughters, money is not the issue; morality is."

"That's...not what...I'm concerned about your spiritual well-being," Pastor Ashton stammered, shoving his hands in his pants pockets. He retreated several steps as Henderson pressed forward.

"I understand exactly your concern," Henderson continued, pushing Ashton aside. "Thank you for the beautiful words about Polly today. Now, if you'll excuse me, I have other guests to greet."

The men wove in and out of the crowd.

"Henderson, sorry, son. Hell of a loss." Henderson's uncle, James Westchester, greeted them at the door.

The wounded civil war vet and United States congressman, visiting from DC, extended his hand in sympathy. A second handshake from James's son, Herman, followed, a member of the Pennsylvania state house. Besieged by grievers, sounds of *Congressman will you look into...* and *Congressman, I need a favor* replaced the traditional, *Sorry for your loss.*

Henderson's father had wished for him to enter politics with James. Henderson preferred wrangling cows and horses to wrangling rats and snakes.

"Uncle, Cousin Herman, thank you for coming. You are correct. Hell of a loss." Henderson's forehead furrowed as he shifted from side to side. "Polly glued this family together."

"I may have some good news, Nephew. Perhaps this evening I shall join you for dinner? Say, at seven o'clock?" With a smirk, James shook Henderson's hand a second time. "Tonight, then, Nephew."

James departed, leaving Henderson and Ben staring in disbelief.

"That was bold, even for a Westchester! Washington arrogance.

One of the reasons I stayed on the farm." Henderson pursed his lips as his uncle departed. "Come on, Son, shall we say our good-byes to the rest of this group?"

To the family's relief, the exit of Congressman Westchester signaled the conclusion of the funeral gathering. A mass exodus ensued. Henderson's brood formed a reception line as guests expressed one final gesture of condolence, then traveled back to town or neighboring farm.

∞∞∞∞

Henderson discharged a low, guttural moan as he surveyed the food on the dining room table. "Thank God this is over." Cook began clearing the platters of cheese, sandwiches, and cakes. The two housemaids gathered scattered crystal and china. Ginny and Levi collected soiled linens.

"Everyone, into the library. Cook, that includes you and the other house staff."

Trudging in front of family and employees, Henderson led the parade down the hall, past the parlor still filled with flowers, and into the left-wing office. The employees scurried, tossing their things in the kitchen and washrooms to follow the children into the room.

"Father, is this really necessary?" Tildy challenged. "I'm so tired. I wish to go to bed."

Henderson turned and stared, but his steely eyes seemed to have no effect on her. "I shall assume that your physical and emotional state causes you to forget your place. Today I shall overlook this question."

Henderson's lips drew into a grimace. Ben looked at his sister, raised his eyebrows as he mouthed, *Stifle yourself*. Fred bit his lip and exchanged a look of fear with Levi. Olive, the caboose, clomped along, tugging her brother Fred's hand.

Heavy cerulean silk draperies, drawn closed, cast an ominous gloom inside the dark-stained, wood-paneled library. Henderson flopped into his padded leather desk chair, pushing stacks of unopened ledgers across his expansive mahogany desk, littered with papers.

Ginny and Tildy sat on a cobalt blue velvet chaise. The others either stood or joined the youngsters on the floor. The mood set, Henderson began.

"Okay. I'm not happy about what I have to say. First I want to address how things will be moving forward, without your mother. I shall not employee a governess for Olive and my grandchildren. The mothers oversee their own." Henderson paused. "Tildy, Olive is your responsibility. She'll be good practice for what is to come."

"Father!" Tildy blurted out.

"There's more. James and Herman are coming back for dinner tonight." The family echoed a universal groan. Cook's mouth dropped open. "Cook, do we have anything other than leftover finger food in the pantry? I know supplies are low."

"You can't be serious," Tildy quipped, forgetting her manners again, inciting another group moan. Ginny instantly slithered to the opposite edge of the chaise.

"Matilda, I'll not repeat this. Hold your tongue." Droplets of sweat formed on Henderson's brow. "Ben, Clyde, Levi, I need you to join us tonight. Bessie shall feed the remaining family."

"Happy to help, Father." Bessie nodded in agreement. "Leftover sandwiches and cakes in the cottage everyone."

Tildy groaned. Henderson turned his head slowly toward his defiant daughter. "Matilda, as punishment, you're in charge of Olive, permanently." Tildy fumed, neck turning red.

Interrupting Tildy before she could reply, Ben asked. "Do you know why Uncle James wants to return?"

"You were standing with me. I have no idea," Henderson snarled, jaw clenched, teeth showing. Running his hands through his hair, he sputtered, "Any other stupid questions? Cook, can you prepare dinner for six people tonight? Seven o'clock?"

The mantle clock chimed four times.

"Yes, sir. Dinner shall be ready at seven, but I'll need some extra help. Sir, may I take Ginny or Tildy, or both?" The cook nodded to the other staff members. "We have cleaning to finish before we start cooking. May we leave now? Plenty to do."

"I'm not watching Olive, and I'm not helping cook dinner." Tildy spat the words at her father.

"You, young lady, shall peel potatoes and scrub vegetables, or you may move out tomorrow," Henderson hissed, teeth still clenched. "You wonder why the Jamisons disfavor you. No one wants a girl with a sharp tongue. God knows I've tried. Jamison wouldn't take you for the entire US treasury. Now, march. Take Olive."

Tildy's green eyes turned dark. "You bribed Jamison? With what?"

"Never mind that, now. We have work to do. Go help Cook, and your sister. Don't forget to keep Olive with you."

Olive followed the conversation from father to sister and back.

She scooted behind Fred for protection. Clutching the back of his arm, Olive whispered to her brother, "Freddy?"

Grabbing the child's hand, Fred said, "Father, Olive can stay with me tonight. Is that fine with you?" She beamed in appreciation.

"Do what you please. If you wish to save Tildy today's punishment, do so." Henderson threw his hands in the air. "Just keep Olive out of my sight."

PORK BELLY

*G*inny removed three leaves from the polished mahogany
dining room table. Its fully extended ten feet accommodated nightly meals for the entire family, unnecessary
tonight for only six diners. Draping her grandmother's intricate hand-
crocheted tablecloth over the top, she lay linen napkins edged with
more crocheted lace at each place setting. Polly's Haviland Limoges
and Georgian stemware, recently washed, sparkled in the afternoon
sunlight.

A matching mahogany sideboard boasted two silver caddies. The
flatware, already polished for the funeral, reflected starbursts on the
ceiling as Ginny placed them on the table. They were heirlooms
engraved with a *W* and the family crest; Henderson inherited the set
from the previous two generations. A handsome room, the luxurious,
usually brilliant green and rose-colored Morris Artichoke wallpaper in
the dining room was looking dull and dated—despite its recent instal-
lation and extravagant cost—in reflection of the dark mood of the
family today. Polly's portrait hung above the sideboard. Commis-
sioned by Henderson after Clyde's birth, the oil was draped in black
cloth.

Ginny removed the draping to expose a beautiful blonde, wearing a high collar lace and linen blouse with a pearl necklace. Her curly hair was pulled into a loose bun, while several tendrils cascaded down her forehead. She sat straight-backed, regally. Neck and head held high, her full lips curved into a slight smile, but her pale blue eyes twinkled, mischievously, as if hiding a secret.

"I love this portrait of Mother," Ginny said with a tear. "I hate seeing it covered."

"She is beautiful," said Levi as he rearranged the ceremony flowers into a table centerpiece; fresh stems of sunflowers mixed with lavender, daisies, and hollyhocks, with grapevine cascading down the Bavarian crystal vase.

"I think this is presentable for the honorable congressman James Westchester," Ginny sighed, wiping her eyes on her dress sleeve. She nervously filled silver candlesticks with new tapers, then grinned gently at her brother. "Levi, you have a real talent for flowers."

"Hold your tongue. If anyone asks, tell them Fred did the arrangement." Levi snickered as he swept up debris.

"I'm sure Father is exhausted. This dinner is such an imposition." She paused. "I guess either Bessie or I shall be considered the female head of household now." Turning away from Levi, Ginny bit her lip, then sighed. "I don't really want it, but Bessie is...not as *refined* as Tildy and me. Tildy's not up to the task."

"Ginny, don't fret; you'll make a splendid hostess. You are so much like Mother: kind, caring, and gentle." It was Levi's turn to hide his face.

"Come on, little brother." Ginny motioned toward the butler's pantry. "Shall we check on kitchen progress?"

"Rather, I think I'll check on Fred and Olive. They may be hungry. If you need me, I shall be hiding in our bedroom." Placing several cookies on a plate, he climbed the rear staircase to the left wing, the children's wing.

"Coward," Ginny snorted at him.

"I think not!" Levi said, stopping on the stair. "Have you tried to contain Olive?" Levi jumped in the air, flinging his arms in an imitation of his sister.

"She's not that bad," Ginny said. Levi responded by emitting gagging sounds.

The inside house kitchen flourished with action. A long trestle table was cluttered with trays of leftovers to be sent to the cottage for tonight's dinner. Potatoes and carrots filled a six-foot long, deep, trough-like sink. A large cast-iron coal stove occupied one entire corner of the room, with a matching stove in the outside kitchen, used for cooking and baking in the heat of summer. For convenience, a small potbelly stove heated the kettle. Several side rooms of larder and pantry shelved all of Cook's essential supplies.

Household finery, china, crystal, linens, silver, and such were stored in the butler's pantry, a hallway-like room separating the inside kitchen from the dining room. Built-in cabinets with glass doors displayed collections accumulated over many generations.

House staff bustled in a frenzy of activity. Ginny glanced outside where feathers flew about, sticking to wet potato peels. Cook masterminded a creative meal from their meager larder with the addition of two freshly beheaded chickens. Tildy's hair, pulled away from her face with a scarf, escaped the constraints of her bun. Sweat dripped from her forehead.

"If I have to peel another carrot, I shall scream," Tildy groaned as Ginny approached.

"You poor, overworked soul." Ginny thrust a wagging finger in her sister's face. A carrot whizzed past Ginny's ear, landing in the corner.

Cook looked at both Westchester girls, then shook her head, silent witness to many such exchanges. She wondered how Polly's influence failed to penetrate either daughter's brain.

"Matilda, five more carrots to peel. Please cut them into slices; then, you may go. I'll julienne them."

Ginny lifted a tray of finger sandwiches and cakes. "Tildy, I must help Bessie with our supper and check on my baby. Bring the youngest three, and don't be late." Waving goodbye, Ginny slammed the rear screen door. Tildy stuck out her tongue and stomped her foot.

∞∞∞∞

The house servant suppressed a yawn as she poured wine. Henderson motioned for dessert. The woman retreated to the butler's pantry, waiting for additional cues.

James and Henderson sat at opposite heads of the table with Ben and Levi on Henderson's left, Herman and Clyde on Henderson's right. The smell of cinnamon and nutmeg permeated throughout the room as staff distributed the meal's final course.

"Marvelous peach cobbler. Splendid meal, Henderson, simply splendid. I knew you could rise to the occasion."

James's voice echoed in the large room. Shimmering rays from the wall sconces and table candles danced, creating an ambiance contradicting the diners' temperament.

"And just what occasion is *that* Uncle? Today is not the most convenient day for a dinner party," Henderson said, no longer capable of civility.

Uncomfortable with the nuances of societal dining, Levi looked across the table for guidance. Clyde placed one hand on the table and gently shook his head.

Unintimidated, James continued, "You may or may not know that I am now the chairman of a congressional committee that works closely with the Secretary of War. The purpose of this committee is to fortify both the US Army and Naval forces." James puffed out his chest, slipping his thumbs through his suspenders. "Roosevelt wants to beef up our military. Ensure a continuous supply of qualified officers for the next ten to twenty years."

"No, I knew of no such appointment, but pray, what has this to do with me?" Henderson's steely gray eyes stared at his uncle.

"Patience, Nephew. Of course, Teddy is partial to the Navy. He'll oversee the Annapolis reinforcements himself. That leaves me with the Army."

Henderson emitted an exasperated whistle through pursed lips. Sitting upright in his chair, he gestured for brandy, then strummed his fingers on his snifter, provoking the crystal to ring out.

"If you allow me to finish, I shall get to my purpose straight away. Your melancholy is apparent. And unappreciated."

James returned Henderson's stare. Levi, Clyde, and Ben held their breath, waiting for flying objects.

"Please do continue, Uncle. Just know that your presence tonight is as unappreciated as my attitude."

"Touché." James guffawed. "Currently, an agriculture appropriations bill is in Congress. I guarantee a significant government contract for your farm if you promise to help my committee. Pork belly, openended." James sat back in his chair, slightly easing tension. Henderson followed suit, then swirled and sipped his cognac.

"I am neither a politician nor do I care to be one. I made that clear to your brother, twenty years ago." Henderson recalled the argument on his twenty-fifth birthday with his father. James had won the federal election and left his state office vacant, to be filled by Henderson. Henderson refused; Herman accepted. "What crazy notion have you that I may be of assistance?"

"If I'm to boost the Army, I must secure suitable candidates for West Point Military Academy. I need to provide necessary officers. I have no young sons. Herman produced only girls. However, your two youngest boys exemplify the perfect cadets. Your family is affluent, prominent, respected. The boys have pedigree parentage..."

"Stop right there." Henderson held up his hand. "You promise a government farm contract, starting now, if Fred and Levi attend West Point when they come of age?" Rubbing his palms together, Henderson cocked his neck. Without looking at Levi, Henderson stood, thinking out loud. "The younger boys working the farm is only temporary. They must eventually make their own way in the world.

An ongoing contract shall afford me money to hire extra workmen." Extending his hand, he said, "Uncle, you have a deal."

Levi let out a ghastly groan. Under the table, Ben placed his hand on Levi's knee.

"Steady, Levi," Ben uttered in a low voice. Levi's face drained of all color.

Henderson winked. "I assume you shall be the one to ensure their acceptance, Uncle?"

"Absolutely. I'll prepare the paperwork on my return to D.C. Consider it done. They shall be automatically enrolled after high school graduation. How old are they?" For the first time that evening, James bothered to look in Levi's direction. James smiled. Levi did not.

"Father?" With a deep breath, Levi braved speech. The boy trembled.

"Never mind, Levi. You and Fred will need an education. The farm belongs to Ben and Ben's son. Clyde shall share in managing the enterprise; however, I shall not divide it into smaller parcels. This estate was never to be yours, nor Fred's." Turning to James, Henderson continued. "Thank you, Uncle. You saved me a fortune in education fees. Schedule Levi to begin in three years, 1908," Henderson paused, then counted on his fingers, "and Fred in 1911. Well done!" As an afterthought, he added, "I do apologize for my agitation. This solves two of my problems. Any idea what I'm to do with my three girls?" His muscled abdomen vibrated with a hardy laugh.

"Sorry, Nephew. I envy you not, concerning your three daughters. They are a challenge that even the great Teddy Roosevelt would hesitate to solve."

4

NOW I LAY ME DOWN TO SLEEP
WESTCHESTER ESTATE, 1911

*T*ildy held Lizzy's hand as they crawled through the break in the fence that separated the Jamison farm from the Westchester farm. Brushing several blades of grass from Lizzy's dress Tildy said, "Remember, you mustn't tell anyone that we visited Daddy today."

"Yes, Mama. Will we see Daddy again next week?" Lizzy unwrapped the piece of candy given to her by her father, Tommy Jamison.

"Yes, darling, but it is our secret. Now hurry, we are due in the nursery."

Tildy's five-year-old daughter, Elizabeth Jamison Westchester, Ginny's seven-year-old son, Samuel, and nine-year-old Olive shared the nursery. The room was the largest in that wing of the house. Tildy served as a governess while Ginny managed household affairs.

The left upper wing contained four bedrooms with a shared bath: the nursery, Clyde and Sally's room, the girls' room, and the boys' room. Three years previous, Clyde married sixteen-year-old Sally Thompson. She was yet to produce a child.

Lizzy and Tildy scurried up the backstairs to find both Samuel and

Olive eating cookies. Olive read a book while Samuel played with blocks.

After greeting her roommates, Lizzy picked up her doll, cradling it in her arms. "Hello, Dolly." Lizzy rocked her arms back and forth.

Olive snatched the heirloom porcelain doll from Lizzy. "I want that doll," she screamed.

Lizzy held tightly. Olive tore it out of her arms, then threw it across the room. The doll's white face cracked; her dainty hand shattered as it hit the plaster wall. Lizzy wailed.

"Olive! Look what you've done—you killed Mother's doll!" Tildy yanked her sister's arm and dragged her out of the nursery while swatting her behind.

Olive scrunched her nose in a look of defiance and deliberately passed gas. Lizzy ran screaming to her mother.

"Olive, why are you such a brat?" Holding Lizzy, Tildy sat down on the floor. "What prompted this behavior? She's not even your doll. Dolly belongs to Lizzy." She caressed and kissed her daughter's head. Olive glared at Tildy's affection, which held for only Lizzy.

"Olive, what shall I do with you?"

The previous six years raising three children had taken their toll on Tildy. She spent too many hours brooding in frustration, secretly rendezvousing with Tommy Jamison, longing to be his wife.

Olive looked at her sister, sitting in the corner, and kicked her hip. The kick produced its intended effect. Tildy bent over, sobbing uncontrollably. She rocked back and forth, squeezing Lizzy.

"Oh Lizzy, what a cruel fate we suffer. Your Daddy loves us. Why won't he marry me?" Lizzy tried to wiggle free as she looked at her mother.

"Don't cry. I love you, Mama." Tildy clasped her daughter more tightly and wailed louder.

Olive glared, then spun on her heel and stomped down the hallway, escaping into Fred's room.

∞∞∞∞

"I don't know what to do with her," Tildy whined at dinner as she relayed the events of the day.

"Have you asked her what's going on?" Her children being slightly older, Bessie resorted to logic. Both Ginny and Tildy ticked their tongues.

"Do you hear yourself? She's nine. This is *Olive* I'm talking about. She's always been obstinate." Tildy's eyes glazed over. "We need to rearrange the bedroom situation. Especially with Fred leaving. Clyde and Sally should be living in the right bedroom wing. Why do you need all that space to yourself, Father?"

"I do not care to hear women complaining about children at the dinner table." Placing his fork on his dinner plate, Henderson grabbed his stomach. His narrowing eyes darkened, flashing a warning. "All this babble gives me indigestion."

"That's right, Father, ignore the fact that Olive is spiteful, deceptive, hurtful, and spoiled." Tildy's tongue took flight. "Mother indulged her too much, now look at her," she said, flinging back her head.

Henderson's clenched fists pounded the table. His wine glass toppled. "Enough! Do not disparage your mother." He brushed aside the maid as she tried to sop up the spill. "Get out. All of you. Get out of my house."

Some found refuge on the porch swing, others in rocking chairs. They sat waiting for Henderson's eruption to subside.

Ginny offered, "I'll make arrangements for the room swaps. But Tildy, when will you learn to hold your tongue? Who do you think Olive mimics?"

"I have no idea what you are talking about."

Clyde and Sally hid rolling their eyes at each other. Leaning close to his wife, Clyde whispered, "I shall prefer living in the right-wing. Much-needed privacy for starting a family." He grinned as a blushing Sally poked him in the arm, giggling.

Fred, head lowered, ventured back into the dining room. "Father, may we finish dinner? I leave tomorrow. I shall like one last meal with the family."

"What's that, last meal? Don't speak such nonsense." Henderson frowned and scratched his head.

"Not literally. You know what I mean. Before I head off to West Point." Engaging his father's gray eyes, Fred watched them soften. Fred moved closer to Henderson. "I shall miss family gatherings in this space." Together, they savored the beauty of the room, Polly's flair.

"Yes, Son. I am sorry. I am lost, without your mother, when it comes to my female family members. Of course, we shall resume eating, as long as the women control their tongues." Henderson swallowed his wine, relaxing back into his chair. "Round them up."

Laughing as he rejoined his siblings on the porch, Fred invited, "Come back in. He's calmed down. But for God's sake, Tildy, stop complaining about your entitled life."

∞∞∞∞

Fred's door hung open as Olive walked to the bathroom for her nightly routine. On her way back to the nursery, she stopped and knocked. Looking up from his book, Fred beckoned her to enter.

"Freddy, may I sleep in here tonight? In Levi's bed?" Her sad eyes peeked up from her hanging head. She stared at the blue and brown patchwork quilts and tan walls, immersed in masculine comfort.

"Yes, you may, Olive. In fact, I shall enjoy your company." Evading a solitary night before his travel, he motioned his sister to come to him. Olive ran over to her brother, threw her arms around his neck, and sobbed. Fred tumbled backward from the impact.

"Why do you have to leave? Why did Levi have to leave?" She clung tightly. "I don't understand. I don't want you to go."

"Dear sister, is that why you bullied Lizzy this morning? Are you so distraught?" He returned her hug. "I don't really want to go either, but I have no choice in the matter. I'm eighteen now, and ready for college. I need to continue my education. Learn about the world." Fred wasn't sure if he was convincing Olive or convincing himself.

"Will I go to college?" Blue innocent eyes peered at him. Olive climbed onto the bed.

"No, sweetie. You will find a wonderful husband and get married." His arms circled her to pull her near. He cozied into her chubby, preadolescent body.

"But Ginny and Tildy didn't get married. Are you sure I'll get married?" This caused Fred to laugh. He rose, lifted his sister, and swinging her in circles, chanted a nursery rhyme. Olive giggled in delight as she flew around the room.

"Oh, Freddy. I love you. Never forget that I love you." Olive planted sloppy smacks on Fred's cheek.

"I shall remember, dear Olive, I shall. Now let's get you tucked into bed." Fred gently placed Olive under the quilt of Levi's bed and kissed her forehead. Her face radiated up at him.

"You're getting heavy. By the time I come home, you'll be all grown up. Now, close your eyes, and dream of ponies and flowers." He tucked the bedsheets under her cotton nightdress.

"First, I have to say my prayers." Olive scrambled out, kneeled beside the bed, and chanted, "Now I lay me down to sleep, I pray the Lord my soul to keep. If I should die before I wake, I pray the Lord my soul to take. God bless Papa. God bless Levi. And God bless Freddy, my only friend in the whole world. Keep him safe away from harm. Bless him with a Heavenly Charm. Amen." She jumped back into bed. "Okay, now I'm ready for sleep. I love you, Fred."

She was out within the minute. Fred watched the child sleep for a moment before resuming his packing. As he folded the last of his trousers, tears dropped from his eyes. Stirred by the moment, Fred grabbed a piece of paper and pencil then wrote a message for Olive. Placing it in an envelope, he tucked it into his suitcase. The outside was addressed, *To Olive, in the event I never return.*

5

DOWN THE TRACKS

*O*live, Ginny, Samuel, Fred, and the chauffeur, Jake, clambered out of the Model T. They stood on the outdoor platform awaiting the afternoon train to New York. Other groups clustered together, chatting in hushed undertones. A whiff of sage and allspice drifted past with the approach of additional passengers and a sausage lunch. Billowing patches of dust swirled around them as crisp dry air, smelling of straw, hinted at autumn and the colder days to come. Olive clung to Fred; her nose nuzzled into his shirt, savoring his musky scent. Samuel, sensing something wrong, clung to his mother.

A dozen other passengers waited to board. Always on time, the afternoon eastbound train made several stops in Johnstown, Altoona, and Wilkes Barre/Scranton before crossing state lines and heading into New York. He would spend a night in the city, then take a morning train for West Point tomorrow. Brother and older sister awkwardly engaged in small talk while they waited.

"When is Christmas break?"

"I don't have my schedule yet. How shall you rearrange the left wing?"

"Not decided. What time do you arrive?"

"Around three in the afternoon. Where shall I sleep when I come home?"

Olive cocked her head to the side as she listened to her siblings. Putting an end to the nonsensical conversation, she asked, "Fred, tell me what you are going to learn in your new school?" She brushed a clump of mud off the wooden surface and squatted.

Fred, happy to discuss something meaningful, sat down on the platform, embracing the fleeting comfort of the child under his arm.

"All the normal subjects, and I shall also be learning how to fight a war." The simple answer startled him.

"Where is the war?" asked Olive, as she smoothed her gingham dress over her legs in an attempt of juvenile modesty.

Fred hugged his sister. "There is no war—that I know of, at least. Just because I learn how to fight a war doesn't mean that there will be a war."

"Then why learn how to fight?" Her brow wrinkled between the blonde pigtails.

"You never know when you may need the skill. It's like learning how to swim, or ride a horse. You don't do it every day, but someday you may need to know how." Fred rubbed his sister's back. "Do you understand what I am saying, Olive?"

The world stood still, for brother and sister, if only for a few seconds.

"I think so, Fred. We have the Ford to take to town, so I don't need to ride my pony. But maybe someday I'll need to go to town, and the Ford's not here. Then I'll go by horseback."

The train whistled as it approached Campbellsville Depot, breaking the spell. The front cowcatcher raced toward them like a medieval siege weapon. Screeching brakes belched a hiss of steam that tasted of metal.

"You got the idea," Fred said, tapping her nose. "Now here comes the train. Give me a big hug and kiss. I love you, little sister." Fred lifted her and kissed her on the lips. Placing Olive on the ground, he moved on to Ginny. "Well, Big Sis, this is it. Take good care of Father. I love you."

"Be safe, Fred. See you at Christmas." Ginny bit her lower lip.

Climbing up the steps, Fred hesitated. He stared deeply at the familiar town and the people he loved before crossing the threshold to board the train. He chose a window seat. Sticking his head out of the window, he waved to his clustered family until the train curved around the hillside.

Ginny, Samuel, and Olive snuggled together on the ride home, taking turns blowing their noses. In the front, a few muffled sniffles were heard between shifting gears.

6

UPPER LEFT CUT

*F*red's departure ushered in the end of summer and the beginning of a new school session for the younger children. Celebrating a December birthday, an excited Lizzy was eager to start her first year. She joined Samuel and Olive as they walked the half-mile to the one-room schoolhouse. The trio kicked stones, jumped puddles, and picked weeds as they skipped and sang down the winding country path.

Bea Thompson, Sally's younger sister, traveled from Campbellsville to teach the local farm children. Grades one through eight were taught in the single room. After grade eight, the rich and lucky male students continued their education at Campbellsville High School. Most girls concluded their book learning, the elite going on to a finishing school emphasizing the social arts. Lower class boys found a job, while the girls awaited marriage.

Welcome Class, written on the large chalkboard, greeted the Westchester children as they entered the room through the side door. A cloakroom, with hooks for winter wraps, was strategically placed behind the chalkboard, saving valuable space. About thirty desks filled the room. A massive world globe stood to the left of the teacher's desk, with an American flag on the right. Three oversized, double-hung windows, flanking both walls, created a cross breeze while illuminating the space.

Samuel placed an apple on the teacher's desk. Olive rolled her eyes as she guided Lizzy to a desk in the front of the room, beside another first grader. "Sit here, Lizzy. I'll be right over there." She pointed across the room to where some older students gathered.

Lizzy's lip quivered. "Olive, I'm scared." She hugged her new slate and pencil case to her chest.

"It's fine. Samuel and I shall be close by." Looking at the little boy sitting next to Lizzy, Olive asked, "What's your name?"

"I'm Johnny." Lizzy relaxed. Johnny's frightened pale face matched Lizzy's.

"I'm Elizabeth Jamison Westchester." Gaining confidence, Lizzy stood, grinning as she chanted her full name. An older boy overheard Lizzy. Curious, he joined Olive and the two youngsters.

"What's your name?"

The boisterous demand frightened Lizzy, and she slid behind Olive.

"Her name is Elizabeth Jamison Westchester," Olive said. "Who are you?"

Children strode over toward the commotion. Most of the class watched Olive. The boy ignored her, staring down Lizzy.

"My daddy says that your mother's a whore." Nose to nose, the boy shouted the slur at Lizzy. Bursting into tears, she ran to Samuel, leaving Olive with the unknown accuser.

"You take that back." Olive pushed the boy backward. Stumbling over Johnny's desk, he regained his balance. Students gaped in awe.

"I'll not take back the truth." He pushed Olive in return; she remained upright.

"Tildy is not a whore." Olive clenched her fist and wound her arm. Thrusting her hand up, she smacked him square on the chin. The boy hit the floor with a thud, just as Miss Thompson appeared from behind the chalkboard.

"Stop fighting! What is going on here? Everyone, to their seats.

Olive, young man, come outside with me," Bea Thompson, small in stature, commanded. "I said outside, *now*."

Olive scowled at the prostrate boy, spun on her heel, and stomped out the door. The boy rolled onto his side. Pushing himself up and rubbing his chin, he followed Olive and Miss Thompson out of the room.

"Sit. Both of you. What is this all about?" Both children responded immediately to Bea's stern tone. The children sat on a wooden bench; tiny Bea towered over them. One large oak tree suspended a swing. A seesaw and several distant picnic tables completed the school grounds.

"Young man, who are you?" Bea asked. "Where do you live?"

Olive cut in. "He called—"

"Olive, I asked this boy a question. You shall have your turn." Bea looked at the boy's bloody lip and handed him her handkerchief. "Now, who are you?"

"I'm Leonard Lewis. We're new here. My daddy works at the Jamison farm." The taste of his own blood sickened Leonard. He doubled over, then spit. Glaring at Olive, he continued, "This bitch hit me."

"Leonard Lewis, you watch your language, or you'll go home with a sore lip *and* a sore bottom." Bea produced a ruler from her apron pocket. Leonard recanted.

"*She* hit me." Leonard poked his finger in Olive's chest. Olive swatted it away.

"What did you say to aggravate Olive?" Bea continued, knowing Olive's volatility.

"What does 'aggravate' mean?"

Olive jumped into the conversation. "What, are you stupid? 'Aggravate' means to make me mad at you."

"That's enough, Olive. I'm talking to Leonard. If you don't control your impulses, I shall have you sit at a picnic table while I speak to you each individually."

"I said that Lizzy's mother is a whore," Leonard said.

Taking a deep breath, Bea controlled her inclination to deposit a second blow onto Leonard Lewis's chin. "Do you know what the word whore means?" Bea looked deep into the boy's eyes.

Leonard hung his head. "No, Miss Thompson. It's what my daddy said."

"Then why did you use a word that you don't understand?" Olive shifted in her seat.

"Olive, do you know the meaning of 'whore?'"

"Ah, no, but I know 'aggravate.'"

Bea suppressed a grin. "If you didn't know the meaning, why did you hit Leonard?"

"I didn't like the tone of his voice. He put his face right up to Lizzy's face, scaring her. Then he yelled and called Tildy that name. No one talks to a Westchester like that. Not to Lizzy, not to Tildy, and especially not to me."

"Leonard, apologize to Olive for what you said. Then go inside and apologize to little Lizzy. If I catch you bullying my students, I shall expel you. Am I clear?"

"But she hit me!"

"Am I clear?" Bea placed her hands on her hips, her voice raising up a pitch.

"Yes, Miss Thompson." Tail between his legs, Leonard admitted defeat. "I'm sorry," Leonard mumbled.

"Louder. What are you sorry about?" Bea prodded.

"I'm sorry for saying bad words and for pushing you." Leonard refused to look at Olive, whose squinting, ice-blue eyes terrified him.

"Olive, apologize to Leonard."

Convinced of her innocence in protecting her family, Olive objected. "But—!"

"You don't hit people when you don't understand the language they use." Bea hated punishing Olive. Although she did not condone force, she understood defending the weak.

Forty eyes peered through the school windows.

"Oh, okay." Olive let out an exaggerated sigh. "I'm sorry for hitting you. But don't you *ever*—"

Bea Thompson cut off the threat. "That's enough."

Grabbing both children by the collars, Bea dragged them into the classroom. The class scrambled back to their seats.

∞∞∞∞

Tildy ran to meet the children as they returned home from school. All three skipped and laughed as they entered the gate. Scooping Lizzy up in her arms, she twirled her around. Olive and Samuel continued toward the house.

"Oh, my big girl. How was your first day of school?" Tildy squeezed her daughter tightly.

"It was exciting, Mommy. I recited my numbers...well, up to ten, and I learned how to write some letters." Lizzy showed her mother the slate with the letters a, b, and c written on it.

"Did you have fun?" Tildy pressed for more while glancing at Olive for confirmation.

"A mean boy scared me. But Olive took care of him. She hit him." Searching arms, legs, and face, Tildy examined her daughter for signs of abuse. "Stop, Mommy. You're tickling me."

"Olive, Samuel. Here please." Tildy called to the older children. "What is Lizzy talking about? A boy frightened her; you hit him? Olive Westchester, how dare you fight at school—and on Lizzy's very first day?"

Glowering at her older sister, Olive met Tildy's gaze, turned, then stomped into the house.

"You come back here, you little brat," Tildy called out. Picking up a pebble, she threw it in Olive's direction,

"Mommy, don't yell at Olive. She saved me." Lizzy understood enough of the day's activities to recognize Olive's protection.

"Nonsense. Olive's such a nasty one. Oh, you sweet thing. Let's go in and see if Cook has an after-school treat ready." Tildy bundled Lizzy in her arms, showering her with kisses as she carried her into the kitchen. Olive, on her way to snatch an afternoon snack, watched the open display of affection from the butler's pantry. Biting her lower lip, she retreated up the back stairs to her room.

∞∞∞

"Father, you really must do something about Olive. She got into a fight today. It's only the first day of school."

Ben, Bessie, and their children, Ben Jr., and Nellie, as well as Clyde, Sally, Ginny, and Tildy, with Henderson at the head, assembled around the dining room table for dinner. The youngest children were already fed in the nursery. The aroma of fried onions filled the room as Cook served a first course of green tomatoes.

"Tildy, all you do is whine. You take so little responsibility." Henderson's large hand quivered, resisting the urge to wad into a fist. "For God's sake, stop. I'll deal with her if you can't."

"I think you need to hear Olive's side of the story before you accuse her falsely." Sally, already aware of the events of the day, jumped to Olive's defense.

"Why do you always take her side?" Tildy ran her hands across the sides of her head. Olive possessed ample power alone; she needed no support.

"I'm only saying that there are two sides to every story. Bea spoke with me after school; I'm happy to share our conversation." Sally glanced at Tildy, who sat frowning.

"That's not necessary, Daughter-in-Law." Henderson scowled at both women. "*I'll* deal with Olive, if the women of this family are incapable."

Looking to Clyde for support, Sally braved, "You need to listen to Olive before passing judgment."

"Fine, go get her. Let's hear what she has to say." Henderson rested his elbows on the table as he stroked his cheek.

Ginny summoned the child. Confused, Olive entered the dining room. She glanced at her father, then at Tildy. Father smiled; Tildy did not. Olive stood statuesque.

"Olive, I understand you hit a boy today at school." Henderson's baritone voice grumbled the question. "Do you care to explain yourself?"

"Truthfully, I'd rather not talk about it." Olive observed her father's face for a sign of understanding. The twinge of a smile changed into a frown as Henderson crossed his arms.

"Well then, I suggest you take a seat and tell us anyway. Immediately, young lady." At Henderson's command, Olive sat down beside Sally, across the table from Tildy. "Enlighten us."

Olive hesitated, then asked, "What's a whore?"

The family gasped.

Henderson raised his hand, then lowered it with an exhale, pausing a minute before continuing. "Enough of that language, young lady."

"Olive, please tell us why you want to know the meaning of that word?" Ginny gently asked the child.

"For goodness' sake, Ginny, she's an uncontrollable brat. Why do you coddle her such?" Tildy said with a head fling. Olive ignored her older sister.

"No! First, tell me what it means. Then I'll tell you what happened today." Determined to control her destiny, Olive refused to back down.

Sally struggled not to smile. "A whore is a promiscuous woman who has relationships with men for money. Do you understand?"

"Is 'promiscuous' like a floozy?" Olive's question evoked several chuckles.

"Yes, a floozy, but a floozy who takes money from men," Sally simplified.

"Then I was right to hit him. Leonard Lewis called Tildy a whore." Matilda choked on her food; her eye twitched uncontrollably. "He said it to Lizzy. Right in her face. It really scared her. So, I knocked him out."

Henderson laughed, amused with Olive's spunk. "You knocked him out?"

"Yes, Papa. I made a fist then hit him in the chin. He went flying down onto the floor. No one is going to talk about Westchesters like that in front of me and get away with it." Olive jumped off her chair and thrust her hands to her hips, widening her stance.

Henderson nodded in approval. "How old was this boy?"

"According to Bea, the same age as Olive and about twenty pounds heavier," Sally interjected.

"Well. Damn and tarnation. You hit him to defend the Westchester name?" Henderson deliberately surveyed his children's faces. No one showed emotion except for Tildy, who flung back her head in self-pity. "Olive, do you sleep in the nursery?"

"Yes, Papa." She raised her chin and met his gaze.

"From now on, you shall have your own room. And you shall join the adults for evening meals." Standing, Henderson circled the table.

Tildy moaned. "She's only nine."

"I'll be ten next month. I'm not a baby anymore," Olive interjected as she retook her seat.

Henderson stopped behind Olive, placing his hands on the back of her chair; he beamed. "Ginny, see that Olive moves into a separate bedroom. I don't want her sharing with anyone. And I no longer want Tildy as her governess."

"I'll make the arrangements tomorrow, Father. May I move Clyde and Sally to the right-wing?"

Sally hid her pleasure. Clyde pinched her leg under the table. Olive noticed both.

"Of course, make room for my little champion." He moved on without touching the child.

The family looked at their father in disbelief. Olive sat tall in her chair, chest forward, longing for her father's caress—however, still celebrating her first right of passage.

7

MUSICAL CHAIRS

*G*inny emptied the chest of drawers as the maids carried clothing to the right wing. The blue and green striped wallpaper, appropriate for Clyde and Ben as adolescents, was now faded and worn. Dark blue, homespun draperies fluttered in the open window, exposing frayed hemlines.

"Sally," Ginny asked her sister-in-law as she planned their new lodgings. "Do you mind helping me with your things?"

The simple task of sorting personal belongings seemed monumental to the privileged daughter of Henderson Westchester.

"Of course not. I'm so excited to finally have some privacy." A half-smile formed on Sally's face. Ripe with the urge of parenthood, Sally elated in the move.

Ginny looked befuddled. "But you already have a private room, although it is in need of an update."

"We are not soundproof. I shall enjoy romantic evenings while we try to expand the family." Both women giggled. Sally continued, "If I can hear you and Tildy, you can hear me."

"Ah, it's been so long. Do you believe conceiving Samuel was my last time?" Ginny admitted as the color rose in her face.

"He's almost eight." Sally tilted her head. Lowering her voice, she asked, " Whatever happened to his father?"

"Mother knew, no one else." Ginny folded and refolded a blouse hastily. "The circumstances shall remain my secret."

"We all know Tildy's story; no one knows yours. I don't mean to pry or gossip." Ginny remained silent; Sally leaned in to whisper, "*Speaking* of Tildy, I believe she is sneaking out to see Tommy Jamison."

Taking the bait, Ginny asked, "Do you think Tildy is still involved with Jamison?"

"I see her coming home from the direction of Jamison's farm most afternoons. Sometimes Lizzy is with her."

"Sally, are you spying?" The women giggled again. "It wouldn't surprise me if Tildy were seeing Tommy. She's been crazy about him since they first moved into their farm."

"There is so much about this family that I don't yet understand," Sally admitted. "For example, why does Tildy hate Olive so? She isn't *that* terrible a child. She's inquisitive, maybe headstrong, but truly brilliant."

"Olive was forced on Tildy after Mother died, and Tildy was pregnant at the time. I think her *female nervousness* with the pregnancy set the tone." Ginny mimicked Tildy's head fling; Sally snickered.

The women worked and laughed, preparing to exit the left-wing and enter the right-wing. Each carried a stack of clothing into the third-largest bedroom on the newer side of the house. Henderson's and Polly's separate rooms shared a bathroom, while a second hallway bath serviced the other two bedrooms and any visitors. The move not only gave Clyde and Sally a more private bedroom but also a private bathroom. The house's original two small bedrooms, between the wings, were currently used as a sitting area and for storage.

Sally gasped as she entered the room. Pale green silk draperies swayed in the breeze from the open windows. Lavender sachets to scent the drawers lay waiting on the dresser top. Yellow floral wallpaper, a white wicker rocking chair, and an Aubusson wool rug softened the dark wood framework and floors. The full-size iron sleigh bed displayed a yellow and white flower, garden pattern quilt.

"Oh, this is moving up in the world." Sally placed her items on the quilt. Running her hand over the silk draperies, she grinned.

Ginny frowned. "Don't let it go to your head. I am still running this household."

Three hours later, Clyde and Sally occupied a new home.

"I'm beat. Sally, will you finish up in your room? I need to think about how I'm rearranging the nursery." Ginny sat in the rocking chair, holding her head as if in pain.

"You're not dismantling the nursery, are you?"

Ginny tilted her head to the urgency in Sally's voice. "Are you pregnant?"

"Not yet. But I intend to be before Christmas. We'll have every opportunity with this new room." Sally winked.

"Then, I guess the nursery stays. I think I'll move into your old room, although I do intend to redecorate. Olive moves to the boys' room. Samuel can move in with me. He's getting too old to share with a little girl. Lizzy can either stay with Tildy or in the nursery, Tildy's choice."

Sally looked puzzled. "Don't you want a private room? As the woman of the house, you deserve one."

"I'm not sure how to arrange things otherwise." Ginny looked perplexed.

"Give Samuel a room. Lizzy may either share with Olive or stay with Tildy. Olive won't mind."

"But Father said... "

"For God's sake Ginny. Make a decision," Sally concluded.

Ginny caught her breath and held it. She left Sally and walked back to the left-wing of the house. Sitting down on the edge of her old bed, Ginny folded her hands over her eyes. Tears ran down her arms. Sally didn't completely comprehend the gravity of Henderson Westchester, nor the responsibility of running a large, complicated house. Too many moving parts. What Ginny really wanted to do was take Samuel and move away, far away from the family. She bowed her head in prayer to Polly.

Mother, why did you leave us? I need you. I don't want to run this house. I want my own life. How am I to venture out without money, without Samuel's father? Please, show me a way.

∞∞∞∞

"I don't know how mother coped," Ginny confessed to Tildy, sitting on one of the single beds in their old, shared room.

"Now look who's being dramatic." Tildy offered no compassion to her sister. Tildy offered no sympathy to *anyone*, except Lizzy. "You're the chosen one, running Father's house. You have an illegitimate child, same as me, yet no one calls you a whore." Flinging her head, she dared her sister to contradict.

"Stop. I can't tolerate you any longer, Tildy." Ginny clutched her hair, pulling it up and out of the ties. Her brown locks fell over her face. "Will you ever grow up?" Standing, Ginny grabbed a stack of blouses as she retreated to her new space, Clyde and Sally's old, outdated room. She stuck her head out her door as she shouted, "Because you are so miserable, Tildy, Lizzy moves in with you. Samuel shall stay in the nursery for the time being. Olive shall sleep in the boys' room alone. And by the way, I know you are seeing Tommy Jamison." Ginny slammed the door shut, sat down on the bed, and cried.

Tildy stammered a denial, then set about writing a long letter to Jamison. She needed to warn him of their discovered triste.

Olive ate with the adults that evening. Her head swiveled, trying to follow and comprehend the conversation. Observing them, she noticed Ginny sitting silently, her eyes red. Tildy's tongue cut as usual, but her hands twitched. Ben stammered as he reported directly to Henderson on the status of the farm, while Sally grinned like the

Cheshire cat. Having always wondered what happened during the day, Olive realized these details were empowering.

"Corn in the northern fields... ripe apples... canning... bringing in the herd of cattle... baling wheat for winter... "

Slightly overwhelmed, Olive sat quietly, eating her dessert, sorting through the evening's arbitrary information.

"Olive, you haven't said much this evening. Do you enjoy your new, grown-up status and new room?" Henderson finally addressed his youngest child.

"Oh, Papa, yes. Thank you. I haven't moved into my new room yet. Ginny says tomorrow."

Henderson threw Ginny a scowl. "She's not moved?" Ginny shook her head no.

Unperturbed, Olive continued, "I'm trying to get it all straight, everything that was said tonight. I think I'll go back to my room and write the most important things down."

Ben cast a cautious look at Clyde, who offered the same in return.

Henderson chuckled. "Boys, I think we must be on our best behavior. Little Polly has arrived."

Olive furrowed her brows. "Who is Polly?"

They all looked at Olive in amazement. Henderson, no longer smiling, answered. "Polly was your mother. Her name was actually Philomena, but everyone called her Polly."

"I'm a little Polly?" The declaration puzzled Olive. Memories of her mother settled like a thick fog in her brain.

"For God's sake. Not in the least." Tildy belted as she tossed her head back, in typical Tildy fashion. She again drew her father's disapproval.

"Ginny, tomorrow after school, share some of your mother's stories with Olive. In fact, it's time to go through her closet. See what can be used by or altered for the women of the house. Display her jewelry. I'll go through it before dinner tomorrow, and distribute it." Henderson rose slowly, then touched Polly's portrait. "Six years is long

41

enough to hold onto the physical. I'll always have her memory." He left for his office, to drink cognac.

All joviality lost; the family dispersed to their appropriate bedrooms. Olive sat alone in the dining room. She studied the pattern of the wallpaper, china, and crystal. She noted the placement of the silver, the fabric of the draperies. Lastly, she memorized her mother's likeness, then went upstairs to bed, her last night in the nursery.

8

PRECIOUS GEMS

*G*inny unlocked the door to her mother's room, expecting it to need a good dusting. Instead, it glistened. Fresh daisies filled the vase on her nightstand. Her white iron bed was covered neatly with a new quilt. The aroma of lavender lingered on the stiffly starched linens. Polly's yellow satin robe hung over her vanity dressing chair, waiting to be donned at the end of the day. Her silver comb, brush, and hand mirror along with crystal perfume bottles scattered beams of light in every direction. The wooden dresser top sparkled, reflecting trinket boxes and Polly's jewel case. Entering her mother's walk-in closet, Ginny hummed as she sorted through her mother's belongings. Memories flooded over her like breezes from the past. Articles of gowns and gloves conjured images of Polly, the belle of the ball. Ginny gently cradled a pale green, silk gown, the dress Polly wore on her last Christmas alive.

Having the same build as Polly—tall and thin, with slender arms—Ginny inventoried items that would soon occupy her closet. Being shorter, with no patience for hemming, Matilda would most likely pass on the clothing—unless she could bribe either Sally or Bessie to sew for her. Bessie and Sally would pick last, if pick at all.

During her search, a stack of papers tied with a ribbon fell out of a shoebox. Numerous scantily scented letters, several tin-type photographs, and a certificate of membership from the Daughters of the American Revolution comprised the cache. Ginny lay them on the bed in a pile for Henderson's inspection later that evening.

Caught up in a world long gone, Ginny had lost track of time. Olive knocking at the door startled her.

She jumped before saying, "Come in, Olive. How was school?"

"Good. I didn't hit anyone today." Olive giggled. "This is a beautiful room. It's so...purple."

Ginny chuckled. "Mother loved lavender and daisies. Purple and yellow." Remembering her question, she added, "I should hope you're not fighting. Please do me a favor? I need to pull out Mother's jewelry. Will you retrieve a silver tray from the butler's pantry? I shall arrange Mother's items so Father may easily review them."

"Sure, Ginny." Olive skipped down the rear staircase. After several minutes, she returned and offered Ginny the tray and a cotton towel.

"Why the towel?" Ginny avoided eye contact with her younger sibling.

Olive shrugged her shoulders to the obvious answer. "So that we neither scratch the tray nor the jewelry."

"Oh. Good idea." Embarrassed by her lack of forethought, Ginny grabbed the tray and walked to Polly's dresser.

Ginny opened boxes and cases, creating an elegant display of wealth for Henderson to survey, as Olive sat on the wool pile rug, thumbing through the stack of papers.

"What are the 'Daughters of the American Revolution?'" Olive looked up from the papers, searching her sister's face.

"Mother was a member." Ginny remained expressionless.

"I can see that from the certificate. What is this organization?" Olive lay down the membership certificate and scratched her head.

"To be a member, you must have a direct ancestor who fought in the American Revolution. Do you understand what that is?" She turned her back to Olive.

"Yes, silly. I know all about George Washington, the Declaration of Independence, and the Constitution. America wouldn't exist if we didn't fight the Red Coats for our freedom." Standing, Olive confronted Ginny. "Do we have an ancestor that fought in the Revolutionary War?"

"We must, otherwise Mother could not have joined." Shrugging her shoulders, Ginny continued sorting Polly's clothing.

"Who are they? Do you think Father knows? Can I join?"

"How should I know, Olive? I think you must be older to join. My, you ask a lot of questions. Why don't you ask Father tonight at dinner?"

Taking a stance, one hand on her hip, Olive proclaimed, "I shall, if there is time. He said last night he wanted to distribute Mother's jewelry tonight. Maybe I'll wait until tomorrow." After a moment, Olive softened her voice and added, "You are to tell me about Mother, remember?"

Heeding her father's request, Ginny shared several stories with Olive about Polly. "Mother loved flowers, especially daisies. She planted all her flower gardens to include special varieties not common to this area." Ginny paused to recall specific details. "I remember once, she had Father order her a plant that came the whole way from California, transported on ice."

Olive sat quietly, fingering one of Polly's scarves as she listened.

"I remember one year—I was younger than you—Father took Grandmother Sinclair and Mother on the train to New York City. A shopping trip." Ginny sighed. "They came home with trunks full of purchases and gifts. It was glorious. I was just learning to trot; they gave me a beautiful porcelain figurine of a prancing horse."

Olive gaped in awe, "I've never seen that. Where is it?"

"It's wrapped and tucked away. Someday I'll give it to Sammy." Ginny continued, "Mother had a gift for numbers; she helped father with his books, keeping the ledgers. None of us possess such an aptitude for arithmetic."

"What was she like, as a person?" Olive's voice cracked.

"Oh. She was a lovely person." Polly's absence and Ginny's sentimentality allowed for potential exaggeration. "Ever so kind, always there with a smile. I miss her so much." Ginny lowered her head, sobbing quietly.

For the second time in two days, Olive's head went spinning with new information about her family, especially her mother. She excused herself, retreating to her new room. Munching on a hidden cookie, she waited for the dinner bell, thinking about what it would be like to have Mother around. Someone to hug and kiss you each morning, to tuck you into bed at night. Someone to soothe away your tears and heal a skinned knee.

∞∞∞∞

Henderson washed and changed clothing before dinner. Exiting the bath on Polly's side, he appraised the clothing and the tray of jewelry assembled by Ginny. Caressing several of Polly's favorite items opened waves of memories. He stared at her elegant jewelry, some given to her by Henderson, some inherited from Polly's mother. The shimmer of a perfectly matched strand of pearls dominated his attention. The ancient gems from the sea were Polly's most prized possession. Fingering the pearls, he dropped them into his jacket pocket.

"Ginny, come here, please," Henderson called.

Ginny had been waiting in an overstuffed wing chair at the top of the grand staircase. The landing, part of the original house, connected the two additions outside of the original bedrooms.

"Here, Father." Entering her mother's room, now occupied by her father, evoked an alien feeling in Ginny. Neither of them belonged here.

"Ginny, do with the clothing as you see fit. I imagine most will fit you. Tildy can alter some. Whatever you and Tildy discard may be given to first Bessie, then Sally. Is anything suitable for Olive?" Clutching a pair of gloves, Henderson inhaled the sweet leather, still infused with Polly's perfume.

"I'll save several of the smaller blouses for Olive. She's growing like ragweed and starting to slim down, while filling out up top." Ginny blushed, "Thank you, Father. Mother's clothing is exquisite." She hugged Henderson. He stood stiff, unresponsive to her embrace.

"Take the clothing with you. They no longer belong in this room. As far as this jewelry goes...you take her garnet ring, the one with which I proposed marriage. It is the most valuable item on the tray." Ginny almost dropped the ring as Henderson tossed it at her. She scrutinized the tray. *Where are the pearls? They are more valuable than the ring...*

"Ginny, please wear the ring tonight, and bring the tray to the dinner table." Henderson fidgeted, touching each piece with a lingering caress. He lowered his voice. "I shall present my gifts during dessert. Oh, and—thank you for doing this." Ginny squirmed, uncomfortable in the moment of spoken, nonphysical gratitude.

∞∞∞∞

Henderson's entrance to dinner lacked its normal boisterous aplomb. He quietly took his seat, allowing other family members to claim center attention. The mellow mood loosened tongues at dinner, promoting lazy conversation. Tildy sneezed, complaining about her allergies. Sally applauded their new bedroom while Clyde smiled in agreement. Ben troubled over the harvest. Clothing alterations obsessed Ginny and Bessie. Ben's children shoveled food into their mouths. Invisible to the family, Olive sat quietly for the second consecutive evening.

With the aroma of cinnamon, the maid finally served apple pie. Conversation ceased as the long-awaited moment arrived for Henderson to distribute Polly's objects of adoration.

"I see you are all in eager anticipation." Henderson held himself high. Ambling to the sideboard, he reached for a horsehair fob and pocket watch. "Bessie, this is for you, as my oldest son's wife."

"Thank you, Father." Bessie fingered the watch, pleased with her gift.

"What!" Tildy shouted in contempt. "That should be mine! If Ginny gets Mother's ring, I should have her watch. Yes, Ginny, I see you wearing the ring."

The mood soured. Henderson tasted bile. Grabbing an unadorned gold brooch, he handed it to Tildy. "This, Matilda, is more than you deserve."

Tildy glowered at Bessie, who quickly handed her prize to Ben for safekeeping.

Reaching again for the tray, Henderson chose an item. "Sally, you may have Polly's rhinestones. Of all the women in this family, you are most likely the one to make social conquests. Here are the matching earrings. A fitting polish for evening attire."

He turned to face his oldest daughter. "Ginny, along with the ring, I want you to have the gold and emerald brooch. It was a favorite of your mother."

"Both Ginny and Sally get two things!" Tildy objected again, wildly flinging her arms. "Why do you favor Sally so? She's only been in this family for three years. I'm the one who watches the children; Sally does nothing but make eyes at Clyde."

"Matilda, you may leave. Take these earrings for safekeeping. I want Lizzy to have them when she gets older." Henderson handed Tildy a pair of black onyx earrings. "Now be gone."

She grabbed them and the brooch and marched out of the room, slamming every door on her way.

Watching Tildy, Olive sat quietly, praying to receive a gift. She wanted a keepsake from her mother, even though Mother was only the vaguest of memories to her. Henderson walked to his youngest daughter.

"Olive." She turned to look up at her towering father. "This is for you."

He reached into his jacket pocket and pulled out the string of pearls. Ginny, Bessie, and Ben gasped.

"Pearls are precious gems from the sea, Olive," her father explained. "Like diamonds, they are rare and valuable, growing inside an oyster until they are big enough to string. Just like you, growing from a child to a woman." He placed the pearls around Olive's neck. "A beautiful necklace for a beautiful girl."

"Oh, Papa." Olive jumped down from her chair. "I will cherish these as long as I live." Bursting into tears, she hugged her father. This time, Henderson accepted the embrace.

Stunned family members sat in silence, then dispersed. No need for gossip, now—there would be plenty of time to discuss the evening's events in the privacy of their rooms.

At Olive's request, the boys' room was unchanged. Ginny boxed Levi's belongings, moving them to the attic. Using the empty chest of drawers, Olive stowed her clothing and treasures. Fred's clothing remained.

Sitting on Fred's old bed, Olive carefully removed her pearl necklace. Covering it with a scrap from an old flannel shirt, she hid the pearls in a drawer. She snuggled under the brown and blue quilt. A faint scent of Fred and the hug from her father quieted her restless soul. She felt peaceful and secure, for the first time in her young life. As Olive slept, she could smell her mother's perfume, sweet, floral lingering whiffs. She felt her touch as Polly brushed her hair, singing softly, while taming Olive's curls into a braid. Her pearls around her neck, Polly smiled at her daughter, then said, *I love you*. It was the first time Olive dreamed of her mother.

9

ONE POTATO, TWO POTATO, THREE POTATO, FOUR

*F*or two days, Tildy stomped around the house, slamming every available door, making her displeasure known to more than just Olive. Ginny sulked. Although given a precious ring and brooch, she coveted her mother's pearls. Bessie remained in the cottage, except for evening meals—which were often eaten in silence. Sally and Olive were the only happy recipients of Polly's treasures.

Eventually, the turmoil over the pearls dissipated as harvest dominated life at the Westchester farm. Twenty hired field hands, two housemaids, and a cook fell short of work demands. Everyone pitched in, including the children. Acres of corn, wheat, hay, and orchards occupied Ben's every moment. Clyde oversaw the livestock, horses, steers, milk cows, pigs, and lambs. Henderson struggled, even with the help of his foreman, to fill orders and keep the books.

The women set aside their daily sewing and needlework, replacing it with preserving fruit, vegetables, and making jams and jellies. All children were given two weeks' vacation from school to help with kitchen chores.

"Olive, will you go to the root cellar and bring up more jars?" Cook shouted over the buzz in the kitchen. "Take Samuel to help you carry."

"Come on, Sammy." Olive grabbed the boy's arm, dragging him out the door.

Looking at the entrance to the dark, dank storage space, Samuel declared, "I'm not going down there. I don't like spiders."

"Don't be such a baby. Brush aside the webs and step on the bugs." She tugged as Samuel resisted. "Oh, for goodness' sake, I'll go down first to clear the way. You follow."

Satisfied he was safe, Samuel waited for Olive to lift the heavy double doors of the bulkhead, brush away the cobwebs, and stomp on a few spiders before he climbed down the outside stairwell.

The root cellar was built during the 1850s, before the second house addition. Originally a small cave used to store wine and alcohol, Henderson's father excavated the area, reinforced a ceiling, leveled the dirt floor, and added rows of shelving. Two kerosene lamps hung at either end of the room, casting deep shadows with minimal light. Spiders, crickets, centipedes, and other assorted crawling creatures thrived in the dark dampness of the farthest reaches of the cellar. An enhanced ventilation shaft was installed nearest the double doors, providing dryer storage area for root vegetables and fruit. The area also accommodated the empty jars and baskets, waiting to be filled and reused.

The children loaded four baskets full of jars. Olive balanced one in each hand; Samuel needed both hands for one basket. Olive clicked her tongue.

"Muscle up, Sammy. If you can only carry one basket at a time, you're coming back down with me. We'll need to empty these and refill them—that is, if you want to eat this winter." Samuel blankly stared at Olive. She shrugged her shoulders.

Sally met the children at the kitchen door. "I'll take these jars over to the summer kitchen to clean them before we use them."

The summer kitchen, a detached, smaller replica of the inside kitchen, was used to prevent heat buildup and potential fires in the main house. The Westchester kitchen contained a large coal stove similar to the house stove, an expansive narrow table, and an eight-foot-long deep sink, great for small animal slaughter, cleaning large quantities, and, of course, canning season.

"What are we making today?" Olive asked as she swiped a stowaway spider off her apron.

"Peaches. Tomorrow we have string and yellow beans, I think. Then beets and apples. Jams and jellies follow tomato sauce and juice. Lastly, we'll use green tomatoes to make chutney."

Olive volunteered, "Why don't I make a list of our products, in the order in which we intend to prepare them? Then I can add the number of pints or quarts we preserve. Cook will have a better idea of our supplies, and less food will spoil."

Sally smiled. "That's how we used to do it at my house. I never suggested it to Ginny. I don't think she likes me much. Bea is right; you are a smart little girl." Sally patted Olive on the shoulder.

"I'm not little, and I'm not afraid of Ginny. I'll talk to Cook." Olive grinned as she clomped into the kitchen, ready to take charge. Cook smiled while Olive explained her idea.

"I love the idea," Cook said. "That's how Polly used to run the farm."

Ginny, who was slicing peaches in the corner, glared at Cook. "If I'm doing it incorrectly, why didn't you tell me?"

"My dear Ginny, it's not my place. How old were you when your mother passed? Twenty? Twenty-one? How many years did you help with this process? You've had plenty of time to learn. It's your duty to run the farm. I take orders from the mistress of the house, not the other way around." Cook returned to her crate of peaches.

Ginny sulked as she worked.

Olive scoured her father's office. She found a new ledger and returned to the kitchen, where she sat tall at a side table and made lists of products according to Cook's order. When she finished, she wrote the date at the top of the first column.

Cook stopped to prepare dinner while the rest of the crew continued peeling, pitting, and slicing peaches. Less daylight meant working through dusk. With all ambient light fading, Olive recorded fifty quarts of peaches. A banner crop and fifty more quarts tomorrow ensured plenty to sell and plenty for family consumption.

Long workdays ordained casual harvest meals. A hearty soup, thick bread, and sausages satiated the hungry group. Of course, the dinner would include a dessert. Henderson required a sweet to end his day.

"Who is the thief amongst you?" boomed Henderson as he slurped a spoonful of soup.

Ben looked at his father, then at his son, hoping him innocent. "Whatever do you mean?"

"Someone stole my new ledger. Who's the thief?" Henderson scanned faces as he repeated the question. Nine sets of lungs held their breath.

Olive broke the silence. "I am the thief, Papa." She sat tall and scrutinized her father's face.

Tildy chortled. "Now you've done it. Not so high and mighty now, are you?"

Defending her action, Olive offered, "I took it to make a list of our canning. We need a running inventory of our supplies, Papa."

Cocking his head, Henderson met Olive's eyes. "*Never* enter my office without being invited. *Never* take a thing from my office without being told. Do I make myself clear?"

Olive broke eye contact. Slouching in her chair, she whimpered, "Yes, Father. I'm sorry, Father."

"Ben, are we sending someone to town tomorrow for supplies?" Henderson's gaze remained on Olive.

"Yes, Father. Ben Jr. is going."

"Add three ledgers to the list. See that Olive gets one of them. I'll take the other two."

Olive hesitated, then took a deep breath before adding, "Ben, we also need more sugar, vinegar, and salt. And another two dozen canning jars."

Henderson was shocked that it was Olive, not Ginny making the request. "Is that true?" Henderson looked at his oldest daughter.

Ginny shrugged her shoulders, her fingers and toes going cold. "I'll have to check with Cook." Ginny excused herself, then left the table.

Upon her return, Ginny admitted, "Yes, Father, we need sugar and salt. Vinegar. Everything Olive requested."

Tildy flung her head and guffawed. Bessie bit her lip.

"You're head of the house, Ginny," Henderson lectured. "Why do you not know this when Olive does?"

In a state of panic, Ginny grabbed a slice of bread then excused herself again.

Proud of herself but unsure of her status with her father and the rest of the family, Olive decided to sit quietly while she finished her soup.

The meal ended in silence. One by one, the diners retreated to the sanctuary of their rooms. Olive, making a habit of leaving last, sat studying her mother's portrait.

How would Mama make things right?

∞∞∞∞

Work intensified daily. Long hours of toil produced sore muscles and restless nights. Jars stacked the root cellar, filled with necessary food to sustain the family throughout the winter. Next week the children would return to school, forcing the older women to complete any residual work without extra help.

Olive, charged with inventory, exited the root cellar with her ledger in hand. Having completed her list of old stock, it was time to shelve the new product.

"Come on, Sammy. Let's go. You can hand the jars to me so I can count and place them on the shelf." Olive encouraged her nephew.

"Oh, Olive, down there again?" Samuel shifted back and forth.

"I killed all the bugs. Bring a stool if you want to sit." Picking their way through the many baskets and jars, Olive started in the back. After moving the old product forward, Samuel handed her jars, one at a time. She placed the newly preserved food in the rear.

"Okay, Sammy, count the total number of jars. I'll record it in my ledger." Olive already had a count of the older stock ready.

"Ah, Olive, do I *have* to count?" Samuel whined.

"This isn't schoolwork; this is farm work. Now count." Olive grinned, then referred to her ledger. She already knew what his answer should be.

"...fifty-nine, sixty..." Samuel glanced down the row of jars, then looked at Olive, scratching the top of his head with both hands. "I don't know if I can count this high."

"Can you count to one hundred? Then you can count my jars," Olive spurred on Samuel. "Don't lose your place."

"We have eighty-seven jars, Olive." Proudly jumping off the stool, Samuel asked, "What's next?"

"Eighty-seven jars of what?" Olive assumed the role of Samuel's teacher in the absence of school.

Samuel squinted in the dim light, trying to distinguish between moss green or flaxen yellow. "I think they are yellow beans."

"Perfect. Now on to green beans." Olive shifted to the next shelf. Samuel sighed.

The two children worked all day, rotating stock, stacking, and counting. When they finished, a clear path through the root cellar appeared. Only baskets of apples, potatoes, turnips, sweet potatoes, onions, winter squash, and rutabagas littered the floor.

"Great job, Sammy. Shall we report our numbers to Cook?" They left the cellar, wiped a few lingering cobwebs from their clothing, then entered the kitchen.

"Cook, do you think we have enough food to last the winter?"

Olive's serious face surprised Cook. Grabbing two cookies, Olive handed one to Samuel and sent him on his way. She took a bite of the other while she waited for Cook's response.

"Why do you ask? It was a good crop this season." Cook wiped her hands on her apron and sat down beside Olive. Olive opened her ledger.

"We have a full cellar, but we also have a large family. Have you seen how much Ben and Bessie's kids eat? I swear, they eat five times as much as me, and I like to eat." Olive paused, making sure she had Cook's full attention. "Do you feed the farmhands?"

Olive's questions amused the wily old cook. "The men go home for the night, except the foreman. He lives with his wife in a cottage on the property and shares our supplies. I usually send something light to the fields to supplement everyone's packed lunch. Old man Westchester, your grandfather, started that during the war between the states."

"Do we have more hands now? More than before?" Olive made notes in the back of her ledger as they talked. "How many jars of peaches do you use to make one cobbler for the main family? How many jars of beans do you use for one casserole? Have you counted the total number of items in each straw basket?"

The interrogation lasted at least thirty minutes. Cook answered best she could.

Olive concluded, "I think the boys need to count and repack the baskets and barrels. I need a more accurate idea of what's on hand. Will you ask them to do that, Cook? They'll listen to you, not to me."

Cook agreed to obtain the requested basket counts, although she doubted the boys would be compliant.

To Olive's surprise, she received the numbers two days later. In the evenings, after supper, Olive studied her counts. She used her slate and chalk to calculate supply versus demand. When she was sure of her conclusion, she made her move.

Late Sunday afternoon, the day before school restarted, Henderson sat at his desk, examining his ledgers. He ran his hands through his hair, leaving ridges. He swore to himself.

Olive knocked on her father's door.

"Father? May I speak with you?" Olive lingered at the door awaiting an invitation to enter.

"What do you want? Can't you see I'm busy?" He looked up briefly, scrutinizing Olive.

Unrelenting, she continued. "I'm sorry to trouble you, but I made a discovery. I think some changes are in order to help prevent waste and provide better food quality, while saving money."

"Nonsense. We had a plentiful harvest, better than the past three years." Waving his hand at her, Henderson dismissed Olive.

"Please, Father, may I show you?" Determined to prove her point, Olive pushed the threshold of her father's patience.

"Fine. You have ten minutes. Make it quick, little missy," Henderson said, hissing the invitation through pursed lips.

She entered the room, closing the door behind her. Henderson scowled at the bold action. Walking to her father's desk, she pulled up a chair and opened her ledger.

Ninety minutes later, with disheveled hair, Henderson opened the library door. He carried Olive's list of last year's wasted food due to lack of proper storage rotation. Her calculations were on the cost of purchased seasonal vegetables, savings to be realized if off-season vegetables were grown on property in a greenhouse, and several other ideas to conserve produce and maximize production.

"I'll make the announcement tonight at dinner." He looked at his almost ten-year-old daughter. "When is your birthday?"

Olive stood, perplexed. Finally, she offered. "Next week. My birthday is October 29."

"Splendid. I'd rather you be older. Easier for the others to digest."

Giving her father a last discerning look, she turned and walked down the hall.

"Good work, Olive! We'll begin building the hot house tomorrow," Henderson yelled after her.

"Harumph." *What's the difference between nine or ten, when I'm correct?* Without looking back, she continued walking.

∞∞∞∞

Having completed the harvest raised high spirits; the dining room filled with laughter. Talk consisted of the annual Campbellsville harvest social and another successful year for the Westchester family farm—one of many. Now with Olive's plans, provisions for continued prosperity were ensured. Cook prepared a celebratory feast. Conversation and wine flowed freely.

Before the entrée was served, Henderson clinked his knife against his goblet. A hush fell over the table. "I have a special announcement to make this evening." Henderson sported an unusual smile. "I am making some changes around here. Cook, please join us."

Cook, who was waiting in the butler's pantry, quickly entered the dining room.

Ben tilted his head. "Father, we haven't discussed any changes. Did you and the foreman make them without me?"

"Are you being defensive, Benjamin?"

Ben gulped. Never a good sign when Henderson used his full name.

"I made the changes myself, if it's anyone's business. This is my farm; I shall do as I please." Henderson baited the family for additional comments. "All of you live here by my good graces, which I may withdraw as I see fit."

"I'm sorry, Father. Of course, it's your farm," Ben acquiesced, appeasing Henderson.

"Thank you for agreeing." His sarcastic smirk thwarted further interruption. "I have decided that Olive will help me with my accounting. She shall also oversee ordering kitchen and household supplies. If you need anything, take it to Olive. She has my full confidence to either approve or deny your request according to our collective needs." He waited for his words to settle. The family looked at each other astonished.

Tildy was the first to blowback. "Olive is nine years old. For God's sake, Father, be serious. Are you going senile?" Astonishment morphed into numbness. Did Tildy really just accuse Father of senility?

Henderson's voice boomed. "Matilda Elizabeth Westchester. Why do you try me so?"

Olive sat unmoving in her chair as all faces flipped from

Henderson to Tildy to Olive. Tildy recoiled, then fell quiet. She mumbled an unintelligible apology.

"Virginia, do *you* have a problem with my decision?" He caught Ginny's eyes briefly before she lowered them.

"I'm surprised, Father, but if this is your wish, then I am fine with your decision. If you are reassigning my responsibilities, is there some other way I may assist the farm?" Ginny continued to avert her eyes.

"Of course. You shall continue to be our hostess. Olive is neither old enough nor is her demeanor suited for the task. She outshines you with farm organizational skills, and she shall help me behind the scenes, with the bookkeeping, the numbers. But Ginny, you'll be the face of the family, with half of your mother's responsibilities. Olive shall have the other half, a great aid to me." Henderson turned to Ben. "Ben, we'll discuss actual farm adjustments tomorrow morning. Olive has several marvelous ideas."

Olive allowed herself to smile. She looked at her mother's portrait, whose curly, long blonde hair was pulled loosely away from her face. Olive decided it was time to eliminate her little girl pigtails.

"Sally," Olive braved speaking. "Will you braid my hair for school tomorrow? One big braid down the middle of my back."

"With pleasure, Sweetie." Sally fancied having a powerful family friend, even if she was only ten. Her alliances with Ginny and Tildy were dubious at best.

The partnership established, Olive crossed her arms, reveling in the day's accomplishments.

10

ROCK-A-BYE BABY

*W*arm October breezes from the south shifted to blustery northwestern December winds. Farm life, now catlike, readied itself for the somnolence of winter. The children no longer walked to school. Jake dropped them off as he drove Ben Jr. to high school in Campbellsville.

Henderson deemed basic education mandatory for girls and boys alike. Even Ginny and Tildy completed eight years of formal education before enrolling in the local Madison finishing school (perhaps not Henderson's best investment, concerning Matilda). The same opportunity would be afforded to Nellie, Olive, and Lizzy when the time came.

Miss Thompson invested extra attention to her star pupil. Olive excelled in all subjects, especially in math, and Henderson reaped the benefits—Olive's ledger never left her side. Polly's youngest protegee managed the house as tightly as a coiled snake. Olive blossomed through her newfound responsibility, while her relationships grew with Sally and Henderson.

With Christmas only two weeks away, lethargy yielded to excitement. After working with her father nightly, Olive retreated to her room, writing lists of necessary holiday preparations. With school in recess, Olive relished some extra time to complete her many tasks.

Tildy and Ginny set about decorating the large house. Using wheat paste and colorful paper, the children made garlands for the tree. Benny allowed Samuel to help tie together pine boughs to hang around the entry doors.

"Cook, please compose a list of provisions needed to outfit our holiday lauder. Benny shall fetch the supplies tomorrow." Cook enjoyed her lessened responsibility due to Olive's ability. Now that she no longer had to spend so much energy supervising Ginny's incompetence, the kitchen returned to its glory days of old.

After skipping down the upstairs hallway, Olive knocked then waited for her new best friend to answer the door. Sally, still in bed, welcomed her to enter.

"Sally, it's noon; why are you so lazy today? Get out of bed." Olive ran into the room to kiss Sally on the forehead. "We have work to do. What smells in here?" she asked before she noticed the bucket.

"Olive, my tummy is queasy today. I think I shall remain in bed." Sally smiled at an unsuspecting Olive.

"Oh my, do you have the flu? I'm sorry I yelled at you." Olive turned around and quietly left the room, closing the door behind her. She never saw Sally's grin.

Downstairs, Olive warned the family. "Dearest Sally has the flu; stay clear unless you want to be sick for Christmas."

Ginny giggled to herself then climbed down from the step stool, pulling Olive aside. "Olive, I think we need to talk. Shall we go up to your room where it is private?"

"Sure, Ginny. Wait until I make a cup of tea to take to Sally. The honey may settle her stomach." Olive turned toward the kitchen.

"Have Cook put a little ginger in it. She'll understand. That's what Sally needs."

Olive looked at her sister skeptically. *How does she know what Sally needs?*

Sally was sitting in bed when Olive arrived. She delivered her gift of tea and cookies to the bottom of the bed, trying to keep her distance from the sick patient.

"Olive, you don't have to avoid me. Ask Ginny to explain." Sally grinned.

"She is already waiting in my room for me." Olive paused. "What's wrong, if it's not catchy?"

"Ginny will explain. Everything is fine, I promise."

Olive left the right wing of the house and walked slowly down the hall, trying to delay whatever Ginny had to say.

"Climb up on the bed and sit beside me, Olive." Ginny looked Olive up and down. "It's hard to believe you are only ten. You've grown tall and thin, like Mother and me. And all that responsibility you handle so aptly." Ginny shook her head in disbelief. "Do you understand where babies come from?"

The simple question stumped Olive.

"I know it takes a mommy and a daddy. I've seen the horses give birth. Ucky." Olive feigned vomiting. Ginny grinned.

"Well, little sister, Sally and Clyde are going to have a baby. Sally is pregnant. Sometimes when women are pregnant, they get sick. It's called morning sickness because it usually happens when you wake up."

Olive pointed to the clock. "It's noon. This isn't morning sickness for Sally."

"For Sally, morning sickness is lasting most of the day. She found out two days ago that she was with child...just like how Mary was with child at Christmas."

Olive shrugged her shoulders and snorted, then quickly corrected Ginny. "It's *not* like Mary. God was the daddy for Mary, not her husband. Father reads this Bible story to us every Christmas, don't you remember?"

"Fine, you are correct. Clyde is the daddy in this case." Ginny inhaled, wishing to escape this discussion. "There is more that I need to tell you. The way you're growing, things may change for you sooner rather than later." Reluctantly, Ginny explained more to her sister about pregnancy and a woman's monthly courses.

Olive sat with her mouth hanging open. Her terrified wide blue eyes never blinked, quietly waiting for Ginny to finish. She braced her hands on the bed to keep from toppling over.

"Ginny, is there any way I can prevent this—what did you call it? The curse of Eve?" Olive's question was more of a plea.

"I'm afraid not. Every woman suffers from this monthly. When you see red spots on your panties, come to me right away. Don't be scared. I'll help you."

This was the first time Olive could remember Ginny ever showing her motherly affection. Tildy was her early governess, and Ginny was always too busy with the house or Samuel to pay her much attention. The sisterly bonding and the realization of a lifelong curse sent Olive into an atypical fit of tears.

"Don't cry, Olive. It's not so bad. You'll get used to it." From the look on her face, Olive knew Ginny lied.

"Ginny, Mama died when she was giving birth. Sally won't die, will she?" Her sobs intensified.

"No, Sally won't die. She is young and healthy. I had Samuel, and I didn't die. Tildy had Lizzy, and she didn't die. Sally shall be fine. By the end of next summer, we'll have a new little Westchester in our family."

Olive stilled her sobs. "Should we make Christmas gifts for Sally's baby? Do you think I can knit a baby dress before Christmas?"

"Slow down. I'll teach you how to knit dresses, but there is not enough time before Christmas for you to make a gift. Why don't you make the baby a different kind of gift, and save the knitting for later?"

Re-energized, Olive jumped off the bed. "I'm knitting Fred a scarf. That's pretty hard. I already know how to embroider some. I'll make the baby a bib for Christmas."

Olive peeked into her sewing kit then proceeded to compile another list for Benny's shopping trip.

∞∞∞∞

Olive sprinted into the dining room. Dinner had already started. Running up to Clyde, she threw her arms around his neck.

"I'm so excited!" Olive jumped from one foot to the other before taking her place at the table.

"Sorry we're late. I'm guilty of sharing your news with Olive, Clyde," Ginny confessed. "I also explained other womanly things, as a precaution."

Henderson looked up from his plate. "What? Womanly what? I shall have no such talk at my dinner table."

Ginny shushed Olive before she could elaborate. "Of course, Father. Olive knows all."

"For goodness' sake. Did you tell her everything? She's only ten," Tildy screeched. Turning to look at Olive and Clyde, she noticed Sally's absence. "Am I the last to know? Sally's pregnant?"

Ben's children snickered. Clyde blushed as Olive answered her sister. "Yes, Sally is expecting a baby. Baby shall be born next summer, and we all better make it a Christmas present this year."

Henderson exhaled. "I'm sorry. I feel responsible for the creation of this leviathan."

"Levia... what?" asked Olive. "Father, may I use your dictionary after supper?"

"Yes, Olive. You may, although you may not like what you find." Henderson and his brood chuckled. Olive joined them, too excited to care.

"Father," Ben changed the subject, "When are the younger boys arriving home?"

"I think on the twenty-second." Henderson scratched his ear.

Ginny flinched. "Oh, I'll need to prepare a place for them to sleep. Perhaps I'll move Samuel in with me over the holiday, Olive can sleep in the nursery, and the boys will have their old beds. Is that okay with you, Olive?"

"I'm so happy Fred is coming home; I'll sleep on the porch!" She emphasized her resolve with a fist to the table.

Henderson roared with laughter. "Like I said...she's my creation."

11

DECK THE HALLS

*E*very day looked more like Christmas. Olive and the children worked diligently to create wonderful treasures for each family member.

After three days of sewing, Olive exclaimed, "This family is getting too big. It takes far too long to make gifts. I don't remember spending this much time last year."

Samuel and Lizzy continued gluing paper. Every so often, Samuel licked his fingers to taste the paste.

A commotion at the back door alerted the children to new and exciting events. They scurried out of the nursery, Samuel's room, down the back staircase and into the kitchen.

"It's here! It's here!" Olive jumped up and down as she surveyed the trail of needles.

"What's here?" asked Lizzy.

Urging them on, Olive commanded, "Follow me, you'll see." The trio darted into the parlor. Skidding to a stop, just inside the doorway, they squealed in delight.

"It's as big as a bear," Samuel exclaimed.

"It's as big as a monster," Lizzy said, remembering her monster nightmares from last night.

"No, it's as big as our pear tree," Olive said, making the most logical assessment.

The massive blue spruce filled an entire corner of the room, the same corner from which, years earlier, Polly and baby said good-bye at their wake. Joining hands, the children spun in wild circular dances, chanting *Three more days till Christmas*. Nellie joined the spinning while Ben Jr. stopped working to enjoy their youthful enthusiasm. He thought himself too mature to join in such a display, but he was secretly as excited about the holiday as the children and his sister.

Sufficiently dizzy, the twirling stopped as the four tumbled on top of each other, laughing and giggling. Olive rolled over onto her back, arms outstretched.

"Aww. All we need is snow. Then we can make snow angels." She moved her arms and legs back and forth. Lizzy and Samuel did the same.

"What's all this noise about?" Henderson teased. "I hear you with my office door closed."

"Grandfather, it's three days till Christmas." Lizzy popped up and began jumping in front of Henderson. "Santa is coming!" Her glowing eyes twinkled, as if she were from the poem.

"Is that a fact?" The holiday softened Henderson's crusty old shell. "I have another surprise."

As soon as he spoke the words, the front door opened. A young man stepped into the vestibule and closed the outer door before opening the foyer entrance.

"Fred, Fred!" Olive ran to greet her brother, but when she saw who it was she could not disguise her disappointment. "Levi, where's Fred?"

"Hello, little sister." Levi gave Olive an up-and-down. "Not so little anymore. My, my, you must have grown three inches since last Christmas."

"I am not little. I help father with his bookkeeping. I also maintain our supply ledger. Where's Fred?" Olive stomped her foot to reinforce her statement.

"Well, I'm glad to see you also." Levi patted her on the head, dropped his bag in the entranceway, then walked into the parlor to greet the rest of the family. Olive gaped after him.

Levi embraced his nephew, niece, and father—but at a thump on his back, he turned. "Olive, ouch. Why did you hit me?"

"You didn't answer my question. Where is Fred?" Her nose was in his chest.

"Excuse me? How dare you be so bold? Have you not learned yet that a woman's place is in the shadows?" Levi turned to his father. "What are you teaching her?"

"Meet Olive Leviathan Westchester." Henderson bowed, waving his hand toward his daughter.

"Stop it, Father, I know what you mean. I'm not a multi-headed monster." Her blue eyes flickered. Samuel and Lizzy gasped at the word monster.

Lizzy ventured, "Is Olive really a monster? Does she live under my bed?"

"Of course not. Monsters are not real." A furious Olive spat. "Where is Fred?"

"Tildy, reincarnate?" Levi beckoned to his father.

"Not exactly. Dramatic, hardheaded, but extremely bright. Leaves Tildy in her dust." Henderson smiled. "I suffer the consequences for an exceptional office helper. Besides, she reminds me of Polly in too many ways."

Levi frowned. "This," he said, pointing to Olive. "Is nothing like the mother I remember."

Hearing Levi's words, Olive whirled around. "I am like Mother. Look at her portrait and look at me. I do resemble her! You're a mean, despicable brother. "Looking Levi directly in the face she screamed, " Where is Fred?" Olive spun on her heel and clomped out of the room.

In her bedroom, Olive crawled under the blue and brown quilt of Fred's bed. His scent long gone, she searched for some remembrance of her beloved brother. *Why didn't Fred come home? Why was Levi so cruel?* She struggled with the idea of despising Levi. *Should she?*

He might be mean, but he was still nicer than Tildy...however, he did ignore her. *So be it.* Holding tightly to the quilt, she cried herself to sleep, missing Fred.

∞∞∞∞

"Olive, wake up." Sally was shaking her shoulder. "Dinner is starting. You're late, sweetie."

"Oh, Sally." Olive smothered her with hugs and kisses. "I'm so glad you are well enough to join us tonight. I've missed you so much."

"Come on, get yourself washed up. I'll make your regrets for being late." Sally kissed her on the forehead and left the girl dressing for dinner.

"I apologize, Father, for being late." Olive entered the dining room; taking her seat across from Levi, she scowled.

"She eats with us?" Levi questioned.

"That's enough from you, Levi. West Point has not taught you humility, I see." Henderson hushed his son. "Let's all be a little tolerant this holiday. Olive earns her place at this table, more so than most of you. I'll have no more disparaging words about her."

"Thank you, Father." Grateful eyes expressed her pleasure.

"And you, young lady, watch your Ps and Qs. I'll not tolerate a bickering family. This holiday shall be a joyful, happy time."

Henderson has spoken, and so it shall be.

Light conversation filled the remaining meal, comprised mainly of catching Levi up on what he had missed. Clyde announced Sally's pregnancy to him, Ben reported on a banner harvest, and Ginny explained the sleeping arrangements.

"Levi, pray—now that your sister has returned, do tell us why your brother did not return home this holiday." Henderson finally requested an answer to Olive's burning question. Olive, who sat silent most of the meal, came to attention.

"The Commandant declared at the last minute that no plebe shall receive leave over Christmas. Fred must remain on campus with the rest of his class for extra training." Levi waved his hand, "I have no idea what caused it, but one of his classmates must have committed a terrible infraction."

"I wish he had written to tell us such. I'd ship a package to him. I'm sure he'd welcome a batch of Cook's famous shortbread cookies."

"Levi." Olive looked at her brother, eyes filled with contrition. "Will you take Fred's gift from me back with you? I worked all fall making it."

"Yes, Olive, gladly." Levi looked at his father, then back to Olive before saying, "I am sorry I shouted and treated you so poorly. In all honesty, when I first saw you at the door, you did remind me of Mother. So much so that I may have been overcome with grief. Whatever the trigger, my actions were unbecoming of an officer in the United States Army. My sincere apologies."

Henderson's face glowed with approval.

"Oh Levi, do I really remind you of Mother? That makes me happy." She glanced at her mother's portrait. Olive's mood improved as she exposed two rows of teeth in a grin. "You're not terribly mean, though maybe a little. But I do miss Freddy so." Olive ran over and hugged her brother. "Welcome home, Levi, and Merry Christmas! Now, let's all trim the tree."

WE, THE PEOPLE

*B*en Jr. and Nellie carried crates and boxes of Christmas items down from the attic, leaving them in the entryway. Ginny and Tildy sorted objects according to function. Whiffs of cinnamon and nutmeg filtered in from the kitchen.

"Samuel, Lizzy, settle down." Tildy's tolerance was none improved due to the holidays. "Stop jumping up and down." Tildy flashed Olive a look as if to say, *Help me with these two*.

Olive ignored the look. She was too busy stringing paper garlands and clipping glass birds to the boughs. Two strings of electric lights added a shimmering glow. Although the entire house was not yet adapted to electricity, the parlor, dining room, kitchen, library, and Henderson's bedroom had power. The conversion of the remaining gas lights was scheduled for the spring. Henderson splurged on the electric tree lights; they cost over twelve dollars each strand. However, he considered it a worthwhile investment to prevent a fire. Two years ago, the neighbor's house burned to the ground because of lit candles on the tree.

"Father, we shall see you in the morning. Bessie, the children, and I need to decorate the cottage." Ben motioned for his family to depart.

Hugging the group goodnight, they left, walking arm in arm the five hundred yards to their modest home. Ben kissed Bessie on the cheek.

"I love Christmas," Bessie responded in kind.

Excitement mounted in the parlor as the big house transformed into a scene from a Currier and Ives lithograph.

Sally bent over, picking up a box of tree ornaments, she placed them on a side table.

"Sally, I don't want you to exert yourself. Don't lift; please play some carols instead." Clyde helped his wife to the piano stool. Producing a stack of sheet music, he opened *The Holly and the Ivy*.

"She's not an invalid," Tildy snorted. Every family member clicked their tongues at Tildy, unable to control her outbursts despite the celebration. Sally ignored her sister-in-law by playing.

"Matilda, please. Don't alter my mood." Henderson glared at his middle child, wondering why she always acted out. "Let us hear *God Rest Ye Merry Gentlemen* next, please."

Music filled the house as the Westchesters sang along to their favorite Christmas songs. Clyde and Levi hung holly wreaths on every window. Ropes of pine draped over the inside and outside double doors. Layers of crystal, glass, paper, and wood adorned the tree. Rays of light from the silver star mounted at the top reflected into the corners of the room. Festivities ended with freshly baked gingerbread and hot cocoa, consumed in front of the roaring fire, as *Silent Night* floated from the keyboard.

"The only thing that could make this night more perfect," said Henderson, "is Polly."

His sad eyes glowed in a rare moment of family pride. His heart filled with love as he looked at the assembled crew. Tonight, he was at peace.

"And Fred. Don't forget Fred," added Olive.

"Yes, and Fred. Shall we call it an evening? I must rise early tomorrow to see the farmhands. Who wants to help me hand out Christmas birds?" Thinking Levi would offer, Henderson was surprised to hear a female voice respond first.

"I'll help you, Father," Olive volunteered.

∞∞∞

A frosty wind blew at five o'clock, the morning of December 24, 1911. Olive wrapped a woolen blanket around her coat as she climbed onto the front of the wagon. The nares of her nose stuck together.

"Good morning. Cold one, today." Henderson yawned as he took the reins. "Shall we be off? The sooner we finish, the sooner we shall be eating Cook's flapjacks." Covering their legs with a second blanket, he spurred the team forward.

The light workday for the farmhands consisted of feeding the barnyard animals, cleaning horse stalls, and gathering eggs. Then, tending to market sales, the foreman Kendrick usually closed around two in the afternoon.

Hearing the screeching wagon wheels, the men assembled outside the barn. "They're here," someone shouted. Per tradition, the higher the rank, the larger the bird. However, this year, Olive budgeted and finagled discretionary money so that every man received at least a twenty-pound bird.

"Olive, please do the honors." Henderson looked at the stack of freshly slaughtered geese, ducks, and turkeys. "Gentleman, this year, Westchester Farms wishes you Merry Christmas with your choice of bird, all of which are similar in size."

Approving looks passed through the group. Murmurs of *I knew we had a good year*, and *This will feed my whole family* were heard. One by one, the men approached the wagon.

"Merry Christmas. May God Bless." Olive, sitting on the wagon bench, distributed according to each man's request, handing each a bonus jar of peach jam.

Kendrick Jones approached last. The foreman generously offered to take any type of leftover bird.

"Mr. Jones, I have one of each left, a turkey, a duck, or a goose.

Your choice." Olive smiled as she handed him a jar of jam. "Merry Christmas to you, sir." Olive turned, waiting for Kendrick's decision.

"In that case, make mine a fat goose." He searched the face of his surly old boss for a clue to this year's generosity. Henderson gave none.

"Here is your goose, and here is a small token of thanks." Olive handed Kendrick an envelope. Kendrick opened it to find a twenty-dollar bill.

"Mr. Westchester..." Kendrick stammered at their generosity. "I am flabbergasted."

Olive spoke first. "Mr. Jones, you provide a valuable service to our farm operation. We appreciate all you do." Henderson laughed as Kendrick eyed the youngest Westchester child, Olive.

"Yes, she is only ten. Yes, she understands this business better than either Ben or Clyde. Too bad, she's a girl."

"What does being a girl have to do with anything?" Olive looked at both men with a wrinkled, clueless forehead. "I can do just about everything the men can do, except for heavy lifting." Her foot thudded on the floorboard.

Henderson flicked the whip, and the horses headed back to the house. "Olive, although I support your basic education and appreciate your help, the world does not always treat women kindly. Women *require* the protection of a husband. You are more like your mother than you realize. She was bright, organized, and strong-willed. A great asset to her husband." Olive touched her father's leg. "I want to be like my mother, even if I don't remember her. Telling me this is a wonderful Christmas gift." Olive lay her head against Henderson's shoulder as they rode home.

"My dear daughter. Your mother was *my* asset. You will be another man's asset. The world shall disallow you as a woman to be your *own* asset."

"But Father, I don't want a husband. I am capable and competent on my own." Olive pouted. "I shall be my own asset."

"Today, you are my daughter. Now let's go home to breakfast."

∞∞∞∞

Calm settled over the household as morning faded into afternoon. Chores finished; the family gathered in the parlor. Slipping under Sally's arm, Olive cuddled her friend. Clyde joined them on the settee. Samuel and Lizzy played a game of Tiddledy-Winks on the floor, Tildy claimed the piano, and Ginny embroidered a last-minute gift. Henderson and Levi entered last, as Cook served a late afternoon tea. All the rest of the staff was off duty.

"How did you manage to find a cucumber this time of year?" asked Levi as he took several sandwiches and cakes from the tiered platter. Cook smiled then looked at Henderson to answer.

Henderson grinned at Levi then at Olive. "Come Levi, follow me. Olive suggested growing them enclosed in glass. We built a large greenhouse. It has extended the growing season for many of the herbs, flowers, and vegetables that would die with the first frost."

Ginny added, "We even have ripe tomatoes and lettuce for Christmas dinner."

Levi was in awe of the massive structure, twenty feet wide, fifty feet long, neatly tucked out of sight behind the kitchen. Windows on levers tilted out and up to promote airflow and control temperature. A steam boiler heated water that flowed through iron pipes buried in the soil. Benches and tables were filled with pots of ornamental flowers and herbs. Shiny red fruit hung from several dozen tomato plants. Vines full of green beans, cucumbers, and squash were trellised on cord. Raised beds of spinach, lettuce, onions, garlic, beets, and carrots thrived in nutrient-rich soil that reeked of manure.

"It's a marvel! And this was solely Olive's idea?" Levi asked, as he and Henderson returned to the dining room.

"Yes, she's a clever girl. It brings in exceptional off-season income, from those folks who can afford such a luxury." Henderson's compliment surprised Olive. "Kendrick helped design the plumbing and ventilation, but the rest was, essentially, Olive."

Levi studied his littlest sister. Creative child. *She's matured in the year since last Christmas. She'll make some man a valuable wife.*

"Levi," Olive asked, seeing her brother studying her, "Do you study the Revolutionary War at West Point?" She pulled a knit blanket over herself and Sally.

"That's a silly question. Of course, we do. West Point was a Revolutionary War fort; Benedict Arnold was commandant. What's your curiosity?" Levi looked at Olive, to his father, and back to Olive. "Don't they teach you this in school?"

"Yes. I want to know about our family that fought in the war. I saw Mother's certificate from the Daughters of the American Revolution. I would like to know about my pedigree."

Henderson jumped up. "I have a couple books and some papers on this topic. Let me get them for you." Returning from his office, Henderson placed two bound books and a file of papers on Levi's lap. Blowing away the dust, Levi opened the file.

"These belong to *your* ancestor, Father, not Mother's." Levi sneezed as he sorted through the stack.

"You *both* have Revolutionary ancestors?" Olive began bouncing up and down.

"Honey, you're going to have to sit still unless you want me bedridden again," Sally whispered. Olive's bouncing reduced to intermittent.

Levi began reading the handwritten entry.

The 1700s—Colonial Pennsylvania
Gregor Campbell's family immigrated to the colonies from Edinburgh, Scotland, in the early eighteenth century. His parents sailed to New York harbor but decided to settle in the Philadelphia area. The Campbell family were always town dwellers. Gregor's father was a shop- and innkeeper. Campbell's "Tartan Inn" was popular with the Scottish and Irish populations of the colonial city. Born in

Pennsylvania, Gregor, a native colonial, was privileged to education and the colonial gentry's life. As a young man, Gregor dabbled in local politics. At the time of the Revolution, he was a respected magistrate. The Campbell family lived in a large, two-story brick home on two acres of land. The grounds consisted of formal gardens outlined with boxwood hedges, a rose garden, a cutting garden, and a vegetable garden. The Campbells were not slave owners; however, they were quick to employ indentured servants. Colin Westchester also immigrated from Scotland, although he was British. Colin's father was stationed in Inverness, Scotland, in 1727. Unlike most officers who left their families in London, Col. Westchester thought it would be an exciting adventure for his young wife to follow him to Scotland. Lady Westchester lived in luxury at Inverness castle. Her husband was always close at hand. It was no surprise that she found herself with child before the end of the decade. Master Colin was born and raised in the Highlands by native Highlanders. He loved the beauty of the land. Colin knew no other life; in his mind, he was part Scott.

By age sixteen, with his father's help, Colin was presented a commission in His Majesty's army. Colin and his father proudly represented the Crown, even if it meant a skirmish or two with their Scottish friends and neighbors. They were, after all, the ruling country. That is, until the battle of Culloden. Father and son were disgusted and appalled by the quickness, ferocity, and outright slaughter of the Highlanders that they both resigned their commissions and sailed for the colonies. Upon arrival, they declared themselves Scotts, despite their contradictory last name. While living peacefully on a farm in Berks County, Pennsylvania, Colin was the first in line to sign up for the Patriot forces when the colonies began revolting against the Crown. Due to his knowledge and skill in warfare, he was immediately given a commission and the rank of Colonel. Gregor Campbell was also quick to side with the colonists for independence. Despite being a man of learning, he worked his way up through the ranks. He finished the war as Lieutenant Gregor Campbell, serving under his fellow Scotsman, Colonel Colin Westchester. At the end of the Revolutionary war, Gregor was given land, same as Colin Westchester, in west-central Pennsylvania. West-central Pennsylvania was already populated by settlers following the Forbes Road and the army to Fort Duquesne during the French and Indian war. Colin received thirteen-hundred acres; Gregor, four hundred acres. The men were friends; therefore, they found it easy to together cultivate a new community of villagers and farmers. The acreage was about eighty miles east of Fort Pitt, twenty-five miles north of the former Fort Ligonier, and ten miles west of the former Fort Palmer. Westchester took to farming, dreaming of the Scottish Highlands while Campbell designed a town. Campbell's town was laid out in a large grid fashion featuring generous lots. Gregor set himself up as magistrate, built a large house, and hoped to entice eastern colleagues in joining him on the frontier. The Conemaugh River flowed directly through the center of the grid. The town offered beautiful vistas of the surrounding Allegheny Mountains and ample river access for industry.

Campbell and Westchester both retained contacts in eastern Pennsylvania. They convinced friends to journey across Pennsylvania to their new land. For those patriots looking for space either in a town or on a farm, west-central Pennsylvania was a popular destination, although Indian raids were not uncommon. The construction of the National Highway made it accessible. Irish and Scotts migrated to its scenic, picturesque hills and ridges. Campbellsville soon attracted many Germans living in the eastern cities due to the resemblance to the fatherland's Mosel river valley. Gregor sold one-acre village lots while Colin sold fifty-acre farm plots. Per Gregor's design, large houses were soon built in the corners of each grid segment. Gregor opened an inn for travelers and troops on their way to Fort Pitt and beyond. The Germans opened a store and a

lumber mill. The Irish opened eateries, farmed, and prospected for
coal. The Scotts farmed and opened a woolen mill. The river
provided easy access for light industry to the newly born town. The
families intermarried. Thus, the town and country grew, along
with America's heritage.

"Who wrote this? These records are astonishing. Colin was, what....your great-great-grandfather?" Tildy was showing an attentiveness quite out of character. "How do the Campbells fit into our history?"

Chuckling at her interest in family heritage, Henderson provided answers. "The Campbells are your mother's family. One of the original Campbell girls married a Sinclair. Your mother's maiden name was Sinclair."

"So, your grandfather, a thousand times back, and mother's grandfather, a thousand times back, were the first people to settle in the area?" Olive could barely contain her excitement. "When I'm old enough, I can join DAR *twice!*" Sally gave her a pinch; Olive tried to sit still.

Ginny stopped sewing. "Sweetie, I don't think it works just like that. You only join once."

Olive's animation infected the group.

"Maybe I'll join. The Jamisons are an old family. That may help me gain their favor." Tildy uttered her thoughts out loud as she pounded a chord.

"Tildy, that is shameful. Join because you are proud of your heritage, not because you want distinction." The ten-year-old lectured her twenty-five-year-old sister.

"I don't want distinction. I want a husband."

Boisterous conversation grabbed the attention of Samuel and Lizzy. Lizzy cozied up to her mother. During the exchange, the innocent child gazed at Tildy and suggested, "Maybe Santa will bring a husband for Christmas?"

Tildy leaned over and kissed Lizzy's head. "My darling daughter, that sounds like the perfect gift."

Giggling stopped as the family quieted. Setting aside family records and thoughts of years gone by, they focused on ancient history, the celebration of Christ's Birth. All the while, they enjoyed the comforting scent of smoke from the fire, the harmonic chords of the carols, and the crunch of crisp butter cookies until bedtime.

13

I HEARD THE BELLS ON CHRISTMAS MORN

*O*live rolled over, pulling the quilt over her ear. She caught a whiff of frying bacon as she snuggled into her pillow. The aroma dispelled her fuzzy visions of dreams as she sat upright in her bed.

"Merry Christmas!" Olive called. Her greeting echoed through the second floor. Replies of *Go back to sleep* and *Just a few more minutes* were mumbled in return. The wish was welcomed only by Lizzy and Samuel, who both ran into Olive's room and began jumping up and down on her bed.

"Do you think Santa found our house?" Lizzy's nightgown caught around her legs as she tumbled onto Olive. The children giggled in excitement.

A yawning Tildy poked her head into the room. "Olive, why so early?" Turning to Lizzy, she said, "Run, now, tend to your bathroom duties. As soon as you finish, we shall go downstairs. Mind you, though; we must wait for the others to join us before we look under the tree." Wrapping her shawl around her shoulders, she shivered in the early morning chill.

"But Mama," Lizzy objected. Looking to Olive for some support, she asked, "Olive, make her change her mind." Lizzy folded her hands in hopes of reinforcing her plea.

"Those are the rules, Lizzy," Samuel said. "Grandfather's law. Like it or not." Trying to comfort his cousin, Samuel hugged Lizzy. She pulled away.

"Well, I say '*not*,'" Lizzy said, running off the bed. She wrapped her body around Tildy's leg, begging for a change in the verdict. Picking up her child, Tildy kissed her hair while Samuel and Olive looked on.

"Don't worry, sweetie. I think we can placate you with some bacon, and maybe a cookie from the kitchen." Then, turning to the other two children, she ordered, "You other two, let's get moving."

Tildy carried a giggling Lizzy down the hall, leaving Samuel and Olive staring at each other.

"Come on, Sammy, let's get ready and go downstairs. Don't forget to dress for services."

Eating a thick piece of bacon, Henderson arrived to find Samuel and Olive sitting on the settee. Munching on cookies, they tried not to soil their church clothes. He burst into a Santa-esque chuckle.

"You know, children, the requisite is to behave *throughout* the year, not only on Christmas Day." Walking to the settee, he kissed each on the forehead, wishing them Merry Christmas. "Now, where are the others? If they hurry, we may have time to open one gift before morning services instead of waiting until after dinner."

As he uttered the last words, Olive heard the pealing church bells. A call to worship echoed through the valley and over the hills. Faithful from every station of life journeyed to one of the many Houses of God. The Westchester family traveled to Campbellsville to attend the First Presbyterian Church.

"Oh, too late for presents now. Hurry, all. We must leave soon," bellowed Henderson. "Cook, are you coming along?"

Cook appeared, flinging her wool cape over her shoulders. "Yes, sir. I shall ride in the buggy. I believe Jake has the Ford ready and waiting." Cook called out, "You in the kitchen, everything is set. Just needs tending. I want to walk into the house after church and be ready to eat." A meek, *Yes, ma'am,* replied from both housemaids.

"Come along children. Why should you wait for the buggy? They who lag shall be cold today. You shall ride with me."

His smile was infectious. Holidays suited Henderson. Samuel and Olive thrilled at Henderson's unexpected invitation.

Olive whispered to Samuel, "Grab your coat. Claim your spot." They quickly jumped into the automobile.

Walking up the path between the cottage and the main house, Ben and Bessie's family watched Henderson leave with the youngsters.

"Now that is odd," Benny said to his sister. "Have we ever ridden with Grandfather to church?" Ben Sr. hung his head, relinquishing his pecking order to his ten-year-old sister.

"Never mind. Two buggies await us. We'll be second to arrive."

The Westchester brood, known as "Easter and Christmas Christians," vainly strolled into the Campbellsville Presbyterian Church. The stained-glass windows, draped with lengths of ground pine, sparkled in candlelight. The aroma of pine and fir floated throughout the worship area. An embellished circular advent wreath filled the pulpit. Today, Pastor Ashton would light the Christmas candle.

Henderson led the children to the front pew. Already occupied with devoted attendees, Henderson stared until they relinquished their seats to the master of Westchester Farms. The act was repeated with the occupants of the second pew.

"Jake, sit behind us. Save the entire row for my family." As the opening hymn played, the remaining family filed in, filling the sanctuary's first three pews.

"O come all ye faithful, joyful and triumphant!" Olive and Samuel belted out the words of the carol as Campbellsville proclaimed the birth of their Savior.

∞∞∞∞

"Fine sermon. Fine sermon," Henderson repeated as he shook the pastor's hand. "Splendid Christmas morning to you." Helping Olive with her coat, he ushered her forward toward the door.

"Merry Christmas to you also, Mr. Westchester. Who is this fine-looking girl? She favors Polly." Pastor Ashton's patronizing smile betrayed his knowledge, as he reached to touch Olive's arm.

"Perhaps she does. Thank you, now we must be off." Henderson forcefully removed the pastor's grip on Olive. Anxious to collect his brood and be on his way, Henderson plotted their escape.

"Henderson, is it too much of an imposition for your daughters to attend weekly service? Like they did when Polly was alive?" Ashton moved slightly to the right, blocking the doorway.

"Pastor, it is of no consequence if they attend. You'll find my semi-annual gift in the collection plate. I'm sure it's adequate." Henderson dismissed the request, hurriedly gathered his family, and pushed past. "Merry Christmas, Ashton. Until Easter," he called from the Ford.

∞∞∞∞

"Hurry, hurry," Lizzy tugged at her mother. Coats were hung three-deep on the entrance hall-tree as the family piled into the house. "I want to see what Santa brought."

"Just a peek," said Tildy as Lizzy pulled her into the parlor.

"We feast, first. Everyone, into the dining room," yelled Henderson. "Come, children."

Food crowded the ten-foot table, along with thirteen Westchesters. A bowl of fresh holly, flanked on each side by candles, set the table aglow. Pine aroma mixed with spices and herbs brought the scents of the outdoors inside.

Privileged to the dining room only on two high holidays, Samuel and Lizzy found seats beside their mothers. Foil-wrapped Christmas crackers lay across each plate.

Picking up the banded cylinder, Lizzy asked, "What do I do with this?"

"Silly, don't you remember last year?" Samuel questioned. "Watch. You hold both ends, then pull hard." The cracker popped. Lizzy jumped. Inside, a folded paper crown waited to be donned. Samuel unwrapped his crown and placed it on Lizzy's head. She squirmed in appreciation.

"Now, you pop yours and give me your crown." Samuel placed Lizzy's fingers in each end, helping her find the strings.

"Why is there a crown inside?" Lizzy mused as she unfolded the thin paper.

"For the Birth of Jesus, the King. Kings wear crowns," Samuel explained as if the answer were obvious. "We wear a crown to honor Him today on His Birthday."

"Ooooooh." Lizzy thrilled as the family laughed and popped their crackers.

Their feast was fit for a king. Pumpkin soup with biscuits began the day of gluttony, to be followed by roasted goose, bacon-fried potatoes and turnips, sautéed green beans topped with toasted almonds, rum-glazed carrots, spit-turned pork shoulder, cinnamon apples, and pickled beets. Booming with reverberating sound, the Westchester dining room witnessed peace on earth and goodwill to men, for at least one afternoon.

The Christmas tradition of a day-long meal ended with an assortment of cakes, pies, sweets, and eggnog in the parlor. Finally, after an entire day of waiting, Lizzy, Samuel, and Olive gathered around the tree, ready to open gifts from Santa.

The family waddled into the parlor, found a seat, and marveled at the beauty of the tree.

"I believe this is the most spectacular tree ever," admitted Ginny. She cuddled a less-than-willing Samuel at her side.

"Father, we have waited all day. May we begin?" Olive, trying to move the evening along, received appreciative looks from Samuel, Lizzy, Benny, and Nellie. "I want to distribute my gifts first."

"All right, you may begin. Ginny, Tildy, will one of you play the piano?"

"I'll play, Father," Sally spoke. "Ginny and Tildy both have children with whom to share this evening. Next year, I'll have my little one, so I shall play tonight." Tildy looked at her sister-in-law, mouthed a guttural thank you, then squeezed Lizzy.

"Wait, before you begin, open this. It's for the baby." Olive handed Sally a package wrapped in brown paper, tied with a red ribbon.

"Thank you, Olive." Sally unwrapped the gift carefully, so as to reuse the paper. Inside she found a linen bib, hand-embroidered with a "W." "Did you make this yourself?" Sally looked lovingly at Olive.

"Of course I did, silly. You're my best friend in the world, except for Fred. I can't wait for this baby to be born."

Hugging Olive, Sally sniffled then blew her nose. "It's perfect. Look at me. I'll not be able to see the sheet music." She tried to laugh. Olive reciprocated the hug. "I love you, little Olive."

Olive looked at Sally, with her pale blue eyes and held so tightly that Sally winced. Then Olive sat down under the tree. "Someone else go; I'll finish my gifts later." She sat, tears trickling down her face, staring into space.

A stack of packages accumulated in front of Olive. She sat quietly and waited, watching others open their gifts. The family received a collection of knitted socks, scarves, mittens, gloves, and shawls given by Sally, Ginny, Tildy, and Bessie. Lizzy and Samuel dispersed a menagerie of animal-like glued paper creations.

Samuel delivered Olive's packages on her behalf. She had purchased a length of white linen over the summer and fashioned handkerchiefs for the family, each embroidered with their first initial. Sock hand-puppets for both Samuel and Lizzy sported embroidered eyes, noses, and a tooth.

"Time for Santa's stockings. Samuel, will you help me?" Henderson grabbed each hanging stocking, handed them to Samuel, who distributed one to each family member. Items removed, one by one, triggered oohs and aahs from the family. Identically filled, each stocking held a bottle of Coca-Cola, a pack of Wrigley's Spearmint gum for the adults, Wrigley's Juicy Fruit gum for the children, Jergen's lotion for the women, Bag Balm for the men, and a bright, plump orange hidden in the toe.

Ginny opened the lotion bottle, rubbing it on her hands. "Stockings are the best gifts."

"Your mother always favored those items." Somewhat wistful, Henderson permitted himself to recall ghosts of Christmas past.

All gifts dispensed; Olive reluctantly unwrapped her stack with encouragement from her family. Looking at Ben and Bessie as she flung a bright red, knit scarf around her neck, she said, "Thank you." Tildy gave her a pair of socks. Holding up a chiffon and lace blouse, she exclaimed to Ginny, "My, Ginny, this is exquisite. Where did you find this? Certainly not in Campbellsville?"

"It was Mother's blouse. I altered it to fit you." Ginny looked at her father for approval.

Sally halted her playing to say, "Open ours next." Olive found a long wool skirt inside. "To go with the blouse."

"I always wear dresses and pinafores. These are grown-up clothes."

Beside herself, Olive stared at the adults. Fingering the lace of the blouse and studying the pleats of the skirt, she conjured a fuzzy vision of her mother.

"I declared you an adult this fall, didn't I?" Henderson asked. Tilting his head, he gently sighed.

"Yes, Father, but these are too beautiful for me." Holding up the garments, Olive ran the fabric across her face. "The blouse is so soft. But it looks too grown-up for me."

"I treat you as an adult. You help as an adult; you may also dress like an adult—for special occasions, at least." Henderson laughed.

"Thank you. Maybe, for a special occasion, I shall also wear my pearls." Olive smiled for the first time since Sally's proclamation of love.

"The pearls will complete the outfit, perfect little lady," declared Sally. Tildy let out a harrumph.

Less-talkative Levi decided to join the conversation. "Here is a gift from Fred..... and me." He handed Olive a package that felt like a book. She ripped off the paper to uncover a copy of Jack London's *Call of the Wild.*

"I love this story, Levi. Thank you. Please thank Fred for me. I'll write him a note, but do tell him that I love the book."

"I shall, Sister. The book was Fred's idea." Olive clung to it. Then she opened to the first page: First edition, 1903, inscribed, *"To my dearest little sister, I love you more than life. Fred."* It was evident that *"and Levi"* was added as an afterthought, by a different pen. She clutched the book to her chest, holding it tight.

"Oh, Freddy, I love you too." Overcome with emotion, Olive doubled over, clinging to her knees. Several moments passed before she composed herself enough to add, "I love you also, Levi."

"Well, I do believe I'm upstaged." Henderson handed Olive another package, another book. Inside was a dictionary, *Webster's New International*, 1909 edition.

"Father, my own dictionary? But you have one in the library already. This is extravagant."

"Olive dear, my dictionary was my father's. It contains one-fifth of the words in this new edition. Our scholar needs proper reference material." Henderson opened it to the first page. "It's also inscribed. *'Christmas 1911, your loving father.'"*

Dazed with unidentified feelings, Olive stood. "Merry Christmas, everyone. Please excuse me; I'm up to bed."

"But Olive, we haven't had our eggnog yet." Lizzy fussed with her new doll. "I'll let you play with my dolly."

Moved by her daughter's generosity, Tildy offered to teach Olive a new embroidery stitch.

Olive said nothing as she looked at her family. She was speechless, trying to remember if anyone other than Fred ever confessed loving her. She was too young to remember her mother's love, positive her father conveyed only approval and disapproval. Sally's declaration and

Henderson's inscription bewildered and confused her. She turned, hesitated, then went up to her room. Alone in her bed, Olive wept into the long hours of the night, struggling to comprehend unfamiliar feelings of love, kindness, and compassion.

14

WE THREE KINGS

*E*piphany signaled the official end of Christmas. The weeklong visiting of friends and family—and the expansion of Westchester waistlines—concluded. School and heavy farm work, machine repair, herd branding, and lambing season began in the morning, along with staff dismantling all holiday decorations.

The Westchesters' interpretation of Epiphany—a mixture of folklore, old-world customs, and family traditions—differed from most rural Pennsylvania residents. Mock gifting of gold, frankincense, and myrrh concluded this family's holiday. Cook prepared a light meal, packed for travel. Symbolizing the Wisemen's journey, the family bundled up in their coats, hats, and mittens to walk to the ancestral graveyard on the hill. Once there, they placed holly and pine, representing myrrh, at the base of each gravestone. Picking a spot to sit, they laid out blankets, plopped down beside the graves, and ate their picnic meal. The outing ended with a memorial service. After singing a few carols and saying prayers for the departed, they headed back to the house.

Emulating years past, Henderson lingered at Polly's grave.

Polly dear, you would be so pleased with little Olive, he thought. *She is so much your twin—bright, spirited, headstrong.* Henderson chuckled to himself. *I don't know how to love her. I must catch myself at times to remember she's just a child. I want her to be you, but you are gone. Sometimes I look at her, and I'm filled with rage —not from her actions, but at myself for my inability to be the father she needs...and because she's not you. Forgive me, Polly. Sleep well.*

Upon arriving home, Henderson gave each of his family and house staff a small gold coin. At the conclusion of the celebration, the family gifted Cook a large box of imported spices, symbolizing frankincense. The spices must last throughout the year, since they were replenished only on Epiphany.

Tildy hovered over the fire, warming her hands. "Brrrr. It's a cold day. I'm glad Lizzy and Samuel stayed inside."

"So am I," Ginny said. "Today is such a solemn day for the family. Though, I was surprised to see Levi leave last week. I expected him to stay until today; after all, this is a family tradition. And with a rather lame excuse to—" A loud, continuous banging on the door disrupted Ginny's small talk.

"Who the hell is that?" Henderson pushed his daughters aside, determined to put an end to the rude knocking.

"Mr. Westchester! Mr. Westchester, we need your help." The appeal was delivered by a stranger. "Please hurry. Hitch your buggy."

"Who are you, man? What is this all about?" Henderson scowled at the intruder who dragged snow into the outer vestibule and interrupted his holiday.

"I'm Nate Lewis. I work at the Jamison Farm. There's been a terrible accident. Please hurry."

Jamison caught Tildy's attention. She ran to the door, asking, "Is Tommy okay?" Nate looked at Tildy, rolled his eyes, then turned back to Henderson.

"Please, Mr. Westchester. We must leave now."

Henderson pulled on his coat and gloves. "Ginny, have Jake hitch the wagon and rally Kendrick. Quickly now. I have no time to gather details; however, I fear I may be returning home late."

He rushed out the door. Running to the barn, Henderson jumped into the wagon seat as Kendrick and Jake hitched the horses. "Jake, take the car to town, summon the doctor back to our farm."

"Follow me," yelled Nate as he galloped across the frozen field toward the Jamisons' property. With the wagon in hot pursuit, the three men crossed the barren expanse.

On the edge of Henderson's neighbor's property was Lucas Jamison, lying on the ground. His right leg was bent underneath his body. Bone jutted through the skin of his left arm, broken at the elbow. He had been thrown to the back and the side, and the tilt of his neck forewarned impending doom. A horse whinnied softly, startling Nate.

"Did you bring a gun?" Henderson asked Kendrick.

"Yes, sir. You thinking to shoot the horse?" Kendrick loosened his holster.

"Let me take a closer look." Henderson approached the collapsed animal. He lay on his side, trying to lift his head to Henderson. "Easy boy." He stroked his nose. Inspection revealed two broken legs. "Shoot him. Put him out of his misery." Turning to Nate, he asked, "What the hell happened here?"

Nate continued to stare at his boss. The gun fired; Nate flinched.

"What's that, Mr. Westchester?" Nate mumbled, barely perceptible.

"I asked you what happened to cause this calamity." The man was still unresponsive. Henderson grabbed both of Nate's shoulders and shook. "Get hold of yourself, man."

"We were out riding," Nate began. "Mr. Jamison just bought this stallion beauty. It was a Christmas gift for his son. Mr. Jamison and I took him out for some exercise. We hit an icy patch, right over there." Nate pointed to an ice-covered bed of rocks, three feet from where Jamison lay. "We were in a full gallop. Mr. J. was in the lead. His horse skidded and fell. I had just enough time to stop." Nate bent down to his boss. "I got help, sir. You gonna be alright. Mr. Westchester's here now." Nate held Jamison's right hand. "It's gonna be alright."

Jamison mumbled a few inaudible words. Using all his energy, he muttered, "Henderson."

Henderson kneeled, placing his ear close to Jamison's mouth. "Tell Tommy it's okay to marry Tildy."

His eyes rolled back into his head, and he was gone. Henderson's face drained of all color.

"What did he say?" Kendrick looked at his ghostly pale employer.

"He said to tell Tommy to marry Tildy. That son of a bitch," Henderson whispered as his face regained all color, then turned bright red.

Nate defended his boss. "Mr. Westchester, that's not very Christian of you, calling a dying man a foul name." Nate took Jamison's limp left hand, tears welling in his eyes.

"Jamison isn't dying. He's dead. For seven years, this ass prevented Tommy and Tildy from being together. He made my sweet, innocent granddaughter a bastard child. I tried to bribe him with fifty acres, for Polly's sake. The son-of-a-bitch refused. Fifty goddam fertile acres and he said no."

Henderson walked away from the scene. Distraught, he wasn't sure how to proceed. Kendrick motioned to Nate to help him load the body into the lorry. The night was falling; they need not linger in the cold air. The men hoisted the corpse of Lucas Jamison onto the back of the wagon with minimal trouble.

"You think you can bring your men out tomorrow to bury that horse?" Kendrick asked Nate. "Who's your crew chief?"

"Ah, I am. That was my Christmas gift. Old man Timmons retired after harvest. Mr. J. took three months deciding who would take his place. Told me last week. That's why I'm here today. You know." Nate waved his hand at Kendrick. "Always on duty. Moved my wife and son into the chief's bunkhouse last week." Nate looked from the dead horse to the dead man, to Kendrick. "I done got myself in a full mess."

Henderson lumbered back to the wagon. Joints stiff from the cold, mind stiff from Jamison's revelation. "Nate, ride home to the Jamison house," Henderson said. "Fetch Alva and Tommy. Bring them over to my place. They'll stay the night, so have them pack an overnight bag.

HI, HO, THE MERRY O

*J*ake drove the Ford into the driveway. Ralph Paulson hurried up the path to the house. Tildy, Ginny, and Olive waited for him inside. Tired from the day's exposure and her pregnancy, Sally retired to bed with Clyde.

"Allow me to take your coat," Ginny offered as she placed the doctor's hat on the hall-tree. "Father has yet to return."

"Who's been injured?" Paulson looked around for a patient.

"We have no idea. Jamison's man came an hour ago, pounding on the door. He said there was an accident. That's all we know. Please, sit, doctor. May I bring you some coffee or tea?" Ginny failed at numbers; however, she excelled at hospitality.

Tildy, already waiting in the parlor, walked back and forth, wringing her hands. "Not Tommy, dear God, please not Tommy," she prayed as she paced.

"You'll wear a hole in the carpet if you don't sit down," Olive instructed. Tildy burst into tears.

"I snuck out to see Tommy last night. He intends to sell his new horse for money. We are planning on running away. Taking Lizzy and maybe going to Pittsburgh. Oh...oh...I finally get to marry my love and...Oh...oh..."

"I knew you were sneaking around with Tommy Jamison," accused Olive. "You have been all along, haven't you?" Olive looked at her sister with disdain. "If Tommy had half a spine, he would have married you before Lizzy was born."

Tildy held her hands over her ears and screamed. "Shut up! Shut up, Olive! You loathsome brat. I can't stand you!"

Olive began, "Well, the feeling is—"but Ginny stepped in, cutting Olive off mid-sentence.

"Not in front of the doctor, please," Ginny said. "Have some decorum, both of you. Act like adults, if that's at all possible."

Instead of ringing for service, Ginny spun on her heel, leaving to order tea and cookies from the kitchen directly. Olive took a seat across from Tildy. She sat quietly until she heard the squeaking wagon wheels.

"They're home. Tildy, allow me to investigate, please. I'll come to get you if I think it's safe for you to view." Olive gestured civilly, despite the personal attack. Tildy grunted.

The front door burst open. Henderson, Kendrick, and Nate carried a body draped in a blanket. Tildy caught a glimpse and fainted.

"Dr., you tend to whomever just came in. I'll revive Tildy." Olive cradled her sister's head in her lap, fanning her with the newspaper. "Ginny," Olive called out to the kitchen. "I need a glass of water along with that tea, please."

Dr. Paulson hurried to the entrance. Henderson shook his head.

"Who is it?" the doctor asked.

"Lucas Jamison. Riding accident. Had to kill the horse, two broken legs. Jamison was alive when we arrived, but not for long. Poor sot broke his neck with the fall, not to mention his arm and leg."

Paulson pulled back the covering. "Your diagnosis looks to be correct on all three accounts."

Henderson spotted Olive peeking around the corner. "Olive, help us. Move over a couple of chairs, something on which to place the body." Olive dragged chairs from the dining room, which she covered with towels. The men lowered the body for Paulson to make a more thorough examination.

"Hmm." He pressed on Jamison's chest. "Broken ribs too, and probably a punctured lung. He never stood a chance." Paulson closed the corpse's eyes, then drew up the covering. "What about the widow?"

"Widow?" Tildy staggered to the parlor doorway, her face as white as a sheet. Wringing her hands, she asked, "Who is dead, Father?"

"Lucas Jamison." Henderson considered his next move, unsure of Tildy's involvement with Jamison, the younger. Tildy began laughing hysterically. Olive and Henderson watched as Tildy clutched the molding of the threshold, then collapsed to the floor.

"Lucas, not Tommy." Tildy folded her hands. Laying there, she raised her head to the heavens, praying giddily, "Thank you, God. Lucas, not Tommy."

"For God's sake Matilda, control yourself. The widow Jamison and her son are on their way over here. If sympathy is an impossibility, at least be empathetic." Henderson scorned his daughter.

"Tommy is coming here?" The laughter stopped as abruptly as it started. "And Mrs. Jamison?" Tildy sputtered a litany of gibberish before darting to a mirror to inspect her reflection.

Ginny arrived with a tray of cups, saucers, a tier of snacks, water, and a teapot. "I'll place this in the parlor and order another pot of tea. Please help yourself."

"Father?" Henderson looked at Olive, who was engrossed with the dead body. "Are we leaving him here? In the middle of our foyer? I covered the seats with towels, but will he not bleed, now that he's out of the cold?"

Paulson chuckled, slapping Henderson on the back. "You have a real bright one here. Ever consider sending her to medical school?"

Henderson gazed at Olive. "Medical school? Nonsense, Ralph." Shaking his head, Henderson poured himself a cup of tea, repeating, "Medical school. My heavens. A girl in medical school."

Olive gawked at both men, awaiting an answer about Jamison.

The last thing she wanted to do was scrub blood from the needlepoint chair cushions.

"Henderson, I believe your daughter has a point. Perhaps we should move the body to a more respectable bed. Alva shall suffer enough of a shock. Let's not make it worse." Dr. Paulson looked around for an alternate resting place.

"If we set up sawhorses in the cold room off the kitchen, it may slow decomposition. It's not outside, but it's cooler than the foyer. Mrs. Jamison won't freeze, but Mr. Jamison won't thaw," Olive offered.

"Brilliant. Henderson, I tell you, this one deserves higher education."

∞∞∞∞

Another thirty minutes passed before Nate arrived with Alva and Tommy Jamison. Embracing each other for support, mother and son crept down the hallway to view their dear, departed Lucas.

"I can't look. Tommy, is it your father?" Alva turned, eyes closed, burying her head in her son's chest. Dr. Paulson uncovered the upper body. Tommy gasped, clinging to his mother.

"Don't look, Mother. It's Father." Tommy rubbed his mother's back. Tildy watched from the kitchen window.

Gathering strength and resolve, Alva straightened. Turning to face her dead husband, she inhaled slightly, at first sight. Caressing her husband's head, she kissed his lips.

"Dear, dear Lucas. What shall I do without you? Tommy is too weak and inept to run the farm; how shall I survive alone?"

"Mother..." Tommy released his grip on Alva's arm. Stepping back, he glared at his mother. Tildy ran to Tommy's side, wrapping her arm around his waist. She met Alva Jamison's icy stare.

"Don't you be getting any crazy ideas of marrying my son, now that Lucas is gone. I won't stand for it. Do you hear me?" Alva sputtered, glaring at both Tildy and Tommy.

Tildy peered, studying Alva. "What did you say? It was *you*, wasn't it? You are the one who kept us apart. Not your husband. He did it for you, didn't he? You wicked woman." Tildy spit the words at the widow, then gazed at Tommy. "Did you know it was her?"

At a loss for words, Tommy looked from mother to lover.

Incensed, Tildy punched his shoulder. "Was it her? How could you? You said you wanted to run away. Tommy?"

Tildy continued punching Tommy, who did nothing to make her stop.

Henderson grabbed his daughter's arm. "Enough, Matilda. I think we need to go into the parlor, have some tea, and talk. Lucas uttered a dying request."

Spinning around, Alva grabbed Tommy's arm. "Do not allow this tramp to cloud your judgment."

"You better stop right there, Mrs. Jamison. I'll not have you disparage my daughter in my home. Now please, let us move into the parlor. I have some information to share with this group."

Alva, Tildy, and Tommy walked single file into the parlor. Alva took a seat opposite Tildy and Tommy. An icy chill pervaded, despite a roaring fire. Tildy's eyes radiated fury as she peered at Alva Jamison. To defuse the tension, Ginny offered tea, which was graciously accepted, but not consumed. Olive, hoping to remain inconspicuous, slipped into a corner. Nate Lewis stood in the entrance, feeling uninvited.

"Listen closely. All of you. Lucas spoke his dying words to me. Nate and Kendrick are my witnesses. Isn't that right, Mr. Lewis?" Henderson addressed the doorway. The name "Lewis" caught Olive's attention.

"Are you Leonard Lewis's father?" Olive faced Lewis with an icy gaze.

Nate reevaluated his first impression of Olive. "Yes, why do you ask?"

"This is for you." Olive walked over to Lewis. Planting her feet apart, hand on her hips, she kicked Nate Lewis in the shin. "That's for calling Tildy names."

"Why you little..."

"I'll remind you, Mr. Lewis, you are a guest in my home." Henderson turned to Olive. "Is that the father of the boy you clocked on the first day of school?"

"Yes, Father," Olive answered. So much for staying inconspicuous. Henderson laughed.

"I believe, Mr. Lewis, you earned that kick. We shall deal with you later. However, do you attest that Lucas spoke his dying words to me?'

"Yes, sir." Nate rubbed his leg and glared at Olive.

"Tildy, I believe you may be correct about your assessment of Mrs. Jamison. It was Alva—or else Lucas had a *Coming to Jesus* moment. Or both." Tildy squinted fire at Alva. "The last thing Lucas said on this very earth was, '*Tell Tommy; it's okay to marry Tildy.*' I swear...right hand to God, those were his words."

Henderson raised his arm toward heaven then glanced at Nate, who nodded in agreement.

"Mr. Westchester's right. That's exactly what Mr. J. said. He spoke them words, then died."

Alva Jamison let out a screech. "He wouldn't. He would never go back on his word to me!"

Lizzy and Samuel, disrupted from their sound sleep, wandered downstairs to investigate the commotion.

"Tommy, no! Over my dead body!" Alva stood and took her son by the shoulders. "Tommy, you mustn't. I forbid it."

Blank-faced Tommy did not respond.

Rubbing her eyes, Lizzy climbed onto her mother's lap unnoticed. "What's Daddy doing here?"

Alva screamed again. "She calls you 'Daddy?'"

Frightened by the noise, Lizzy began whimpering.

"Of course, she calls him 'Daddy.' He is her father." Furious, Tildy challenged Tommy for support. "Will you sit there doing nothing? Your daughter needs you. I need you."

"Never. Neither of you shall step foot in my house." Alva stood, flinging her arms toward Lizzy and Tildy.

"Mrs. Jamison, I hate to dispel any of your ideas; however, with the death of your husband, the farm automatically passes to Tommy," Henderson said calmly. "Women in this county are not entitled to own property. Lucas may have written provisions in his Will for your care; however, the farm rightfully belongs to Tommy." Walking to Tildy, Henderson took her face in his hands. "Do you want to marry this man? If so, you have my blessing. For that matter, you have Jamison's blessing."

"Tommy?" Tildy raised her hand, ready to strike the younger Jamison's face. "Stand up to her. She no longer has your father as an ally. Or are you as weak as she implies?"

"Tildy...Mother...Stop. Please, both of you, stop." Tommy caught Tildy's wrist and held it in the air. "I can't deal with either of you at this time. My father lies dead outside the kitchen, and the two of you rudely engage in a catfight. Excuse me a moment."

Tommy lowered Tildy's hand. With a slow gait he exited the parlor, making his way to where his father lay. Kneeling beside the corpse, he prayed for three requests: the repose of his father's soul, the wisdom to oversee a farm, and the strength to deal with two crazed, opposed women.

Tildy and Alva fidgeted, avoiding eye contact, while Henderson and the others sat quietly, in hopes of preventing additional confrontation.

After ten minutes, Tommy returned. "I have come to a decision. First, I suggest we sit quietly, say some prayers, then return home." Motioning to Nate, Tommy continued. "We shall not stay the night. Nate, ready the auto immediately."

Tommy walked over to Tildy, taking her in his arms. He kissed her, a deep, passionate kiss. Alva gulped air, watching in alarm. "Tildy, I'll be back in the morning. We shall plan our wedding for the late spring, or early summer. Give proper time for mourning."

"But Tommy..." Tildy reached to stroke Tommy's face. She was met with the glint of love as he smiled sweetly. "We've waited long enough."

"No buts. Yes, we've already waited too many years, Tildy, but I promise I'll not disappoint you. We shall allow time for Mother to grieve before she relinquishes the house to you."

Astonished by his own bravery, Tommy met Alva's eyes, daring her to object.

"Mr. Westchester," Tommy continued. "Thank you for your help and kind generosity. I am in your debt. Mother, please thank the Westchesters. Let us return home. You and I have much to discuss."

Tommy reached for Alva. She turned to Tildy, then to Henderson. Hatred beamed through the slits of her eyes. "I shall never live in the same house as a Westchester."

Brushing away Tommy's arm, she marched outside and into their vehicle. Nate cranked the motor to depart.

Watching through the window, Henderson commented, "I guess young Jamison has more *man* in him than I thought. Tildy, are you finally ready for that wedding?"

Tildy sobbed with joy. "Yes, Father, I am so ready," she said as she hugged and rocked Lizzy.

The child smiled at her mother and said, "Santa *did* bring you a husband for Christmas!"

SPRING IS BURSTING OUT ALL OVER

*S*now and cold made way for rain and wind of early spring. Sleepy winter days yielded; the frenzy of farm life renewed. Olive discarded sewing on linen for accounting in ledgers again, spending after-school hours in the company of her father's desk. Henderson, Kendrick, Ben, Clyde, and Olive worked tirelessly, assigning grazing pastures, scheduling planting, reviewing crop rotation, repairing machinery, and the many additional tasks of running a successful farm. Ginny, Tildy, and Cook planned a wedding extraordinaire, while Sally prepared for her child's birth.

The month of March guaranteed several significant but quickly melting snowstorms. Crocus peeking through the remnants of dirty snow welcomed abundant farm activity. April rains washed away the last of winter and softened the ground for planting.

Sally's belly morphed into a watermelon-sized protrusion. Several months yet until her due date, the family speculated the idea of a conception date miscalculation. The women's fingers flew at a furious pace, completing both layette for Sally and trousseau for Tildy.

"Sally, good morning." Olive knocked on her bedroom door, as she did every morning before school. "Time to braid my hair. I brought you some tea." Olive carried in a tray of tea and morning sweets. Sally typically consumed a morning snack before eating a full breakfast.

"Come in, Olive. I've been waiting for you." Sally shuffled to open the door, then waddled back to her dressing table.

"Goodness. Your belly looks bigger this morning than it did yesterday." Olive sat on a stool after handing Sally a cup.

"I feel like I shall pop any minute, although over two months remain."

Olive reached over to rub her tummy. As she touched Sally, the baby jumped.

"It kicked!" Olive's blue eyes widened in amazement. "Oh, there it goes again!"

"I know, this baby has been extremely active. It kicks in all directions. I don't know how it manages, but it kicks my left side, then punches my right side. Arms and legs must be going at the same time." I'm sore inside from all the movement. Sally drank some tea, then rubbed her belly. "Come hurry, or you shall be late for school."

Olive's attachment to Sally grew more profound every day. She often joined the sewing klatch after completing her father's work, and through it she learned intricate embroidery stitches, how to crochet, and improved knitting skills. By spending hours in her room stitching when she should have been sleeping, Olive stashed a sizable stack of baby clothes. She hoped to present a large, boxed gift to Sally and Clyde at the baby's Christening.

Olive's braid intact, she, Samuel, and Lizzy began walking to school, enjoying the brisk spring morning jaunt. Olive now towered over the other children. Having grown four inches since fall, her upward spurt resulted in a tall, slender, lovely girl who looked and acted more mature than her ten years. Compared to Nellie and the other two twelve-year-old girls in the school, Olive, though two years younger, claimed the distinction of being the most adultlike. Unfortunately, this further ostracized a child who already spent much of her time alone. She intimidated the other students and had no friends her age, neither girl nor boy.

"Olive, will you come to the board, please?" Bea called on her star student. "Explain how I arrived at the answer to the problem written on the board."

Olive drummed her finger on the chalkboard as she studied the equation. Mindlessly placing her fingers in her mouth, she swirled her tongue, wetting her mouth after the taste of chalk. "Yuck."

Exercising careful consideration, Olive said, "Miss Thompson, your answer is wrong."

"What? Mind your manners Miss," Bea warned.

"But look..." Olive pointed to two different errors, one in multiplication, the other in addition.

Bea studied the equation, feeling a flush of embarrassment when she realized Olive was right. Displeased with being bested by a student, she tried to salvage her pride as she erased the board.

"Fine. While I make the correction, please explain to the older class how you use the plus, minus, and times tables when calculating your ledger entries."

Olive approached the chalkboard, opened the mock ledger, and began writing. The girls rolled their eyes while the boys fidgeted as she explained her calculations. Unappreciative of their lack of attention, she turned to the class.

"How many of you boys intend to manage a farm when you grow up?" Most hands went up. "Then listen." Olive clicked her tongue and shook her head in frustration and disgust. "Stupid boys," she mumbled.

On the way home from school, Leonard Lewis caught up to the Westchester children.

"Olive, Olive, wait." Olive ignored Leonard. "Please, wait up."

She spun around, stomped her foot, then halted. "What do you want, Leonard Lewis?" Gritting her teeth, she glared at her peer.

"I'm hopin' you can help me with some of my figurin'. My papa says you're smart." Leonard clasped his hands behind his back, embarrassed to ask a girl for help.

"If I remember correctly, your papa says a lot of things, mostly untrue." Olive turned to continue walking.

"Wait, Olive. I don't pick up numbers like you. I wanna learn," Leonard pleaded.

"If you genuinely care about learning, then I recommend you ask Miss Thompson to help you. She's a nice teacher. I'm sorry, Leonard, but I do not have the time to help. I have too many chores and household duties," Olive politely declined, telling the truth.

"You just don't want to help a boy." Leonard stepped forward. With his chest only inches away, Olive felt his hot breath on her face.

Olive stepped back, putting space between them. "That's not true. I simply do not have time to help you." Leonard leaned in. "Leonard, leave me alone. Back up. Do you remember the last time you got too close to a Westchester?"

Lizzy's mouth hung open, grinning in admiration, Samuel stepped forward to help, if needed.

Olive, grabbing Lizzy by the arm, dragged her down the path away from Leonard. Samuel lagged behind as the trio traveled several yards before Leonard reacted. Incensed by her refusal, Leonard took a running leap, ready to tackle.

Samuel called out, "Olive, watch yourself!"

Responding too slowly to the warning, Olive fell in the mud with Leonard on top of her. Samuel grabbed Lizzy to keep her away from harm. Before Leonard knew what was happening, Olive rolled him over and began pelting his face on both cheeks with her fists. She connected a right punch to his eye. Leonard pushed her off, but Olive climbed back on top, straddling him, unleashing a barrage of fists and kicks. Leonard screamed for help.

Samuel whispered to Lizzy, "Run back to the school and get Miss Thompson. Hurry, Lizzy. Olive's going to kill him."

A crowd of onlookers gathered as Leonard screamed and Olive hit.

"Stop this! Immediately! I said, *stop this!*" Bea called when Lizzy returned with her. She pulled Olive away from the bloody boy.

"Olive, enough of your belligerence. Why are you fighting? Look at you. Covered in mud and blood." Bea turned to Leonard. "Did you provoke this encounter?"

"No, Miss Thompson." Leonard dropped his mud-covered face to avoid eye contact.

"He's lying. He did so," Samuel and Lizzy said in unison.

"I suspected as much." Bea took Leonard by the ear. "Now Leonard, try to answer my question with the truth. Did you start this fight?"

"Yes, Miss Thompson. I jumped Olive. But she deserved it." Leonard crossed his arms in confirmation.

"No, she didn't." Lizzy stomped both her feet, spraying mud. "All Olive said was that she was too busy to help him with his numbers. She said he should ask you to help, Miss Thompson."

Some of the other children snickered. One older boy mumbled, "He asked a girl to help him?"

Olive regained her footing. She brushed off as much mud as possible. Glowering at Leonard, Olive sputtered in his face.

"I *am* too busy to help you right now. Every day I go to school, do my chores, help my father with the farm books, eat dinner, then stitch for my sisters. One is getting married; the other is having a baby. I don't have time to play; I don't have time to practice my piano. I don't have time to *read.* All I do is work, so please, leave me be! Ask Miss Thompson to help you. She's the teacher." Olive grabbed Lizzy and Samuel. "Now you've made me late *and* dirty."

The trio continued down the path toward the farm.

Bea Thompson scattered the rest of the children, retaining Leonard. "Why was it necessary to attack Olive? I'd think one knock-out should have taught you otherwise. I'm afraid, young man, this is grounds for dismissal. I warned you at the beginning of the school year that if you bully my students, you are out."

"Please, Miss Thompson. I want to learn my numbers. That's why I asked Olive. She's smart," Leonard pleaded.

"Yes, she is smart." *Too smart for her britches*, thought Bea. "However, you have no reason to attack her. She has chores. Do you?" Bea thrust her hands on her hips.

"Not as many as Olive, for sure." Leonard hung his head. "My daddy's right; I'm a stupid good-for-nothing lout." Leonard sat down on the ground, burying his head in his hands.

"Nonsense. You just need to try harder." Bea looked at Leonard, who hung his head, tears falling. "Do you deserve another chance, Leonard Lewis?"

"Oh, yes, please, Miss Thompson." His eyes implored with eagerness. "I'll study real hard."

"I'm more concerned about you fighting. Can you control your temper?" Bea Thompson grabbed the boy by the shoulders, her eye latched onto his.

"Yes, Miss Thompson. I can do that. I promise."

"This is your last chance, Leonard. One more fight and you are gone. Understood?" Against her better judgment, Bea Thompson allowed Leonard to continue. He was a minor inconvenience. Her real problem was the insecurity and threat she felt from Olive's intelligence.

Olive raced into the house after feeding the chickens, avoiding contact with the adults. Quickly washing and changing clothes, she ran down the rear staircase, grabbed a cookie, and headed to the office.

"You're late," Henderson said, not bothering to look up as she entered.

"Sorry, Father. I stayed after school." Olive sat in her usual spot, pulled out a ledger, and began adding and subtracting the columns of Henderson's entries. Not wanting to provoke her father, she deliberately avoided mentioning another scuffle with Leonard Lewis. The two worked until the dinner bell rang.

"Better go wash up. Don't want to keep hungry animals waiting." Henderson walked out of the room, not once looking in Olive's direction. Exhausted from the physical and mental exertions of the day, Olive closed her book, leaned back in her chair, and immediately fell asleep.

∞∞∞∞

During the dessert service, Sally asked, "Where's Olive?"

Turning to look at her empty chair, Henderson defensively answered, "She was right behind me when we left the office."

Ginny went upstairs to search in her bedroom. Empty. Finding the youngest children in the nursery, she interrupted their playing.

"Sammy, Lizzy, have you seen Olive?"

Samuel rolled his eyes. "No, silly, she eats with you."

"Yes, dear, but she missed dinner tonight."

"Olive never misses food. Especially dessert," Samuel said.

"Maybe she was tired after the fight," Lizzy assessed.

"Shhh, Lizzy!"

"Oh, and what fight would that be?" Ginny asked with a smile, inviting a response. "You may tell me. Neither of you shall be in trouble. Sammy?"

"Oh, brother, Lizzy. Olive is going to be mad now." Facing Ginny, he said, "Leonard Lewis jumped her after school."

"Yes, and I ran back to tell Miss Thompson," Lizzy said.

"Don't yell at Olive. It was Leonard's fault. He asked Olive to help him with his numbers. She said no, 'cause she has too much to do. He got mad, and came at her from behind." Samuel crossed his arms while Lizzy nodded in agreement.

"Did she get hurt?"

"Nah, just dirty. Olive pummeled him. He had a bloody nose, black eye, and fat lip when she finished." Samuel looked at his mother. "I hope I can fight that good someday."

"We'll worry about fighting later. Will you both search the rooms up here to see if you can find her? If you do, bring her to the dining room." Ginny was already walking down the hallway.

"She's not in her room," Ginny said, making her way back to the dining room. "The children are searching in the other bedrooms. Maybe she's still in the office?"

Ginny looked at her father, who shrugged. Sally tried her luck. She waddled through the parlor to the library, where she found Olive curled up in her chair. Sally did not disturb the peaceful, slumbering child.

Lumbering back to the dining room, Sally said, "She's in the library, sound asleep, poor dear."

"Why is she so tired?" Henderson said. "She never sleeps through a meal."

"She has a lot to do."

"Nonsense. She comes home from school every day, works with me on her numbers, then eats dinner," Henderson said.

"She does her chores before she helps you, Father," Sally said.

"What chores are those?"

"She feeds the chickens, gathers eggs, and weeds the garden before she helps you in the library." Sally paused, hearing the list aloud for the first time. "She does seem to have a large responsibility around the farm, for a ten-year-old."

"She's only ten?" Henderson's eyes squinted as he cocked his head. "What do the rest of you lazy sots do around here?"

Ben and Clyde mumbled, "We run the farm, Father."

Ginny stammered, "Father, I'm the hostess."

Sally, Bessie, and Tildy said nothing, looking at each other, guilty of frittering away their days.

"May I ask why she has taken on so many duties?" Henderson boomed the question at the group. Foreheads rippled in dismay; they hesitated.

Finally, Sally braved the answer. "Because of you, Father. You keep asking her to do tasks, and she keeps doing them. She'll never deny you if you keep asking."

"Poppycock. You are mistaken, Daughter-in-Law." Henderson's

chair scraped the floor as he stood. "I expect whoever caused this problem to remedy it, immediately."

Storming out of the room and into the foyer, he grabbed his hat, leaving the family staring at each other in bewilderment. Henderson slammed the front door, then strolled down the path and up the hillside to the family graveyard.

The house was dark when he finally returned.

∞∞∞

Sally was the first to speak after Henderson's exit. "I think it's about time for Samuel and Lizzy to take on some chores to help Olive out."

"Oh, of *course* you do. You don't have a child yet on which to dump extra duties," Tildy snapped back.

"Stop the drama, Tildy. Lizzy can feed the chickens. Samuel is capable of collecting eggs and weeding the vegetable garden," Sally challenged.

"You are equally capable of feeding the chickens," Tildy snapped.

Ben interrupted long enough to gather his family in hasty retreat. Ginny sat quietly, neither supporting Olive nor mentioning the fight.

Clyde defended Sally. "Tildy, in case you haven't noticed, Sally can barely bend at the waist. Why don't you get off your lazy behind to help? The wedding isn't for another three and a half months. How much preparation do you need for a wedding night that occurred seven years ago?"

"Why you...!"

Awakened by voices, Olive wandered into the room, rubbing her eyes. "Where is everyone? Why are you arguing?"

"We're arguing because of you. Always because of you." Tildy poked her finger in Olive's chest, flung her head, and stomped out of the room. Sally rushed to Olive's side, wrapping her arm around the girl.

Trying to pacify her, Sally said, "Ignore Tildy. She's nervous about the wedding."

Olive smiled. "Tildy is always nervous about something," she said, then looked around for a platter. "Is there any food?"

17

THE BLESSED EVENT

*C*rocus, daffodils, tulips, and lilacs unhurriedly gave way to roses. As summer wore on, the gigantic expanse of Sally's belly and resulting back aches caused her even more difficulty standing upright. She gained precious morning sleep with school in summer recess, however, as she was no longer required to braid Olive's tresses. Samuel slept in Ginny's room temporarily while the nursery was converted to accommodate an infant.

Olive's more menial duties were distributed to Lizzy and Samuel. She gladly taught them shortcuts to performing their newly acquired chores. While free from braiding duties, Sally capitalized on reinforcing her new family allyship with Olive by devoting an hour each evening to enriching Olive's creative skills, especially on the piano.

∞∞∞∞

One lazy June afternoon, Sally and Olive sat at the piano while Olive worked on her dreaded scales.

"Olive, you shall be capable of playing carols this upcoming Christmas," Sally praised.

While playing a scale in F major, Olive played B natural rather than a B-flat. As she depressed the key, Sally groaned, doubling over.

"Was it that bad? I just missed one key." Olive laughed nervously as she turned toward her teacher.

Sally's face was pale. Olive noticed her wet dress and a puddle on the floor. "Did my wrong key trigger your bladder?" Olive giggled.

Sally moaned; her fingernails dug into Olive's arm.

"Call the midwife. Call Clyde. The baby is coming." Standing up, Sally steadied herself on a chair. "I'll be upstairs. I should have a few minutes between contractions."

"Goodness," Olive stammered without breathing. "What do I do? Sally, what do I do first?"

"Olive, calm down; I'm the one having the baby. Get Ginny and make the calls. I'll be waiting upstairs." Sally wobbled to the staircase, leaving a trail of water behind her.

Olive ran through the kitchen, shouting, "Ginny, Cook, Tildy! Everybody, it's time! Gosh, it's time!" then out the back door, heading to the barn. "Clyde, Clyde! Come now, it's time!"

Clyde pivoted to see the frantic girl running in and out of the farm buildings, yelling at the top of her lungs. The entire farm now knew that Sally was in labor—even though Olive had never announced exactly *what* "time" had arrived.

Jake drove to fetch the midwife, while Ginny wiped Sally's brow. Tildy sat, waiting to be given orders.

Clyde knocked at the door. "Sally, may I come in?" Tildy rolled her eyes while Ginny nodded. Olive stood in the corner, biting her fingernails.

"Clyde, come in for just a minute. It's started, but it may be several hours before the baby comes," Ginny granted permission.

Clyde shyly entered the room, approached the bed, then kissed his wife in front of the gathered women.

"My beautiful Sally. I love you so. May God protect you today and bless us with a healthy child." He whispered his prayer aloud. From the back of the room came a whimper from Olive. "Oh, little sister, she'll be just fine. Don't you worry," Clyde soothed as Sally groaned with another contraction.

"You better leave now, Clyde. We'll take good care of her." Ginny's smile assured her brother. Clyde stroked Sally's hair, kissed her cheek, then exited.

The ordeal lasted throughout the evening. The women took turns eating their supper, providing continuous help for the midwife. In the dining room, directly below her bedroom, the men could hear her sighs and screams during each contraction.

Five hours into the process, Clyde climbed the stairs reluctantly. He flashed back to that fateful day, seven years prior, when he lost his mother. As Clyde knocked on the door, Sally shrieked. He hesitated then rapped again.

Olive opened the door. "Not now, Clyde. They say the baby's almost here." She grabbed his arm and squeezed. Her body trembled. "Sally's doing fine." Olive's voice cracked. "She's tired from pushing because the baby is taking its good old time arriving."

"Get him out of here," screeched Tildy. "Give us some privacy."

Hearing Tildy, Clyde's eyes implored Olive for reassurance.

"I'm as afraid as you, Clyde. I wouldn't lie to you. But so far, she's fine." Olive shut the door as the midwife announced, "Here it comes. Push Sally, now push."

The baby's cry was heard downstairs. The men gathered in the dining room breathed a sigh of relief until another piercing scream followed.

"Something's not right." Clyde jumped and ran toward the staircase. On his way up, he met Olive coming down. The girl was ghostly white. "What's the matter Olive? Is she bleeding? Tell me!" Clyde shook her shoulders. Olive stood looking in amazement.

"There's another baby. It's a litter. You are having twins." Olive sat down on the step, seemingly as exhausted as Sally. The men cheered. Henderson poured a round of brandies for everyone.

"I'm sure the women shall be joining us soon as mother and babies settle in for the night." Motioning to the housemaid,

Henderson ordered new glasses for those busy with the process of birthing.

"Olive, is the baby a girl or a boy? Do I have a grandson or grand-daughter?" asked Henderson.

"The first one is a girl. I don't know about the other. All I saw was the head sticking out." She stood slowly, gripping the handrail. "I think I shall be sick for the rest of my life. You'll never catch me having a baby."

Olive went to the sideboard, poured herself a brandy, then downed it in two swigs. She poured the second drink and collapsed into a chair as the men roared in laughter.

∞∞∞∞

Another hour passed before the room was tidy and clean. Midwife, Ginny, Tildy, and Bessie left mother and children alone. The men were several drinks ahead of them when they retreated to the parlor. Henderson passed around glasses.

"Clyde, you have two healthy babies, a boy and a girl," the midwife announced as she covered her shoulders with her shawl. "Mother and babies are fine. Sally is resting now. She had a long, painful evening."

Clyde hugged the midwife. "Bless you. Thank you for keeping her safe." Handing her an envelope containing her payment, he stopped and grabbed it out of her hand. "Oh my. I never thought. I owe you double. Wait—Father, may I borrow some cash? I don't want to disturb Sally." Clyde's face colored bright red.

"Mr. Westchester, don't be silly. You pay by the pregnancy, not the baby." The midwife, embarrassed, blushed, matching Clyde.

"Nonsense," bellowed Henderson. "That's the most absurd thing I've ever heard. Of course, we shall pay by the baby."

Henderson left. Returning from his library with extra cash, he handed it to Clyde as he whispered, "There's some extra in there for her. No need to repay me, son. I'm pleased as can be that all are healthy."

The women settled in, sipping their brandy.

"What a glorious day." Bessie snuggled into Ben's arm. "Where's Olive?"

"She made it through the second baby crowning. That was enough for her." Tildy laughed. "I'm amazed that she did so well at ten years old."

The men howled.

"She's passed out in the dining room. She came down, pale as a ghost, and drank two brandies. Within minutes, she was out." Clyde chuckled. "You should have seen her face."

Ginny sipped her drink. "Actually she handled things quite well for her age. Witnessing your first childbirth can be very traumatic. No wonder the poor thing went for the brandy."

"She is a very odd creature, isn't she?" Henderson uttered. "I see Polly in her, in so many ways. Her confidence, reliability, intelligence, and gruffness."

"What do you mean, 'gruffness?'" Ben looked questioningly at his father. His eyes were slits, brows furrowed. "Mother had no gruffness."

"Ahh, Benjamin. She may not have shown it to you, but your mother had an edge about her. It made her capable and so...*exciting*. Unpredictable. Olive has that same edge." He rubbed his hands through his hair. With red eyes, he continued, "I miss her so. Sometimes, when Olive is working with me, I forget she's not Polly. I forget that Olive is only ten. She's growing so tall." Tears flowing freely, Henderson permitted a rare moment of vulnerability. "Oh, children, your mother would have been so happy tonight." He clasped his hands to his heart.

The children kissed their father goodnight as he sat crying tears of happiness for Clyde, tears of sadness for Polly.

No one bothered to carry Olive to bed.

18

I BAPTIZE THEE, IN THE NAME OF

*O*live knocked gently on the door. She whispered, not wanting to awaken a sleeping baby. "Sally, do you have time to braid my hair before the Christening?"

"Oh, not today. I'm simply too busy with the twins. Maybe Ginny can help." Olive watched, smiling as Sally dressed the twins for the day's celebration.

The babies wore heirloom Christening gowns. Sally had originally only prepared for one child, laundering and starching a Christening garment which had been used by every Westchester living in the house. Made of fine French cotton, the forty-five-inch skirt boasted tucks and pintucks, suitable for either gender. A hand-embroidered "W" filled the bodice. The name of each Westchester baptized in the ensemble encircled the hem of the slip, row after row, added for each generation of use.

The shock of the second baby sent Sally scrambling for another gown. She decided to use Polly's family heirloom. Ribbons, made from inserted French lace, filled the hem of the Sinclair gown. Tiny pearls were incorporated into the hand-smocked bodice, and silk lace flowers resulted in a feminine garment destined for the baby girl.

Ginny was occupied in the dining room, unable to help Olive.

"Tildy? Lizzy?" called Olive. No one answered.

Olive tried her best to braid her own hair, crisscrossing her blonde locks back. The intended smooth, tight braid ended in an unruly collection of sprouting squiggles.

"Fiddlesticks." Unwrapping her cherished pearls, she snapped the clasp without incident. "At least that worked." Admiring her reflection in the mirror, she said out loud, "I am old enough to be a Godmother." Silently, she added a little prayer: *Please, God, let it be me.*

"Samuel," Olive yelled across the hall. "Hurry, the pastor will be here soon. We need to be downstairs waiting." Dressed in a new pair of short pants and knee socks, Samuel hooked his suspenders as he walked down the back stairs. He spied Olive in the foyer.

"Wow, Olive, you look all grown up. Why are you wearing big girl clothes and jewelry? Is that your Christmas blouse?" Samuel gave Olive an up and down glance. The eight-year-old's smile indicated his approval.

"Sammy, lower your voice. Do you know who Clyde and Sally picked to be Godparents? Has your mother mentioned anything?" Olive took Samuel by the arm, pulling him away from the rest of the family. "Think hard."

"No, Olive. The only thing Mommy said was that they will announce the Godparents today, same time they name the babies," Samuel whispered. "This is fun. Are we on a secret mission?"

"Sort of," replied Olive. "Don't say a word to anyone. I really want Sally to ask me. She's my good friend." Olive guided Samuel down the hall, away from the family gathered in the parlor. "Keep your ears open. Tell me if you hear anything."

"Sure thing, Olive. Pinky swear." Samuel raised his little finger, crossed it with Olive's. Their oath was sealed.

Suddenly, Olive stopped short. "Sammy, I forgot my gift. Don't let them start without me."

She ran back upstairs. Lugging an oversized box, she teetered, holding onto the railing. After setting down the box in the foyer, she hurried into the parlor, just as the pastor began to speak.

Clyde, Sally, the twins, Bea Thompson, and Ben Jr. stood in front of the pastor. Olive's heart dropped. Tears formed behind her eyes but did not fall.

Bea held the baby girl.

"Do you, Beatrice Thompson, swear to raise this child in God's Holy Church?"

"I do." Bea kissed the baby's head. "Sweet darling, Aunt Bea is here for you always."

"I Christen thee Penelope Rose Westchester. In the Name of The Father...The Son...and The Holy Spirit." Pastor Ashton splashed the baby with water three times, signifying the Holy Trinity. Olive stood in shock in the back of the room, watching in silence.

Ben Jr.'s turn. Pastor Ashton asked him the same question. "Do you, Benjamin Westchester Jr., swear to raise this child in God's Holy Church?"

"I do."

Olive blanched. *He doesn't even attend Sunday services!* She allowed the tears to fall.

"I Christen thee Sinclair Henderson Westchester. In the Name of The Father...The Son...and The Holy Spirit." Again, Pastor Ashton splashed the baby with water three times.

The family cheered as the babies cried. Bea and Benny paraded around the room, presenting their new spiritual charges. Formal introductions to the twins were made by each family member taking turns holding the babies. Olive hung back. Sally noticed the girl sitting in a corner.

"Little Sister-in-Law, I thought you would be enjoying today's merriment? Why such a long face?" Sally reached for Olive, who pulled away. Puzzled, Sally offered the baby. "Why don't you hold little Penny? She's your niece."

"I know she's my niece. I am her aunt, just like Miss Bea." Olive turned her body away from Sally. "No, thank you, I don't care to hold her. I think I'll go upstairs and change. This blouse is itchy."

Olive stood, excusing herself. Smuggling a plate of food from the dining room, she retreated to her bedroom, where she opened her precious copy of *The Call of the Wild*. Remaining in her bedroom, she read the rest of the afternoon.

∞∞∞∞

Clyde and Sally commenced opening gifts as the family munched on tea sandwiches and sweets. The surprise of the second baby evened out the gift preparation for either a boy or a girl. Little dresses, tiny shirts and shorts, socks, jumpers, bibs, and blankets scattered across the settee. A stack of cloth diapers—oh, the diapers—tumbled over as they added the third dozen. The proud parents giggled and cooed at their offspring as the Godparents held them on display.

Lizzy and Samuel enjoyed the festivities, having contributed by picking flowers to decorate the rooms. Spotting a large box in the corner of the foyer, Lizzy pushed it over to Sally.

"Look at this! Open this one next, please." Bent at the waist, Lizzy grunted as she pushed.

"My goodness, who is this box from? There is no card." Sally looked around the room for an indication of ownership. Seeing none, she asked again, "Where did this come from?"

Not sure if he should tell, mostly since she was not in the room, Samuel waited several moments before disclosing, "That box is from Olive."

"Olive? Such a large gift?" Sally searched the room to thank her. Finding no Olive, she asked, "Where is Olive? She said she was just changing her clothes."

"Oh, Olive is always disappearing," squawked Tildy. "That child is never where she is supposed to be. Go on, don't make us wait. Open it."

Sally reached inside the box, pulling out two matching, knit, cable stitch blankets. "How odd. They match. Why would she knit two? The twins were a surprise to everyone, including the midwife. How did she know to make two?" Then, inspecting them more closely, she added, "Nice stitching."

"She didn't know," Samuel offered. "She stayed up all night this past week to finish the second one. She wanted them to match, to be special." The family responded with silence.

Next in the box, Sally found a dozen diapers. Matching knit booties, matching embroidered bibs, and several mismatched bonnets revealed many hours spent in a labor of love.

"How did she ever find the time?" Clyde wondered aloud. "And where did she get the money?"

Henderson solved the money question. "I pay her a stipend to help me with the books. It's not much, mind you. If I were to pay an accountant, I'd be spending thirty times more. She has some money."

"She obviously spent it all on us." Sally snuggled the soft blankets against her cheek. "Such a kind child."

Tildy guffawed. "Olive, kind? Must be post-pregnancy hallucinations. Olive is kind only when it benefits Olive."

"Like I said last week, she's an odd creature." Henderson poured himself a brandy. "Time for something stronger? To my new granddaughter and grandson, Penelope and Sinclair."

Glasses clicked, conversation soared, and the Westchesters celebrated.

All except Olive, who sulked alone in her room, wondering why she was so unappreciated.

19

LOVE THY NEIGHBOR

*T*ildy folded laundry while Lizzy played in the corner. "Now that all this baby nonsense is over, I can get on with planning my wedding," Tildy confided in Lizzy. "Are you excited, Lizzy? We are going to live with Daddy soon." Tildy fussed, refolding a blouse. "I hate the way the maid does this. When I finally leave this place and run my own house, I'll have things done exactly my way."

"I don't want to leave this place. I like living here, Mommy." Lizzy clung to her doll.

"You may take your dolls and toys with you. And you'll have your very own room. Mommy will be sleeping in Daddy's room after we move." Tildy threw the slip on the floor in disgust. "Argh, why does she fold the top down instead of the sides in, first?" Picking up the clean undergarment, Tildy wrinkled it into a ball, throwing it into the dirty laundry pail.

"But I'm scared. That mean lady who lives in the house doesn't like me." Lizzy shook her head back and forth. Jumping on her bed, she snuggled under the quilt. "I'm staying here."

"She's your grandmother. Of course, she likes you; how could she not?" Tildy squeezed her daughter. "You are so cute and sweet."

Lizzy giggled. "You're tickling me, Mommy." Lizzy stopped

laughing to continue pleading her case. "Every time we visit Daddy, she always grumbles. And she has so many rules. Take off your shoes, don't run in the house. Don't pick the flowers. Wash your hands. She always says, 'wash your hands.'" Lizzy paused before continuing. "'Don't touch that; you'll break it.' 'Wipe your feet.' 'Keep your hands away; that is special.' Geez...she never runs out of rules." Hands on her hips, Lizzy stuck out her chin as she finished her litany.

"Your Daddy will deal with her. He promised me." Tildy inspected her ring finger, now dressed in an emerald. "When you are afraid, just look at Mommy's ring. Daddy bought an emerald because he said it matches Mommy's eyes. It shows that Daddy loves us, and wants to make us happy. Your Daddy shall take care of us."

Scrunching her face, Lizzy changed the subject. "Will my name change?"

"Why would you ask such an unusual question?" Tildy stopped folding and watched Lizzy.

"Olive said..."

"Oh, I see." Turning her attention to her work, Tildy dismissed the thought of her sister. "Ignore Olive. She's a troublemaker."

"Mommy. Olive said that instead of my name being Elizabeth Jamison Westchester, it will change to Elizabeth Westchester Jamison."

Turning back to her daughter, Tildy scratched her neck. "Oh. I hadn't thought of that."

"Olive said that you wouldn't have thought of it." Lizzy's eyes never left her mother's.

"Why, that little brat..." Instantly, her face turned bright red. Tildy walked toward the door.

"Mommy, please don't yell at Olive. I like Olive." Jumping up, Lizzy ran to her mother, grabbing her skirt. Tildy stopped. Scooting Lizzy back into the room, Tildy followed.

"Well...Once I am married, you shall be spending much less time with Aunt Olive. *Much* less time."

∞∞∞∞

The road leading from the farm was full of ruts and ditches. Sitting in the front of the Ford, Olive bounced in anticipation as she rode with Jake to the train station.

"Miss Olive, please stop bouncing. I beg you. I'll be seasick." Jake's face already glowed green. "This road is bad enough..." He thrust his head out of the open window.

"I'm sorry, Jake." She tried to quiet her legs. They seemed to take on a life of their own. "I'm just so excited to see Fred."

Jake smiled, then gasped for air.

Coming home for the wedding, Levi and Fred were due on the three o'clock train. Both soldiers had remained in New York during the offseason. Levi was working as a law clerk and planned to attend law school after his service requirement. Fred spent the summer working on campus, in the library. Enjoying the luxury of reading for hours on end, Fred only left the building to eat and sleep.

The vehicle pulled up as the train rolled into the station. Olive pictured the cowcatcher as having a wide smile. She jumped out of the Ford before it came to a complete stop. Running to the platform, she pushed her way to the front of the crowd.

At five feet, six inches tall, Olive could see the train clearly as the passengers disembarked. Dressed in his cadet gray, Fred crossed the threshold. Olive's heart fluttered and her stomach turned flip-flops. Immediately, Olive went into motion.

"Fred! Oh, Fred!" She ran to him, throwing her arms around his neck before he descended the bottom step. "Freddy, I missed you so." She kissed both cheeks. Greedily, she inhaled his scent, no longer present on her quilt.

Laughing and stunned by such a greeting, Fred eased his sister away. "Look at you. My goodness, you've grown at least five inches since I saw you last." He wrapped his arms around her waist. "Come here, out of the way." They moved to an empty area of the platform. Fred lifted Olive and swung her around in circles.

He stopped, gasping for breath. "You're not only taller, but heavier, too. What are they feeding you?" Fred collapsed onto a bench. Olive joined him, giggling uncontrollably.

"Oh, Fred. How I miss you. Why do you stay away?" She placed her head on his shoulder. Feeling the bulge of his muscle under his shirt, she added, "You've gained some weight too, at least some muscles. Tell me about New York."

"As I said in my letters, the Hudson River valley is beautiful." Fred stroked Olive's hair as he chatted.

"But we live in a beautiful river valley also. The Conemaugh is not a large river, but we have gorgeous hills on either side." Olive motioned to the rolling green hillsides that surrounded the town. "When do classes begin? Can you stay awhile?"

As they walked back to the Ford, Fred said, "I have to be back in two weeks. Olive, where are your manners? You haven't even greeted Levi." Fred glanced at his brother, who was loading luggage into the back of the Ford.

"Phooey, I saw him at Christmas. He could care less about me." She hugged Fred again. "Freddy, I love the book. I know it was really from you. Levi added his name as an afterthought, didn't he? Did you like my scarf?"

Fred's face reddened, "The scarf is a godsend. The wind whips down that river. How did you know what color yarn to use?" Fred walked on; Olive tugged until he stopped.

"Uncle James told me. I started knitting it as soon as you left. It was my first knitting project. Geez, I pulled more stitches out than I put in." Her confession reminded Fred of her young age.

Giving her the once over, Fred shook his head. "You look like Mother. Has anyone told you that?"

"Levi said as much at Christmas. I think it made him mad." Her blue eyes latched onto Fred's gaze. "I'll be eleven in two months. I'll be in sixth grade." She squeezed Fred's hand. "Freddy, will you talk to Father for me? I want to go on to high school in Campbellsville. Then

I want to go to college, maybe study mathematics or attend medical school." Her eyes pleaded.

"My, my. That is an honest, lofty ambition. A woman doctor? Wherever did you get such an idea?"

"Dr. Paulson said I would make a fine doctor." Olive looked up at her brother, a toothy grin covering her face.

As they finally arrived at the Ford, Levi greeted his sister and gave her a peck on the cheek.

"Hi Levi, welcome home." Olive clung to Fred. "Levi, sit in the front. I want to sit with Fred in the back."

"Yes, ma'am. I see you're still bossing everyone." Levi sat down beside a smiling, no longer green-faced Jake.

At the house, a robust Henderson welcomed both young men. He swept them into his office before they had a chance to see the twins.

"Sit men, both of you sit. I want to hear all about your adventures, your studies, and your conquests." He winked as he poured drinks. Both boys blushed.

Fred began, "Father, it's an all-men school. We have no conquests."

"Speak for yourself, Fred." Levi chuckled, punching his brother's shoulder. Henderson raised his eyebrows.

"You do say now! Who is she, and where did you meet her?" Henderson rubbed his hands together. "Out with it."

"Her name is Sylvia Flossman. She works in New York City." Unconsciously, Levi licked his upper lip.

"Works? What kind of lady worth her salt works outside of the house?" The crease of his forehead confirmed Henderson's disapproval.

"She's a vaudeville actress." Levi dropped his head to hide his sly smile and the red in his cheeks. Fred grinned. Henderson choked on his brandy, spitting it across the room.

"An actress! Levi Westchester. A floozy actress?" Henderson glared at Levi. "I send you to get an education. Instead, you find a tramp."

"No, father, it's not like that. She comes from a respectable family from upstate New York...Saratoga Springs." Levi stumbled over his choice of words. "I ask that you keep an open mind. She is studying drama and literature at Barnard College."

"Her family permits her to work in vaudeville, and they also send her to college? What kind of people are they?" Henderson braced himself with both arms, leaning over Levi.

"Obviously, her family is more progressive than you, Father." Levi tried to stand; Henderson prohibited him.

"Father," Fred said. "The idea of higher education for a woman is not so farfetched. I believe Olive wishes to attend college."

Having chosen an inopportune moment to champion his sister, Fred caught Henderson's attention.

"What? Olive, college? What kind of nonsense is this? It's bad enough for Levi to court a college woman. His can be a short-term fling to fulfill certain *manly* needs. But for me to educate my daughter beyond finishing school? My job is to prepare her as an acceptable wife, to find her a respectable husband who can provide for her. College? Poppycock!" Taking several steps back, Henderson placed both hands on his waist. Glowering at his sons, he spun and walked out of the office, muttering, "Send them away...heads full...stupid ideas...educating a woman..."

Levi burst into roaring laughter. "I do believe, Brother, that you have ruined things for The Queen." Levi slapped Fred on the back. "Good job."

Levi followed Henderson out of the room. Fred sat alone, hands covering his face, dreading what he would tell Olive.

20

DEARLY BELOVED

*T*wo days later, Tildy's long overdue wedding day arrived. Guests sat on chairs in the Westchester front yard, fanning themselves on the hot August afternoon. Keeping the attendees to immediate family limited the chair search to thirty.

Olive knocked on Sally's door. "Sally, will you braid my hair?" She poked her wild locks into the opening.

"I'm sorry. I don't have time; I must dress the twins." Turning her focus back to Sinclair, Sally added, "Ask Ginny."

Wandering down the hall, Olive knocked on Ginny's door. No answer. The next option was Tildy. After a few moments' hesitation, taking a deep breath, Olive knocked.

"Whoever you are, you better have a good excuse for interrupting me," Tildy said through the door, her voice tense with stress.

"Tildy, it's Olive. Will you braid my hair?"

"No. Go away. Lizzy, stand still. I can't fix your hair if you fidget so." The anxious bride fussed over her daughter. "We must be ready in ten minutes."

Olive absentmindedly walked into her room, now being used by Fred and Levi. Dressed in his cadet uniform, Fred buttoned his jacket.

"Oh, Fred, I'm sorry. I forgot you were in here."

Head hung, she walked over to her dresser. Reaching for her brush, she began the chore of controlling her curls by herself. After three unsuccessful attempts at braiding, she sat down on the edge of the bed. Holding back tears, she began the fourth attempt with her hair.

"Olive, sweetie, maybe I can help?" Fred took the brush. Drawing it through her hair, he calmed the curls by grabbing them in his large hand.

"You start at the top with a few strands, then keep adding more hair as you go. I don't care if I have sprouts sticking out for school, but I want to look nice for Tildy today." Olive smiled at Fred as he patiently stroked her head with the brush, mastering the art of braiding. "Sally used to do this for me, until she got pregnant. Now she's been too busy with the babies. She used to be my friend. But not so much anymore."

Fred kissed the back of her head.

Pleased but surprised by the kiss, Olive turned to face her brother. "What was that for?"

"Sit still. You'll ruin my masterpiece." Fred chuckled as he chastised Olive. "I promise to braid your hair every day for the next two weeks, my dear sister," he said lovingly.

Brother and sister went outside, arm in arm. Taking their seats in the second row, they joined Samuel and Benny, who nodded at Olive. Wearing her mother's blouse and pearls with expertly braided hair, Olive looked older than Nellie—much older than "almost eleven."

The family gasped as Henderson and Tildy walked across the lawn, down the aisle to join Tommy. Clad in an ecru, embroidered lace dress with a wreath of daisies crowning her dark hair, the twenty-six-year-old was stunning. A bouquet of daisies and sunflowers hinted at the end of summer. Lizzy walked in front of her mother, tossing daisy petals to escort the bride.

Tommy Jamison beamed. Alva Jamison, sitting in the front row, scowled. A low hiss escaped her mouth as Tildy and Henderson passed. Ginny, Tildy's witness, smiled. The best man, Tommy's cousin, gaped open-mouthed at Tildy's beauty. Henderson handed his daughter to Tommy as he kissed Tildy's cheek. Then, grabbing Tommy's arm, he whispered, "It's about time," as he took his seat in the front row across the aisle from Alva.

"Dearly beloved," began Pastor Ashton. Tildy's smile was radiant throughout the ceremony. For seven years, she had dreamed of this day. Finally, nothing could come between her and Tommy. "Do you, Thomas Lyle Jamison, take this woman, Matilda Elizabeth Westchester, to be your lawfully wedded wife?"

The ceremony was a blur to both Tommy and Tildy. The only thing they truly understood was the pastor saying, "I now pronounce you man and wife. Please kiss your bride."

A cheer erupted as Tommy embraced Tildy. Alva sat straight-faced, arms crossed in front of her body. The guests flocked to the newlyweds, offering congratulations and envelopes of money before heading inside to enjoy Cook's treats.

Rather than a full meal, Ginny planned a formal English Tea. The dining room overflowed with sandwiches, cookies, and sweets. Fruit punch, served in Polly and Henderson's crystal punch bowl, coffee, tea, and lemonade refreshed the hot crowd.

Olive allowed the crowd to thin out before approaching Tildy. She carried a parcel, wrapped in silver paper. Tommy did a double take as she walked toward them.

"Tildy, Tommy, I wish you a lifetime of happiness," she said, as she handed Tildy the gift. "Please open it now." A rosy complexion camouflaged Olive's youth.

"Oh, Olive, I have other guests to greet. I can't be bothered by your silly gift." Even on her wedding day, Tildy unleashed her tongue at her sister.

Surprised by the outburst, Tommy said, "Tildy, she's your sister."

"Please, Tildy?" Olive insisted, as she held the gift in front of her.

"Oh, all right." Removing the paper, Tildy discovered a blank ledger book. "For goodness' sake, a ledger?"

Olive stood her ground. "You'll be running your own household now. You'll need this. But look inside, please."

"If I must." Tildy opened it to the first page, titled "Jamison Farm Records." In the binding crease was a crisp twenty-dollar bill. "Where on earth did you get twenty dollars?" asked Tildy.

Biting her lip, patience running thin, Olive scrutinized Tommy. "I hope you realize what you are getting into with her. Save the money for an emergency. Don't let her spend it frivolously...and...*you're very welcome.*"

"Olive, you are exasperating." Tildy flung her head so hard that her crown of daisies flew off. "Oh now look..." Tildy scrambled to replace her headpiece before she was seen by others. "Tommy, help me!"

Olive spun on her heel and clomped away.

∞∞∞∞

The rest of the afternoon and evening, guests ate and drank. Henderson employed a local group of musicians to play dance tunes and gigs. The family took turns dancing with each other on a wooden dance floor installed on the closely mown lawn. Olive's favorite partner, Fred, quickly became everyone's favorite partner.

"Olive, may I have this dance?" Olive spun to see Henderson extending his hand as dusk fell. Jars filled with lit candles suspended from the porch roof; trees and arbors swayed in the gentle evening breeze.

"With pleasure, Father." She accepted his hand as she twirled into the crowd of dancers.

"You look very grown-up, tonight. Such a resemblance to your mother." Henderson expertly spun her around the floor. "Not much of a dancer though," he said with a grin.

Olive flushed. "I'm pleased to be like Mother."

"Well, you are. More than you know, child...more than you know. It won't be too long, maybe five or six years, before we celebrate *your* wedding." Henderson flashed a charming smile at Olive and continued

131

without allowing Olive to reply. "With your beauty, all the young boys will be asking for your hand. Promise me that you'll be a good girl and wait to have babies until *after* you are married. Not like your sisters. A deal, my Olive?" The dance over, Henderson commenced looking for a new partner.

"Father, wait." Olive caught her father's sleeve. "What do you mean, 'five or six years?' I'll still be in school." Staring directly at him, she said, "I want to attend Campbellsville high school, and then go to college."

"Don't be silly, girl. You'll go to a finishing school, just like your sisters." Henderson snickered, dismissing her. Walking away, shaking his head, he continued laughing. "Where does this girl get such ideas?"

Olive's limp arms dropped to her side; her mouth hung open. *I have three years to convince him otherwise. I shall not be married in six years. I shall go to college.*

Fred waltzed over to whisk his sister back onto the dance floor. "Come on, Olive. The prettiest girl here can't be allowed to stand alone. Shall we dance?"

Seeing Fred was enough to mollify her mood. Olive smiled, grabbed her brother, and danced late into the evening, allowing herself to think happy thoughts.

MY MOTHER'S KEEPER

"*L*izzy, we're home," Tildy shouted as she entered the Jamison house on return from her week-long honeymoon in West Virginia.

Much smaller than the Westchester mansion, the Jamison place consisted of an entry hall, a parlor, a moderately sized library/office, a dining room, and a kitchen on the first floor. The second floor hosted four bedrooms and one bath. Their only servant, a cook, slept next to the kitchen. Unlike the Westchester servants, who slept on the spacious third floor, the Jamison attic was just that: an area for rafters and unwanted items.

"Lizzy, where are you?" Tildy yelled again. "Mommy's home."

Tommy dropped their luggage in the foyer and looked around the house. The dining room sideboard was bare of all items: no silver decanter, no crystal vase, no candlesticks. Tommy opened the drawers of the cabinet; they were also empty of all contents.

"Tildy, something is very wrong here." Tommy said as he anxiously rushed in, completing a room-to-room inspection.

"Where's my daughter?" Tildy's voice was now a screech. As she screamed, Nate knocked, opening the front door.

"Welcome home, Tommy....ah, I mean Mr. Jamison." Nate hung

his head at his faux pax, waiting for an invitation to enter. "Did ya have a good trip?"

"Nate, what's going on here? Were we robbed? Did you call the police?" Tommy motioned for him to join them in the dining room. "Where's my mother?"

"Never mind Alva, where is Lizzy?" Tildy interrupted.

"Mrs. J., Miss Lizzy is at your pa's house. She's fine. Been stayin' there all week while you been gone." Moving closer to Tommy, Nate avoided eye contact with Tildy.

"Why is she at my father's? I thought Mother Alva wanted time to get to know her?" Tildy's voice raised a full octave as she took hold of Tommy's shoulders. "I want my daughter."

"I'm afraid Mrs. Alva had different plans." Hands in his pockets, Nate searched for the proper words.

"Nate, stop this aimless gibberish. Tell me what's going on." Releasing Tildy's grip, Tommy approached his foreman. "Get on with it, man."

"I'm trying, Mr. Jamison. Mrs. Alva packed up the house and moved to her sister's in Ohio. She took all her belongings—her wedding gifts, all her clothes, all her jewelry—and left the day after your wedding." Nate bit his lower lip. "Think she planned it all along."

Tommy collapsed in a chair as he ran his fingers through his hair. Tildy stood speechless, unsure if she felt elation from Alva's disappearance or disappointment over losing the opportunity to boss Alva around in her own home.

"Where's the cook?" Tildy sniffed the air. "I'm starving. Why isn't supper ready?"

"Mrs. Alva took her, too."

Tommy looked at his wife. "You'll have to scrounge through the larder and make dinner tonight, Darling. We'll hire another cook as soon as we can find one."

"Cook? I don't know how to cook. We'll go over to my father's for dinner tonight. They'll be anxious to see us. Besides, I need to gather

Lizzy." Tildy removed her traveling gloves. After tossing them on a chair, she untied her hat.

Struck with a thought, Tommy jumped up. Running upstairs, he entered the largest bedroom, his parents' bedroom, to find it completely empty of all furniture and articles. "No!" he screamed.

"Tommy, what's wrong?" Tildy rushed to her husband's side, abandoning Nate to continue pacing in the dining room.

"All of our money is gone. All of it." Tommy motioned his arm around the empty room. Blue and yellow striped wallpaper, once camouflaged by heavy, dark furniture, fashioned an unfitting circus air.

"What do you mean, all of it?" Tildy tugged at his sleeve. "Tommy, the bed is gone, not the money, right?"

"My father kept his cash in a box, hidden in his chest of drawers. I put our wedding money in the same box, thinking it would be safe. Mother took it. Furniture, box, money. We're broke." Tommy walked to a spot on the floor covered in dust.

"How much money are you talking about? Why the hell isn't the money in the bank?" Spittle flew from Tildy's mouth, her body shook.

"Father never trusted banks." Tommy collapsed to the floor, crying. "Mother is right; I am a failure."

Sitting beside him, Tildy yelled, void of compassion, directly into Tommy's ear. "How much?"

"Five thousand dollars. And the two hundred we got as wedding gifts. I counted it before we left." Burying his head in his hands, Tommy moaned.

"Five thousand, two hundred dollars. You're a stupid idiot to trust her." Tildy slapped him across the face. Tommy stared at his wife as if viewing a stranger. "Why would you not secure the money before we left?"

Tildy's blood froze at the look she received from Tommy. Rubbing his face, he stood slowly, snarling, "Shall we retrieve Lizzy?"

A silent ride to the Westchesters' followed. Tildy left Tommy in the car as she ran into the house.

"Lizzy, Lizzy, Mommy's home." The girl raced down the back stairs and into her mother's arms. Tildy lifted her, smothering her with kisses. "Oh, how I missed you. Did you have fun while I was gone?"

"It was just like living here. I always have fun." Lizzy shrugged her shoulders as she answered her mother. "Where's Daddy?"

"Oh." Tildy turned to see if Tommy followed her inside. "He's coming."

Hearing the ruckus, Henderson strolled out of his office. "Ahh, the newlyweds return. How was the new resort?" Henderson searched the room. "Where's your husband?"

Tildy clicked her tongue. "On his way." She continued kissing Lizzy.

"Don't tell me the honeymoon is over already?" Henderson chuckled, knowing Tildy's tone.

"What if it is? Does it matter? I'm stuck now, aren't I?" Setting Lizzy down, she patted her bottom, shooing her out of the room.

"Darling daughter, you were stuck seven years ago when you decided a chaperone was unnecessary." Laughing casually, Henderson relished seeing his caustic daughter.

"Stop, Father. I care not for lecturing tonight. We're staying for dinner; please tell Cook." Tildy tossed her head.

"What, you're not ruling over your table on your first night home? Relegating Alva to an inferior role?" Thoroughly enjoying the banter, Henderson failed to recognize the magnitude of Tildy's anxiety.

Her face quivered, Tildy could tolerate no more. She draped herself over her father, sobbing colossal tears. Alarmed at her uncharacteristic display of sensitivity, Henderson ushered her into the parlor. Pouring her a brandy, he asked, "Now, tell what this is all about."

Before Tildy answered, Tommy entered. "It's my fault, Mr. Westchester."

"For goodness' sake, either address me as Father or Henderson, whichever is more comfortable." Giving the couple a lengthy stare, he continued. "What is your fault, Tommy? What has my daughter so troubled?"

"May I have a drink?" Tommy swallowed the entire contents in one gulp. "My mother stole all of our money."

"Your mother did what?" At full attention, Henderson poured another round. "According to the will, the farm is yours—as is the money. She is not legally entitled to your property. Wait—I'll get Levi."

Leaving the couple alone, Henderson went in search of his son. Tildy and Tommy avoided eye contact. Tommy breathed deep, laboring gulps to calm his nerves, while Tildy whimpered softly.

Tildy was the first to speak. "Tommy, I'm sorry. I didn't..."

"No, Matilda. I'm the one who's sorry. You finally have your wish; you snatched your husband. However, bear in mind that possession of a husband does not guarantee a happy marriage." His sorrowful eyes betrayed his wounded soul.

The men returned to find Tommy and Tildy sitting on opposite sides of the room, staring in different directions.

"If I understand correctly," Levi reiterated, "your mother took property belonging to your father. She is entitled to her jewelry, her clothes, all personal property. She is not entitled to joint gifts, such as wedding gifts, house, land, farm equipment, or proceeds thereof. Neither is she the owner of the money. You are entitled to sue to regain what is rightfully yours."

Henderson offered, "Son, if you need money to hold you until you settle this mess, don't worry. That's what family does. I have you covered. Knowing your stubborn mother, she'll try to delay this as long as possible." A slap on Tommy's back substituted for a handshake.

Tommy breathed a sigh of relief. "She's determined to interfere in this marriage. She stopped it seven years ago, and now she's trying to stop it again." Pausing, Tommy comprehended his words. He wiped his sweaty hands on his trousers as he reached for Tildy. "Darling, please, I do not wish to fight. My mother is trying to place a wedge between us, don't you see?"

"Tommy, do you remember when you first moved into that farm? You and your father toured the field closest to ours. I was there. I watched you from behind the fence. I fell in love with you that day; I was six years old. I shall always love you." Tildy smothered his face with kisses.

"Enough. Save the affection for the privacy of your own home." Henderson walked to his cashbox. Withdrawing several hundred dollars, he handed it to Tommy rather than Tildy.

"Thank you, sir. If I may ask, what does Mother have against the Westchesters?" Tommy braved walking to the dining room.

Henderson thundered with laughter, "Jealousy. That is a story for another day. Now let's eat."

THE HOUSE ON THE HILL

"Olive, help me with the crate." Tildy issued a demand, rather than a request. Traveling to Ohio for retribution, Levi and Tommy hoped to return by the week's end, with a resolution in hand. With Fred heading to West Point, Levi to New York City, both held tickets for the Friday train. Tildy ransacked the Westchester treasure stash for interim supplies.

"She took her china and crystal. I have some mismatched plates in the kitchen. Nothing worthy of a dinner party." Tossing newsprint and straw, Tildy covered the attic floor with packing material. "There has to be an old set of china up here someplace. Don't we have Grandmother's?"

"For goodness' sake, unless you intend to clean up this mess, be neater." Olive shook her head, fearing she would be tasked with tidying up after Hurricane Tildy. "Really, Tildy, I don't have time for this. Fred leaves in four days. I intend to spend as much time as possible with him." Olive brushed straw from her hair. Climbing down the third-floor staircase, she called back to Tildy. "Did you bother to inventory the *Jamison* attic? Maybe you only need to rampage your own home."

Tildy only replied with an angry groan. Olive stopped on the second floor and peeked into her bedroom.

"Fred, let's do something fun," Olive said, climbing up on the bed beside a reading Fred. "You only have a few days before your return to New York. I want an adventure."

"I have two pages to read in this chapter, but then we can. What would you like to do?" Fred read as Olive considered her options.

"Can you drive?" Peeking over Fred's shoulder, Olive teasingly reached for the book.

"I've driven. I haven't practiced much." Fred winked at his sister. "Now stop it. Allow me to finish."

"Let's go into Campbellsville. I never get to go to town. Maybe we can have a soda drink at the drugstore?" Jumping off the bed, Olive grabbed her hairbrush. "Phooey, I'll allow my hair to do whatever it wishes."

"You look fine. I can drive that far. Sounds like a grand idea." Closing his book, Fred laced his shoes. "I'll tell Jake that we have the car, in case Father is looking for it."

Olive and Fred giggled as they bounced down the country lane. The front tire slipped into one rut, sending the car spinning and forcing Fred to downshift. Gaining control, he stopped while the laughing continued.

"Oh, Freddy! I need to run into the woods. I've laughed so hard I may have wet my pants." Olive hid behind a tree and squatted. Leaping back into the seat, she hugged her brother. "I haven't had this much fun since last year. I wish you didn't have to return to school. I do miss you so, Fred."

"Don't be morose. Today, we conquer Campbellsville! Forward ho, troops!" Throwing the Ford into gear, they bounced and laughed until they reached the main road leading to town.

The Campbellsville drugstore soda counter was a local gathering spot. A druggist prepared medical mixtures and concoctions in a small rear room, while the front of the establishment was a store for miscellaneous whatnots. Greeting cards, thread, needles, fabric, proprietary medicinals, dime novels, hair combs, penny candy, and stationary filled the shelves on the right side of the building, while a soda fountain, including counter service and booths, occupied the left.

Fred slid into a booth. Olive sat across from him. "What's your pleasure, Little Sister? A banana split? A soda drink?" Handing her a menu, he watched her eyes widen in delight.

"I want a chocolate malted milk. Yummy, that sounds good," Olive said, salivating.

Motioning to the clerk, Fred ordered, "Two chocolate malts," then to Olive, he added, "Good choice."

As they waited for their order, several local factory laborers entered for an interim refreshment. Spotting Fred, the men, covered in grease and grime from head to toe, stopped to chat. Olive held her breath to lessen breathing in the smell of sweat.

"Hey, Fred. Haven't seen you in a while. Aren't you at the Point with Levi?" Glancing at Olive, the man continued, "Who's this pretty filly? I haven't seen her around."

"This 'filly,' as you call her, is my sister, Olive." Fred scrunched his face and shook his head at the man. "Olive, may I introduce Tobias Bailey. Tabs started high school with Levi."

"I'm sorry, Fred. Meant no disrespect. She sure is pretty."

Olive blushed. Fred kicked her under the booth.

"Pleased to meet you, Mr. Bailey." Olive reluctantly presented her hand, which Tabs kissed in greeting.

The clerk delivered their malteds. Turning to Tabs, she asked, "The usual, Tabs?" A beaming, toothless grin greeted his affirmative nod.

Tabs stood at the booth until Fred said, "Where are my manners? Would you gentlemen care to join us?" Jumping at the offer, Tabs lowered himself beside Olive. Immediately on his feet, Fred held up his hands. "On this side, please." Fred motioned for Tabs to acquiesce; he and his companion faced the Westchesters.

"I don't believe I know your friend," said Fred.

"My apologies. This is my cousin, Wyeth Bailey. We work at the foundry together. We're on a break between a double shift."

"Mr. Bailey, Fred mentioned that you began high school with Levi. Did you not complete the course work?" Olive casually asked the stranger.

"No, Miss Westchester. Family matters required me to find a job. Happily, I found a position in the foundry. I work as many doubles as I get. The mines pay more, but the foundry's not as dangerous."

"My Uncle owns that shop," Olive said. "Have you met him? Congressman James Westchester?"

"No ma'am, I haven't met the honorable congressman. And yes, ma'am, I am aware of your status in the community." Tabs felt the heat rising in his neck.

"Olive, don't be rude." Fred pinched her leg. Olive stared blankly; she spoke the innocent, unintentional insult as a simple statement of fact.

Wyeth grimaced. "I believe we've bothered these good folks long enough, Tabs. Let's leave them be." Standing, Wyeth carried his soda and sandwich while pulling his reluctant cousin to a different booth.

Fred whispered to Olive, "You really must not be so blunt, Olive."

"But Freddy, I'm always to the point. I don't know how to be any other way." Her face concealed any remorse.

"And, perhaps, that is why our siblings rebuke you?" Fred took her hand. "Sister, brash actions from a man are received as competence; however, from a woman they are simply impolite."

Finally, Olive's face reddened. "Fred, I did not intend to insult those men. I was simply stating the truth, making conversation." She lay her head on Fred's shoulder. "Did I make a mess of things?"

"Cheer up. Drink your malt. You'll learn the art of socializing. It takes practice. You certainly do not have a good role model in Tildy." Disparaging Tildy made Olive laugh.

"Yes, I shall blame Tildy. My dramatic, ill-tempered older sister. May she and Tommy get what they deserve." She raised her glass in a sarcastic toast.

"Oh, you wicked cat."

Wyeth and Tabs recoiled with paranoia as Olive and Fred burst into hysterical laughter.

"Fred, may we take a walk around Campbellsville? I do enjoy escaping the farm, but my visits to town are too infrequent. Father rarely permits me to accompany Benny on supply runs. Says it's a waste of my time."

Paying the check, Fred escorted Olive out of the drugstore. "Perhaps we shall do this again tomorrow?"

Tabs watched their exit closely as they walked arm in arm, intrigued by the mysterious Westchester daughter.

Walking down the main street, they passed an assortment of businesses. Dry goods, milliner, butcher, baker, cobbler, and Dr. Paulson's office filled the expanse of two blocks. Next to the river, the blacksmith, granary, and foundry were located on the lower street.

Fred admired the green hills surrounding the town. "Look how the sunlight reflects through the leaves. Fall is around the corner." Fred sighed wistfully. "I'm reluctant to return to West Point."

"Why? Don't you like West Point? You used to love school." Olive, startled by the statement, wrapped her arm tighter around Fred's.

"I do love school, but not the students. Someday I shall tell you about the horrors of plebe hazing, but not today." Fred paused before adding, "I would rather study literature than war. I want to write, perhaps become a journalist. The military is not my choice of study." Fred reached for Olive's hand. "Shall we change the subject? Look at these beautiful houses. Not as big as our grand home, however, very respectable."

"I want to live in town. I should, really. The doctor ought to have her office in town." Olive motioned to Paulson's office. Then she pointed to a sizable, three-story corner home, presumably the largest house in town. Located on the uppermost street, it stood guard over the entire valley. "I want to live in a house like that. One year at Christmas, Father brought us into town. That house was lit with candles in every window. Absolutely stunning."

They meandered for an hour before returning to the Ford. "Well, Olive, I hope you enjoyed the day, but we ought to be heading back. Father shall be looking for us."

Olive snuggled into Fred's arm. "I had the most wonderful day. Thank you." She hesitated before she continued, "If you truly dislike West Point, please speak to Father. Perhaps he'll permit you to transfer schools. You'd make an excellent writer."

Fred frowned. "I'll think about it, dear Sister. I believe the situation is beyond my control. Father and Uncle James signed an agreement. Levi and I attend West Point; Father's awarded a government contract."

"Oh, Freddy. Did Father ask you first?" Olive frowned, chewing on her fingernail.

"Ha. What do you think, Olive? Does Henderson Westchester ever consider his children's feelings?"

"I'm so sorry. Father certainly tries to control our lives. I hope to be the one to change his ways. I have three years to change his mind about my attending high school."

"Good luck, dear Olive." Fred kissed Olive's forehead, looped his arm around her waist, and guided her back to the automobile.

Cherishing each other's company, Fred and Olive spent the next three afternoons enjoying chocolate malts at the Campbellsville drugstore. Every day, Tobias and Wyeth Bailey cordially greeted the Westchesters when they stopped during their work break. However, the conversation started and ended with "*Hello.*" Obscuring his stares, Tabs observed the youngest Westchester daughter with mounting interest.

TREASURE HUNT

*R*eturning to her new home, Tildy commenced setting up a house. Although she never admitted such, she heeded Olive's advice and searched the Jamison attic for treasures. To her surprise, Alva had stashed crates of china, silver, and crystal in the back corner of the attic. Perhaps her lorry exceeded full capacity with the bedroom suite. Whatever the reason, Tildy claimed possession of the fineries.

Levi and Tommy returned from Ohio late Thursday evening and went straight to the Jamisons'. Tildy met them at the door, the light fading and breeze blowing, a signal of the new season. Summer's short, sweet visit would soon give way to a long autumn and winter.

"Well, did you get the money?" Hand on her hips, hair pulled off her face with a bandana, she looked a fright—absent was the well-dressed, precisely groomed diva.

"Not even, 'Hello, was your journey safe?'" Eyeing her appearance, Levi asked, "My God Tildy, what happened to you? Married one week, and already you let yourself go."

Tommy reached for Tildy as Lizzy ran into the room. "Daddy, Daddy!" She jumped into Tommy's arms. He twirled his daughter until she begged for him to stop.

"How did I allow Mother to keep me away from the joy of such a greeting?" Tommy kissed his daughter, then his wife. Handing Tildy a box, he smiled. Tildy rubbed her hands together before taking it from him.

Tildy licked her lips. "You got it back?"

"We had to compromise. I gave Mother the bedroom furniture, which is rightfully ours, in exchange for the box." Tommy beamed with the pride of accomplishment.

"Did she know the box's contents?" Opening the case, Tildy began counting the money.

"Yes. She knew, but she didn't have the key." Tommy's eye twinkled as he dangled the key in front of his wife. "She was adamant that we split the money."

"Did you?" Tildy dropped as many bills as she counted.

"No. You may stop. It's all there; Levi and I counted it." Bending to pick up the fallen money, Tommy noticed Tildy wearing his work boots.

"Darling, is this a new fashion?" Chuckling, he brushed straw out of Tildy's hair.

"Stop it, both of you. I've been working."

Levi reached to feel Tildy's forehead, then feigned to faint. "You must be ill. Tildy doesn't work!" The trio laughed. Levi continued, "I insisted she return their wedding gifts; however, she swore she didn't have them."

"She doesn't have them." Tildy waved toward the dining room. "I found them. That's why I look like this. I've been upstairs, in the heat of the attic, stomping on spiders. But I discovered a treasure trove."

"Clever girl," praised Tommy. Tildy glowed, accepting total credit.

"Are we required to provide for her?" Tildy's question, directed to Tommy, was answered by Levi.

"Good question. You are not. If Alva had remained in the house, she would have been your responsibility, financially, for room and board. However, because she willingly chose to leave the property, she is on her own. Jamison's last will and testament made such stipulations."

"So...she is totally out of our lives? I never have to deal with that dreadful woman again?" Tildy pirouetted on the toes of her boots.

"Tildy, you are speaking of Tommy's mother. Have some respect." Levi chastised her brazen tongue.

Tommy laughed. "My dear wife, my mother is a fiend. I agree with you, Tildy. She worked for seven years, cajoling Father to support her, telling me dreadful lies to keep me from my love and my daughter. I'm elated to have her gone."

"I believe this warrants a celebratory drink. Tommy, have you any brandy?" Levi searched the dining room for signs of a carafe.

"Yes, we do. I set it up in the library, just like my father. I'll pour." Tildy returned with three crystal snifters of brandy. "Oh, and I found a new cook. Levi, stay for dinner?"

"Thank you; however, this is my last evening before returning to New York. I shall spend it with Father." Levi glanced at Tommy. "May I ask Nate to drive me home?"

"With my pleasure. Brother-in-Law, you have done us a major service. We are indebted. I thank you."

"Who knew you were so talented?" Tildy kissed his cheek as he exited. "Do have a safe journey."

"I shall, Sister. If I were licensed, I'd be handing you my invoice. Perhaps next time." Instead, Levi extended Tommy his hand in a jovial shake.

∞∞∞∞∞

Westchester mealtime without Tildy was a calm, pleasant event. Cook prepared a feast in honor of both sons. Conversation flowed. Henderson, in high spirits, spoke casually of autumn and the harvest to follow.

"I trust you shall both be joining us for Christmas this year?" Henderson's question was answered by complete silence. Levi sat stoically, while Fred squirmed in his chair. "What? Neither of you intend to return for the holiday?"

"I'm spending my holiday in the city, Father." Facing Ben rather than his father, Levi added, "Soon I shall be assigned my first command. This visit may be my last visit home for some time."

Trying to slow his heart rate, Henderson inhaled several deep breaths. Ginny watched her brothers as she pushed her food around her plate, while Ben and Clyde gulped their wine. Olive's eyes darted from sibling to sibling.

Levi laughed nervously, "Father, don't make such a big deal out of it."

"Don't make a..." Locking his jaw, Henderson placed his hands flat on the table. His face burned red. "You've been home for several weeks and you're just telling me *now?* I sent you to military school to become a coward, Levi Westchester? Is that what they teach you? To avoid the truth?" Blood vessels in his neck protruding, Henderson turned to Fred. "And what about you? What's your sad story?"

Sitting beside Olive, Fred squeezed her hand under the table. "Father, I hoped to change schools over the holidays. Levi is more suited to military life than I. Perhaps I shall transfer into Yale or Penn to study literature, and..."

Henderson's pulsing veins stopped Fred mid-thought. Rising slowly from his chair, Henderson hammered the table with his fists. Plates and goblets rattled.

"You may not transfer to Yale. You may not transfer to Penn. I signed an agreement with my uncle and the United States government that the two of you attend and graduate from West Point. By God, I'll honor that agreement. You'll both graduate, and you'll both serve your country as required. Do I make myself clear?" The dining room chair toppled and fell as Henderson pushed away from the table. Storming out of the room, he called, "Good night to you and safe journey."

"That went well." Levi's voice quivered. "You have a knack, little brother. You ruined college for Olive, and now you ruined life for yourself. Now, if you'll excuse me, I must pack."

Olive searched her brother's eyes for an explanation. "What does Levi mean, you ruined college for me?"

"Oh, Olive, I'm so sorry. I mentioned it to Father, as you asked. He was not receptive to the idea of your education. Please forgive me." Tears filled Fred's eyes. He trembled as he wept, distraught with failing his sister.

"Freddy, don't. It's not your fault that Father is stubborn." Olive wrapped her arms around Fred's neck. The two of them hugged, crying together.

THE NEXT MORNING, Levi, Olive, and Fred found themselves on the train platform in Campbellsville again. Fred and Olive held each other tightly while saying goodbye.

"Please think about returning for Christmas. The holiday is not the same without you, Fred."

"Do not hate me, but I think I shall remain in New York. I do promise to come home for at least two weeks each summer." Fred hugged Olive, reluctant to let go.

"Freddy, I can never hate you. You are my only true friend. But...please don't squeeze so hard. You're going to crack my ribs."

Fred released the pressure; Olive inhaled. "Ahh. Much better." She gazed directly into his face, "If you shan't return, promise to write to me every other week. I'll accept no less." Her foot hit the ground to seal the contract.

"I promise, little sister. Now kiss me, and permit me to board. Father will be none too happy if I miss this train." Fred swooped in for an embrace.

"Safe travels, Levi. I love you, Fred." Two handsome men, cadet and officer, climbed the steps as they waved goodbye.

FRUIT OF YOUR LABOR

OCTOBER, 1914

*T*he cyclical rhythm of harvest and holidays remained consistent over the next two years. Olive, in eighth grade, continued to excel in school, calculate her father's accounts, and occasionally babysit the twins. Both Sally and Tildy were excitedly expecting February babies. Fred visited for two weeks each summer and faithfully wrote to Olive, as promised. Farm life moved from one day to the next.

Mealtime, the only time of the day that the family gathered as one, was their opportunity to share and bond.

One evening, during dinner, sixteen-year-old Benny asked, "Who's going to the Harvest Dance?"

"I am!" Olive, the first to respond, shot her arm into the air. "I bought a new dress. Blue chiffon with a flounced overskirt."

"Olive, I was hoping you would babysit the twins. Clyde and I would like an outing before the holidays, before the next baby arrives." Clyde nuzzled his wife's neck as she spoke.

"Sally, find a different babysitter. I'd rather attend the dance. I'm celebrating my thirteenth birthday that weekend. Not that anyone remembers my birthday around here."

Olive huffed. She searched the table for support, but no ally was found. Samuel, age eleven, still ate with the twins.

"You're starting to sound like Tildy." Clyde kissed Sally's cheek as he defended his wife's request.

"Who can tell me the date of my birthday? You have three choices, now that I've disclosed it's the weekend of the Harvest Dance." Her eyes darkened as she quizzed her family.

"Olive, really!" Sally protested the inquisition. "Don't be silly."

"Anyone?" Olive brought her fingers to her mouth as she stared. Shaking her head, Olive concluded, "I thought as much."

Henderson tried to cover his lack of knowledge. "We know it's close to Halloween."

Laughing, Benny added, "Because she's a witch?" The entire table giggled. Olive pursed her lips.

"Oh, so I'm a witch, am I?" Olive allowed tears to form but did not allow them to fall. "Tildy is the witch. However, if you wish me to be one, I shall gladly accommodate you. Clyde, Sally, find another babysitter for the night of the dance, and every future time you need one. Benny, next supply run, unload the truck yourself. Ginny, track your own kitchen supplies; I'm too busy with chores, school, and studying for entrance exams." Olive clenched her legs together to steady her shaking body.

"Entrance exams for what?" Henderson lifted his head, interested in rejoining the conversation.

"Entrance exams for high school placement. I may be able to skip ninth grade by placing into tenth. Father, I have mentioned this before."

"Young lady, yes, you *have* mentioned this, and we've been over this point numerous times in the past." His shoulders tensed as he grabbed his head with both hands. "You shall go to a finishing school starting next fall. I need to groom you into an acceptable wife—tame your tongue. Do you wish to catch a suitable husband?" Henderson placed his hands on the tabletop indicating the subject closed.

"Father, you miss the point. If I get an education, I shall not have to worry about a suitable husband because I'll be capable of caring for myself." Olive stood.

"Naïve thinking, Olive. It may work in theory; however, society is not ready for independent women, no matter how much the suffragettes preach. This conversation is over. Do *not* mention it again. Am I understood?"

"Are you really serious?" Olive gazed directly into Henderson's eyes. "You intend to deny me after all I do to help you?"

"Yes. Now this is done." Henderson returned to eating his meal. Olive walked to the head of the table. Standing beside her father, she leaned on her elbows, her nose in his face.

"It is not done. If you insist that I waste my intelligence, then I'm afraid I must insist on a pay raise for my bookkeeping."

"What? Olive, you try my patience." Food sprayed out of Henderson's mouth, splattering Olive. Grabbing his napkin, she wiped her face. "This is extortion."

"*Au contraire*. I demand to be paid for my services. What would an accountant charge?" No one answered her question, too awestruck to speak. "Father, I asked a question. What would you pay a male accountant to keep your ledgers?" She tossed the napkin into his plate of food.

Moving slowly, Henderson gazed at his daughter, then hissed an answer. "Probably fifteen to twenty dollars a week. For a good one."

Olive gasped, expecting less. "You only pay me one and a half dollars a week. Am I a good accountant, Father?"

"Yes, you are excellent. Better than your mother. Our books are perfect." Thinking the conversation concluded, Henderson pushed away his dish and summoned more wine.

"Fine, then I wish to be paid ten dollars a week for my accounting skills." Maintaining her stare, she conceded. "I should get fifteen, but the five dollars is for my room and board. I'll pay for my keep. I provide significant help with chores and other farm duties, equal to my siblings to earn my birthright in this family. I shouldn't need to pay, but I shall. Either you give me ten dollars a week, or you let me attend high school. Do we have a deal?"

"Why, I never..." Henderson's tanned skin glowed a shade of orange. "You are impertinent and ill-mannered, Olive Westchester."

"Do we have a deal?" Olive's voice carried into the kitchen.

Henderson pushed Olive aside. "You'll be paid."

He jeered, storming out of the room, mumbling to himself.

"Olive, my goodness, that was bold. You become more like Tildy every day," Sally reproached.

Ginny nodded in agreement. "How do you have the nerve to demand such from Father? You need to mind your manners."

"Do either of you provide fifteen dollars' worth of additional services to this farm each week?" Disappointment in Sally spread over Olive's face.

"My father does," offered a defensive Benny.

"And your father is paid a salary, and shall inherit the farm. And you shall inherit it after him. You are working to maintain your future. This family reinforces the adage of 'every man for himself.' I have no future without an education, so I demand money for my services. It's simple economics."

Clyde whispered to Sally, "The birthday fits the description." Olive's mouth fell to the ground, heartbroken when Sally laughed.

HAPPY BIRTHDAY

"Mail call," Samuel yelled as he dropped letters and packages onto the tray. The family made a mad dash to the entrance hall table. "Here, Olive." Samuel handed Olive a box. "It's from Fred."

With sparkling eyes, she ran to a chair and ripped off the paper.

"What is it, Olive?" Samuel hurried over and sat on the floor at Olive's feet.

Olive discovered a copy of *The Mutiny of the Elsinore* by Jack London. "Oh, I love reading Jack London's books. Freddy is so good to me." She opened the book—another first addition. Fred's inscription read, *To my darling sister Olive, on the event of becoming a woman. Happy thirteenth birthday. Love, Fred.*" She hugged the book. "Fred always remembers my birthday."

Running upstairs, she placed it on the shelf beside her copies of *Call of the Wild* and *White Fang*, then she jumped onto the bed to begin reading Fred's letter.

Samuel shadowed her. "Olive, will you read the book to me?"

"Sammy, after I am finished, you may borrow it and read it yourself. Mind you, take good care of it." Olive patted Samuel on the head.

"Thank you. What does Fred have to say?" Samuel leaned over her shoulder to glance at Fred's letter.

"News of Levi. He accepted a peacetime army posting in Virginia. He teaches math at Fishburne Military School, twenty-some miles from the University of Virginia, where he is in law school. That's always what Levi wanted, to be a lawyer. Good for him."

"What should I be, Olive?" Samuel's face glowed as he watched Olive read.

"I'm not sure. Why don't you make a list of all the things you like? Maybe the list will help you decide. We'll talk about it later." Olive continued reading.

"The letter goes on to say Levi bought a car and that he and Sylvia Flossman are engaged to be married. That's odd. Why didn't Levi tell Father himself?"

"Who's Sylvia Flossman?" Samuel stretched out on the bed, making himself at home.

"Well, Samuel, I don't know that either. Fred enclosed a newspaper clipping from New York. It's from the society page announcing the wedding." Olive squinted to read the newsprint. "Goodness. The wedding is next week. Who gets married in November? And why aren't we invited?"

"Let's play spy. I'll ask my mom." Jumping into action, Samuel leaped to the ground and ran down the backstairs, leaving Olive to finish reading. Olive listened to his feet quickly descending the stairs. Minutes later, Olive heard a slow *clunk, clunk, clunk.* Samuel returned, less enthusiastic. He knocked before entering.

"Samuel, why are you knocking? Just come in." Olive looked up from her letter.

Sheepishly, Samuel sat down on the bed. "Olive, you're not going to like what I have to say."

"Why's that, Sammy?"

"The family is going to the wedding. But you're not." Samuel hugged Olive. "I'm sorry."

Olive allowed the information to register. "Levi didn't invite his own sister to his wedding. Is everyone going except me?" Her head cocked to the side in disbelief.

"Mommy said Grandfather, Mother, Uncle Ben, Aunt Bessie, Aunt Sally, Uncle Clyde, Aunt Tildy, and Uncle Tommy are all taking the train to New York. Benny, Lizzy, you, me, and the twins stay home. Miss Bea is coming to watch us."

Olive kissed Samuel's forehead. "Thanks, Samuel. I think you better leave now. Please close the door and ask Cook to send up a dinner tray."

Putting down the letter, she walked to the shelf to retrieve her gift. Neither thoughts of the Harvest dance nor tomorrow's birthday visions alleviated the pain of betrayal. Olive ate dinner in her room, feigning a fever.

Why?

She gripped her knees and rocked herself to sleep, all the while managing to cling to her new book.

∞∞∞∞

"Happy birthday, Olive." Samuel handed her a bunch of freshly picked wildflowers. Olive sat on the bench swing that hung under the grapevine arbor, reading her book. The leaves of the vines, typically providing shade from summer heat, were now brown and shed on the ground. Olive was wrapped in her shawl to dispel the chill in the air.

"Samuel, how sweet. Thank you."

"You're welcome." He kissed her cheek. "Are you still going to the Harvest Dance, tonight?"

"I sure am. Wouldn't miss it. Tonight is my birthday celebration, of sorts." Olive tried to ignore the nagging ache caused by the news of Levi's wedding.

"May I have a dance?" Samuel shyly lowered his head, embarrassed to ask.

"You may have the first dance and the last." Olive smiled at her caring nephew. Achieving his objective, Samuel left to complete his morning chores. Olive remained on the swing, reading her new book and licking her wounds.

Around eleven o'clock, Ginny called out, "Olive, are you going to do any work today?"

"No." The one-word answer offered neither explanation nor justification.

"Olive, stop being so obstinate. I need help ordering next week's supplies."

"I'm off today. I am reading." Olive returned to her book.

"If you help me, I'll let you ride with us tonight," Ginny said, resorting to bribery.

"No, thank you. I'll walk to town if I must." Turning away, Olive pulled the shawl tightly around her shoulders.

She read into the late hours of the afternoon. About four o'clock, she joined the family in the parlor for tea.

Ginny rolled her eyes as Olive entered. "How nice of you to finally join us." Olive glanced at Ginny, then poured a cup of tea. Choosing several snack items, she sat beside her father on the settee.

"Father, it's Saturday. May I have my week's wages?"

Henderson grumbled but walked to his office. Returning, he handed Olive fifteen dollars. "Here." He thrust the money in her face.

"You gave me too much. I only asked for ten," she said, counting the money.

"I'm well aware of your request," Henderson grunted. "Damn it. You are correct, and you earn this. Take the full amount. You need not pay room and board when none of my other children do so. By God, you are a trying soul."

"Is *that* why I'm not going to New York next week?" The family stared at each other in surprise.

"How did you find out about New York?" Ben posed the question.

"Come on, Ben, I'm not stupid." Olive met eyes with each of her siblings and her father. "I truly wish to know why I am not going." Tears hovered below the surface. "And why you kept it from me."

Henderson spoke first. "Olive, it was not our decision to exclude you. It was Levi's."

"Yet you, as head of this family, did nothing to convince him otherwise." Her gaze moved to her Father. "Did you?"

"No, I did not." Henderson dropped his eyes.

"Thank you all for championing me." She spat the words. "Did Levi explain my exclusion? Is there an overpowering reason to ban his sister? Or does he simply hate me?"

"Olive, the invitation stipulates an *adult only* wedding and reception. His handwritten note explicitly stated all guests need to be twenty years of age or older."

"You considered me an adult at age ten, seating me at your table. Instead of showing me the invitation outright, you found it necessary to hide it from me. Am I that volatile? Please excuse me. I must dress for the dance." Grabbing several sandwiches, she left.

Henderson painfully watched his explosive daughter leave the room. *Polly, what the hell am I to do with her?*

Sally called out as Olive ascended the staircase. "You mean you are not watching the twins, tonight?" Confused, Sally exchanged questioning glances with Clyde. Olive answered by clomping upward.

DO SI DO

*A*t five thirty, Olive began her four-mile walk into Campbellsville, giving herself plenty of time to arrive at six thirty for the dance. She wore her school shoes and coat over her tea-length dress while carrying her dance shoes and a lantern to illuminate the often-dark country road. Vehicles began passing her after she had traversed a mile. First, Sally and Clyde drove past. Finding no available babysitter with the whole town attending the social, the twins were in tow. Next came Ben and family; neither vehicle stopped to offer a ride. Lastly, Henderson, Ginny, and Samuel approached in the Ford, with Jake driving. The Ford shifted gears, then stopped.

"Olive, please get in. You don't need to walk," Henderson implored. "I am not comfortable with you traveling this lane alone late at night. Ride with us."

Olive ignored her father and walked on. "Miss Olive," Jake spoke. "Why don't I drop Mr. Westchester and Miss Ginny off in town, then come back for you?"

"Thank you, Jake. I appreciate and accept your offer." Olive covered another mile, trying not to focus on Ichabod Crane before Jake returned to collect and transport her.

"Thank you for the ride, Jake. Now I shall be rested and ready to dance." Olive closed the car door.

Once they arrived, as she moved toward the town hall, Jake called out, "Happy birthday, Miss Olive. Thirteen is a special day." Olive stopped mid-stride. Running back to the Ford, she kissed Jake on the cheek.

The Harvest Dance, Campbellsville's method of bidding goodbye to the growing season and welcoming the holidays of Thanksgiving and Christmas, drew crowds rivaling combined Easter and Christmas church services. Sights and smells of fall engulfed the stairway and rocking chair-filled porch of Campbellsville's social hall. The town and surrounding farms' central meeting place, the social hall hosted weddings, meetings, festivals, and various other events. Tonight, bales of hay, carved pumpkins lit with candles, and garlands of dried apples, stacked, strung, and strewn, greeted the partygoers.

The smells of cinnamon and nutmeg flooded over Olive as she entered the sizable room. Combing the long hall for Samuel, she found him in a corner bobbing for apples with other youngsters his age. Olive scurried across the floor.

"Come, Samuel. Shall we dance?" Samuel flushed, wiping water off his face. He grabbed Olive's hand, dragging her onto the floor for his first dance, a slow waltz. Samuel counted *one, two, three* as he stepped to the beat. When the musicians ended the song, Olive asked, "Do you have a dance card, Sammy? Come, we must get ours."

"What is a dance card, Olive?" asked Samuel as they walked past tables filled with candy apples, pies, jams, and jellies, on sale by the local churches and civic groups.

"You enter the name of your partner on a line for each dance. Then you know with whom you shall be dancing, or if you are sitting out."

"Oh," Samuel said, "Good idea." Olive ushered Samuel to the hostess, who handed her a dance card for her dime entrance fee.

"Did your mother pay for you?"

Samuel shook his head no.

"Here is another dime, for Samuel. He needs a dance card, also."

Samuel radiated. "Now, go ask ladies to dance. Wait, put my name on the last line. I promised you first and last."

Samuel skipped across the floor, stopping at Sally, Tildy, Bessie, Nellie, and Ginny with dance requests. Olive grinned as she watched his delight.

"Is that your brother, Miss Westchester?" A man's voice sounded behind her.

Pivoting, Olive faced Tobias Bailey, who was wearing a clean pressed shirt and smelled of laundry starch and shaving soap. It took a moment to recognize him without his cap. A bush of brown, wavy hair sprang from his head, making him appear taller than five feet, five inches.

Tabs handed her a drink. "May I offer you a cup of cider?"

"Thank you." Olive accepted the cider. "Samuel is my nephew. My younger brother died at childbirth, along with my mother." Embarrassed by sharing such personal information, she blushed and drank.

"I'm sorry...I pray your dance card is not full." Tabs drew nearer. Olive stepped back.

"Quite the contrary; I just arrived." Flattered, but cautious of the attention from an older man, Olive sought an appropriate retort. She found herself tongue-tied.

"Then, with your permission, may I occupy several lines of your card?"

"Certainly. I am celebrating my birthday today. I intend to dance the evening away." Olive smiled, handing Tabs her dance card.

"Well, then, happy sweet sixteen, I presume."

"Ah, something like that." Olive blushed, deliberately hiding her real age.

Tabs wrote his name on Olive's card, and her name on his. "Thank you. I shall look forward to our dances; however, I must go. This dance is already taken."

A stunned Olive stood staring. Henderson slid beside his daughter. "Olive, who is that old man?"

Olive jumped. Henderson gently grabbed his daughter's arm.

"Father! I didn't hear you. That is Tabs Bailey. He asked me to dance." Her face drained itself of most color.

"Be sure to share your dances with younger boys, too, not just the old men. If I dare say so, you are the prettiest girl here. Your dress matches your eyes." Henderson touched her face. "Should have no problem filling your card. Now, allow me to write my name on several lines. By the way, you shall return home in the Ford with Ginny and me. This is not a request."

Olive looked at her father and then at Tabs. "Yes, Father. I shall."

Henderson returned her card. As he left, boys formed a line, all waiting to twirl Olive across the floor. Olive beamed, excited by all the attention. She bewitched several of Benny's classmates, whom Benny promptly teased. Even Leonard Lewis braved an invitation to spin Olive around the room. Henderson taught her the nuances of a three/four waltz swing and sway, while Ben demonstrated several new square dance moves. Olive glowed. Sixty minutes passed before she encountered an empty dance space.

"Thank goodness I have a break." A thirsty Olive hurried over to the punch table to gulp two cups. Finding a chair beside Ginny, Olive rubbed her calves as she enjoyed the quick respite.

"You've been occupied this evening. Thank you for paying for Samuel's entrance. I never imagined him wanting his own dance card."

"He's eleven. Of course he wants to be a man." Olive rolled her eyes at Ginny, wondering why she did not recognize the obvious. They shared civilized small talk about the party refreshments for several minutes until Tabs approached.

"Miss Westchester, I believe this is my dance." Tabs extended his hand.

Ginny looked at her card. "I'm sorry, you are mistaken."

"Forgive me, Miss. The other Miss Westchester, Miss Olive, is next on my card." Olive took his outstretched arm as Ginny quickly inhaled. Glancing at her card, Ginny sadly noted several lines void of names except for those of her father and brothers. She watched Olive, Tildy, and Sally enjoy the evening and felt desperately alone.

I really must escape and make a life for myself, she thought. *Or I shall always be overshadowed by my sisters.*

Ben, Clyde, Benny, Henderson, several boys from Olive's school, anxious young men from Campbellsville High School, and even Jake continued to spin, loop, whirl, and spiral Olive. Fearful of losing his turn, Tabs diligently arrived a minute before each allotted time slot.

The evening flew by, literally and figuratively. At midnight, the band announced the last dance. A waiting Samuel proudly reached for Olive's arm.

"You are the most popular girl at the dance, Olive. And I am a lucky boy to get the last dance with you." Samuel beamed. His waltzing skill had improved from the evening's practice; he now counted to himself.

After the final number, the musicians packed their instruments as the patrons gathered their belongings.

"Miss Westchester, may I see you home?" Tabs Bailey asked. Henderson swooped in to rescue his daughter.

"Thank you, sir. However, she is quite young. I, her father, shall see her home. Come, Olive." Henderson stared at Tabs, defying him to make a move as he placed his hand on Olive's back.

Olive flashed Tabs a smile. "Thank you, Mr. Bailey, for the enjoyable dances. Perhaps next time."

"It was my pleasure, Miss Westchester." Tabs's gaze followed Olive to the car, admiring her stunning, tall, thin silhouette.

As Jake closed the door, Henderson scowled at Olive. "Like hell, 'next time.' That man is old enough to be your father."

"I was only being polite. And he's Levi's age."

Olive sat in the backseat with Samuel and Ginny, neither of whom noticed her glimmering face. She savored the evening by dancing and re-dancing the entire night in her head. Her imagination ran wild as she realized her effect on men.

I don't need my family to be a Princess, she thought. I can manage on my own. My, what a perfect thirteenth birthday.

27

WE ALL SCREAM FOR ICE CREAM

*T*wo days later, Monday afternoon, Samuel and Olive waved from the platform as the family boarded the train to New York. Jake waited at the Ford.

"Are you ready for some fun, Sammy?" Olive draped her arm over his shoulder as they walked back to the car, her smile a mischievous grin.

"Fun?" asked an intrigued Samuel, falling into step with Olive.

"Yes. We have a full week without anyone bossing us around."

"What about Miss Bea?"

"She'll be here at night, but she will have things to do right after school. She's only really here to make some extra money. It'll be you, me, Lizzy, Penny, Sinclair, Cook, and the two maids, who watch the twins most days, already. Sally pretends she's too tired to chase after them. Benny and Nellie are staying alone in the cabin." Olive rubbed her hands together. "If they're going to exclude us, we're going to bend the rules."

"Olive!" Sammy covered his open mouth with his hand. "You're bad."

"So they tell me." Olive bent over to whisper in Samuel's ear.

"We're not really going to be bad, but I'm requesting Cook make all our favorite foods. And we'll stay up later than usual."

"May we have chocolate ice cream?" Samuel salivated at the thought.

"Ice cream every day, chocolate, peach, vanilla, caramel, whatever flavor you wish. It's cold enough to put the churn directly into the stream; the cream will freeze without buying extra ice."

"Yummy! I like being bad your way." Sammy giggled.

The week progressed without incident, other than the children consuming too much ice cream. The flavor of the day changed nightly.

Bea Thompson arrived promptly at six o'clock to eat dinner, including ice cream, with Samuel and Olive; Lizzy and the twins were fed earlier. Envying her sister's leisurely lifestyle, Bea prepared her lessons for the next school day after supper, serving little purpose with the children other than a goodnight kiss. The maids bathed the twins and Lizzy, while Samuel and Olive tended to their own grooming needs. By retiring for the evening by nine thirty, Bea facilitated unchaperoned time, permitting Samuel and Olive to retreat to Olive's room. Most evenings, the duo played board games, checkers, card games, or read stories of Sherlock Holmes aloud. Every night before sleep, Olive looked in on Lizzy and the twins.

On Thursday, having grown accustomed to a new, luxurious way of life, Bea neglected to look in on the twins when she arrived, assuming staff had taken care of their needs. As usual, after saying goodnight around nine thirty, she climbed straight into bed, avoiding a nursery detour.

A few hours later, fatigued from overeating and lost sleep, Olive and Samuel decided to call it an early evening. Per her nightly routine, Olive peeked into the nursery. Upon discovering an empty bed, she raced into Samuel's room.

"Sammy, is Sinclair with you?" Olive looked in the corners and behind the heavy draperies.

Already snuggled under his quilt, the interruption startled Samuel. "No. Why would he be in here?"

"Well, he's not in his bed."

"Where is he?"

"Sammy, don't be daft; that's why I'm here. Come on, hurry, get dressed. We need to find him."

Olive ran to Bea's room and knocked on the door. No answer; only a purring sound came from inside. Knocking louder, Olive called out.

"Miss Thompson! Wake up. Sinclair is not in his room." Now directing Samuel, Olive added, "Sammy, go get Cook and Jake. Kendrick, too. We must find Sinclair." A few moments later, a yawning Bea Thompson opened her door.

"What's all this clatter about? Olive, go to bed." Bea stretched, then tightened her shawl over her shoulders.

Olive clicked her tongue and rolled her eyes. "Was Sinclair in his bed when you checked him tonight?"

"I don't like your attitude, Olive. I didn't look in on the twins today." Bea admitted.

"You didn't? What purpose do you serve here? ...never mind. He's not in his bed. Get dressed and help us look for him." Without hesitation, Olive ordered her teacher into action before scampering down the staircase.

"I beg your pardon, Olive—how about some respect? I shall not take orders from a child."

"We're not in school. This is my house. Get dressed and help us," floated up the stairs in reply.

Olive left Bea stammering on the second-floor hallway as she grabbed her coat and raced out the door.

Kendrick, Cook, and Jake searched in separate areas. Olive and Samuel took a lantern, heading off together.

"Where does he like to play, Sammy? Do you know?" Olive asked, as they shivered in the cold November air.

"He's two and a half. I don't play with him." Still groggy, Samuel struggled to stay with Olive.

"When you were that little, where did you like to play? Think,

Samuel. Sinclair could be in danger." The cold night air and Olive's pleading aroused Samuel's brain. "Sammy, where does a little boy play?"

Taking a deep breath, Samuel said, "Let's look down by the spring house. I used to play there all the time. Maybe he went there thinking he'd find more ice cream."

"Brilliant, Sammy." Olive didn't wait for Samuel to finish; she raced down the path to the spring house. Tripping over an exposed root, Olive fell, scuffing her face and wrists. The cold air stung her bleeding face and her wrists throbbed. She shook her arms and quickly got up, ignoring the pain. Olive continued at full tilt toward the spring. She yanked at the door; it resisted opening. She pulled again; the hinges squeaked and moved as Olive stepped into the cold, damp enclosure. Her nostrils stuck together.

Shining her light into the stream, she called out, "Sinclair, honey, are you in here?"

No answer. She listened as the water babbled over the rocks. Then she heard the whimper, a soft cry coming from someplace inside. She waded into the cold water, scanning for the source of the voice. Feet burning with cold, she called again, waiting to hear a tiny moan. Searching close to the churn, she saw a pint-sized hand. The child's body was completely submerged, leaving only his head above water.

"Sinclair, grab hold of me. Can you see me?" Shining the lantern on her face, she clutched the child's arm and pulled. Losing her grip, she tumbled backward, landing on her backside in the water. Sinclair's soaking wet clothes rendered him dead weight. Mustering all her strength, Olive yanked, dragging the boy out of the rushing stream. His ice-cold body shivered, chilled through. Taking off her coat, she wrapped the little boy, rubbing him to stimulate blood flow.

"Samuel, I have him," she called. "Go get the men. Tell Cook to boil some water and heat some soup."

Carrying the toddler, Olive lumbered toward the house, singing softly in his ear. He lay limp, groaning. Jake and Kendrick reached

Olive at the same time. Kendrick took Sinclair into his arms while Jake threw his coat over Olive.

"You're a brave girl, Miss Olive. Let's get both of you inside and warm. Kendrick, I'm off to get the doctor." Jake patted Olive's back. "Good job, little Miss."

Olive scrunched her nose and cocked her head, staring blankly at the men. "I did what needed to be done. That's all."

Once inside, Cook inspected the baby, his lips and fingers blue from cold. Bea, finally dressed, met them in the entranceway.

"Olive, grab extra blankets. We need to warm him slowly." Cook barked additional orders for the housemaids to make tea and a thin broth. "He should only sip the broth. You," she said, pointing to Bea. "Take off his wet shoes and socks, and rub his feet. Olive, you rub his hands."

"Excuse me? Who are you to order me?" Bea gave Cook an incredulous glance. She tried to maintain an air of authority as tiny beads of sweat formed on her brow. "I am the substitute head of house this week."

Olive pushed Bea away, "If you're going to be useless, Miss Thompson, move aside. Sammy, rub his hands. I'll rub his feet."

"Olive, Cook, I demand some respect from this family. I am an educated, respected member of the community." Bea stood upright, hands on her hips, shouting her mandate.

"This is not the time for excess pride, Miss Thompson. A child's life is at stake," Cook quipped as Samuel and Olive jumped into action.

By the time the doctor arrived, the little boy's frozen fingers and toes had slowly turned from light gray to white to pale pink.

Dr. Paulson and Jake burst into the foyer as Sinclair began to revive. He sat propped up, sipping some chicken broth.

"Looks like someone's quick thinking saved this little guy's life." The doctor smiled at Olive. "Jake relayed the events of the evening. Bravo, Olive. Now, if I may, I want to inspect for myself to be sure we have no hidden issues." Dr. Paulson gathered the child, carrying him upstairs for a full examination. Halfway up the stairs, he called back down, "Olive, I'll tend to your face and hands after I look at Sinclair."

Olive stared at her teacher, hesitated, then spoke. "If you had done your job by looking in on the twins, we could have avoided this. Do you understand that he almost died? Your nephew and godson almost died because of your negligence." Olive splattered spittle over Bea's face.

"You insolent little..."

"Stop right there, Missy." Cook halted Bea's slur. "That's enough. You may take your leave. You are no longer needed. I shall see that you are paid through Wednesday. My staff and I shall care for the children. The only thing you provided this week was an extra dirty plate to wash. Now get out."

Olive giggled.

"That laugh, Olive Westchester, just got you expelled from school." Bea seized the opportunity, as she donned her coat, to solve a problem and to speak the last word.

"You can't do that," Olive challenged with ice blue eyes.

"I just did. I'll send any personal items home with Samuel tomorrow." Bea spun on her heel and slammed the front door.

Stunned, Olive looked at Cook. "What did *I* do?"

Cook embraced Olive before answering. "You embarrassed her. She's saving face."

Olive slowly sat down, placing her head in her hands. Samuel rushed to her side. "Don't worry, Olive. Grandfather will make it okay."

Jake, Kendrick, and Cook stared at each other, knowing all too well that Bea Thompson and her entitled social class had allowed pride to punish good deeds.

With Sinclair warmed and back in his bed, Dr. Paulson joined the group in the foyer. "Why all the long faces?" Paulson looked from Olive to Samuel, to Cook and back. "Sinclair is fine, thanks to Olive's care and fast thinking."

"Well, tell that to Miss Thompson. She just kicked me out of school." Olive was visibly crying.

"Don't you worry, young Olive. You have four adults here to support you. We'll defend your story." Dr. Paulson lifted Olive's hand. "Allow me to clean your wounds. You saved that boy's life tonight. You're a star."

28

TRUTH OR CONSEQUENCES

*T*he train from New York arrived on Saturday. Olive and Samuel waited at the house for the family's return. Jake and Kendrick filled the expanse of the entrance hall with luggage. Tildy and Tommy were the first to arrive, followed by Clyde and Sally.

Lizzy jumped into Tommy's arms. "Daddy, Mommy! Yippie!" she shrieked with delight.

"Did you have a fun week?" Tommy asked his daughter as he threw her into the air.

"Daddy, we had ice cream every night. A different flavor. Thanks to Olive," Lizzy praised.

"That wretched girl." Tildy rubbed Lizzy's belly as she glared at Olive. "I hope you didn't get a tummy ache."

"Only once," admitted Lizzy. "It was worth it."

"I'll bring down the twins. Is Bea up with them?" Sally called out.

Olive supplied a monotone, "Bea's gone home."

"Odd, I thought she would wait to greet us." With the twins retrieved, Sally and Clyde hugged and kissed their children. Pushing Sinclair's unruly hair out of his face, she noticed a smudge. Upon closer inspection, the smear revealed a bruise on Sinclair's forehead. "Sweetie, what happened to your head?"

The child answered with one word. "Olive." Handing Sinclair to Clyde, Sally stormed over to Olive.

"What did you do to my son? Why, you little brat! Why is his head bruised?" Sally slapped Olive across the face. Shocked by the attack, Olive stood silent, unable to comprehend Sally's actions. Sally slapped her a second time. Roused to defend herself, Olive kicked Sally's shin.

"Why are you hitting me? I didn't do anything," asked a bewildered Olive. She studied the crazed Sally, unable to understand her friend's attack.

"You marked Sinclair's face. How could you be such a brute to your nephew? I always suspected you had a dark side, but I gave you the benefit of the doubt."

Notwithstanding the physical and mental attack, Olive lashed back at Sally. "Dark side? How dare you. Dark side...What about my own bruises?" Olive displayed her wrists and cheek. "I love those children. I should have been their godmother, not Bea. She doesn't care for them." Olive backed away, premeditating her next defensive move.

"Oh, now it comes out. You're jealous. And to think I considered asking you to be godmother for our new baby. What a mistake." Sally reached for another slap, round three. Olive caught her arm, twisting it at the elbow.

Sally cried out. "Stop! You're hurting me. See? I'm right. She is vicious."

"I'm only defending myself from your unprovoked assault, you two-faced witch. You pretended to be my friend. Was that just to be accepted into this family? Now that your children secure your place, I'm dumped? Sinclair almost died Thursday night because—"

"What do you mean, 'almost died?'" Sally grabbed Olive's shoulders and shook her violently. By now, the entire family, Cook, and Jake encircled them.

"Let go of me!" Olive pushed Sally. "It's not my doing; it's your sister's. Ask Cook, or Jake, or Dr. Paulson."

Henderson moved in to separate the women.

"Dr. Paulson? He required the doctor?" Sally shook with rage; her entire body flushed red.

"Stop this catfight immediately. All of you, into the parlor, to sort this out." Henderson tugged on Olive's sleeve. "You better be in the right, young lady."

Olive stopped, shook her arm free. "Why do you always think the worst of me? All of you do." She met each one's eyes individually. " You, Sally, jump to conclusions after a toddler says my name. I've never done a thing to any of you except be smarter and work harder." Henderson reached again for Olive. She tore free, ran up the steps. "I hate you all! You have no idea how much I despise you. The lot of you —rot in hell!"

Ginny tried to stop her.

"Let her go," Henderson growled, asking in a stern voice, "Jake, Cook, do the two of you know what happened the other evening to Sinclair?"

"Yes, sir." They spoke in unison. "Kendrick also," added Jake.

"I want every detail."

The family gathered in the parlor. Agitation prevailed, despite the crackle of a burning fire and sweet smell of cherry wood. Sally and Clyde sat, clinging to the squirming twins. Hands folded on her lap, Ginny chose to hide in the corner. Henderson and his employees occupied center stage.

Pointing to each individual, Henderson barked, "Out with it, each of you. Recant the events of the accident."

Kendrick, Jake, and Cook extolled Olive's quick thinking that saved the boy while accusing Bea of neglect. Sally's anxiety increased as she listened. Her entire body trembled with rage.

Henderson spoke first. "Perhaps we owe Olive an apology."

Jake risked insubordination. "No 'perhaps' about it. That girl is a hero. She's been mistreated here."

"I don't believe you." Sally shook as she defended her sister. "Bea is Penny's and Sinclair's godmother. She would not neglect the children."

"I'm sorry you feel that way, Mrs. Westchester; however, Miss Thompson served no purpose this week," Cook said, defending Olive. "My house staff tended to the children. Bea ate dinner, prepared her lessons, then retired. Olive and Samuel were more help than she. And it was Olive who checked the twins every night. Good thing too, otherwise that boy would be dead."

Sally grabbed Clyde's arm. "Clyde. I simply will not live in this house anymore. They wrongfully disparage my sister. I shall no longer suffer this family's snobbery."

"Sally, you're overcome with emotion. There is absolutely no reason for us to move." Clyde enfolded his wife. She pushed him away.

"My mind is set. We shall move into town." Sally lifted both toddlers, squeezing so firmly they squirmed and squealed.

"Mommy, not so tight," Penny protested. Sally freed the children.

"Clyde, you'll have to figure a way to make it work, this move. It's settled. Please arrange for our transfer before Christmas." Snatching the twins by the hands, she said, "This family has never accepted me!" She retreated to her room.

"Sally, don't be unreasonable," Clyde objected.

Henderson raised his hand. "Clyde, Ben, into my office."

∞∞∞∞

Henderson knocked on Olive's bedroom door. He listened. After a few minutes of silence, Olive answered.

"Who is it?" Her raspy voice lacked energy.

"Your father." Henderson shifted, unfamiliar with admitting wrong.

"I wish to be alone." Olive blew her nose then pulled her blankets over her head.

"We owe you an apology, Olive."

"It's too late for an apology." Olive rolled onto her side, facing the far side of the room.

Henderson rubbed his forehead. "You are an obstinate brat."

"That doesn't sound apologetic to me. Now leave."

Henderson laughed then knocked gently. "Olive, open the door."

"Bea Thompson kicked me out of school. Did they tell you that?"

Henderson sucked air through his teeth. "What? Why did she expel you?"

"I laughed."

"You laughed? Olive, open the door. I don't want to stand in the hallway."

"Too bad." She waited a moment then continued, forcing her point one last time. "*I* want to go to high school. But now I'm kicked out of elementary school, for one laugh. After I saved Bea's behind by rescuing Sinclair. Seems like we don't always get what we want around here. Now goodnight...I'm still mad at you. I despise Sally and Clyde, and I hate Levi."

"You are tenacious. We'll discuss this tomorrow. Goodnight, Olive. I'll speak to Sally and Clyde." Grinding his teeth, Henderson departed for his office.

Olive called after him, "Don't waste your breath. I'm going to despise them for the rest of my life."

29

KILL THE FATTED CALF?

*O*live stayed in bed later than usual. She arrived in the kitchen around eight, scrounging for food.

"Cook, sorry for the late arrival." She rummaged through a few bowls on the table. Finding only apples and dry biscuits, she asked, "Any chance of breakfast?"

"Would you care for bacon, eggs, and toast, Miss?" Not minding the interruption, Cook hoped to reward the girl's bravery.

"Would I? Sounds delicious." Instead of eating in the dining room, Olive sat down at the kitchen table while waiting on her breakfast.

The bell, originating in Henderson's office, rang for service. "Your father wants more coffee. Do you mind taking it to him?" Cook asked, deliberately orchestrating the meeting.

"I'd prefer not to, but for you, I shall make an exception. I'll be back in a minute to eat."

Olive lifted the tray, carefully balancing it as she walked to the other end of the house. She entered the office to find Henderson, Ben, and Clyde seated among a stack of papers and ledgers.

"Oh, Olive. Good, you're up. I need you to join this discussion," Henderson said, as Olive placed the tray on his desk.

"I have nothing to say to you. My breakfast is waiting. Excuse me." Olive turned to retrace her steps.

"Olive, as our farm accountant, I require your presence. Join us after you've eaten." Without looking up, Henderson ordered his employee daughter.

"Fine. I shall return," she complained as she stomped back to the kitchen.

∞∞∞∞

"One more piece of toast, please, and another egg," Olive asked Cook, trying to maneuver a delay of the inevitable.

"Miss Olive, I'll make you another egg if you are truly hungry. However, I have my doubts." Cook questioned the girl. "You'll not avoid this. My Pappy always said, 'chin up and get on with it.'"

"Fine." Olive expelled a long breath, poured a mug of tea, and trudged to the office.

Upon entering, she sat on the edge of the settee, away from Clyde. Trying to avoid eye contact, she glanced at the paperwork piled on the floor. Deeds, last will and testaments, contracts, and various other essential farm documents dotted the rug.

"Thank you for joining us, Olive. We need to discuss Clyde's request, and I want your input from a financial viewpoint." Olive grunted in response. Henderson continued, "Clyde has asked for his share of his inheritance."

At that statement, Olive met Clyde's blushing gaze with a smirk.

Ben protested, "Clyde, we've been over this before; Father wishes to keep the farm together as one unit."

Clyde shifted in his chair. "Well, without money, how am I to move?" He nervously intertwined his fingers.

"Ben, throw another log on the fire, please." Cracking his knuckles, Henderson continued reading a contract. "There is no need to move."

"*You're* not married to Sally." Clyde coughed, choking on his words. "She squanders our money."

Olive harrumphed, rolling her eyes. Walking over to the fireplace, Olive finished Ben's job by stoking the logs. The fire sprung to life, filling the room with warmth and casting a red glow on Olive.

"Olive, any notion on the subject?"

She thought for a few minutes, then asked, "What exactly do you want, Clyde?"

"The money sum equivalent to my inheritance." Clyde's eyes challenged Ben to object.

"So, you want Father to pay you for something that is his...not yours?" Olive waited for the question to land, then continued. "You do understand Clyde, that as the second-born, according to the will, you are entitled to nothing, same as Levi and Fred. The younger boys were sent out to make their own way in the world. I suppose you are welcome to do the same." Olive looked at Henderson. "Is Clyde free to leave and make his own way, Father?"

Henderson rolled in laughter. "Levi only pretends to be the attorney; I believe we have our own attorney, and a better one, right here. She is correct, Clyde; you only assume you are entitled because it is my longstanding wish for you to be an active participant in the management of this farm. You were never written into the will. The property is still mine, and I am free to change my intention whenever I choose to do so. I intend for Ben to inherit the entire parcel."

Looking at Olive, Clyde fumed. "He listens to your every word. You encourage him to exclude me."

Olive stood quietly by the fire. "Don't be absurd, Clyde. Father is his own man; he wards over all of us. I only state what is contained in the legal documents. You get nothing."

"Why, you devil she-witch! How dare you threaten me with disinheritance? You are pure evil."

"You blame me as if I'm Father. Grow some manly parts; call *him* a devil, you spineless coward." She waved the poker in Clyde's direction, who moved behind Ben.

Henderson continued laughing. "By God, you are the spunkiest of the Westchesters, Olive. It is a real pity you're a girl. If you were a man you'd accomplish greatness. But you shall make some lucky man a hell of a wife."

Olive stood, directly facing Henderson. "You slander my gender one more time, and I shall surgically convert every man in this house into a female. You praise my capability, yet you prohibit me from achieving my full potential due to my sex. I do not find this amusing, and I shall hold a grudge until my dying day."

She sat back down. Henderson quickly sobered.

"I prohibit your education because you, my dear, are rude, ill-mannered, quick tempered, and prone to outbursts. Yes, you are highly intelligent, but your education is lacking in etiquette, demeanor, and proprieties. This void shall not be filled by a high school curriculum, only by that of a finishing school. My decision has little to do with your gender—purely your personality."

Olive bit her upper lip, her dark eyes slits of fire, unaccustomed to chastisement. She took several deep breaths before continuing. "Back to the problem at hand. The farm cannot afford a large cash payout. It also cannot withstand being carved into smaller pieces, not without reneging on our government contracts. The only answer I see is for Clyde to build himself a house someplace on the property while he continues to work the farm."

Henderson looked at Olive, then to Clyde. With a scowl across his face, he asked, "Do you have money enough to erect a structure, Clyde?"

"No."

"What the hell do you do with all the money I pay you?" Henderson grimaced.

"I have...ah, expenses. Sally..."

"Spineless simpleton." Olive leaned toward Clyde, who darted farther behind Ben.

"That's enough out of you, Olive." Shaking his head in disgust, Henderson added, "What did I just say about your outbursts?"

Henderson turned to address Clyde. "You live in my house free of charge. You use my vehicles, fuel, stables, and supplies, yet you foolishly squander your salary. Sir, you are out of luck, and are free to leave with nothing. Should you choose to stay, you may eat from my table and sleep in my house and work on my farm." Motioning to Ben, Henderson said, "Refile this paperwork, please. Olive, I'll see you in your room after supper."

30

THE PRODIGAL DAUGHTER

*S*unday dinner arrived more quickly than usual, due to tension and the drama of the morning. The family gathered in the dining room for their first family meal since their return from New York. Conversation lulled—no one was in the mood for congeniality.

"I think it's time Samuel joins us for dinner." Wanting a friendly companion, Olive broke her long silence. "Sammy's eleven. I joined this table shy of ten."

"Ginny, your sister presents a valid argument. Samuel is no longer a child. It's high time he is educated on being a Westchester and farm administrator." Henderson chewed his cake as he commented.

"Yes, it is time for Samuel to cross over into adolescence, but Father, what future does Samuel have on this farm?" Ginny, hunting for reassurances, asked Henderson.

"I guarantee he will always have a paying position," he said, as he took another bite.

"In what capacity? As a farmhand? Perhaps a foreman?" Shaking her head, Ginny caught her breath then added. "Never as an heir. He's too far down the line to inherit. And I forbid him to attend a military school like Levi and Fred, although Levi is doing well for himself. Have you read the papers lately? Europe is—"

"The unrest in Europe won't impact us," declared Henderson.

Ginny hesitated then added. "I've been thinking...*wanting* to do this for some time. Samuel and I are moving out."

Cake splattered across the table onto Henderson's neighbors. "You're what? And just where are you going?"

"I spoke with Aunt Clare at Levi's wedding. I'm moving to Philadelphia to live with her. Her son moved to Los Angeles. She is aging, needs someone to help her. I volunteered. Samuel shall have the opportunity to attend college on the east coast when the time comes."

"When do you intend to leave? What about your promise to me, as acting hostess?"

"I hope to move next week. I'd like Samuel to be settled in school before the holidays."

"Just when did you think you'd mention this to me? I don't like surprises. Did you plan to slip out in the middle of the night without a goodbye? Christ's sake, woman. Take some time to think this through."

"I have, Father. I've wanted to escape for several years. I need to make a fresh start for myself." Ginny dropped her head.

"'Escape.' You make this sound like a prison. You desire a fresh start at thirty?" Henderson ranted.

"Yes, Father. At thirty. I do not want to be alone my entire life. I want Samuel to have a happy family life."

"What do you call *this*? *This*, Missy, is a family." Henderson motioned to everyone seated around the table. "Are you saying we are not happy?" The blood rushed up through his neck.

"Are we happy? Who here is truly satisfied with life on Westchester Farm?" Ginny scanned her siblings, hoping for support. The group collectively held its breath.

"I've heard enough. *Be gone.* With that attitude, you are no longer welcome in my home. I pray Clare understands what she signed up for. She'll be paying for that college education you mentioned."

Henderson slammed his fist on the table in front of Ginny, then exited the room.

Olive sat dumbfounded, staring at her sister. Samuel, gone? What kind of nasty tricks were the gods playing on her?

In desperation, she exclaimed, "Samuel can't go, Ginny."

"Why not? Of course, he can."

"I won't allow it."

Ginny chortled. "You have no more power over me than Father."

Something inside Olive snapped.

"You are foolish, Big Sister," she said. "Father is all-powerful. Over you, over me, over all of us." Olive glanced at Clyde and Sally. "Do you honestly think you can escape? No one can. You'll come crawling back." With a long sigh, Olive added, "Levi is the only one to dodge Westchester chains. As much as I hate him, bravo, Levi." She clapped her hands together in slow applause.

Olive stood. Walking to Sally, she stood behind her chair. "Did Clyde tell you about the move?" Olive leaned in, singing directly into Sally's ear.

"No. What about our move? Is everything settled already?" Sally smiled in anticipation.

"You bet it is." With a sinister timbre, she added, "You aren't moving. You spend your money foolishly and you are forced to stay here." Her lips formed a menacing grin.

"Clyde, what is Olive talking about?" Sally pulled on Clyde's arm.

Shaking her loose, Clyde left the room without a word.

"Clyde, Clyde!" Sally began crying. "Don't you dare leave, Clyde! Tell me what's happening!"

"Shut up." Olive pulled Sally's head backward by her hair. Discharging a guttural growl, Olive loomed over Sally. "You deceitful traitor. Grow up. Deal with the fact that your husband is a weakling. You'll be living here until your dying day. Look on the bright side; you may become our household hostess, unless Bessie wants it. Do you, Bessie?" Olive released Sally's head; it went flying forward.

A stunned Bessie shook her head back and forth. "I didn't think so." Olive sneered. "Easier to hide in your little cottage, away from the main house crazies."

Ginny flinched as Olive walked to her side of the table.

"Don't think you'll be getting a monthly stipend, Ginny. I shall ensure you don't. *That*, my sister, is the price you'll pay for taking Samuel away from me. Although—ha! I must thank you, Ginny. I have escaped a Henderson encounter because of you. He'll not want to speak to me this evening. Oh, Sally, don't worry. When Ginny leaves, I'll arrange for you and Clyde to occupy the entire left wing. That's as close as you'll ever get to owning a house. I'll take your room in the right wing."

As she sauntered up the front staircase, the remaining diners heard a sort of cackling coming from the hallway.

KETUBAH

*T*he week flew past quickly as Ginny and Samuel prepared for their journey across Pennsylvania. Olive remained angry at Ginny for taking away Samuel.

Olive called from her bedroom, across the second-floor hallway, "Samuel, I received a surprise letter from Fred. I only wrote to him last week. I didn't expect a reply so quickly. Would you like to hear it?"

"Sure. I hate packing. I'll gladly take a break." Samuel slid beside Olive on the bed. "I don't know why, but Mother's heart is set on moving. I think she is lonely."

Olive harrumphed. "Aren't *we* all alone, too? So, she selfishly takes you away, makes *you* the lonely one to satisfy *her* needs. Typical Westchester behavior."

"Olive, why are you so angry?" The boy looked at Olive with sincere concern.

Olive peered into Samuel's eyes and pondered. Placing her arm around his waist, she said, "I'm going to miss you, Sammy."

Picking up the letter, she began reading.

Dear Olive,

   I hope this letter finds you well. I'm sorry to hear about school.

185

Adult egos are an overly sensitive subject. I have learned this the hard way. I missed seeing you at the wedding. I hope you understand that I fought with Levi over your ostracization. He was in the wrong, and I let him know so.

It was a strange—well—different ceremony from a Presbyterian wedding. The evening before the wedding, they celebrate a Ketubah, an actual marriage contract. Entirely fitting for an attorney. The bride, groom, and their parents must sign before the couple is permitted to be wed. Sylvia is bright and beautiful, just like you. I predict you'll be best friends—that is, if Levi ever allows the two of you to meet.

Olive, Levi's changed. He's overcome with pride and ambition. He forgets his humble beginnings.

Olive stopped reading. Shaking her head, she commented, "Humble beginnings? A Westchester? Fred is delusional. There is nothing humble about being born a Westchester. We are the elite of Campbellsville."

She continued reading.

It's a big world out here, Olive. We grew up thinking that we are elite, but we're not. We are merely average American farmers. Levi has lost sight of this. I fear his ambitions will someday be his demise.

Enough of my philosophy. Graduation approaches quickly. I sincerely hope you'll consider making the journey to West Point. I want you by my side when I am presented with my commission. Please think about attending. Most likely, I shall be sent off directly to my first assignment.

Be well and do take care of yourself. I'm happy to hear that Father finally compensates you appropriately for your office work. Keep up your studies. Perhaps I shall help you find a way to continue your education.

In anticipation of your next communique, your devoted, loving brother,
Fred

Olive folded the letter, placing it back into its envelope. Walking to her dresser, she slipped it under a ribbon which tied a stack of notes together.

"Are those all from Fred?" Samuel surveyed the inch-thick stack.

"Yes, and you better write to me and start your own stack. Understood?" Smiling at Samuel, she softened her tone. "I really shall miss you. Let's have the same arrangement I have with Fred, and write each other every other week. Pinky swear?" Olive extended her little finger and looped it around Samuel's.

"Pinky swear." He kissed Olive's cheek, then left the room to continue packing as tears streamed down his face.

∞∞∞

Tildy, Tommy, and Lizzy joined the entire Westchester family for dinner the evening before Ginny's departure. Apart from the twins, everybody crowded around the dining room table. Cook prepared the equivalent of a holiday feast.

Samuel and Olive enjoyed a private conversation while the family talked about Ginny's adventure.

"Samuel shall attend a private school called Friend's Select," Ginny answered Tildy's question. "We're so fortunate for the opportunity. Aunt Clare has a large Victorian with staff in the exclusive Rittenhouse area. She needs a companion, of sorts, to run her household—which will be my job."

"Friend's Select. Sounds like a Quaker school?" Laying down his knife, Henderson paused cutting his meat.

"Yes, but they provide a respectable education." Ginny's voice cracked. She pulled Samuel's chair closer to her.

"We're Presbyterian, not Quaker." The matter-of-fact comment indicated the end of the discussion. Henderson resumed attacking his pork chop.

Olive snorted. "Presbyterian? Father, you're nothing. All you do is tithe to keep in good civic standing."

"Watch your tongue, young lady." His mood declined rapidly with the continuation of the conversation.

Olive laughed.

"You never learn, do you, Olive?" Henderson sneered at his youngest child. "Your inappropriate laughter often creates trouble for you, yet you dare risk more?" Turning back to Ginny, he added, "Will Samuel be expected to attend Quaker services?"

"I believe so. They are gentle people." Ginny averted her eyes. "Aunt Clare is a Quaker."

"I don't care if Benjamin Franklin and William Penn themselves are part of the congregation. My grandson shall be raised Presbyterian. Both mine and Polly's families were always Presbyterian, and we shall continue the tradition. I should have never allowed Levi to stray from the flock. It ends with him. Do you understand? All of you, do you hear what I'm saying?"

"Well, I had a choice of this fine Quaker school or a public school, possibly filled with riff-raff."

"Ginny, get your story straight," Olive challenged. "Think about it logically. You just bragged that Aunt Clare lives in an exclusive part of the city. There's little chance for low-class riff-raff in an elite public school."

"You don't know that for sure." Less confident of herself, Ginny aimlessly pushed her food around on her plate.

Tildy seized the opportunity to stir the pot. "I see nothing has changed here. Olive's tongue is still as sharp as a knife."

"Oh, Sister dear, it's sharper. Want to know why?" Olive, blue eyes turned to ice as she thrust her face at Tildy. "I no longer care what any of you think of me. It used to bother me; I tried so hard to make this family care for me. I tried to be..." Something caught her attention. Olive gazed at Polly's portrait, leaving her sentence unfinished. Her mother returned the stare, noting all the changes to her darling baby that had been made over the last ten years.

Silence followed as the diners watched Olive walk to Polly's portrait. Olive traced the outline of her mother's face with her index finger as a calmness flowed over her body.

Turning to the table, Olive declared, "I am retiring for the night. Samuel, please stop in before you sleep. I wish to say goodbye. Ginny, I'll bid you safe travels. You are a disappointment to me." ·

Shocked, the family buzzed criticism of the thirteen-year-old. "How dare she be so rude? She's a brat. That tongue shall be her downfall. Bitter child."

Only Henderson sat quietly, engrossed in thoughts of Polly, and how his youngest daughter emulated her.

∞∞∞∞

The knock on the door found Olive dressed for bed, reading a book with her mother's pearls around her neck. "Come in, Sammy."

Samuel entered shyly.

"Why the hesitation?" Olive patted the quilt inviting him to climb up onto the bed. "Shall I read to you this evening, one last time?"

Tears poured from Samuel's eyes. "I don't want this to be the last time, Olive. I'm afraid to leave." Samuel hugged his aunt, his friend. "Philadelphia is a big city. I like living on the farm."

"I know Sammy. I'm saddened by your leaving. But your mother is set on this move." Olive jumped out of bed. Walking to her dresser, she retrieved a bulky package wrapped in brown paper. "Here, Sammy, this is for you."

"But I don't have anything for you, Olive." Samuel buried his face in his hands.

"Come on, open it." Olive coaxed. Samuel carefully removed the paper to reveal three books: *The Adventures of Sherlock Holmes*, *The Memoirs of Sherlock Holmes*, and *The Return of Sherlock Holmes*.

"Oh, Olive! I can't accept these. They are some of your favorite books, your prized possessions." Samuel gently fingered the front of each book.

"They are, but I want you to have them, to remember me by. Remember the times we spent reading them together." Olive handed Samuel a linen bookmark. "I embroidered this for you. Never stop learning, Sammy. Never." She embraced the boy. "Now leave. I shall not go to the station tomorrow morning. Write to me, my friend." She kissed his cheek, then closed the door behind him.

That night, Olive slept fitfully, clutching the bag containing her mother's precious pearls. The next morning the commotion of Ginny and Samuel's departure awakened her; however, she kept her word. Olive did not see them off. Instead, she remained in her bedroom for the rest of the day.

RING, RING

*N*ovember and the first weeks of December dragged by without school to occupy her time. Henderson now refused to offer his influence to have her reinstated. Olive spent hours rearranging the second-floor rooms, relinquishing the left wing to Sally and Clyde. Sally accepted the suite of rooms as her new home. She and Clyde claimed the large nursery for their room, while the twins moved into Ginny and Tildy's old space. Sally redecorated Samuel's room to be the new nursery in plenty of time before her February due date.

Deciding she no longer wished to share space in her father's office, Olive converted a bedroom at the top of the front staircase, part of the original house, into her private library office. Choosing the largest of the two rooms, she stripped the wallpaper, painted it pale blue, then rummaged the barn and attic for a desk, bookcase, desk chair, and lounge chair. Since the room was not yet wired for electricity, she confiscated several oil lamps and a gas chandelier. By placing the desk in front of a large window overlooking the rear yard, she was provided ample daylight and beautifully spun evening shadows on the navy wool rug. Once Jake cleaned the fireplace and flue, Olive was open for business.

Henderson knocked on Olive's office door late in the afternoon. A fire crackled, throwing heat and shadows. Surveying Olive's new space, he commented, "The room is cozy. Tell me, Olive, is there a justifiable reason why you wish to leave my office?"

"You just answered your own question. It is *your* office, not our office. I want my own space." Keeping her back to her father, Olive gazed out the window.

"What if I have a question, or need you to explain something?" Henderson paced the hallway.

"You walk, or call up the steps. My door is usually open."

"Olive, my office is in the far corner of the left wing. I shall not inconvenience myself every time I wish to ask you a question. This is unacceptable." Henderson's voice deepened into a growl. He stopped pacing and stood in the center of the doorway, glaring at Olive.

"Then I suggest you improvise. Install a speaking tube between the two rooms. Better yet, purchase two telephones. It won't kill you to modernize." She continued writing without looking up.

"May I enter?" Henderson asked. Olive motioned him in. He sat on the lounge chair. "I'm thinking it's time for you to begin finishing school."

Olive sucked air through her front teeth, then turned to face Henderson. "What shall I learn in finishing school that I don't already know?"

"They'll teach you the finer things in life. Grace, patience, humility. Improving your stitching, music, piano, how to run a household with staff..."

Olive cut him short. "My stitches are finer than Tildy's, I play better than Bessie, and as for running a household, how dare you even *suggest* that skill can be improved upon by a silly girls' school? If I am to succeed alone as a woman, humility and patience shall not provide success. You know which school I wish to attend. It's Campbellsville High School, or NO school." Olive searched her father's face for a softening on his position. There was none. Expelling a long sigh, she continued, "I see. If you'll excuse me, Father, I have some work to complete while I still have light."

"You could stand to learn some manners, you are stubborn, obstinate..." Henderson mumbled on his return to his office. As he entered, he rang the bell for Jake.

Jake knocked, then waited for an invitation to approach. "Yes, Mr. W., may I do something for you?"

"Jake, call the workmen to have the rest of the second floor wired for electricity. Complete Olive's office first. And I want two telephones installed—one in my office, the other in Olive's office. I'm not walking up the stairs every time I need to communicate with *her*."

"Do we need Miss Olive's approval for the additional outlay of capital?"

Henderson sneered. "Is this not my farm? Do as I ask; Olive shall benefit. I'll request a line item be included in next year's budget for powering the barns. For now, we finish the house. You may leave."

"Yes, sir."

∞∞∞∞

Holiday preparation paled in comparison to previous years. Sally and Clyde exerted a token effort to delight the twins. Henderson and Ben scouted and marked the tree to be cut and placed in the parlor. Olive grumbled, "Bah humbug," contributing minimally. She spent hours in her new office, either working for her father or studying the dictionary. A meager supply of reading material was dependent on Benny's willingness to cart books back and forth from the high school library.

Sally reluctantly called up the stairs to Olive's open office door. "Olive, will you help me hang the inside garland?"

"No, and you should not be climbing ladders. Get a farmhand to drape them." Olive turned back to her writing. "Now, I have work to do, if you don't mind."

"I don't have the authority to order the workmen," Sally whined.

"Nonsense. I just gave it to you. Now leave me alone; get the men to do the heavy lifting." Olive condensed a stack of papers, placing them on the corner of her desk.

"Olive, will you make the request?" bellyached Sally. "I'm not permitted."

"For goodness' sake. You're pitiful. You sound like a bleating goat." Olive rang the bell for Jake, who appeared within several minutes.

"Miss Olive, how may I help?"

"Please have several of the men assist Sally in hanging the household greeneries. For some reason, the twit fears asking herself."

Jake smiled before answering. "That's because Mr. W. instructed the men to answer to only Ben Sr., Kendrick, himself, and you. Mrs. Sally, Mrs. Bessie, and Ben Jr. may not order the staff."

Jake's reply piqued Olive's interest. "Curious. When and why?"

"Last week. It seems Mrs. Sally overstepped her bounds by asking a worker to babysit the twins on the maids' day off."

Olive burst into laughter. "The lazy sloth. No workman shall assist her listless mothering attempts; however, she is pregnant, so climbing is unwise. See to it that the Christmas decorations are placed according to her instruction. Thanks, Jake."

Tildy, Tommy, and Lizzy joined the Westchester brood for holiday dinner. The room whirred with sound while Tildy and Sally clucked about their impending births. The absence of Ginny, Samuel, Levi, and Fred seemed apparent to only Henderson and Olive.

The conclusion of dessert signaled relocation to the parlor, gift exchange at hand. Sally collected the sleepy twins, who immediately revived with the noise and the lights. Henderson encouraged Olive to play carols during the delivery of presents. Eggnog consumption was in direct correlation to the conversation's decibel level, drowning the piano melodies.

"Sinclair, Penny, look here. Santa left you a present." Clyde failed to distract his children, who were shaking a cocoa tin full of shiny pebbles. Clyde grumbled to Ben, "Why spend hard-earned money when a piece of rock entertains?"

"Clyde, they are children; you were the same," Henderson said. "If I recall correctly, each and every one of you, except for Olive, preferred rock-filled tins over their gifts from Santa."

Tildy scoffed. "Figures. What did the special, *Miss Better Than Thou* choose?"

"She was happy with picture books." Amused by Tildy's annoyance, Henderson handed Olive a wrapped gift. "Olive, from me. You are always the easiest of my dog pack to buy for."

Olive placed the cumbersome box on the piano bench next to her. Pulling off the paper, she discovered a box imprinted with a large, black, bell-shaped logo.

"What is this?" Carefully lifting the lid, she found a crank model telephone. "My goodness, you listened. You bought a telephone."

"I purchased two telephones—one for my office, and one for yours. They shall be connected after the holiday." Voices ceased speaking as awareness of the device spread around the room. "I did it for selfish reasons, Olive. I'm too old to be chasing down the hall every time I wish to speak to my accountant. It would be unnecessary, if only you'd stay in my office—but so be it."

"Thank you, Father. I do appreciate this gift." She felt the weight of the mouthpiece. "And, please. Let's have a truce. We've discussed the reasons for my move." Her tongue was tempered by the celebration of the Lord's birth.

"You'll be the first farm in Campbellsville to own a phone. What a status symbol," Tildy said, then whispered to Tommy, "Should we have one installed, also? Dr. Paulson's office has one, and with the baby coming...?"

"I'll look over our financials to see if we can afford one." Tommy rolled his eyes at his pretentious wife. "Are you sure you don't want a phone simply for prestige?"

Tildy scoffed. "I'm pregnant, Tommy!"

Unimpressed with Tildy's pride, Henderson returned his attention to Olive. "Agreed, Olive. We shall call a truce today. Suspend the playing; there are other gifts for you under the tree."

Wool stockings from the Jamisons, a cotton blouse from Ben and Bessie, a silk under slip from Clyde and Sally, Dutch chocolates sent by Ginny, pink angora gloves from Levi and Sylvia, and a Waterman fountain pen from Fred filled Olive's pile.

Scrutinizing her stash, Olive declared, "For being such despicable people, these are wonderful gifts. I appreciate and thank each of you for your generosity."

"The Queen expresses appreciation. It's a Christmas miracle," mocked Tildy.

Henderson flashed Tildy a warning. "Olive, this package was delivered yesterday. It's addressed to you by a hand of which I am unfamiliar." Henderson reached under the tree for her last gift. "Do you know who sent this?"

The handwriting was, somehow, familiar; however, Olive did not immediately recognize it. She removed the newspaper wrapping to reveal a rabbit's foot suspended on a copper chain. An enclosed note read, *May your days be filled with the best of luck. With admiration, Tobias Bailey.*

"Who is Tobias Bailey?" asked Sally, Tildy, and Bessie in unison.

"Not that old man you were dancing with at the Harvest Dance. Tell me it's not." Henderson grabbed the note from Olive's hand.

"Father, I fear it is one and the same, though I did not encourage this attraction. I have neither seen nor spoken to him since October." Shocked and flattered, Olive inspected the fur. "It looks to be homemade, don't you think?" She handed the charm to her father. She understood a factory laborer's inability to purchase a fancy gift and appreciated the effort to create something homemade.

"I believe so. Not my approach to impressing a girl...not that you have my permission to be courted by Bailey. Although it does raise an interesting topic. If you choose not to attend a finishing school, perhaps we should start looking for a suitable husband within the next year or two."

Olive tucked the rabbit's foot into her skirt pocket. "Stop, Father. I shall not agree to a marriage. I'd rather remain single and simply work as Westchester Farm's accountant."

"I'll suspend this discussion for a future date," Henderson acquiesced. "More eggnog, anyone?"

Dazed by the gift and attention from an older man, Olive, entrenched in thought, sipped a glass of spiked eggnog as Henderson dispersed his favorite, the Christmas stockings. Jovially, Henderson threw a handful of Hershey kisses into the air, laughing as the twins and Lizzy scampered to gather them.

"Merry Christmas to my family," Henderson shouted.

"Merry Christmas, Father," echoed the group.

"I welcome the addition of two new children next year. Too many have abandoned our home for a different life," he whispered to himself.

33

PINK OR BLUE?

FEBRUARY, 1915

"*O*live!" The voice originating in the left-wing called out to her sister-in-law. "Please call Dr. Paulson to send the midwife and let Clyde know my time has come—oh!" Sally yelled as her contraction intensified.

"Here we go again." Olive, irritated by the interruption, cranked the phone to ring in the barn. Henderson appreciated the ease in communication provided by the new technology; therefore, a phone was installed in the main barn and kitchen.

"Kendrick?" Olive heard the whinny of horses and a few grunting pigs in the background.

"Yes, Miss Olive?"

"Gather Father and Clyde. Sally's baby is coming." Clicking off, Olive connected to the Campbellsville switchboard for redirection to the doctor. Minutes after the second call, her office phone rang.

"Olive, it's Lizzy; Mommy said her baby is coming. A puddle of water just ran down her leg, but she says she didn't pee. She said to call you. What do I do?"

Olive sat silent. *How am I supposed to know about organizing a double birth? I'm only thirteen!*

"Lizzy, run out and find your father," Olive said, finally. "Tell him to call me immediately."

Olive rang for Jake. "Jake, take the truck over to Jamisons, fetch Tildy, and bring her here." Next, the kitchen. "Cook, boil water, I think...? We have two babies coming again today."

As soon as she hung up, Olive's phone rang again. It was Tommy. "Tildy is on her way over with Jake," Olive said. "Both she and Sally are in labor. Dr. Paulson is already on his way. Grab Lizzy and come over."

Olive waited with Sally until Dr. Paulson arrived, followed by Jake and Tildy minutes later, with Tommy and Lizzy close behind.

"Doctor, Sally is upstairs; contractions are ten minutes apart. Tommy, take Tildy up to Mother's room, since it's already made up."

"Not on your life!" Tildy wailed her objection in between contractions. "She died there, giving birth. I'll not enter that room pregnant."

"For goodness' sake, Tildy. Stop the drama."

Tildy grabbed each side of the door frame as Tommy tried to usher her across the threshold. "I'm not going in there!"

"Alright! Don't you dare drop that baby in the hallway. Let me make up the guest room." Olive ran to the linen closet to quickly dress the bed. Tildy changed clothes and climbed onto the mattress as Dr. Paulson finished Sally's exam.

Entering the second patient's room, he asked, "So, Tildy, is this a conspiracy with your sister-in-law?" A contraction squelched Tildy's reply. "The midwife is on her way. We're going to have an interesting day."

Henderson, Clyde, Ben, Bessie, Tommy, Nellie, and Olive shifted into high gear. Bessie and Nellie assumed responsibility for childcare, sweeping Lizzy, Penny, and Sinclair away to the cabin for an afternoon of play. Henderson and Ben managed to remain working in the barn until dinnertime. Tommy and Clyde crushed a path in the carpeting by pacing between the parlor and office, while Olive, the midwife, and the doctor trampled grooves in the upstairs hallway as they checked on the soon-to-be mothers.

"Olive, please bring me a piece of ice."

"Olive, wipe my brow."

"Olive, rub my feet."

Back and forth ran Olive to satisfy their requests. Finally, after about three hours of crazed demands, Olive ceased to comply.

"Clyde, Tommy, get up here and tend to your women. I'm exhausted, and I'm not their slave." The men heeded Olive's call.

"Men should not be present at a birth." Dr. Paulson chastised Olive and the future fathers. "You two must leave now."

"Why can't they be present? You're a man, and you're here. Tommy and Clyde planted the seed; they should help with the harvest," Olive defended. "Besides, I'm done. Doctor, I have ten dollars saying neither one of these two prima donnas will even thank me for helping today." Olive slapped a ten-dollar note on the hallway table, removed her apron, walked into her office, and closed the door.

Dinner hour arrived without any babies. The family gathered for a light buffet supper of grilled ham sandwiches, hot potato salad, pickled beets, and mulled apple cider. As food piled onto plates, two screams filtered down from above. Tommy and Clyde dropped their dinner. Running side by side, striding two steps at a time, they mounted the stairs. At the landing, Clyde turned to the left as Tommy turned to the right.

"Won't be long now," called the doctor from Sally's room.

"Same here," replied the midwife attending Tildy.

Olive slid out of her office, undetected in the confusion. She scurried down the back staircase and slipped into the dining room to fill a plate. Retracing her steps, she retreated to her office to quietly enjoy her food. Her solitude, however, was short-lived, as a crying baby soon announced its arrival to the world.

Paulson yelled out, "Olive, I need a hand in here, please."

Rushing down the hall to the left, Olive witnessed Dr. Paulson cutting the umbilical cord of Sally's new Westchester girl. Olive swaddled the infant then handed her to Sally and Clyde. Within minutes, another baby's cry echoed from the right-wing of the house. Paulson and Olive rushed in as the midwife finished wrapping baby boy Jamison.

Turning to Olive, Dr. Paulson said, "It seems you are once again the hero of the day. I don't know how we would have handled this without them being in the same house. You have a good brain, young—"

"Don't remind me of what I'm being denied." Olive turned her back to Henderson as he entered the room to meet his grandson. Clomping into her office, she slammed the door.

34

THE GILDED LIFE

SPRING, 1915

*T*he Christenings of Blossom Westchester and Lucas Lyle Jamison, planting, and the thought of spring hastened winter's conclusion. Temperamental March conceded as spring peeked through the thawed earth. Mothers and babies thrived. Olive, a little richer, won her ten-dollar bet with Dr. Paulson, who graciously paid.

Olive's thoughts turned to Fred, his impending graduation, and her trip to New York.

"Father," she asked during dinner in late April. "How long is the train ride to West Point?"

"Why do you ask?" Henderson glanced up from his food.

"I'm attending Fred's graduation. Are you not going?"

"It never crossed my mind." Henderson scratched his forehead, then returned to eating.

Suspect of her father, Olive rested her chin in her hand. "Why not? You went for Levi."

"With everything happening here, I guess I simply forgot." Henderson brushed it off as inconsequential; one West Point graduation sufficient to satisfy his sense of fatherly responsibility.

"Well, I'm going, and if I must travel alone, I shall." Olive pronounced her intent. "Fred specifically invited me."

"Don't be ridiculous. A young woman may not travel that distance without a chaperone."

"Well, then you better come up with one, and soon, because I'll not miss Fred's commission. He trusts I'll be there and be there, I shall be." Olive pronounced her verdict with a decisive nod.

Ben spoke up. "Father, I'd like to take Benny. Olive may travel with us, if she wishes."

Surprised at her oldest brother's offer, Olive agreed to their safeguard.

∞∞∞∞

"I'm so excited. I've never been out of Pennsylvania—or even Campbellsville, for that matter." Olive and Benny, perched on a bench seat, swayed with the train. Ben Sr. sat in first class on a padded chair.

"Me too," said Benny, leg jiggling up and down continuously, keeping perfect rhythm with the click-clack of the rails.

"But Benny, you're sixteen. You have not traveled out of Campbellsville?" Olive's excitement betrayed her tender age.

"Where am I to go? I only make supply runs from the farm to town and back. I'm only three years older than you, Olive."

"Odd, isn't it? You're my nephew, yet you're older. Seems strange for Father to have a grandson older than his daughter."

"That's how it works in large families." Changing the subject, Ben asked, "What do you suppose the Hudson river looks like?"

"Fred described it as looking very much like our little river valley, except some hillsides are higher and steeper. It's all part of the same mountain range." Olive's answer was a simple matter of fact.

"It is?" Benny looked bewildered. "How do you know that?"

"Benny, you're in high school. Don't you pay attention in geography class?"

"Not really. I daydream about girls." Benny giggled.

Olive blushed. "Where do you go to meet girls?"

Benny smiled, "My daily after-school run to the drugstore. The town girls conveniently find excuses to be there every afternoon. I have my eye on several. Father was married at age eighteen; it's nearly time for me to select a wife."

"Goodness. I hope Father forgets about marrying me off. I don't want anything to do with boys, husbands, or babies. It doesn't seem like a happy or practical arrangement to me."

"I thought Tabs Bailey was your beau. Although he is rather old for you."

"I am not courting Tabs," she said, grunting. "I spoke with him once and danced with him twice, maybe thrice. That does not make him my suitor." Olive crossed her arms in front of her body, turned, and watched the green fields and forests pass.

"Fine. Don't talk to me. Grandfather is correct; you are obstinate." Benny twiddled his thumbs for lack of anything better to occupy his time.

"Am I? I'm shocked you understand the meaning of the word 'obstinate,' being so smitten by the gentler sex you're unable to concentrate on your studies," Olive spit back at Ben.

"Why are you angry?"

"Don't you listen to our dinner conversations? Goodness, Benny, all I ever ask of Father is that he allow me to go to high school and then on to college. And all Father wants to do is send me to a finishing school, to teach me useless wifely skills—marry me off to a *proper* husband. I don't want a husband." She sputtered her reply. "Shut up and allow me to enjoy the view."

After about an hour, Olive removed a book from her valise.

"Did you bring a second book that I may borrow?" Benny, tired of doing nothing, broke the silence.

With a huff and puff, Olive handed Benny a book. "Don't ruin it."

∞∞∞∞

The trio of Westchesters disembarked, entering the new Grand Central Station for an overnight in New York City. Olive's neck bent backward at a sixty-degree angle as she examined vast marble pillars, arched ceilings, and carved moldings of oak leaves and acorns, symbols of the Vanderbilts.

"I can't believe this is a train station. These marble floors should be in a palace." She gazed at the gold-framed blackboards announcing the arrival and departure of the day's traffic.

"Look at that four-sided clock," exclaimed Benny, whose gawking equaled Olive's.

"I hear they have a hospital room in the building," added Ben. "Nothing like Campbellsville, is it?"

"Seeing this makes the trip doubly special." Overcome with wonder, Olive's head swiveled left then right, excitedly taking in fantastic sights and sounds. Red capped porters carted their luggage as the family marveled at the station.

"Wait until you see the actual city. Father and I have a special treat for you. We are staying at the Plaza, right on the edge of Central Park, the same place we stayed for Levi's wedding."

"Isn't it expensive?" asked Olive.

"Yes, it is, Olive; however, Henderson—well, Father—and I consider this trip to be a graduation gift of sorts. Ben is graduating from high school and you from primary school, since you refuse finishing school. Both of you work extremely hard for Westchester Farms and deserve a reward." Ben seemed to be gratified by their youthful wonder. "Neither of you experienced this during Levi's wedding. It's a once-in-a-lifetime treat, for the likes of us."

Ben flagged down a cab. "Normally, we'd take a trolley. Today, we go first class."

Olive and Benny continued gaping in awe, mouths open. Despite coughing from motor vehicle exhaust, they stuck their heads out of the cab windows to view the continuous expanse of tall buildings. Nothing prepared them for scenes like the triangular-shaped Flatiron building, the Metropolitan Life building, or the world's tallest, the Woolworth building.

"Boy, you need to be in shape to climb all those stairs," Olive stated naïvely.

"They use elevators. *Now* who is the dummy?" accused Benny.

"Ben, may we ride on one, an elevator, while we're here? Please?" Olive, eyes wide with delight, pleaded with her brother.

"Our hotel has one, Olive. We shall take a ride to our room." Benny and Olive grinned at each other with excitement.

"This is quite different than what I expected. Are other big cities like New York? Look at all the automobiles and people; it's so...crowded."

Ben smiled, "Most big cities are crowded. New York City is second in the world, only to London."

The cab pulled up to a sparkling white building on the corner of the park: The Plaza. Benny and Olive gasped again.

"How many floors are in this hotel?" asked a stunned Olive. "And is that Central Park?" she pointed across Fifth Avenue.

Red-carpeted steps between marble columns, gold gilded doors, and an oval stained glass insert portraying a back-to-back double "P" created sensory overload for Olive. The doorman opened the taxi door. Ben paid the cabby as Olive and Benny reached for their luggage.

"Allow me, Miss," said a porter as he motioned for a luggage cart. Olive, rumpled from the long train ride, smoothed her skirt and hair.

"I feel like a princess walking into a castle," Olive whispered to Benny as she clutched onto his arm. The youngsters followed Ben and the bellhop into the lobby area. Olive inhaled in surprise as she touched a cold marble column while studying the stained-glass ceiling. The aroma of cleaning polish lingered.

"Is every place in New York a palace? I brought my best clothes, some new clothes, and still I have nothing to wear worthy of this hotel." She shook her head in amazement. "We have two maids and a cook, and our home still collects dust. This place is spotless."

"I have an idea," Ben said as he walked to the front desk. "Why don't we all go shopping this afternoon, and buy ourselves some new duds? It won't hurt to spruce us up a bit. We have dinner reservations in the Terrace Room tonight. I'll verify the dress code, just in case."

Olive's and Benny's faces beamed with excitement. "Ben, will we go to our rooms first? I need to use the bathroom."

"Of course, Olive. But there is a restroom over there." Ben pointed across the lobby. "If you are desperate."

"I'll be right back." Olive hurried across the marble floor. When she returned, her face was porcelain white.

"Olive, what's wrong?" asked Benny.

"They have gold spigots, gold flush pulls, and gold gilded mirrors...in the public bathroom!"

"You're lying," accused Benny.

"Go look for yourself." Olive gestured toward the other side of the room.

"Father, I'll be right back. Don't go up without me." Benny dashed to investigate Olive's claim. Upon returning, Benny shook his head in disbelief. "None of my friends will ever believe me when I tell them about this hotel."

Ben's body shook as he chuckled. "Come on, kids. We have more to explore and discover today."

An elevator attendant pressed the button for the sixth floor. Olive grabbed the brass bar to steady herself as the trio moved upwards.

"Sixth floor."

"This is us," Ben said. "Our luggage will follow us shortly."

A trip to their accommodations led to more amazed gawking. Their adjoining rooms were decorated with crisp linen bedding, down comforters, feather beds, ornately carved and gilded Rococo headboards, and a matching pair of Louis XIV chairs. The shared bath boasted two solid marble sinks and a large claw-foot soaking tub. The separate water closet was plumbed with gold flush pulls.

Arms outstretched, Olive plopped onto the bed, sinking into the feathers.

"Ben, I could get used to living like this," she called to the neighboring room.

"Then you better find an extremely wealthy husband, Olive."

"Phooey! I'll earn my own money." Olive forced herself off the bed and walked to the window. Lifting the lower pane, she coughed, "Benny, look out your window. There's a pond in the park, right in the middle of the city," said Olive. "I can see it from my room window."

"That park is mammoth. It looks to be as big as our north cornfield." Benny's eyes were wide and round.

The luggage arrived with two valets as the youngsters viewed the city from the height of six floors.

"Miss, may I help you with your unpacking?" the valet asked. Olive nodded, amazed.

"Ben, I'm never leaving here!"

∞∞∞∞

Soon, they found themselves back in the lobby, Benny and Olive still looking skyward.

"Shall we begin?" Ben urged them to follow. The doorman hailed a cab for the trio.

"Where are we going now?" asked Olive. "Shopping?"

"We shall shop soon, but first, I have a surprise." Ben whispered something to the driver. "Sit back, kids, and take in the view."

Olive noted the multitude of fashion styles displayed in the shop windows and worn by pedestrians as she planned her purchases. They passed through an unsavory section of the city before the cab stopped in the harbor. Ben instructed the cabby to wait.

"Get out, children. There is something I want you to see." Finding it hard to contain his grin, he opened the back door for Olive.

As she exited the vehicle, she looked across the water. Rendered speechless, Olive gazed at the Statue of Liberty, a towering symbol of freedom given to the United States by France. Thinking how the

French were currently suffering horrendous hardships of war, she burst into tears.

"Oh, Ben. She's breathtakingly beautiful—and enormous! I'm overwhelmed with gratitude."

Benny grabbed hold of his father's hand. "It's the most astonishing thing I'll ever see in my whole life. Thank you, Father."

"You are both very welcome. See there?" Ben pointed to Ellis Island. "That is where the immigrants enter the States. They are processed in that building before being granted permission to step on our soil. Many families came from Europe these past fifteen years, looking for work in the mines and mills. Uncle James hires some for his factories, while others work in the steel mills or coal mines."

"I met a new boy after school last year; he spoke with a funny accent. They called him 'Stush.' Do you think he came through there?" Ben asked his father.

"I'm sure he did. I think I know his family. His father, Jan Stanislaw, works at the Westchester factory. Good-hearted fellow."

Olive blocked out all conversation. She was thinking of Fred and the potential danger he may face in the coming months. Mesmerized by the proud lady, she began singing.

"My country, 'tis of thee, sweet land of liberty, to thee I sing."

Benny and Ben joined the second line. "Land where my fathers died, land of the pilgrims' pride, from every mountainside let freedom ring."

By the end of the first verse, all three Westchesters were in tears. They stood humbled, holding hands, engrossed with the magnitude of Lady Liberty's significance.

Heaving a long sigh, Ben prompted, "We better get on with our shopping. I'm grateful to see her again and to share her with you."

They retreated to the taxi. Ben sat in the middle, his arms encircling Olive on the left, Benny on the right.

35

THE CLASS THE STARS FELL ON

"*O*live, Ben, Benny! Over here," Fred called out as his siblings and nephew stepped off the train. Dressed in cadet gray, Fred appeared older, wiser. Over the past four years, he had grown from a boy to a man. Standing erect, he waved. "I trust you had a pleasant journey."

Olive's heart jumped. "Fred!" She ran to her brother. Flinging her arms around him, she spun them both in circles. "Oh, Fred, I'm so happy to see you. I've missed you so." She repeatedly kissed her brother's cheek.

Fred pushed her back. "I want a good look at you," he said. "My goodness Olive, you look like a full-grown woman."

"Chet, you didn't tell me you had such a pretty beau back home." The remark, made by another cadet, caused both Olive and Fred to turn around.

"Hey, Brad. Come over to meet my family. Omar Bradley, may I present my brother Benjamin Westchester, his son Ben Jr., and my youngest sister, Olive."

Brad shook hands with the two men, then took Olive's hand, kissing her glove.

"It's a pleasure, a special pleasure to meet you, Miss Olive." Bradley winked at the girl. "Good thing I have my Mary back in Missouri; otherwise, Chet and I may be engaged in a duel."

Olive blushed bright red. "Pleasure to meet you, Mr. Bradley."

"Easy, Brad, that's my sister you're talking about." Turning to Olive, Fred continued, "And it's *Lieutenant* Bradley, Olive—at least it shall be tomorrow." Fred cuffed Bradley on the shoulder. "Be off with you, scoundrel." Then to his family, "Come, I have a car waiting to take you to your hotel. Olive, did you enjoy your night in the city?"

Olive wrapped her arm around Fred's waist. "Fred, it was marvelous. I bought two new dresses, one for last night's dinner and one for tomorrow's celebration. First we saw the Statue of Liberty—she's spectacular. After shopping we ate in the Plaza Terrace room. It's all white, pink, and gold with actual inside terraces. The salmon was divine." She bubbled, rambling with enthusiasm as she and Fred continued walking arm in arm. "We had baked Alaska for dessert. Did you know the bathrooms have gold spigots?"

Fred chuckled at Olive's joy, then faced Ben. "Big Brother, thank you for coming. And thank you for bringing this little troublemaker." Fred pinched Olive, who clung tighter to him.

"My honor to be here, Freddy. This is a great opportunity for both youngsters." Ben hesitated before adding, "And for me."

"Here's our car." The foursome took their seats: Ben in the front, Fred between the youngsters in the back. "Your hotel is nothing like the Plaza, but you'll have clean, comfortable beds and a hearty breakfast. There is a dinner tonight at the officer's club for cadets and invited families. It's hosted by West Point's Commandant; I'll gather you around six o'clock. Olive, you might want to wear that dress from last night." Fred's eyes sparkled as he spoke to his sister. "Ben, I assume you have a formal suit with you."

"Wow, I'm excited," Benny chimed in. "Formal clothes two nights in a row."

∞∞∞∞

The family settled into their modest room, a far cry from the opulence of the previous evening. Olive found a hair salon to help with her unruly locks, while Ben and Benny walked along the Hudson until it was time to dress for the evening. A car arrived at the prescribed time to transport the Westchesters to West Point. As Olive crossed the front threshold into the club, talking stopped, cadets stared, and Army brass smiled. A picture of elegance, Olive wore a dark plum, off-the-shoulder, crisscrossed shawl top gown with a handkerchief hemline, her mother's pearls, plum-colored T-strap heels, and elbow-length silk gloves. Her curly blonde hair was coiffed high on her head and tied in matching silk ribbons. Several whimsical stray curls dangled down the sides of her face, softening her profile. Olive portrayed a dazzling vision.

Fred rushed to her side. "Olive, you look stunning." He kissed her cheek. "Come, all of you, our table is this way." Fred led his family across the freshly oiled parquet dance floor. They passed the orchestra playing a cacophony of sounds as they tuned their instruments for a repertoire of dinner music. A flash from the photographer's booth startled Ben, who headed to the bar on the opposite side of the room. Finally, all arrived at a cluster of round tables draped in white linen, accommodating eight diners.

"Who shall be eating with us?" asked Benny as he fidgeted with his tie.

"Edwin Kimble and family. He's a brilliant man, second in our class," Fred said with admiration.

"Fred, you're also gifted," argued Olive proudly.

"Not like Edwin. I rank in the thirties. He'll be studying with the Army corps of engineers, reserved only for the top-ranking grads from our class."

Kimble, a handsome cadet with a long, thin nose had brown hair, slicked straight back and thinning along the temples. He, along with his guests—a slightly plump, graying, middle-aged woman and an equally attractive man of about eighteen—arrived as Fred finished speaking.

"Hello, Chet. May I introduce my mother, Elvira Kimble, and my brother, Kenneth," Kimble said as he eyed Olive. "Mother, Kenneth, our table companion: Fred Westchester."

"Pleased to meet you, Mrs. Kimble, Kenneth. And this is my family...my brother, Ben Sr., my nephew, Ben Jr., and my beautiful sister, Olive."

"She certainly is," said Kenneth. Olive blushed, extending her hand for both young men to kiss.

"Shall we sit?" Kimble held Elvira's chair. Fred reached for Olive's, but he was outmaneuvered by Kenneth.

"Allow me, Miss Olive." The gallant Kenneth Kimble assisted in seating her.

Each place setting was adorned with a personal menu, dance card, and individually wrapped chocolate truffle, displaying the West Point seal and motto: "Duty, Honor, Country." A gold eagle was the focus of each floral centerpiece.

"I see we are dancing this evening," said Fred. "Olive, may I be the first name on your card?"

Olive gleefully handed her card to her brother. "I hope you intend to occupy several lines, Fred—or do you wish to be addressed as Chet?" She giggled at the nickname. Fred blushed.

"Save a dance for me," Benny and Ben chimed in unison.

"Miss Olive, if I may be so bold—and with Chet's permission—I shall happily add to your amusement tonight. May I, Chet?" Kimble solicited.

"Consider the same request from me," added Kenneth.

Like the harvest dance, Olive's card contained six names on twelve lines within minutes as other unattached cadets queued, seeking her partnership for a whirl, spin, or twirl.

"I'll be entering these hallowed halls as a plebe in the fall," Kenneth mentioned to Olive during dinner.

"Congratulations," Olive answered politely. Preferring to talk to Fred, she moved her chair closer to her brother, achieving a more comfortable conversational position.

"Fred, are you worried about the events in Europe?" Olive asked. "I worry you and Levi shall be sent away."

"Don't worry, Miss Olive," offered Kimble. "The trouble is Europe's trouble. President Wilson has no intention of sending troops."

"Even considering the sinking of the Lusitania? I certainly hope your assessment is correct." Olive squeezed Fred's arm. "If my big brother travels to Europe, I intend to tour along with him—unless he's taking his new bride, of course." Olive flushed at her presumption.

"There is nothing I should rather do than escort my little sister throughout the capitals of Europe."

"I suspect many men are willing to accompany you, Miss Olive." Kenneth's charming smile intensified the red of Olive's already colored cheeks.

"Do you know where you'll be stationed?" Wishing to divert the attention, Olive whispered in Fred's ear.

"I do. Brad and I are both to be sent to defend the border with Mexico." Olive flinched. Fred stroked her hand in reassurance. "We shall be stationed at Fort Bliss."

"Do you leave immediately? Is there actual fighting?" Her brow wrinkled.

"A skirmish or two, nothing serious. I have four weeks to report. I'm packing my belongings, sending some home and some to Texas." Fred paused. "I'm visiting Levi for a week, then heading down. I'll not be stopping at the farm."

Olive slumped into her seat. "Fred, why do you never come home to visit us?"

"Shall we walk to discuss this, dear Olive?"

Fred took her hand and led her to the veranda, overlooking the Hudson River. Olive noted to explore the view in daylight. The scent of roses, vining on trellises, filtered through the evening air.

Strolling side by side with Olive, Fred confessed, "I'm evading Father. I shall tell only you the reason why, but you must promise to never repeat it. Promise?" Fred turned to face his sister, clutching her hands.

"Yes, Fred, I shall keep your secret. I *am* curious." She lay her head on Fred's shoulder.

"Father forced me into attending West Point." Hearing his own words aloud was cathartic, like releasing agony. His muscles relaxed slightly.

"Yes, I know. He signed a contract with Uncle James. The farm benefits immensely from the resulting sales. We've spoken of this before."

"Well, I resent being a pawn. I hate it here; I've always hated this place. As a plebe, I endured horrific hazing rituals." Fred recalled being bound and thrown into the river—a presumed test of athleticism. "Once, I thought I would drown."

Turning in shame, Fred hid how his relived torture showed on his face from Olive. He pushed other torturous memories of plebe hazing from his mind.

"Was it the same for everyone?" Releasing his hand, Olive reached for Fred's face. "Look at me," she said, touching his cheek.

"The athletes were spared the worst of it, but you know I'm not athletic." Fred moved away to hide his embarrassment. "I blame Father —even despise him for it. I return home once a year purely to see you, dear Olive; otherwise, I'd avoid Westchester Farms at all costs."

Olive tucked herself under Fred's arm. "I'm so sorry, Freddy. Father is a tyrant, driving you, Levi, and Ginny away, denying me the chance to develop talent. Please continue visiting once a year, for my sake. At least until I am old enough to travel alone. I can't bear the thought of not seeing you."

Fred paused before answering. Weighing the pain of not seeing Olive against the agony of being in his father's company, he said, "I shall, Olive. I promise to continue my visits until you reach adulthood. Shall we return? Listen, I believe I hear the clink of china. After all I've been through, I'll not miss my graduation meal."

Taking Olive's hand, Fred steered her through the throng of humanity that was the class of 1915.

The meal began with a crab croquette, followed by tomato shrimp chaud froid, and lemon sorbet to cleanse the palette. An entrée of chateaubriand, asparagus, and roasted potatoes gave way to assorted cheeses. Each course was accompanied by appropriate wines.

White-gloved waiters served peach melba as the Master of Ceremonies announced, "Ladies, Gentlemen, distinguished guests, and cadets, I give you the honorable mayor of New York City, John P. Mitchel."

The young Republican mayor took the podium.

"Thank goodness," said Benny. "I need to stop eating. Geez, that mayor looks awfully young."

Ben grasped his son's shoulder, pulling him close. "Quiet. He's in his thirties. Proves that if you put your mind to it, you're never too young for success."

Mitchell began addressing the audience, discussing the need for decency and honesty in politics and drawing a similarity to the West Point motto of "Duty, Honor, Country."

∞∞∞∞

With speeches and dinner over, staff cleared the tables as the orchestra retuned and readied for livelier dance selections.

"Olive, before we begin dancing, shall we have a photograph taken? Ben, Benny, come along. I shall order several copies of each pose." Fred pointed to the south corner of the room where a photographer from Rochester set up to commemorate the event.

"I'm about to split my gown. May we walk first?" Olive rolled her eyes while pressing her belly. "Cook prepares delicious food, but tonight's food was better than the Terrace room at the Plaza."

"I agree, with both sentiments," added Ben. "I must move."

Fred directed his family outside to the veranda for a stroll.

"It is lovely out here," said Ben.

"Yes, it is! May we return tomorrow so that I may gaze out on the river?" Olive asked.

"Time permitting. At the moment, I think it's time to return inside." Ben motioned to couples circling the floor.

The group went directly to the Kodak booth. Fred posed with the entire group, then alone with Olive. After ordering several copies of each, he took Olive's hand, leading her to the dance floor.

"Shall we dance, dearest Sister?" The orchestra began playing a Chopin waltz. The couple glided across the floor as if floating. "Olive, have you been practicing since Tildy's wedding?"

Smiling at her brother, Olive confessed, "I have been practicing at least a little, Fred. I didn't want to embarrass you. I even learned one tango step."

"Have you changed your mind about attending a finishing school? Are they teaching you social dances?" Fred looked hopefully at Olive.

"Heavens, no."

"So, you're teaching yourself?" he asked as he led her into a promenade. "Both class work and dance?"

"Please, Fred, I prefer to change the subject. Like you, I am hurt and disappointed by Father's single-mindedness. May I simply enjoy my time in your company?"

"Olive, bear with me; don't be angry. We can both consider ourselves victims. However—it occurs to me this evening—we are only victims if we allow ourselves to become so. My road was chosen by others, as was yours, but I've decided that I shall overcome. I shall be the victor when all is said and done." Fred hesitated before continuing, "Olive, do you understand? Determine your own outcome!"

Olive sighed. "I shall consider your comments later. For now, let us simply enjoy this evening and each other's company."

"Absolutely, darling Sister," Fred said as Olive drifted in a fairytale dream, adoring the status of princess.

∞∞∞∞∞

The next day, Graduation Day, spectators took their seats in the stands that lined the Plain, a flat expanse of green surrounded by campus buildings. It was used for more than ceremonial parades; the cadets had received tactical training by spending part of the summer encamped on the very Plain they were now graduating upon. A long grandstand was erected for guests, who were given chair assignments according to their cadet's class rank. Fred, landing solidly in the mid-thirties out of one hundred sixty-some, afforded his family placement in the third row, close to the center; however, his placement did not provide for his own advancement to the engineering corps.

The day smelled of freshly mowed grass as the sun beat down on Olive. She wore a second new, less formal dress. A flowered, wide-brimmed hat protected her face, while straw boater hats with silk grosgrain ribbons shielded Ben and Benny as they listened to the West Point student band play John Phillip Sousa marches.

Olive leaned over to whisper in her brother's ear. "Ben, do you think it permissible for me to remove my gloves? I'm baking in this sun."

"I'm no fashion expert; however, the other women are not removing gloves, so probably neither should you. Think about how hot the cadets must be in their wool uniforms. Here they come."

The musicians quieted as mounted officers rode onto the Plain. They were followed by the young cadets of the class of 1915. All neatly groomed, starched, and pressed with spit-shined shoes, the men marched onto the field, clad in full dress uniform.

"My, they are handsome," admitted Olive.

"I thought you were a sworn bachelorette," teased Benny.

"I am! Shh. The band is playing again. My goodness, that's 'Hail to the Chief,'" Olive said as the crowd stood. She gasped as President Woodrow Wilson entered and took his place on the dais. "Ben! It's the actual President of the United States of America!"

Ben chuckled. "Yes, Olive, it is the actual President. Now you better hush."

After the crowd settled down, Wilson began his speech. He reinforced his policies of economic support to Britain and France, while keeping the country neutral on the prospect of supplying fighting troops.

"Wilson better mean what he says," whispered Olive.

His speech was followed by several West Point administrators, then William Covell, who ranked first in the class. Cadets were called one by one, issued diplomas, and awarded commissions as second lieutenants into the United States Army.

"May I present Second Lieutenant Frederick Westchester, Campbellsville, Pennsylvania," announced the commandant. Fred shook hands and saluted, then turned and smiled at his family. Olive blew him kisses with her hands, Ben and Benny whistled and clapped.

Hats were tossed high into the air, culminating the day as the crowd applauded and cheered their loved ones' lives as a West Point cadet complete. The real world lay ahead.

Fred crossed the parade grounds along with the other new lieutenants, rushing to find his family.

"This ending is all so bittersweet. Four years passed so slowly, yet so quickly." Shaking hands with the men and embracing Olive, Fred bid them goodbye. "I must vacate my quarters. The class of 1919 arrives in several weeks, poor foolish buggers. Safe travels, dear ones. I am grateful you came."

"Fred, promise to continue writing," Olive pressed. "Remember, I love you, dearly."

"And I love you, Little Sister. Until our next meeting." He kissed both cheeks and sent her on her way.

36

PANCHO AND FRIENDS

SPRING, 1916

*O*live ran to the foyer table scanning for mail. Seeing a letter from Fred, she scooped it out of the tray. Grabbing the newspaper, she ran upstairs to her office, slammed the door, and ripped open the envelope. The letter was dated three weeks prior.

Dearest Olive,

I'm sorry it's been several weeks since my last letter. We are engaged in a border war. Pancho Villa attacked Columbus, New Mexico, and Camp Furlong. Over a dozen civilians and soldiers were mortally wounded. My current assignment is to escort a rail transport for the recognized Mexican President Carranza's forces from Eagle Pass, Texas to Douglas, Arizona. I shall attempt to write; however, please be patient if my free time dictates otherwise.

Your loving brother,

Fred

Olive folded the letter. Retying the ribbon, she placed it in her dresser drawer. A second, smaller bound stack of correspondence from Samuel lay in the same drawer. Obsessed with news from Mexico and Europe, Olive scoured the daily newspaper for updates and warning signs. Discussion of fighting filled her evening meal conversation.

"Father, how can you be so sure President Wilson will not enter this war?" Olive's face challenged the table for an answer.

"This again." Wiping his face with his napkin, Ben placed his fork on his dinner plate. "Olive, you were there last summer at Fred's graduation; he admitted as much. He's running for reelection on an anti-war campaign. Must we endure the same discussion every evening?"

"But the situation is changing." Olive faced Ben directly. "Do you take the time to read the papers?"

"Olive, don't worry. Fred and Levi are fine," Benny interjected, naïve and uninformed.

"I don't care about Levi; he has a way of falling into a pile of dung and smelling fresh. Levi is a manipulator. He knows how to work the system. Fred is my worry. He's already fighting Mexicans. I say, let them have Texas."

"Olive! You'd feel differently if they were trying to annex Pennsylvania," Ben said. "Texas has been part of the union since before the Civil War—although they joined the south in that fight."

"My point. They chose poorly in the past. Why should brave northern boys risk their lives fighting for them?" Confident of her logic, Olive stared at the table.

"That is nonsense. US soldiers defend every state in this republic." Henderson defied Olive to object. "What is West Point's motto, do you remember?"

"Duty, Honor, Country," mumbled Olive.

"Exactly. That is just what Fred and Levi are fulfilling. Levi is now part of the Judge Advocate General corps. Even if Wilson sends troops, Levi stays on US soil." Henderson resumed eating.

"I told you, I don't give a damn about Levi!" Olive's scream carried to the kitchen.

"Olive, don't be so crass," Bessie chastised. "That language is not used, especially not at the table."

"Shut up, Bessie." Olive's eyes narrowed to slits. "You're a silly twit."

"That's enough, Olive. There is no need to insult Bessie. You really need to grow up," Ben growled, reaching for his wife's hand.

"He's right, Olive. Hold your tongue. What has you riled so?" Henderson said, attempting to calm his youngest.

Olive threw a newspaper onto the table. "This has me upset."

She pointed to the headline: "US Forces Attacked by Both Mexican Government Forces and Villa's Banditos."

"'Troops are fighting deep in Mexican territory and being attacked by both sides,'" Olive read. "Why? Why does Wilson send more troops south? He's butting into a Mexican civil war, and if he does that, what's to say he won't send troops to France?" Olive clenched her teeth, picked up the paper, and threw it at Henderson.

"Olive, Villa crossed our borders and attacked our towns. Wilson is defending our country—rightfully so. He shall not enter the war in Europe unless we are attacked on our soil. Wilson is sending Europe supplies precisely because the American people will not tolerate our boys fighting a foreign war. As long as the Germans refrain from attacks on US merchant ships, we avoid this war." Henderson spoke slowly and steadily as he gazed directly into his daughter's eyes.

"And you trust the Germans to keep their word?" Not yet pacified, Olive opposed his sensibility.

"Olive, you whipped yourself into a frenzy. Here, drink a glass of wine to ease your anxiety. If you continue this excited state, I'll deny you sight of the paper."

"You think you may ignore the truth? You're delirious, Father." Shaking her head in disgust, Olive sipped her wine. "Bury your head in the sand, but mark my word: this war is coming to Campbellsville."

Reaching his threshold for insubordinate behavior, Henderson stood. "That's enough, Olive. You may be excused. Please leave this table. If you refuse to speak civilly, you shall eat alone in your office. Am I clear?"

"Do and say what you must; it does not change reality." Olive pushed her chair under the table, scooped more potatoes onto her dish, then turned.

"I said, *enough*, Olive. I do not want to hear anything more about this war from you. Go, young lady. Do not return to this table until you can control your temper."

Locked in her office, Olive wistfully fondled the silver-framed photograph of her and Fred, taken last year at his graduation dinner. Olive in her plum gown and Fred in his cadet uniform stood side by side. At six feet, two inches tall, Fred towered a full head over Olive's five feet, seven inches.

"Oh, Freddy," she said as her finger traced his face longingly. "Be safe, dear Brother. Although the rest of them don't seem to care, I love you very much."

∞∞∞∞

Henderson's ostracization of Olive continued, although it was not the punishment he intended. She gladly ate her evening meals alone in her office. Her daily routine of reading the paper expanded. A visit to the Campbellsville dry goods and mercantile resulted in the purchase of the daily *Madison Gazette* and *The New York Times* as supplements to the weekly *Campbellsville Herald*. Continuing to spend her hard-earned money, Olive acquired her own Victrola as well as an assortment of phonograph discs.

She remained happily isolated until one day in mid-July when, taking her usual seat at the table, she motioned for the house staff to retrieve a place setting.

"And to what do we owe the pleasure of your company?" Henderson asked with mild interest.

"Today's paper. Did you see the news from Britain and France?" Olive threw the newspaper on the table, again. "Look at the foreign headlines. On the first day engaged in the Battle of the Somme, the Brits suffered almost sixty thousand casualties. Twenty thousand are dead. Tell me how they can continue without our help if they suffer those losses."

"Good God! Are we back to this? I thought we agreed to your absence if your civility and this topic remains the subject of the evening." Henderson's disgust spread to Ben and Clyde.

"Olive, it was so pleasant without you," Clyde said. "Can you not drop this subject?"

Olive cocked her head with a smirk. "Of course, Clyde, After all, I'm here tonight to listen to the family gossip. All of you dare to ignore world issues, and I shall permit you to live in your fantasy; I'll not speak of it. My main reason for joining you is to hear about your insignificant existence."

Henderson placed his hands on his hips as he stood to address Olive. "Get out. Go back to your office. Your impertinence is insufferable, and I've had my fill of you. If you weren't such a talented accountant, you'd be gone from my house."

She chortled in response. "You'd actually disown a fourteen-year-old girl? After tolerating both Ginny and Tildy's unwed state of motherhood? You'd throw me out for worrying about my brother. You're a real piece of work, Father."

Ben rubbed his eyes, then sighed. "Olive, it's your *attitude* Father cannot tolerate. None of us can. I find it impossible to believe, but it is true: you are worse than Tildy! What triggered this acceleration into defiance and sarcasm?"

Olive's eyes flashed hatred as they latched onto Ben's, then Henderson's. Saying nothing, she strolled into the kitchen. "Cook, it seems I'm not welcome at the table. I shall continue to eat in my office."

37

GREEN RIBBONS

EARLY DECEMBER, 1916

*L*ife marched on for the Westchester clan. Another prosperous growing season resulted in another plentiful harvest. Once again, the long kitchen trestle table was ladened with canning jars brimming with hot water, denoting the start of a winter supply assembly line. Pots full of sauces, jams, and chutneys bubbled on the main stove, while the summer kitchen was reserved for water baths used to seal jar lids.

Immersed in preserving food and still angry with her father, Olive continued isolating herself from family meals, preferring to eat in her office. Engrossed in her work, enjoying minimal free time, she managed to squirrel away a tidy sum of money. Not knowing the expense of higher education, she saved every penny she could, intending to enroll in college one day whether her father supported her or not.

The Campbellsville Harvest Dance found Olive dancing in the arms of Tobias Bailey once again. Tabs continued to leave small, handmade Christmas trinkets for Olive under the Westchester tree, although they were not considered a couple by any modern social standards.

As Olive prepared for her outing to town, she wove last year's gift from Tabs, a green silk ribbon, into her braids.

"Olive, I'm leaving in ten minutes," shouted Benny. "Hurry up. I want to get to the mercantile before they sell out of stock."

Olive glanced at the snow-covered fields out her window, the tops of corn stalks the only visible vegetation. Large flakes fell, coating tree limbs as if frosting them with glistening icing.

"Benny, are we taking the wagon or the Ford?" Olive watched as the fields disappeared into a sheet of white. "I think the wagon is safer. The snow is coming down heavily right now."

"If you insist. I'll have Jake hitch the team...though I was hoping for more driving time." Benny moped as he headed to the barn.

Olive wrapped her wool cape around her shoulders, donned a knit beret and matching gloves, then grabbed a muff and extra blanket in case of an emergency. Climbing into the wagon, she felt an unfamiliar sensation; a smile crossed her face. *The last time I was genuinely pleased was at Fred's graduation*, she thought. Sixteen months ago.

"We're off," Benny announced as he urged the horses forward. "Olive, do you need anything in particular today?"

"I'll help you with supplies, then I shall like to stop at the drugstore for a malted, my favorite. If we have time, may we walk for a few minutes? I do enjoy Campbellsville's Christmas decorations."

"Hoping to see Mr. Bailey?" Benny teased.

"Not necessarily," Olive shared a rare smile.

"Well, a stop at the drugstore suits me just fine. Ingrid Mueller works there. I'm kind of sweet on her." Benny blushed with his confession.

"Is this considered an official courtship?" Olive pried as the wind blew harder. She tucked the blanket over their knees.

"What makes it official?" Benny stopped the wagon.

"Keep moving, silly goose. This storm threatens our chance of any fun time in town. It's 'official' if you have declared to Ingrid the intent to court. And you need her father's permission." Olive laughed. "Men are so daft when it comes to matters of the heart."

"Look who's talking. You're the prettiest girl in the entire valley, but you have no suitors of your own—save an old man," Benny scolded.

"Harrumph. I enjoy being alone. I'll make my way without the help of a man." She slid away from Benny, rebuking him, despite the cold. "And Tabs Bailey is not my suitor."

"Olive, you're a woman. You can't even vote. How can you 'make your way' without a man?"

Stating the obvious only served to agitate Olive. "I don't want to talk about it anymore. Thanks for ruining my day." Olive crossed her arms and tucked her hands into the muff.

"You ruined the day yourself, without anyone's help." Benny cracked the whip to spur the horses as Olive glared straight ahead.

They rode in silence over the country lane. Close hanging trees sheltered them overhead from the flurry. Snow blanketed them as they exited the track leading from the farm and entered the main road for the remaining trek into town.

"Wow, this may turn into a blizzard if the wind increases. Shall we make haste?" Benny broke their silence. Twenty minutes later, they pulled in front of the feed store.

After tying the horses, Benny extended his hand to help Olive from the wagon. She refused, shook the snow from the blanket, folded it, and stowed it under the seat. Olive brushed off her shoulders and stomped her boots, then they entered the store.

Olive browsed through bolts of fabric, selecting a festive red velvet. The clerk cut the required yardage to sew a skirt.

"Do you need anything else, Miss?" asked the clerk, hoping for an additional sale.

"Do you have any white linen, French lace insertion, and small shell buttons?" Olive answered as she checked the shelves for hidden treasures. The clerk pointed to the appropriate display. After paying for her package separately, Olive ordered necessary kitchen supplies while Benny attended to farm needs.

"The wagon is tied out front. Please load and cover our items.

We'll be back in thirty minutes," Benny instructed the proprietor. "Come, Olive, I believe a chocolate malt is on the schedule."

While walking in silence to the drugstore, Benny and Olive enjoyed the privacy of their thoughts. A bell tinkled as Benny opened the door for Olive. They kicked the snow from their boots to minimize water puddles on the black and white tile floor. Both Ingrid Mueller and Tobias Bailey glanced toward the entrance. Ingrid giggled like a schoolgirl. Olive rolled her eyes as Benny ogled the plump-faced blonde.

"Miss Westchester, what a delightful surprise. Do you care to join us?" Tabs immediately greeted Olive as Cousin Wyeth tossed his head in disgust at the interruption of their snack.

"I believe your cousin is unhappy to see me," Olive accused.

Taking her by the hand, Tabs led Olive to their booth. "His opinion is of no consequence. He may leave if he so wishes." Tabs glared directly into Wyeth's eyes.

"I believe I shall return to the factory. Good day, Miss Westchester." Wyeth tipped his hat, dropped two bits on the counter, and left. "I'll see you later, Cousin."

"Forgive Wyeth. He means no disrespect." Tabs smiled radiantly, relishing their chance meeting.

"Of course, he does. His only issue is that I don't care what he thinks," Olive quipped with her usual sass.

"How are your brothers?" Tabs cordially inquired.

"Ha. Levi promotes Levi. Fred is fighting in the Mexican Expedition." Wanting to change the subject, Olive peered at the counter. "May I order a chocolate malt?" she bellowed.

Startled, Ingrid Mueller blushed as she diverted her attention from Benny to her job as a waitress.

"What brings you to town today, in this wretched weather?" Tabs removed his cap, exposing a full bushy head of brown hair.

"We need supplies for the farm. And I'm looking for a few last-minute Christmas items."

Olive and Tabs engaged in polite conversation as Ingrid delivered the malt. Olive opened her clutch to pay.

"Please, allow me." Tabs motioned for Olive to close her purse.

"Thank you, but that is not necessary. I understand you are caring for your elderly mother. I'm happy to pay my own way."

Tabs considered Olive's response, then dropped his head. "Miss Westchester, I realize that we are from different stations in life. If norms permitted our courtship, I should declare my intention immediately, but our social gap is too wide. I do not, simply out of respect for your family. As I cannot do that, please at least allow me to buy you a chocolate malt." Tabs scanned Olive's face for a hint of returned affection.

"I mean no disrespect," said Olive. "I'm sorry to have offended you. I thought I was being considerate of your circumstances."

"Miss Olive, men are prideful and discontented if they are bested by a woman. It may serve you well to remember this—my mother taught me that a man may not be a gentleman if a woman is not a lady."

Olive pursed her lips. "Forgive me, Mr. Bailey, but I care not to be lectured." Olive stood to carry her malt to another booth.

After she was finished with her malt, Olive approached the counter again. "Ingrid, add a dozen peppermint sticks to my order, please." She dropped a dollar on the countertop. "And put Mr. Bailey's meal on my check."

Tabs inhaled, saddened his advice was lost on the young woman. "Miss Olive..."

Olive threw her hand up in a sign of dismissal. "Let's go Benny," she said, as she stormed out the door.

Benny squeezed Ingrid's hand. "Merry Christmas. Maybe I'll see you next week, weather permitting?" She giggled and blushed.

The visit to the drugstore lasted longer than the prescribed thirty minutes. By the time Benny and Olive returned to the wagon, a full inch of snow had accumulated on their cargo. The horses pranced, ready to return to the warmth of the barn.

"We may have waited too long." Benny brushed the horse's manes, secured the rigging, then climbed into the wagon.

"Did you have a productive meeting with Ingrid?" Harassment was lately becoming a favorite pastime for Olive.

"Why are you always so sarcastic?" Benny spread the blanket over their legs. "I noticed that your encounter with Mr. Bailey ended in a difference of opinion."

"There is nothing between Tobias Bailey and me. He is an old man from an inferior social class, not worthy of a Westchester. Now shut up, and let's hurry home."

"Yes, my queen."

"Mr. Westchester." The store owner called as Benny clicked his tongue at the horses. "Wait. A large crate was just delivered for you."

"How long will it take to load?" asked an impatient Olive. "Our journey home shall be slow and treacherous with this snow coming down so quickly."

"Go ahead and load it. I'll not return tomorrow in this weather." Benny agreed to wait.

"I promise I shall delay you for fifteen minutes only. Ned, hurry, repack the wagon to fit this box."

"Make it snappy. We need to get home, straight away!" Olive squawked.

One clerk uncovered and rearranged the parcels while the owner and Ned dragged a crate half the size of the cart bed. The three men hoisted it into the back of the wagon, resulting in the front wheels losing traction.

"What in the name of heaven is that?" Benny asked, fidgeting with the reins while the horses pawed.

"Hurry, Ned, move this forward some. Center it in over the axles." The proprietor glanced at the sky, knowing the risks of the country lane leading to the Westchester mansion. Throwing the tarp over the cargo, he yelled, "Okay now, be off and be careful."

Benny released the brake, flipping the reins to urge the team forward as the wheels slid.

"Yikes. We may need a sleigh today." Benny pursed his lips and clenched his mouth.

"Don't be such a sissy. Just drive. They're expecting us home soon. If we don't arrive, Jake or Kendrick will come looking for us." Olive snapped at Benny but faced away to hide her concern.

The rolling hills of town posed minimal trouble, as the crate's extra weight helped the wheels grip the brick roadways. However, with Campbellsville in the distance, gravel roads transformed into dirt country lanes full of ruts and ridges. They began the journey up the mountain to the Westchester estate.

"It's always easier coming down this hill than climbing up it," moaned Benny, his grip so tight that his hands cramped.

"Hmmm." Olive was distracted, watching the right axle as it skidded and slipped. "Benny, whoa!" She grabbed the reins and pulled back hard. The horses struggled with their footing as the right side of the wagon slid into a ditch. "Son of a gun. We're buried."

"I didn't see that coming." Benny jumped down, inspecting the wheel. "Olive, I am sorry. The axle's still intact, but we are stuck." The wheel was lodged deep in a snow-covered hole, preventing it from moving either forward or backward.

"It's not your fault. How could you see it with all this snow?" Olive pulled her cloak tighter to cut the wind. "But now what?"

"We're in a pickle. You take the reins and pull the horses; I'll try to push the wagon from the back." Benny reached up and grabbed the edge of the cart, securing his grip.

"Why did we ever wait for that ungodly box?" Olive climbed down; she petted the noses of both horses to settle them. "Yell when you're ready."

"Pull now." Benny pushed as Olive pulled. The cart wiggled forward, then backward, settling in the ditch. "Try again."

"Come on, you nags," chirped Olive as she tugged harder. The wagon inched forward. "Push, Benny!" Using all his strength, Benny pushed. Olive yanked the reins, the team powered ahead, and the wagon moved. Benny's hands slipped as he fell flat on his face.

"Christ!" Benny's neck jerked back as his chin and nose hit a snow-covered rock. Blood gushed, turning the pristine snow pink. Olive raced to engage the brake, preventing the wagon from drifting back into the ditch. Then she ran and knelt beside Benny.

"Can you sit up? Is anything broken, besides your face?" Olive rolled Benny onto his back, raised his head, then assisted him to a sitting position.

"I think I broke my nose." Benny bent his legs and raised his arms in additional diagnosis. "But that might be it."

"I think you did, too. It's a little crooked, and it's spurting blood. Here, put your head back. Can you pinch your nose?"

Skeptical instructions, knowing Benny's nose was too tender to touch. Ripping the bottom of her slip, Olive fashioned a bandage. "Benny, this will hurt, but I need to wrap your face. Keep your head tilted." Olive wound the white cotton under his chin, over his head, under his nose, and around the nose again, finally securing it with a knot.

"There. Now let's get you onto the top of that enormous wooden crate. I'll lead the horses the rest of the way home."

Olive replaced Benny's cap on his head. Easing her arm around his back, she tried lifting him. Losing his balance as his ankle buckled, Benny slid down to the ground, pulling Olive on top of him.

"I may have sprained my foot. That really hurt." Benny rubbed his leg.

"You have to help me; I can't lift you alone." Brushing snow off her skirt, Olive struggled to her feet. "Come on, Benny, don't be such a wimp; you can't just sit here."

She didn't hear the man approach until he spoke. "Miss Olive, may I be of service?" Through the blowing snow, Olive saw the form of a man, collar turned up against the wind, hands deep in his tattered coat pockets. She strained, trying to recognize the owner of the familiar voice.

"Mr. Bailey? What are you doing all the way out here?" The Westchesters gazed at each other in surprise.

"I walked out to make sure you made it home safely. All this snow is too deep for a wagon."

Olive blushed, remembering her condescending treatment of Tabs only an hour earlier. "My...that's very kind of you."

"We got stuck," Benny said. "I fell and broke my nose, maybe my ankle too. Olive's trying to help me onto the cargo so she may lead the horses home." Benny squinted through his bandages at their good Samaritan, then moaned in pain.

"Hold on, Mr. Westchester." Despite his diminutive size, Tabs bent over, lifted Benny in his arms, and placed him in the back of the wagon. "Miss Olive, climb up. I'll walk the horses the rest of the way."

"I won't put you out," Olive snipped too quickly.

"I put myself out when I deliberately left town. Please, don't argue. I wish to be gentlemanly, so you must be ladylike." Tabs grabbed Olive by the waist and boosted her onto the bench.

"Well...I never...!" Olive stammered.

"Olive, shut up, and thank Mr. Bailey for his help," Benny groaned from the back. "I need to get home. I'm in pain."

THE COFFIN

*T*he last of their travels consumed triple the usual time. Tabs guided the team, Olive rode in silence, and Benny lamented his clumsiness. Kendrick trotted up to greet them as the wagon and trio cleared the woods, entering the driveway.

Viewing Benny lying in the wagon with a bandaged nose, Kendrick burst out, "What in the name of heaven happened to you? Both your fathers are worried. Why on earth did you go out in a wagon in weather like this?"

"Sorry, Kendrick. It's a long story." Benny offered little in response, trying to immobilize his face.

"Mr. Bailey, how are you involved in this caper?" Kendrick, only a half-dozen years older than Tabs, eyed him with suspicion.

"We ran into Mr. Bailey at the drugstore. He was kind enough to see us home," Olive spouted.

"Miss Olive, was that before or after Mr. Ben broke his nose?"

"Look here, Kendrick. I care not to be accused of foul play. I ran across these two at the drugstore. Knowing..."

Kendrick cut Tabs off. "Ah. Drugstore. Now I understand. Benny, how dare you risk Miss Olive's life just to get a glimpse of Ingrid Mueller?" Arriving at the house, Kendrick jumped off his mount, took the reins from Tabs, and flicked Benny behind the ears.

"Ouch! Why'd you do that?" Embarrassed and in pain, Benny fought to regain his dignity.

"After I set your nose, that slap on the ear will feel like a love tap. It's too snowy to get the doctor out here. No worries—in my line of work, I've done noses a thousand times." Kendrick laughed, knowing Benny's immediate future.

"Kendrick, I'll dock your wages for such insubordination." Benny gingerly climbed down, glaring at Kendrick as he tried to hobble on one leg.

"Benny, you'll do no such thing, seeing how I control farm funds," Olive said. "Kendrick, we are both guilty of this adventure. May we leave it at that?" Olive pleaded. "The less Father and Ben know, the better."

"What is that monstrosity in the wagon?" Kendrick pointed to the tarp.

"I have no idea; however, it is the reason we are late and encountered trouble on the lane," Olive said. The ease with which Olive took charge astonished Tabs. "Please have the men store it in the back-kitchen until we have a chance to investigate. Thanks, Kendrick. That is all."

∞∞∞∞∞

Daylight faded early with the heavy snow. Dusk approached as Kendrick removed the horses and cargo. Individual house lights twinkled inside; the Westchester mansion sprang to life.

Facing Tabs, Olive said, "Mr. Bailey, thank you for your kind assistance. Please join us for dinner? It is late; I'll have a bed and a hot bath prepared for you. You'll spend the evening, and I won't take no for an answer."

"No, thank you, Miss Westchester. I shall return home," Tabs replied, as he turned to retreat.

"Nonsense. Even with a lantern, the night is already too dark—and the snow and wind are terrible." Olive motioned for Tabs to follow; he stood still. "Mr. Bailey, I'm cold and tired. Let us go in."

Benny moaned and interrupted the stalemate. "Go! Both of you. Kendrick shall be ready to set my nose, and he's not doing it out here in this weather." Benny grabbed hold of Tabs's arm. Dragging him toward the house, he said, "You won't win against her. The sooner you give in, the sooner we get warm."

Olive opened the outside set of double doors. Hooks and boot racks lined the front vestibule room that sheltered the main foyer. Another set of doors led to the main house.

"Mr. Bailey, feel free to hang your jacket and boots here." Olive gestured as she draped her coat and scarf. Tabs followed suit, then removed his boots to expose hole-filled socks. He tried unsuccessfully to hide his right foot; a ragged, crusty big toe poked through the tip. Quick to notice the lack of darning, Olive offered, "Mr. Bailey, follow me upstairs. I'll draw you a warm bath and find you some dry clothing. Levi may have abandoned items your size in the attic."

"Oh no, Miss Olive. Only allow me to sit before the fire to warm myself. Then I shall return to town."

Olive frowned, then exhaled. "This matter is settled. You're staying."

Tabs reluctantly followed Olive into the main foyer. He gazed at the sweeping expanse of the carved staircase, polished wood paneling, and inlaid pedestal tabletop, centered in the space. Walking to the table, he ran his fingers over the side of a crystal vase filled with flowers.

Sucking air through his teeth, he said, "This home is breathtaking. Where do you find fresh blooms this time of year?" Tabs's head swiveled as he absorbed the essence of Westchester wealth.

"Thank you, Mr. Bailey. In our greenhouse, we grow cutting plants, vegetables, and herbs all year round. Let's get that bath going, shall we?"

"It's Wednesday. I usually bathe on Saturdays, after the workweek is done."

"Yes, my olfactory glands noticed. I'll wash in my room from the pitcher; you may bathe in my bathroom."

"How many bathrooms are in this house?" Tabs couldn't resist asking.

"Three on the second floor, one on the third floor," she answered simply, as if all homes boasted four bathrooms.

Olive rang for a housemaid. Orders given, she returned to Tobias Bailey. "Now, off you go. I'll find you some clean clothes and socks. Dinner is in forty-five minutes."

A trip to the attic unearthed a trunk full of Levi's clothing, too small for Benny or Fred, but perfect for Tabs. Olive chose a pair of wool trousers, a white cotton shirt, a tan cardigan, brown wool socks, and fur-lined slippers. Leaving the stack of folded clothing outside the bath, she retreated to her bedroom to change for dinner. She chose an emerald-colored skirt and a matching green-and-white striped linen blouse; both complemented her hair ribbon.

Olive arrived downstairs before Tabs. The housemaid prepared a spare room for his overnight stay as Henderson entered the house, the wind still howling outside. Shaking the snow from his coat, he noticed a strange, worn, oily addition to the racks.

"With whom do we have the pleasure of dining this evening?" he boomed as he removed his boots and scarf. "Dreadful storm blowing."

"Tobias Bailey is joining us. Hello Father." Olive moved from the shadows into the light of the center chandelier.

"Bailey?" Henderson shook his head. "We'll discuss this in a moment. Olive, what on earth were you thinking today, going out in this? Benny may not be clever enough to judge the weather, but I expect more from you. Where is Ben Jr.?"

"I'm here, Grandfather." Benny frowned at the insult. He sat in the corner of the foyer, nose protected by a metal scoop-like armor plate, secured with gauze.

Henderson heaved a guttural laugh as he eyed his grandson.

"Kendrick mentioned a broken nose, all over a silly girl." Benny and Olive glanced at each other, realizing their secret revealed. "Did you learn your lesson?"

"Not just for a girl, Grandfather. We needed supplies," Benny stuttered, defending their travel in such nasty weather.

Tabs sauntered down the staircase, interrupting the conversation.

"Ah, Mr. Bailey," Henderson said. "I hear you shall be my dinner guest tonight."

Tabs stopped mid-flight, clutching the bannister. "If that is not an imposition." Tabs sought reassurance by looking to Olive.

"Father, Mr. Bailey shall be staying the night. He's on foot, too dangerous to be out in the elements," Olive obliged. "Like you said, it's a dreadful storm."

"Overnight is not necessary. I'm happy to loan him a horse. Shall we discuss this at the table? Excuse me while I wash for dinner."

Henderson sneered at an embarrassed Tabs, dressed in Levi's discarded clothing. The cardigan provided coverage to the slightly wrinkled shirt. Levi's boyhood trousers fit the slender man perfectly.

"Miss Olive, this is a bad idea." Tabs thrust both hands into his trouser pockets. "The bath felt delightful; however, please return my clothing. I shall be off immediately. It's clear your father does not welcome me."

"Mr. Bailey, I could not return clothes even if I were so inclined. The maids are washing them as we speak. Besides, this is my home also, and you are my guest, so you shall stay."

Olive ushered Tabs into the dining room. Cloth napkins, crocheted table covering, and crystal goblets emphasized the chasm between their lifestyles.

"You eat like this every night? Even weeknights? I have never seen the likes of such finery." Tabs moved into the room, stopping in front of Polly's portrait. "Your mother?" He studied the lines of Polly's face. Olive's body stiffened.

"Yes, she died when I was three. I treasure this painting, not knowing her."

"She's beautiful. Uncanny resemblance." Tabs rested his hand on the sideboard.

"Thank you." Olive touched her face and hair as she gazed at her mother's portrait. "Mr. Bailey, please sit beside me."

The rest of the family filed in. They fussed over Benny's broken nose while taking their seats, then pried into the events of the day. Henderson's arrival signaled the service of the first course.

"You must take back this clothing after dinner," Tabs tried again, whispering to Olive. "This clothing is too fine for me to accept."

"Nonsense. They are Levi's cast-offs. I shall look for more the same size to send with you tomorrow." Olive eyed Tabs. "They suit you," she said, as a matter of fact.

"I am not here for a handout, Miss Olive," Tabs insisted. "I prefer to return them."

"Mr. Bailey, I do not wish to repeat our previous conversation." Olive softened her tone. "I am trying to be ladylike and neighborly, that's all. We no longer use these items; they fit you, so take them. Shall we change the subject, please?"

"Yes, let's change the subject." Henderson glared at Tabs. "Mr. Bailey, why were you following my daughter today?"

"*Father,*" Olive objected. Tabs reddened.

"Sir, I was not following your daughter."

"You most certainly were. From what I hear, you were far up the lane to my farm when you came across the wagon."

"Yes, that is true, however—"

"Then you were deliberately following my daughter. How old are you, Mr. Bailey?" Henderson continued his inquisition.

"Father, enough. Mr. Bailey rescued us." Olive's face flushed.

"I simply want an answer to why he was trespassing on my property."

Tabs rose, lowered his head, and placed his napkin on the table. "Miss Olive. I'm glad I helped you today, but I really must go."

"Yes, you must," growled Henderson.

"No, you must not." Olive stood also. Her blue eyes were icy slits, daring her father to protest. "At least listen to Mr. Bailey's side of the story before you cast him into the frigid night."

Henderson stared at Olive. "Olive, since this is your first evening back at the table, I'll indulge you. All right, on with it, Mr. Bailey."

Tabs looked at Olive questioningly, she held her breath and shook her head. "There's nothing to tell," Tabs answered. "I met Miss Olive and Mr. Ben at the drugstore. I knew they had the wagon and ran the risk of an incident due to the snow. I walked out to ensure their safety."

"Pray tell, why are you so concerned about my family that you would venture out in these elements?"

Tabs inhaled, waited a moment to compose himself, then began. "If you must know..." Tabs found Henderson's eyes, hesitated, then continued. "I care deeply for Miss Olive." Olive gasped at this revelation. "I have for—"

"So, you *were* intentionally following her?" Henderson taunted gruffly.

"Yes, sir, but only to safeguard her. No other reason. Had she found her way home safely, my intent was to simply turn around and walk back to Campbellsville."

"Without announcing yourself at the house?" Henderson badgered.

"Yes, sir." Tabs puffed his chest. "Do not mock me, sir. I mean Miss Olive no harm."

"Back to my question. How old are you, Bailey?"

"Twenty-six."

Henderson choked on his food. "Eleven years older than Olive." Tabs gasped. "Good God, you're an old man."

"Yes." He hesitated before adding, "Admittedly, I thought Olive to be at least seventeen. Her tender age is a shock." He raised an eyebrow as he glanced at Olive. "I am also a poor man, so I admire Miss Olive from afar. She deserves a suitable husband; sadly, I am not that candidate."

Olive's mouth dropped at Tabs's revelation. Sally snickered and whispered to Clyde. Bessie kicked Ben under the table, and Benny opened his mouth as much as his broken nose permitted.

"Father, please stop this conversation." Olive's voice cracked. Henderson ignored her, looking directly at Tabs.

"Well, Mr. Bailey, we finally have come to a mutual agreement. She *does* deserve a suitable husband, not the likes of you. From this day forward, you shall leave my daughter alone. No more trinkets under the Christmas tree, no more Harvest Festival dancing, no more stalking. Are we agreed?"

"We are agreed, sir." Tabs moved towards the foyer.

Henderson called after him. "Stay, eat. You shall leave in the morning, when the weather clears." Turning away to address Ben concerning the farm matter, the conversation with Tabs was considered concluded.

Tabs sat again and ate in silence, head hung, food catching in his throat. He resisted the urge to scratch his wool-irritated legs and feet, not wanting to fidget. Cook served dessert herself, enjoying a peek at the unlikely visitor. As she placed apple pie à la mode in front of Tabs, he shook his head no, then rose.

"Mr. Westchester, thank you for your hospitality. I shall be leaving. Miss Olive, may I have my clothing?" Tabs faced Olive, ready to say goodbye.

"*Your* clothing? What are you wearing?" Another annoyance for Henderson.

"Sir, I passed on a double shift to come directly from the foundry in my soiled work clothes. Miss Olive generously loaned me these items to don after my bath, so that I may be presentable at the table."

"You took a bath here? Olive, have you lost all sensibility? Whose clothes are these?" Henderson waved his arm up and down Tabs as if highlighting a display.

"Father, be generous. Mr. Bailey has on a few of Levi's old high school items, from the attic. All the men in this family are too tall for them. We should have donated them long ago, anyway."

"Mr. Westchester, I do not want your charity. I shall return the clothing."

"Grandfather." Benny mustered courage, then stammered, "Mr. Bailey rescued both of us. It's my fault that we went to town. Olive kindly kept me company. We may have avoided trouble had we not waited for the crate—but then again, that was my decision. Blame me, not Mr. Bailey." Benny felt his underarms sweating. Turning to Tabs, he continued, "Mr. Bailey, thank you for your help. I am deeply appreciative."

Tabs nodded. Henderson stared.

"Let me make one thing clear." Hands on her hips, Olive leaned over the table, peering at her father. "Mr. Bailey is welcome to the clothing, the bath, and the meal. Mr. Bailey shall spend the night, eat a warm breakfast, then borrow a horse to take him into town tomorrow."

"Miss Olive..." Tabs stopped mid-sentence as Olive placed her hand on top of his. Tabs, visibly shaken by her action, withdrew his hand immediately, although not before all diners noticed. Alarmed, Henderson's eyes shot daggers at Olive. "Enough. All of you. This conversation is over!" Olive declared, then retook her seat, never moving her gaze from her father.

Henderson paused. Clenching his teeth, he viewed his wife's portrait, then scrutinized Olive. *Damn you, Polly.* To Tabs's surprise, after several moments of father-daughter eye contact, Henderson complied with his youngest daughter's wishes.

"What's in that damnable crate? Do you know?" Still gruff, Henderson switched topics, grilling Benny, then Olive. "That box is the size of a coffin."

HOPE CHEST

Three weeks of continuing snowfall created a substantial snowpack and the perfect winter wonderland for the holiday season. Two sleighs, draped with boughs of greenery, transported the Westchesters to Christmas morning services. They now awaited the return ride home.

"Come on, Benny, stop dilly-dallying," Ben called to his son, as church bells echoed through the hollows and the choir sang *Joy to the World*. "Time to go."

Benny's head swiveled, searching the retreating congregation.

"Benny, she's not a Presbyterian, you dolt. Ingrid is German. She most likely attends the Lutheran church," Olive correctly interrupted.

Olive climbed onto the bench beside Sally and the children. Four-year-old Sinclair scrambled onto her lap. Bessie, Nellie, and—finally—Benny occupied the opposing bench, while Henderson, Ben, and Clyde enjoyed ample space in the second sleigh.

Tobias Bailey, waiting at the crossroads, motioned for Jake to slow the team. As they passed, Tabs whispered to Benny and handed him a small package.

"What was that all about?" asked Sally, belly protruding, leaving minimal room for the squirming, twenty-two-month-old baby Blossom.

"Nothing." Benny glanced at Olive, denying involvement. "Mr. Bailey inquired about my nose." Metal guard no longer necessary, Benny's face boasted two black eyes fading from purple to green.

"Santa, Santa!" chanted Sally's three children in unison.

"Yes, Santa visited last night. It's Christmas Day."

"Presents!" squealed Penny.

"Things never change, do they?" Bessie smiled gently. "The children make a holiday." She squeezed Benny's hand. "Perhaps I shall be a grandmother soon?"

"Mother!" Benny blushed. However, his ear-to-ear smile was a dead giveaway that he shared her dream.

A more beautiful winter day was hard to imagine. Sleigh bells, horse whinnies, and boisterous children created a festive mood for the journey home. Tommy, Tildy, Lizzy, and little Lucas arrived as the Westchester sleighs approached the house.

"Grandfather, may we go for a sleigh ride before dinner?" Lizzy, now ten, asked Henderson.

"Sounds like a reasonable request. Olive shall accompany the children." Henderson's false assumption was soon corrected.

"No, thank you," Olive said as she folded the blanket and placed it under the bench.

"Go with them, Olive. Penny, Sinclair, and Blossom will ride with Lizzy," Sally said, lifting Lizzy onto the seat.

"I said, 'no.'" Olive glared at Sally.

"Sinclair, ask Aunt Olive to go for another ride with you," Sally unwisely urged her son.

"Not a chance in hell!" Olive retorted. "I have better things to do than babysit a bunch of screaming kids."

"Olive, watch your mouth," Tildy said, never failing to criticize.

"Get the governess to take them—or Sally, why don't you go? Try something different; take care of your own children today." Olive jumped down from the sleigh and clomped inside.

"Olive, wait," called Benny, following her. "Why so melancholy? It's Christmas."

"Sally irritates me. She used me, pretending to be my friend, and still tries to use me to this day. Besides, I miss Fred and Sammy—mostly Fred," she answered, without looking at Benny. "I wish he wasn't so far away."

"This may cheer you." Benny slipped Olive a package wrapped in newsprint. "Hide it from Grandfather. It's from Tabs."

Olive stopped. Facing Benny, she discreetly slid the package into her muff.

"Thanks, Benny. Maybe you're not an ogre."

"Well, you're still a witch," Benny teased. "Merry Christmas, Brunhilda Westchester." Olive managed a smile.

Olive quickly shed her cape, muff, hat, gloves, and boots. Scaling the stairs two at a time, she closed her office door and tugged at the wrapping. A note read:

> To my dearest Olive,
>
> Now that my true feelings are revealed, I must continue my tradition of a small gift from my hands and heart.
>
> Merry Christmas.
>
> Tabs.

Hand-polished, perfectly matched river rocks adorned the top of a hair comb. Olive caressed the stones, contemplating the numerous hours taken to rub and tumble them into shiny, identical orbs. She lovingly placed the comb in her drawer, next to her mother's pearls.

Returning to the first floor, Olive encountered the large wooden crate, placed in the foyer's middle.

"What in the name of...?" Olive exclaimed, as Jake and Kendrick pried at the box using crowbars.

"The box is stamped 'DO NOT OPEN UNTIL CHRISTMAS.' It's Christmas." Jake's excitement grew as the family gathered to witness the unveiling.

"This better be good," grumbled Benny. "My nose still hurts."

"Oh, but I imagine Ingrid Mueller fusses over it," goaded Ben Sr. as he boxed his son's ear.

Finally, all four sides of the outer crate lay open, revealing one small wooden box and a second sizable container.

"Is this a practical joke?" Henderson's patience waned as his stomach growled. "Get on with it, then. Open them both."

The smaller box contained multiple wrapped gifts addressed to each family member. As Jake called out names, Olive's mood soured, not hearing hers. The larger of the inside boxes was labeled *"Handle with care, open gently."*

"I'm too hungry to wait. Let's eat first. That damnable box will have to wait a little longer." Henderson took his seat at the table, nodded to the staff, and dinner was served. Family members scrambled over pieces of wood and scrap to take their places.

"Jake, go ahead and finish the job, then be off to celebrate with your family." Henderson yelled the order from the dining room, as a second thought.

During dinner, the decibel level verged on deafening as women cackled, children squealed, and men snorted.

"I have news," declared Tildy. "I'm expecting again in July. We just found out."

"Another baby? And Sally's expecting, too!" Henderson wiped his eyes. His attempt in hiding his delight was futile.

"Don't you dare decide to deliver on the same day again. I swear I'll leave you on your own," Olive said dryly. Laughter resonated in the room.

The children's anticipation having reached a maximum threshold, the family strolled through the empty foyer and into the parlor for gifts. Twinkling tree lights, stacks of presents, eggnog, and one massive, decorated chest, with *"Olive"* carved on the front, awaited them.

"What is that?" asked Lizzy.

Olive lifted the hinged lid to find cedar lining, a wrapped package, and a letter from Fred. She read aloud,

> *To my dear darling baby sister,*
>
> *It is time for you to fill a hope chest with your trousseau in preparation for marriage. You are a beautiful fifteen-year-old woman. After you finagle your way through college—and I know you shall—young men shall be lining up to ask for your hand; you must be ready. Look to the heart of the chest for clarity.*
>
> *With enduring love,*
> *Fred.*

"What a strange note," Tildy said as she ran her fingers over the wood, carved with eagles, buffalo, antelope, and antlers. "I bet he found this in Mexico; how exotic!"

Olive gazed at the spectacle. Tears fell down her cheeks. She opened the small package that was inside to find a pair of salt and pepper shakers fashioned in the shape of cacti.

"Merry Christmas, Freddy. I love you," Olive murmured as she blew her nose.

"Fred has the right idea; it is time to start thinking about an appropriate dowry and a husband for you, Olive." Henderson jumped at the opportunity to promote marriage.

"For goodness' sake, Father, marry off Benny or Nellie before you start on me. They are older. And like Fred said, I'm going to school first," Olive grumbled.

Henderson ignored Olive. "Clyde, Ben, Benny, take this monstrosity up to Olive's room, please. There is no room in the parlor for a chest plus all the people of this growing family. Make space for the children to run." Flinging his arms in the air, Henderson chuckled as he boomed, "It's Christmas!" as the children climbed on his lap, looking for candy and gold coins.

Olive directed furniture placement to accommodate the dower chest. Lingering, she pondered the meaning of Fred's note. She ran her hand over the wood, looking for an inconsistency. By manipulating the cedar lining, Olive discovered the key in a tiny hole just big enough for a finger. She slipped her finger underneath, and by pulling up, the board shifted, revealing a narrow space below deep enough to hold important papers. She found another two more notes here. However, a false drawer front suggested a larger hidden compartment. She read one note, and stashed the other in her dresser drawer.

Clever girl. Go further, and you shall find a concealed lower compartment that contains my entire life's savings, about $4,000. Please keep it safe for me. Do not show it to anyone, especially our greedy siblings; instead, use it to pay for your schooling. Hire a private tutor to help with high school, then consider college at either Vassar or Barnard. Both are in New York, that you love so much. I have no current need of this money; you may repay me after you graduate.

Merry Christmas.

Fred

∞∞∞

"Olive, come down. The children are waiting to open their gifts," Sally called as she pranced at the bottom of the staircase.

"I see Olive remains the drama queen." Tildy ticked her tongue and shook her head as Tommy and Clyde shrouded rolling eyes.

With her mood improved, Olive carried her Victrola gramophone into the parlor. "Instead of the piano, I thought we'd listen to recordings this year." She cranked the machine and placed the needle on the disc. Crackling sound drifted from the top megaphone. "This is an amazing invention," she said. After pouring herself some eggnog, she sat back to observe the family enjoying the day.

"Yippie!"

"Hooray!"

"What fun!"

"Merry Christmas!"

ANTICIPATION

SPRING, 1917

*H*enderson sat at the table eating alone, allowing Ben and Clyde to tend to the earliest chores.

Olive stormed into the room, interrupting Henderson's breakfast. "Are you reading the papers? They sank another merchant ship. The Germans are going to pull us into this God-forsaken war yet."

Henderson briefly paused chewing his bacon. "Olive, what are you rambling about?"

"The blasted war. Do you read the paper at all?"

"Yes, but the *Madison Gazette* is limited, and the *Campbellsville Herald* doesn't cover world news."

"Here," Olive threw her copy of *The New York Times* at her father. "Read this; you may learn something."

"My God, you are insolent! You grow more bitter every day." Egg yolk dripped off the paper as Henderson lifted it from his plate.

"Why wouldn't I? You stifle me, Fred—my only friend on this earth—is in constant danger, and the whole world has gone mad warring each other. Simply mad!"

"Thinking the world is crazy doesn't give you permission to be mean and angry," Henderson scolded. "How are you reading *The New York Times*? When did you subscribe to this?"

"I ordered it when Fred graduated from West Point. I decided to broaden my civics education, not that there is anyone in this family with whom I may discuss world issues."

Henderson studied Olive's face, the lines of her mouth, the roundness of her eyes, and the slope of her nose. "You are so much like your mother."

"Well, I did not expect that comment. I'm talking about the war, yet you bring up Mother. Yes, I look like her."

"Not just her beauty, but her resolve."

Polly was a bull-headed beast, just like you, Henderson thought. *It took every ounce of extra energy to tether her to the light.*

"Well, Olive, if you permit me to read your paper after you are finished each morning, perhaps we shall have grounds for conversation other than farm finances." Henderson excused himself from the table, mood sullied. Olive remained, brooding over the news.

∞∞∞∞

The afternoon mail brought a surprise letter from Fred. It was addressed to Henderson, not Olive. Seeing the message, Olive grabbed it. Holding it in the air, she ran into Henderson's office.

"Open this, now! I can't believe he wrote to you and not to me—he hates you! What does it say?" Olive's morning agitation increased from the lack of her own letter.

"What? Who hates me, and why?" Henderson frowned at Olive.

"This is from Fred. He did not write to me; he wrote to you." Olive tossed the envelope at her father, hitting him on the face and leaving his skin nicked.

"For God's sake! Settle down, Olive; I'll allow you to read it after I do." Henderson wiped a drop of blood from his face. "You need to control that anger inside of you!"

Using a silver, monogrammed opener, Henderson slit the envelope open and began reading silently.

Father,

I write to you, today, instead of Olive. My news will be upsetting to her; I am asking you to soften the blow. The Germans have been in contact with the Mexican government to form an alliance against the United States. Britain intercepted the telegram; Wilson knows. Most likely, he shall declare war on the Germans before the week is out. To that end, General Pershing is to be transferred from the Mexican Expedition to lead American forces in France.

I shall be promoted to First Lieutenant, travel with him to Europe, and lead my own squad, I assume in the trenches. We leave immediately. I have no opportunity to visit before my reassignment.

This may be my last letter for a while, so I feel the need to make my feelings known. In the past, I failed to find the courage to express my real feelings to you. Here is the truth. I never wanted to attend West Point, and I only did so because of your command. I despise you for it. I hate war, fighting...all I ever wanted to do was write. I serve, forced by you, to honor the Westchester name, and to preserve my country. Levi shall, as he always does, escape this horror due to his role in JAG.

I try to convince myself that I shall not fall victim to others' decisions, however, every day I seem to be less in control of my fate.

Prepare the farm and family for what is to come. Perhaps bring in extra supplies. Europe is a mess. I have no idea how this war shall proceed.

Now, as to my dear sister...Olive is more fragile than you think. Despite her sharp tongue and crusty exterior, she is lost. Please show her some kindness and support her desire to attend college. Such a beautiful child should not be tarnished by the lack of love she desperately seeks.

Today, I am somber, fearing my future. Tell my family I love them, and I fight for our way of life. Tell my darling Olive that she

shall be the shining light that helps me endure each day, for I know
I shall encounter hardship beyond imagination.

    Fred

Henderson placed the letter on his lap. Staring straight ahead, he mumbled an inaudible, "What have I done to my son?" He buried his face in his hands.

"Give it to me! You promised. I insist that I be allowed to read Fred's letter," Olive shouted at Henderson. He did not hand over the paper; instead, he folded it, replacing it in the envelope.

"Olive, shut your mouth—and leave, please. I shall tell the family as one tonight at dinner."

Olive stood and stuck out her bottom lip, hands on her hips, waiting to see the letter.

"Olive, please leave." Henderson slowly rose, walked to the side table, and poured himself a brandy. "Close the door on your way out." Olive spun on her heel, then slammed the door.

Henderson sipped his drink, silently weeping.

∞∞∞∞

Olive joined the evening dinner table, waiting for Fred's news. The family chatted, but she sat silent.

Henderson cleared his throat several times before clinking his fork against his goblet. "Attention, everyone. I have an announcement." The conversation slowly diminished to one or two stray words.

"Fred sent me a communique today; he is headed to France." A collective inhale circled the table. "According to his privileged intel, Wilson shall be declaring war before the week's end."

Olive's eyes filled with tears. Without speaking, she hung her head, burying her face in her hands.

"Grandfather, I thought you said President Wilson is against the war?" Benny asked with dismay.

"Yes, my assumption was false. It seems the United States will join the rest of the world in this nonsensical war. Fred suggests that we make plans to bring in extra provisions as a preemptive measure."

"No one bothered to listen to my warnings," Olive spoke calmly. "I warned you as early as last year that our involvement was inevitable." She rose, pushing her chair away from the table. "Please excuse me. I am no longer hungry."

"Wait, Olive—I want to discuss this as a family," Henderson appealed. Olive laughed hysterically.

"Now you want to hear from us! Never in your life have you accepted an opinion other than your own. You are a stubborn, manipulative bully who rules this family like a dictator. If it weren't for you forcing Fred to attend West Point, he'd be safe. Forgive me for not obliging your request. I'll be in my office." Olive detoured through the kitchen, requested a small plate be sent to her room, and retreated up the back staircase.

Benny scanned Ben's face for a response to Henderson's announcement. "Father, I wish to propose marriage to Ingrid. If there is a chance of me going to war, I should like to have a wife waiting for my return."

"Don't be ridiculous." Henderson's brow furrowed, "No member of this household is going to war. Uncle James will intercede on our behalf."

"All the same, I'm ready for marriage." Benny blushed. Beseeching his mother's intervention, he continued. "Mother, may we plan a June wedding?"

"Benny, does Ingrid reciprocate these feelings?" Bessie smiled gently at her lovestruck son.

"I think so." Benny's beet red neck glowed.

"Then, by all means, propose. A June wedding shall be a delightful diversion," Ben Sr. agreed.

Henderson interrupted the chatter. "Sally, please retrieve Olive. I wish for her to participate in this discussion."

"Me? Father, not me please. Send someone else." Horror shone in Sally's wide eyes.

"Simply retrieve the girl," said Henderson.

"You want *me* to convince her to return? What makes you think she'll consider a request from me?" Sally grabbed Clyde's arm in desperation. "I'm not up to this. The baby is due soon; I don't want to upset it."

"Cowards," Henderson boomed. "I'll get her myself." He stormed up the front stairs, then burst into Olive's office.

"The door was closed for a reason. How rude not to knock." Olive looked up from her writing as Henderson crashed open the door.

"Olive, I demand you join us in the dining room."

"You *demand*? How appropriate." Olive clenched her teeth, seething. Gathering her papers, she stared directly into Henderson's eyes. "I'll rejoin you, and you shall listen to what I have to suggest. Go, I'll be right behind you."

Henderson mumbled to himself as he rejoined the family. *You'd be gone if I didn't rely on you so much.*

The family gazed in disbelief as Olive followed Henderson to her seat. Without waiting for an invitation, she began: "Listen closely and take mental notes. I'll not repeat this. Fred said prepare, so we shall do just that. Who knows if there'll be rationing? Most likely the government will petition each farm to feed the army, so we need to prepare to increase our personal food supplies.

"First off, Ben, have the men double the size of our vegetable garden. Benny, buy an extra twenty-five pounds sugar and salt each week until it becomes impossible to do so, plus canning jars. Another twelve dozen cases should help. I assume it will take the general public several months to realize that war creates a shortage of supplies. God knows it took this family long enough to accept an approaching war. Save every commercial glass jar with a lid. Buy extra paraffin each week to use in sealing jellies and jams. Also, withdraw extra cash each week from the bank. We don't want to run the bank, but we need to have extra bills on hand. Nellie, you and your mother clean out the cold room behind the kitchen. Great room for storage and staging area for extra supplies."

Olive glanced at the group, ensuring she commanded their attention before continuing.

"We'll be isolated on this farm," she continued. "With access to food that most will not have. Benny, if you are seriously in love with Ingrid, marry her now and bring her to the farm. Her family may be in danger after we enter the war. Nellie, do you have a beau?" She shook her head.

"Funny, while you were gone, I asked if I may marry Ingrid," Benny interjected, astonished with Olive's intuitive thinking. "Why will she be in danger?"

"They're German, Benny. People may lash out once we are at war. Discuss living arrangements with your parents. Sally and Clyde may have to relinquish one of their rooms. Even with another baby, three rooms are more than adequate to house your family. Benny, consider moving Ingrid into the main house for added protection."

Olive rambled instructions for another few minutes before stopping. The family gawked at her in silence, mouths open.

"Well, why is no one speaking?" Olive asked finally. Still no response.

Henderson thought carefully, then addressed the room. "Please do as Olive asks, and begin immediately. Add extra ammunition to that list, both for rifle and shotgun. Olive, please communicate with the household staff; Ben, do the same with Jake and Kendrick."

"Oh," Olive added, referring to the scribbles on her paper, "And buy yarn. We'll begin a daily knitting hour to replace our sewing klatch. Nellie, search the third floor for discarded, moth-eaten sweaters that may be unraveled. We'll reuse the wool. The rest of you scour your closets. Penny and Sinclair are capable of rolling string into balls. We can knit socks, scarves, and possibly sweaters; we'll send them to Fred's unit. Sally, contact Tildy and Lizzy. They can join the knitting group; Lizzy's old enough to knit a scarf."

Sally nodded; the rest were silent.

"Does anyone have additional comments? Ideas?" Olive asked the group.

"I'm sure you'll think of anything you've missed. Just like your mother," Henderson mused. "Alright, shall we eat?"

Most of the family picked at their dinner, too melancholy for hearty appetites. Leaving one by one in somber procession, they abandoned Henderson. He sat quietly, pushing his food around his plate as he looked at Polly's portrait.

Forgive me, Polly. I have failed our children.

41

WILSON'S CONSCRIPTION

*F*red's information proved reliable. The United States declared war on Germany on April 6th, 1917, immediately sending troop reinforcements to France. Campbell county, except for Westchester Farms, was in a state of shock.

The Westchesters prepared while Campbellsville remained unaffected, living the status quo. Benny and Ingrid organized a simple June wedding. Although Henderson objected to the venue, preferring the Presbyterian church and the farm, a ceremony was to take place at St. Martin's Lutheran Church, followed by a small reception of immediate family at the Campbellsville social hall.

Benny purchased additional supplies per Olive's design. The garden grew, animals were slaughtered, the meat was salted and stored. Nellie, overseeing the acquisition of yarn, new and recycled, established a daily knitting schedule of two hours. A stack of scarves and socks already piled high in the corner of the parlor.

Two weeks later, on April 19th, Sally, Clyde, Penny, Sinclair, and Blossom welcomed baby Phineas Westchester. Annoyed with yet another birth, Olive barricaded herself in her office and managed to avoid the ordeal of Sally's delivery.

∞∞∞∞

Benny's nuptials approached as the family welcomed June 1917.

"Good morning," Henderson greeted Ben Sr. and Olive at the breakfast table. He walked over to the sideboard and looked inside a chafing dish, finding scrambled eggs and fried potatoes. "Olive, what has you so engrossed in your paper?"

Olive slowly lowered *The New York Times*, a look of shock on her face. "Father, do you remember Conscription from the war between the states?"

"What a strange question. I was born in 1858; however, James spoke of it. You know he chose to serve rather than pay for a substitute to fight in his stead, even though the family certainly could afford to pay. Why do you ask?" Henderson cocked his head, staring at Olive through squinted eyes, he continued. "What are you reading?"

"Congress has abolished the old conscription method. In its place, they have created the Selective Service. All men aged twenty-one to thirty are required to enlist for military service." Olive bit her lower lip. "At least Benny is safe."

Henderson and Ben Sr. reached for the paper at the same time. "Please, may I read that article?" Henderson won the right and Olive offered it directly to her father.

"Well, this may change. The failed target of raising one million men prompted this bill." Henderson was interrupted by Benny entering the room.

"What target, Grandfather?" asked Benny.

"The government needs men to fight this blasted war. They have issued a mandatory enlistment," Henderson repeated.

Benny sat to prevent from falling over. "Me?"

"Not yet, son," Ben Sr. said. "Not yet. You are too young, Benny, and so far Clyde and I are too old."

Henderson winced as he handed the paper to Ben. "My guess is they will lower the age if their target isn't met by this second effort."

The men anxiously took turns reading the article in its entirety.

Worried looks and frowns passed from man to man, who now felt the same angst about the war as Olive.

With a sigh, Benny said, "I'm going to enlist, right after Ingrid and I are married. I'll get her settled in the house, and then I'll go do my part." Benny crossed his arms in front of his body in resolved determination.

"Son, don't do it. Wait until your age group is called," Ben pleaded.

"Father, our family has always heeded the call to service, starting with Great-great-great- however-many-greats-are-needed-Grandfather Colin. I intend to live up to our name, to earn it. I'm certain about this decision."

Leaving the men and Olive, Benny headed out to the fields to share the news with the fieldhands.

"How many of our thirty workers will this affect?" asked Olive. "We need to devise a strategy now. This will impact the harvest."

"Always the practical one." Ben looked disgustingly at his baby sister. "I'm risking a son to this war, and you talk about staffing issues."

"Don't you dare accuse me of not caring. My feelings and needs are deeper than any of you can fathom. You, *all* of you, with your lack of warmth and affection, have molded me to be pragmatic. Fred and Samuel are the only two who understand me. Benny may, also." The words sputtered from her mouth.

"Olive, you call your actions 'pragmatic?' I call them cold and callous. We have not yet had time to digest the impact." Ben grabbed his forehead with linked hands. "For Christ's sake, we're all not as *brilliant* as you!"

Henderson defended his son. "He's correct, Olive. Give it a minute to sink in. We'll get to farm hands soon enough."

Olive rambled on without heeding Henderson. "Well, the town is about to wake up and realize what is happening. Additional supplies shall become scarce. Maybe we can buy this week, but that's it. If it weren't for me, we'd all go hungry this winter. And not one word of thanks! You are pathetic."

She grabbed the newspaper from Henderson and stormed out of

the room; her deepest fears of her family's welfare remained unspoken.

∞∞∞∞

Olive's precise prognostication found Campbellsville in a state of chaos. Families scrambled, too late to stock up on essential supplies. Although absent rationing, the government confiscated all overstock to support the war effort.

Benny and Ingrid were married the next week. After a three-day honeymoon in Pittsburgh, Benny enlisted in the army, scheduled to report in two weeks. Fearing ostracization from their own family, Ben and Bessie determined it wiser for Ingrid to live in the cottage. The shy, chubby-cheeked girl proved helpful in the gardens, in the kitchen, and with the stitching.

Benny's departure day found the entire family on the train platform, wishing him health and safety.

"Son, I'm proud of you." Ben shook Benny's hand.

"Give me a hug, Father. I may not return," Benny said, as he embraced Ben.

"Don't even think that. You must be positive; think of your beautiful bride waiting for you."

"Absolutely!" Benny smiled as he slipped his arm around Ingrid. He planted a sloppy kiss on her mouth. She tried to suppress her tears.

Olive squeezed Benny's hand and said, "Be safe, you foolish dolt. I need you to return to help run this farm." Whispering in his ear, Olive promised, "This family is cold and cruel. I'll see that they don't mistreat your wife."

"Thanks, Olive; I truly love her." Before Benny returned her hug, Olive spotted Tobias Bailey among the multitude awaiting the train.

Olive ran the length of the platform to catch up to him, and when she did she asked, "Mr. Bailey, why are you in uniform?"

Tabs looked quizzically at Olive. "I thought you were the smart

Westchester." He smiled, then added, "I'm in uniform because I am heading to France."

She sucked in the sides of her face. "I'm sorry to see you here. Please be careful over there." Olive leaned over, kissed Tabs on the cheek, and handed him a photograph. "Would you like to take my photo with you? It was taken last year on my birthday. I was going to give it to Benny, but he has a new wife to compel him."

Tabs looked at Olive without taking the photo.

"Am I being presumptuous?" she asked. "You needn't feel obligated; I thought—"

Tabs reached for her hand. Bringing it to his lips, he took the photo. "It is more than I can ask for. I shall keep you next to my heart. Every day you shall spur me on. Miss Olive, may I request the honor of officially courting you, *if* I return?"

Olive searched his tender eyes. "Mr. Bailey, are you still infatuated?"

"No, Miss Olive. I am in love. Although I thought you much older, I have been in love since I first laid eyes on you five years ago." Tabs clutched her hands. "May I have an answer?"

Olive cocked her head to the side. No one other than Fred had ever admitted love for her. "We shall discuss that, Mr. Bailey, *when* you return. Please, you may call me Olive." She hesitated, then added, "And you better write, if you have the opportunity."

"Then please call me Tabs." Tabs pulled Olive close to him and kissed her long and passionately on the lips. His mouth tasted of salt, and his neck smelled of sweat. Olive closed her eyes, savoring her first kiss as a woman.

The train whistle blew, jolting Olive back to reality. Her body tingled from head to toe as she watched the uniforms climb on board. The Westchesters piled into their many vehicles and forgot to check for Olive, who remained at the far end of the station, lingering to watch the train curve around the last bend of the track. Coming back to her senses, Olive found herself alone on the platform.

Typical Westchester behavior, she thought as she began the four-mile walk back to the farm. *No matter.* She meandered home, studying the clouds, lost in her thoughts and fantasies.

42

ONLY THE BEGINNING

EARLY FALL, 1917

*T*he *war to end all wars* raged in Europe. Over sixty countries joined the fighting, on one side or the other. The United States sent ten thousand men a week in support of the allied forces. Olive, in her own war effort, generated a daily schedule that everyone followed. She also encouraged the women to actively read the news in order to stay equally abreast as the men of wartime developments.

Working in the foyer, Nellie finished sealing five crates filled with supplies for the troops as the other women packaged their knitted treasures.

"Fred reported in his last letter that winter in the trenches is cold and wet," Olive said. "We need to get these off to him now if we hope to reach him before Christmas."

"Did you see in the paper yesterday that for thirty-six dollars, we can sponsor a French child?" said newly educated Sally as she guided her twins, who were unraveling an old, knitted blanket.

"Why would we want to sponsor a French child?" asked Nellie.

Olive shook her head, continually amazed at the Westchester women's lack of knowledge. "Because France has been fighting the

German bastards since 1914. Sorry Ingrid, no offense meant. Many French men have already perished, leaving children orphaned."

"My family has lived in Pennsylvania for eighty years. I'm not German; I'm second-generation American." Ingrid, always smiling, flashed white teeth at Olive.

"But Olive, watch your language in front of the children," Sally scolded. Olive harrumphed. "Back to the orphans. I think I'll sponsor one."

"Why don't we all sponsor an orphan?" suggested Bessie.

"I'll add money from Fred. Who wants to contact Levi and Ginny? Eight is better than five," Olive said as Nellie nailed the lid on a crate.

"You're assuming Tildy will participate."

"You're right," Tildy said, as she and Lizzy entered the room. Little Lucas and her newest baby, Marie, were gathered by the governess to play in the nursery with Blossom and Phineas. "On that subject, what *is* Tildy supposed to participate in?"

"We are sending money to help all the French orphans," Sally explained.

"Count me in," Tildy said. "I can't imagine my darlings orphaned, losing their father to war. It's all just so heartbreaking to think about all the men dying."

Ingrid turned her head, hiding the tears forming behind her eyes. Her gaze matched Bessie's.

"Tildy, watch your words," Olive warned. "I'm in no mood for your ignorant attitude today."

"What? I said nothing wrong," insisted Tildy.

"Take care when speaking of our soldiers." Olive scowled.

"Yes ma'am, Madame Dictator." Tildy marched to the opposite side of the room, took out her needles, and began knitting.

As the women worked, one of the maids entered the parlor holding the day's mail. "I have a letter for Miss Ingrid and two for Miss Olive."

"Splendid, maybe Fred has good news," Olive said. Scanning the return address, she corrected her statement. "Well, this is from

Samuel, not Fred. Let's see how it goes in Philadelphia." Olive tore open the envelope and read. "It seems Aunt Clare has succumbed to a bad cold or flu. Her funeral was a week ago Friday. Ginny's services are no longer needed to run the house, and Aunt Clare's son is selling the property. Samuel is unsure if her son will continue to fund his tuition."

Tildy's interest was piqued. "Do you think Ginny will consider returning to Campbellsville? I'd love to see her again."

"Return? Do you not remember Father's reaction when she announced she was leaving?" Olive questioned her sister. "He was none too happy. If Ginny is smart, she'll find a job and stay out east."

"I suggest that rather than speculate, we wait for Ginny to contact Father. Let her make a move before we spoil any chance she may have," Bessie offered.

"I agree with Bessie; we should keep quiet. Poor Samuel. I hope he finds a way to finish school." Olive could relate to the fate of her nephew, who was now a sophomore in high school.

Engrossed in her letter, Ingrid paid little attention to the conversation. When she finished reading, she looked at Bessie, broke into tears, then ran out of the room. Confused, Bessie followed her.

"I wonder what that was all about?" asked Sally. "Olive, who sent the other correspondence?"

"None of your business." Olive looked at the foreign postmark dated a month earlier. She recognized the handwriting, but could not recall the owner. However, she knew it was not Fred's. "Ladies, please continue your work. I shall return shortly." Olive retreated to her office to read the letter privately.

My dearest Olive,

You have no idea how happy I am to address you as such. My ocean journey was most uncomfortable. We were cramped below deck, in a foul-smelling mesh of humanity. The crossing took a total of ten days.

This is my first opportunity to write. I am in the trenches at a place called Passchendaele in Flanders, Belgium. I'm not sure why I'm here, since it's mostly British and Canadians, very few French or Americans.

God, it's wet here. It rains almost every day. The trenches are mud pits. Sometimes the mud gushes over my boots. My feet are soaking wet, with no opportunity to dry them out. Already I have sores on the soles of my left foot. Besides intense fighting, there is a sickness spreading among the men.

I'm sorry to burden you with my complaints. Forgive me. Know that I keep your picture close to my heart and I think of you daily. You are the reason I go on. Please write, darling Olive. Any news from you shall serve to cheer me for weeks on end.

With devoted adoration.

Tabs

Olive sat on the bed, gazing into space for several moments before folding the letter. She replaced it in the envelope after copying the return address, and started a third pile in her drawer. Returning to the parlor, she grabbed five pairs of socks, three scarves, and one sweater from the stack waiting to be packaged.

"I want this smaller parcel to be mailed separately," she requested. "It goes to Belgium, not France."

"Who's the special person to warrant a sweater?" asked Tildy. Olive stared without responding. Thinking about the horrendous conditions shared in Tabs's letter, she wondered what he meant by intense fighting and what he neglected to disclose. After several minutes of pondering, Olive addressed the women.

"Ladies, we must knit faster."

43

JUST SMILE

*C*hristmas 1917 was a somber event. Compared to previous years, the family ate a modest French-themed meal of country cassoulet, crusty bread, cheese, and canned fruit for dessert. Gifts were relegated to children only; the money equivalent for adult gifts was spent supporting the war effort and a second round of orphan sponsorship.

Olive's crates arrived in France, although the family remained unaware. Fred, promoted to Captain, claimed a beautiful cable knit scarf and a pair of soft socks for himself. The smell of the wool and the fineness of the stitching generated dreams of his family who knitted them. He distributed Christmas gifts of dry socks and scarves to appreciative men in his company. News of Captain Westchester's generosity was coveted by the men from other companies—although his gifts did provoke several minor skirmishes over the ownership of a particular style of socks.

Winter turned to spring, and the farm life cycle began anew. Westchester Farms lost about a dozen men to the draft; however, those remaining gladly worked longer and harder to compensate for the fighting patriots. The women continued to knit daily.

Henderson, Ben, and Olive eagerly embraced the new season, innocuously equating spring with new birth and the end of the war.

"Have either of you received letters from our brave soldiers?" asked Clyde at breakfast. Ingrid, always on the verge of crying, shook her head no.

"My last note from Fred arrived over a month ago. I write to him weekly," Olive offered.

"What about your 'special friend?'" Clyde snickered.

"If you are referring to Tobias Bailey, I write to him weekly out of duty to a patriotic friend." Olive sneered. "I also write to Benny. Why must this family be so antagonistic toward each other?"

"Just teasing, Little Sister. *You're* the overly sensitive one." Clyde threw Ben an eye-rolling glance.

Olive glared at her brother for a minute, then diverted her attention to her pancakes.

"Benny's enlistment was a required twelve months, wasn't it?" Clyde asked Ben. "He should be coming home in a couple months, God willing." Ingrid burst into tears, running out of the room. "That poor girl is skittish as a cat.".

"Maybe if you chose more delicate topics to discuss, she'd settle down a little," Olive chastised.

"All you women are difficult. I give up," announced Clyde.

"Spoken like a true Westchester. Don't try to understand the issue, just ignore it." Olive threw her hands into the air mockingly. "All you men are asses. I give up."

She left the table smiling, knowing Ben and Clyde missed her sarcasm and remained cluelessly puzzled.

∞∞∞∞

Farm life maintained some semblance of normality over the next several months. Tildy and Sally's children grew strong and healthy. The twins turned five. In mid-June, a letter arrived for Ingrid reporting Benny's service requirement fulfilled. The girl's mood improved daily as she awaited word of his return.

By the second week of July, Ingrid's nerves began to unravel again due to no news from Benny. Often she sat alone on the grapevine swing with her knitting. One morning, as she stitched on the swing, the wool yarn caused skin irritation from the hot sun and high humidity. Ingrid ignored the itch, knitting frantically, thinking only of Benny. She hummed quietly to calm herself. After several minutes, she noticed someone humming with her. The man's voice came from behind.

She turned in the direction of the sound, then screamed. "Benny! Oh, Benny, it's really you!"

Benny smiled and leaned over to kiss his wife, a sweet, lingering embrace. Then, sitting on the swing beside her in silence, he stroked her hand and lay his head on her shoulder.

"Tell me about your journey back! Why didn't you write to say you were coming? Who brought you from the train station? Do you want a glass of iced tea?" The questions spewed nonstop from Ingrid. Benny sat silent, humming and holding his wife's hand, staring at the garden.

At dinner, the family plus the Jamisons fussed over a reluctant Benny. Ben and Bessie squeezed him tightly. Benny averted his eyes without returning their hugs.

"Welcome home, son."

"Tell us, how was it?"

"Were you anyplace near Fred?"

"Did you visit Paris?"

"How do French girls dress?"

"Did you bring home souvenirs?" Tildy, Sally, and Nellie pried.

Benny only smiled, saying nothing. Olive sat quietly, biting her lip, contemplating Benny's lack of words.

"Maybe we should give Benny a chance to adjust to being back home?" Bessie suggested after ten minutes of intense grilling without answer. "I wonder when Mr. Bailey is returning?" Bessie asked, deliberately diverting the conversation away from her son. "He joined the same time as Benny, didn't he, Olive?"

Olive interrupted her thoughts to answer. "Yes, don't you remember? You stranded me on the platform."

"Did we?" asked Bessie. Olive rolled her eyes.

Henderson took control, interrogating Clyde and Ben about plans to cover the staffing shortage. "Did you see in the paper that they are expanding the age range for the draft—I assume to compensate for the men who have met their twelve-month requirement? The age is now eighteen to forty."

Sally and Bessie gasped. "Clyde, you are thirty-five," Sally whispered.

"Ben is thirty-eight," moaned Bessie.

"Don't worry, girls," Olive advised. "They are issuing dispensation to family men, and Clyde certainly has a big enough family. Ben is too old, with a family, and running a major government supply farm. Father's influence benefits *some* of his family, at least."

∞∞∞∞

Another week passed as harvest approached quickly. Five additional farm hands were called to the draft. Benny spent each day quietly sitting on the swing, humming to himself. Ingrid fretted privately, gladly joining him most days. The couple never spoke, only held hands.

"I'm going to town to see if I can round up some returning veterans looking for temporary work," Henderson said at dinner. "Benny, care to join me?" Benny smiled, and looked down at his plate, saying nothing. He shook his head *no*. "Dear Grandson, you must start living again." Turning to Ben, Henderson asked, "Does he speak at home?"

"No, Father. He sits calmly, smiling, holding Ingrid's hand." Ben wrung his hands together. "I think I need to call Dr. Paulson."

"Give him some more time, please," Bessie asked. "He'll come out of it when he's ready."

The conversation was disrupted by a knock at the front door. The housemaid answered and ushered a man into the foyer.

"Miss Olive, you have a visitor," announced the maid. Olive responded with indifference.

"Are you expecting anyone at this hour?" Henderson, annoyed, disliked mealtime interruptions.

"No. I'll just be a minute."

A stunned Olive entered the foyer to find a uniformed soldier waiting with a bouquet of hand-picked flowers. Tobias Bailey leaned on a cane. Removing his hat, he graciously bowed.

Olive stared dumbfounded before asking, "Mr. Bailey, what are you doing here?"

"Olive! May I still call you 'Olive?'" Tabs grinned, handing Olive the flowers. He kissed her on the cheek; she flinched and jerked away. Releasing a deep sigh, he stepped back, taking in her full view. "You are more beautiful than I remember. You inspired my will to live on most days."

"Mr. Bailey!" Olive exclaimed, as the family gawked from the dining room passageway.

"I hope you'll address me as 'Tabs.'" His brow furrowed at Olive's formality.

"Well, if it isn't Mr. Tobias Bailey," Henderson said with a smirk. "Is that a cane, I see? Were you injured?"

"Nothing serious, sir. A piece of shrapnel from an exploded mortar. I'll live."

"Yes, but will you be able to work? From the looks of this exchange, you still have an interest in my daughter."

"That I do. I am extremely interested in your daughter. I arrived home just this evening and walked from the station. I wanted to see Olive before I greeted anyone else." A perplexed Olive blushed at Tabs's declaration.

"So, Mr. Bailey, considering your correspondence throughout the war, do you intend to ask my permission to court my daughter?"

"Yes, sir, that is my intent." Tabs looked at Olive lovingly.

"Will you be able to provide for her?"

"Yes, I shall provide. Not the elaborate lifestyle she is accustomed to living here, however, I promise she shall never want for love or food. That is, if you and she are in agreement." Tabs searched Olive's face for confirmation. She stared blankly at her father.

"Mr. Bailey, it is your lucky day, for I *am* in agreement."

Olive gasped at the remark.

"Since she seems to be in no hurry to find a husband for herself, it's time for me to do it for her, to push my baby bird out of the nest and into the world." Henderson reached to shake Tabs's hand. "I find no other suitors pursuing her. It seems you win the prize."

"You want rid of me." Olive clenched her teeth. "You're going to saddle me with a husband? How can I make my own way if I'm tied down?"

Henderson burst into laughter. "Are you sure, Mr. Bailey, that you want this spit-fire as your wife? Speak now, for this is your chance to walk away."

Tabs walked over to Olive, took both her hands in his, and said, "I am very sure. I've been in love with you for six long years. Courting you, with the hope of marriage, is the delight of my world." Again, Tabs kissed Olive on the cheek. Again, Olive pulled away.

"Come in, sir, and join us for dinner. Tonight, we celebrate." Henderson clapped Tabs on the back, ordered an extra place set at the table, and welcomed him to eat.

"That's it?" asked Olive. "This is decided between the two of you? Do I have no say in the matter?" Olive looked at her father, then Tabs. "I haven't agreed to any of this."

Henderson stared at his daughter. "My dear Olive, you *had* a say in your future, but you refused to act on it. You were encouraged to attend a finishing school, with the chance to meet more suitable beaus as a debutante. You declined to take that path. Now it is up to me to secure your future. Your communication with Mr. Bailey was friendly. He has made an offer, which I accept. The deal is done."

"You are going to marry me off to Mr. Bailey just because I wrote to him and I have no other male suitors?" Olive shook her head.

Tabs halted, hearing Olive's objection. "Olive, you agreed before I left to fight that I may ask for the right to court. Does this no longer please you?"

"I agreed that we could discuss the idea. It was not a done deal," she stammered.

"Well, darling Daughter, it is a done deal now." Henderson urged Tabs forward.

"Olive, darling, are you displeased?" Tabs asked.

Olive glowered first at Henderson, then at Tabs, her nose and lips pulled into a deformed pucker. After several minutes of staring she said, "Let's eat. I'm hungry," without addressing Tabs's question.

44

M IN THE FIRST DEGREE

everal days passed with Olive still in shock over her fate. She thought back to Fred's comments about avoiding being a victim. Determined to find a suitable solution to her dilemma —despite feeling like a casualty of war—she rummaged through Levi's discards as she planned her escape.

"Nellie, will you help me today?" Olive asked her niece.

"What do you need? Ingrid and Mother are going to town. I promised to keep an eye on Benny."

"I want to sort through some of Levi's old clothing to give to Tabs. He is coming to visit on Sunday. If I'm forced to marry him, he may as well look presentable." Olive scoffed.

"If we bring the boxes from the attic to the swing, I can help. Benny spends most days swinging and humming." Nellie giggled nervously. "Sorting clothes will keep me from worrying about Benny."

"Has he seen Dr. Paulson?"

"Yes, the doctor called it shell shock. He prescribed patience and understanding. He said each man reacts differently to war; Benny is coping by not talking." Nellie scrunched her lips together, contemplating a change in subject. "Olive, may I ask you a question?"

"That depends on the question."

"I, too, waited to attend a finishing school, but I think I shall enroll now. I don't want Grandfather or Father to choose an unsuitable husband, like Mr. Bailey, for me. What do you think? Should I go?"

Olive grimaced. "You dare insult me, then ask my advice? This whole family is crazy. You tend to Benny; I'll sort clothing alone." Olive spun on her heel.

"Olive, I'm sorry!" Nellie sputtered.

Olive never heard the apology; she was already clomping up two staircases. She settled in the least warm corner of the steamy third floor.

After ten minutes of intense sweating, she repacked the crates and dragged them down to the cooler foyer. The open front and back doors created a cross breeze. Sitting on the floor in the middle of the large space, Olive unpacked her crates. She sorted the clothing by size, then by like items, making a dozen piles. *At least I have some suitable garments to give to Tabs,* she thought. *Not that a well-dressed man makes me any more excited to be married.*

A knock came to the door as she worked. Usually, the housemaid answered, but this time Olive jumped up and greeted the stranger.

"I have a telegram, Miss, for Henderson Westchester. Is he here?" the stranger said.

"Henderson is my father. He's in the barn. I'll deliver this to him." Olive reached for the paper as she pulled a few coins from her apron pocket to tip the messenger.

"Thank you. Much obliged. Sorry for your loss." The stranger took the money and walked off the porch.

Wait, what do you mean, "sorry for your loss?" Olive unfolded Henderson's telegram to read:

Dear Mr. Westchester,

We regret to inform you that your son, Captain Frederick Westchester, gave the ultimate sacrifice to the flag and his country when he perished in battle on July 18, 1918. You have our deepest sympathies and gratitude.

Newton D. Baker
Secretary of War

Olive read and reread the short communique five times before collapsing with a thud on the floor. Her heart shattered into a billion pieces, then evaporated, leaving an empty hole in her chest. Greif wretched her stomach; she gagged, then rolled into a fetal position. She grasped her knees, rocking herself back and forth. Eyes burned dry, stinging from the pain that radiated from her head; unable to cry or scream, she continued her dystonic sway. Cook, hearing noise, entered the foyer to investigate. She rushed outside to comfort the girl.

"Miss Olive, what is the matter?"

Moaning in distress, Olive continued to rock, clutching the telegram.

"Jake, Kendrick, Mr. W. come quickly! Olive is having a seizure," Cook yelled as she ran to the barn. The men hurried back to the house to find Olive in the same position as when Cook left.

"Olive," Henderson asked cautiously, "What has come over you?"

Hearing her father's voice, Olive snapped out of her trance. She sat up, tears flowing in torrents from her eyes. Her body trembled. Finding her voice, she screamed, "You! Murderer! You are to blame!"

"Whatever do you mean?" asked Henderson.

Olive scrambled to her feet, charging at her father. Clashing into him at full speed, she pounded his chest using both fists. The thuds echoed. Henderson grabbed Olive's arms, holding them away from his body.

"You selfish son of a bitch! You killed him. He hated you, hated the Army! You and Uncle James, with your agreements over wheat and corn. Fred would be alive if it weren't for your greed!"

Her words registered. "Fred would what?" Henderson held his breath, tears welled behind his eyes.

"He's dead, you bastard! Killed in battle. I hate you; I hate you!" Olive kicked her father's shin. "I shall never speak to you again."

She sank back to the floor, arms extended in Henderson's grasp. She wept and wailed until her throat went raw, no longer capable of making a sound. Henderson released her, and she re-tucked her knees into her arms.

Henderson melted into a rocking chair, holding his head. He sat stoically.

Olive lay on the porch floor, not able to move, not able to cry. News of Fred's death spread quickly among the family. Ben and Clyde went to Henderson.

"Father," Ben said, placing his arm around Henderson's shoulder. "Come, let's get you inside."

Henderson rubbed his face and mumbled, "My darling son."

Clyde took hold of Henderson's left side while Ben held the right. Together, they escorted their father inside to his office. Henderson sat at his desk, head down; Ben handed him a drink, then covered his shoulders with an afghan. Despite it being summer, Ben stoked a small fire to keep Henderson from going into shock, then left him to grieve alone.

The lamenting women feebly approached Olive. Sally and Nellie sat taking turns rubbing her back to no avail. Bessie brought out tea for the group who stayed on the porch with the distraught girl.

"Olive, sweetie, please sit up," Sally pleaded, her facial features stretched with concern.

Nellie tried to take Olive's hand, but Olive tucked it further underneath her body. Olive remained unresponsive, rolled in a ball, rhythmically rocking and moaning.

Benny, hearing the news, stopped smiling and humming. Joining Olive on the front porch, he lay on the floor beside her. Snuggling close, he scooped Olive in his arms and held her tightly.

For the first time in weeks, Benny finally spoke, whispering in her ear, "Don't fret, Olive. Over there, death is better than life. I know the hell he suffered. Trust me when I say, Fred is the lucky one. Death is a blessing."

Thirty words. Benny and Olive lingered, curled together on the porch throughout the night, bound by friendship, bound by pain, bound by an inexplicable grief.

Ingrid came out as the sun set. She covered them with a blanket to ward off the night's chill. After draping the front door in black cloth, she sat in the rocker, wrapping herself in a second blanket, keeping guard of her beloved husband and Olive.

45

DELILAH

Olive remained in her room for the rest of the week, refusing to eat, work, or bathe. Her usually shiny curly hair clumped in greasy strings. None of the family, including a now vocal Benny, enticed her to join the living. She sat in her room, staring at the many books given by and shared with Fred. Letters removed from envelopes were strewn haphazardly around the room as Olive's stained face tearfully read each one.

On day two, Olive removed an unopened letter from the bottom of her cache—Fred's message, sent to her when he was in Mexico, the second note found in the hope chest. It was addressed, "To Olive, in the event I never return." Her hands trembled as she unsealed the envelope. The slight scent of Fred's aroma lingered on the paper. Olive inhaled, allowing it to fill her lungs before she began reading.

Dearest Sister,

I truly hope that you are old and wrinkled when reading this. If you are not, then I have died before my time, which saddens me. I know you are hurting and lost, not having a mother to nurture you. I pledge to shower you with brotherly friendship and love to last a lifetime. Hopefully, I may spoil you with affection in person.

However, if I am gone, I want you to know how similar you are to Mother. I was twelve when she left us. She was a brilliant, strong, opinionated woman, just like you. I know because many times, I witnessed Mother and Father arguing in the Library. I sat reading in the corner, unnoticed, while they yelled and screamed at each other. Their fights always ended with an embrace and a kiss. They loved each other and worked as a team.

Somehow, their strong personalities balanced each other. She tethered his ego; he tempered her strong will. Alone, they are extreme examples of character. After her passing, I watched Father morph into a demanding, controlling demigod, something mother would have prevented.

Olive, find yourself a loving husband to champion you. Someone to place you on a pedestal, worship you for the extraordinary woman you are. Monetary wealth is not necessary for happiness. Wealth is found in the peace of one's heart. You are so much stronger than I am, yet, being older, I am obligated to be your protector. If I'm gone, you must find a substitute.

Darling Olive, I write this as I watch you sleep, an innocent child of nine, the night before I depart for West Point. Your angelic face and loving heart move me to tears. Please stay true to your dream. Search for the love you are missing. Live a full and happy life, and know that I shall always love you and be with you.

With my everlasting devotion,

Fred

Olive re-read Fred's parting letter a dozen times. Tenderly holding the letter in one hand, she retrieved the photo of herself and Fred at his West Point graduation from her dresser. She stared at it, tracing Fred's face with her finger. She barely recognized her gown. Cradling both photo and letter, she crawled under Fred's old quilt, where she remained—eyes red, throat raw—in a postictal stupor, not moving for two days.

∞∞∞∞

"Olive, stop this. You must leave your room to eat," Henderson called gently on his way to breakfast, Sunday morning. "I, too, grieve Fred's loss. Four days is long enough for intense grief. You must force yourself to prod on." His voice cracked. "Olive, please, you'll make yourself sick."

To Henderson's shock, Olive's door opened. Henderson was met with a smelly, ungroomed imitation of his daughter holding a letter opener at his throat.

"Get away from me, you murdering fiend. I swear, I'll slit your gullet, ear to ear, without a single thought of regret. I vowed twice never to speak to you again; I intend to keep that vow. I shall only communicate as your employee. From this day on, I am no longer your daughter. I renounce everything '*Westchester*.'" She spat on his face as she closed the door.

Henderson stood looking through red eyes at the door. Then, to himself, he said with lament, "She'll come around, she must. She's too used to luxury, and Tabs won't be able to provide that for her. She still depends on me, just as much as I need her."

Overhearing every word, Olive tossed a shoe at the door.

∞∞∞∞

Tabs arrived early afternoon, at the scheduled time. He wondered at the black cloth draped over the doorway as a confused Cook greeted him.

"Mr. Bailey, I'm surprised to see you today."

"Why so? Our arrangement is for me to call Sunday afternoons, to join the family for dinner and visit with Olive."

"Did you not receive the news? Captain Fred was killed in battle. Miss Olive is overwhelmed with grief." Cook dabbed her eyes.

Tabs swooned, supporting himself on the doorway as he grabbed for Cook's hand, "Please show me to her room. I did not know; otherwise, I would have come to comfort Olive sooner."

"Mr. Bailey, you may not enter Miss Olive's room without a chaperone."

"This is no time for convention. If Olive is suffering, I must be allowed to console her." Tabs climbed the stairs. "Show me her room, or I shall knock on each door until I find her."

"Top, turn right, first room on the left. I'll not be part of this unseemly encounter." Cook retreated to the kitchen as Tabs hurried upstairs.

"Olive, dear. It's me, Tabs; please open the door." No response. Tabs tried again. "Olive, please, I know about Fred. Allow me to share your pain."

Tabs waited several minutes before the door finally opened. He gasped when he saw his once beautiful betrothed. Olive's cotton nightdress clung to her body with sweat. One side of her usually curly hair lay flat against her head, the other sprang straight out, from her constant tugging. Red, puffy eyes were mere slits, swollen from tears. He gently pushed open the door and carefully stepped over the papers scattered on the floor. Pulling Olive to sit beside him on the bed, he wrapped his arm around her.

"Sweet darling, I'm here. Let go and cry."

Olive convulsed, then sank into his arms. The manly smell of shaving soap intoxicated her as she wept for Fred. Her salty tears flowed nonstop. Olive continuously, rhythmically struck his shoulder with one fist as she allowed the pain to exit her body. Tabs endured the discomfort as he clung tightly. His only action was to hand her his handkerchief.

After thirty minutes of weeping, she pushed away, smoothed back her hair, and blew her nose.

"Are you feeling a little better darling?" Tabs asked as he kissed her hand.

"Is that smell coming from me?" Olive scrunched her nose.

Tabs laughed. "I believe, yes. This time, offenses of the nose are your doing, not mine."

She inhaled deeply, then coughed at the odor, "Goodness. I must bathe before dinner. Are you eating with us?"

"Yes, if I am still welcome." Relieved, Tabs volunteered, "Perhaps I shall join the family below and give you time to make yourself presentable."

Olive looked at her reflection. "Good God! I'm a stinking fright."

"You are filled with grief and beauty." He kissed her cheek before he left.

Tabs waited dutifully in the foyer, avoiding the Westchester family. After forty-five minutes, Olive descended the stairs. Her wet hair was loosely pulled back in a tie, and she wore a cotton skirt and short sleeve blouse.

"You look refreshed and more like your beautiful self," Tabs said.

Olive simply smiled. "Will you join me in a picnic? I refuse to break bread with my despicable father, the heathen. I called the kitchen before my bath to arrange for a basket."

"Sounds lovely, my dear."

"Tobias, I want to walk up the hill to our family cemetery. We picnic there each Epiphany. I should like to eat there today."

"Certainly, Olive. Lead the way." Tabs carried the blanket and basket of food, following Olive away from the house and up the hill to the home of the dead. "What a beautiful view. This is a lovely place to spend eternity."

Olive scowled, "Not if you're only twenty-five, like Fred, or forty-five, like Mother."

"Oh, Olive, let us avoid melancholy. I'm sorry." Tabs spread the blanket on the ground in the middle of the elm trees. "What have we to eat?" He rummaged through the basket, finding beef sandwiches, cucumber slices, and iced tea.

"Tobias?" Olive slid next to Tabs on the blanket.

"Yes, darling Olive?"

Olive did not pose a question; instead, she leaned over and kissed Tabs long and hard on the mouth.

"My, that was unexpected," Tabs stammered, flustered by Olive's boldness. "And very pleasant."

Olive thought back to Fred's instruction, "*find someone to place you on a pedestal, worship you for the extraordinary woman you are.*" Tabs was the only person to ever express unconditional love to her.

"Then this shall be even more pleasant." Olive slithered next to Tabs; her chest pinned his back against a tree. Tabs resisted, pushing her away.

"Please, Olive, my willpower is at a low. Do not tempt me so."

Olive's entire body ached from Fred's death. She felt everything and nothing at the same time. Olive understood the intense love of a brother; could the love of a man, a beau, help fill the void? She knew nothing of intimacy, except that Tildy and Sally seemed to thrive on it. That knowledge spurred her on.

"Oh, but I *want* to tempt you. I am empty. I want to feel. Make me feel again, Tabs." She kissed him again as she unbuttoned his shirt, convinced this act would ease her suffering.

"No, Olive, you must not coax me." Tabs clumsily fastened his shirt.

"Am I not desirable?" Olive sat up, their faces nose to nose, her voice coquettish and coy.

"You are most alluring. It is I who is weak, unable to reject my urge." Tabs trembled with desire. "Please, Olive, stop."

"My heart is hollow, Tabs, void of love. Help me fill it, my dear Tobias, please help me feel love." Olive ran her fingers through Tabs's hair. "Do you not love me?"

"I beg you, Olive, I cannot fight your advances." Making one last effort to dissuade Olive, Tabs slid around the tree. Olive followed, crawling on her hands and knees.

"Stop fighting Tabs. Your war is over." Olive's mouth engulfed Tabs's lips. The poor, celibate veteran, overcome with passion, abandoned his resistance and allowed natural events to unfold. Gently, he claimed Olive's innocence.

Blissfully spent, Tabs lay back on the quilt, ecstatic, every imagined pleasure fulfilled. Olive lay beside him, a single tear in her eye. *Foolish idea*, she thought. She could not bring herself to tell this loving, tender man that her emptiness remained. She was as hollow now as she was before.

She had not found love.

EIGHT ITEMS

*N*ine weeks sped by. Fred's death faded into the distance for everyone in the family except Olive. Although her father tried to engage her in conversation, she avoided Henderson, speaking to him only on the phone about farm concerns.

Tabs loyally visited every Sunday afternoon; Olive received him cordially, but remained aloof. Further conjugal encounters were nonexistent, despite weekly picnics in the cemetery.

"Olive, look below. That looks like an Army sedan in your drive." Tabs pointed to the green car, flags flying above each headlight parked in front of the house.

"Wonder what they want. Maybe Levi finally got his comeuppance." Olive's laugh was guttural, almost sinister.

"My dear, that's not very Christian of you," Tabs rebuked, his tenor voice dropped an octave.

"Well, Levi is no longer Christian. Shall we investigate?" Olive grabbed Tabs's hand—their first physical contact in eight weeks—and dragged him down the hill.

A box, placed on the porch, and an Army Captain awaited Henderson's arrival.

"What have we here?" Henderson asked.

"Mr. Westchester, please accept my condolences. This box contains Captain Westchester's personal effects." The emissary reached to shake Henderson's hand. "His remains are buried in France."

Olive, within earshot, gasped. Her knees buckled as Tabs caught and steadied her. She approached slowly while Henderson thanked the Captain and removed the lid from the box. Olive collapsed on the porch step as Henderson lifted one badly mangled dog tag. Fred's name, rank, and service number were barely readable. Well-worn copies of *The War of the Worlds* by H. G. Wells and *The Picture of Dorian Gray* by Oscar Wilde. A crumpled photo of Fred and Olive together at his academy graduation was inserted in the first pages of a pocket-sized New Testament Bible. Fred's Captain insignia and cap, a folded American flag, and a letter from his commanding officer completed the box's inventory.

Eight items.

Olive's body trembled despite Tabs's embrace. Henderson opened the envelope and read aloud, voice shaking.

Dear Mr. Westchester,

I am Colonel William Cramer, Captain Fred Westchester's commanding officer. It is with grave sadness that I write to you of Fred's passing. Captain Westchester was a valiant brave soldier. His men held him with the utmost love and respect.

Your son died a hero's death. On July 18, 1918, at the second battle for the Marne, a group of German storm troopers attacked our command center, trying to destroy communication between officers and troops. Captain Westchester foiled the attack by lobbing a grenade into a cluster of Germans. Unfortunately, a German grenade landed at his feet. Captain Westchester threw his body on top of the mortar as it exploded, sacrificing himself for the wellbeing of his fellow officers and staff. He saved thirty lives.

Captain Westchester exemplified the essence of an Army officer. You should be proud; he served well.

With my deepest sympathy for the loss of a brave soldier and your son,

Colonel William Cramer.

Hearing Henderson read the letter, Olive sat on the edge of the porch, gagged, then vomited off the side, her stomach rejecting its picnic lunch. Tabs extended his handkerchief, but she swatted away his hand. Tenderly, Tabs leaned over, wiped Olive's mouth, and stroked her hair as tears welled in her eyes.

"Olive dear, steady yourself. Come here." Tabs offered his arm.

Olive stared blankly at both men and the contents of the box. Henderson gazed at the ceiling.

"One small box, containing eight items, sums up a life. How tragic." Her comment barely audible, she turned to Henderson. "This will be your legacy, a dozen insignificant items cataloging your life as Westchester despot."

"Olive, your father suffers also. You must be kind." Tabs reached for her.

Laughing cheerlessly, Olive rose to her feet. Stopping at the garden's edge, she vomited again.

∞∞∞∞

Two weeks later, Levi, Sylvia, Ginny, and Samuel arrived with much fanfare for Fred's memorial service. The entire family, minus Olive, traveled into town to greet them at the station. Sylvia was welcomed into the Westchester family with open arms by Sally and Bessie. Ginny, having aged, sported visible wrinkles around her eyes and across her forehead. Olive ran to the car as it parked in front of the house. She avoided everyone but Samuel.

"Sammy!" She embraced the youngster, pulling him away from the crowd. No one else received a greeting from Olive. "I want to hear all about school and life in the big city."

"Oh Olive, I have so much to tell you." The two made their way to the backyard, sitting on the swing. Sammy talked nonstop.

White, puffy clouds dotted a blue sky. Perfect weather for an outdoor ceremony. That afternoon, Tildy, Tommy, and Uncle James joined the residents of Westchester Farms to pay tribute to their fallen hero.

Olive's entire body spasmed with each round shot during the three-volley salute. A bugler playing taps was echoed by an answering bugle on an adjoining hill. Olive, ready to collapse, found support in Tabs, Samuel, and Benny. The three encircled her body, giving a necessary hand or gentle touch when needed. Ingrid stood, stoic, at Benny's side.

Henderson erected a memorial stone for Fred in the family cemetery. Smaller than Polly's obelisk or the grand stones of previous family heads, the curved monument was carved on top with an eagle, the symbol of West Point.

Olive insisted that Fred's bible, cap, and insignia be buried in lieu of a body. Throwing a rose in the open shallow grave, she retched, ran, and vomited behind a tree.

∞∞∞∞

"Ginny, what are your plans for the future?" asked Sally, as the family retreated to the dining room to eat a light lunch. Olive and Tabs sat in the foyer, picking at a few items on her plate.

"I found another job in Philadelphia; we are staying." Ginny glanced at Samuel's frown. "I'm running a different household, one of the neighbors. Samuel wishes to return to Campbellsville. He misses Olive. Can you imagine?"

"Please, Mother, Olive is my friend," Samuel defended.

"For heaven's sake. Why Olive?" Sally chortled. "She is such a dreadful bully."

"I thought the two of you were bosom buddies?" questioned Ginny.

"You have been gone for too long, Sister-in-Law. Olive showed early friendship potential when she was young. However, she turned out to be just a useful tool, an entrance into the family." Sally snickered at her confession.

Overhearing the conversation, Olive hurled tea sandwiches at both women. "You wicked, two-faced cows," she screamed as she raced to the bathroom, ready to spew her lunch. The women laughed, shaking their heads in agreement, as Tabs chased after Olive.

THE LIGHT

SPRING, 1919

"No. A thousand times, no, I do not want to marry you." Olive angrily deflected Tobias Bailey's weekly Sunday proposal. "This agreement was between you and Father. I want nothing to do with it."

"But Olive, our child shall be born in less than a month. Please, do the right thing, permit me to make you an honest woman."

"Ha. Honest. That is a joke. I am an accountant, and most honest." She pushed Tabs away as he reached for her. "We go through this every week. I shall not marry you."

"Darling, I do not understand. Why would you raise our child alone, in a hostile home, when I can provide love? This is not just your child; it is also mine." Tabs followed Olive through the yard.

"I initiated its creation. I shall take responsibility for it." Olive flung her hands to her hips but automatically moved them to support her back. "I never wanted a husband or a family, that was your agreement with Father. All I ever wanted to do was get an education. I made one silly mistake, and I'll pay for the rest of my life. You need not be obligated to the same debt."

"You are so headstrong. How do you intend to raise a child *and* dream of college?" Tabs uncharacteristically raised his voice. "I do say, you are frustrating at times."

"I'll raise my child on my own, and I'll teach myself." Olive pushed Tabs away as he tried to approach.

"I want this family; I want you as my family," Tabs insisted. "I love you."

"Then you are a fool." Olive spit the words, then spun away.

Tabs followed, discouraged but eternally optimistic. He looked dapper in Levi's discarded clothing. Walking through the garden, she stopped to cut a bouquet of daffodils for her desk. Bending at the waist, she could neither reach the flowers nor stand. She was suspended halfway, big belly prohibiting movement in either direction.

"Blasted...! Tabs, help me stand up. This baby shall not arrive soon enough." Olive struggled to stand erect. Tabs gently attended to her needs as he continued his argument for marriage.

"Olive, you know the pitfalls of growing up with one parent. Do not saddle our child with that burden."

"I grew up without a mother. What I really needed was a mother's love." Olive motioned to the farm. "I got this instead, my father, my curse. This," she said, pointing to her stomach, "shall have all it needs. Its mother. I'll find a way to raise it alone and to get my schooling. I have some money." She added, wistfully, "There must be a way."

"You unjustly accuse me of mimicking your father. He and I are vastly different personalities." Tabs searched Olive's face for a sense of motherly love. "What you refer to as 'it' is a child, our baby."

"Silence, Tabs! No more. Your visits are no longer welcome. I release you of your commitment. Go, and leave me alone." Olive scowled, waddling up the sidewalk, onto the front porch, and into the house. She closed the door in Tobias Bailey's face.

Tabs pounded on the door, "Olive, do not walk away from me—from us! We shall be a family." There was no answer.

∞∞∞∞

Sally heard the moaning as she exited the nursery. "Olive, what's the matter?" Olive sat on the edge of her bed, holding the bottom of her protruding belly with sticky red fingers, looking at the rose-colored puddle on the floor.

"I think it's time. But something doesn't feel right, Sally; the pain extends further than my womb. Will you call the doctor?" Terrified of what was coming next, Olive's face revealed her youth.

"Don't worry, Olive, we'll take care of you. You are going to be just fine." Sally rubbed Olive's back, then made her leave.

Running into the barn, Sally shouted, "Clyde, Olive's time has arrived. Please call Dr. Paulson; there may be a problem. She was bleeding when I checked on her. And call Mr. Bailey. Even though Olive stubbornly refuses to marry him, he admirably insists he wants to be part of this child's life. As much as I hate saying this, I'm going back up to be with Olive."

Bessie, Ingrid, and Nellie joined Sally in Olive's bedroom. Her contractions were coming too quickly for a first pregnancy; however, her cervix was not dilating. Blood covered the bedsheet.

Olive moaned through a contraction; Nellie took her hand.

Dr. Paulson arrived with Tabs in tow. Tabs rushed to Olive's side, taking her hand from Nellie. He spoke softly, soothingly as Olive screamed through another contraction.

"What are you doing here?" Olive asked, bewildered to see a man.

"Tabs, you need to leave," Dr. Paulson ordered. "I don't want a man in my birthing room."

"I am staying. Permit me to hold her hand. I'll keep out of your way," Tabs insisted as he pulled a chair beside Olive's head. Olive leaned her face to his hand.

"This may be traumatic; the baby is breech, coming bottom first," Dr. Paulson said. "Both baby and mother are in mortal danger and the midwife is out on another call. Sally, I need lots of warm—not hot—towels. We must trick the baby into thinking it's still in the womb. If it comes out butt-first and starts breathing, it will drown."

Dr. Paulson barked his orders. On further examination, he realized that an episiotomy must be performed.

"Olive, do not push yet. You must wait." Olive moaned; Paulson continued, "I know it is difficult, but with each contraction you must squeeze your legs together, until Sally returns. Try hard."

"I can't hold back. It wants to come." Olive winced.

Tabs caressed her hand and brushed her unruly hair off her face.

"Am I going to die?" Olive asked, terrified of the pain and the doctor's instructions. She vaguely remembered climbing onto her mother's bed, soaked in blood.

"No, darling, you shall not die." Tabs's calming voice failed its mission; his hands shook with worry.

Henderson, waiting outside the door, overheard Olive's question. "No!" he said. "Not my little Polly!"

"I feel like I shall die!" Olive screeched, as another contraction began. "Tabs, I'm afraid. I don't think I can do this alone."

The women stared at each other as Olive admitted fear. Henderson began to pace the hall.

"You are not alone, Olive. I'm right here with you," Tabs soothed as her contractions quickened. "I'll care for you and the baby."

"Olive," Ingrid said. "I'm here for you, too. So is Nellie. We love you, dear."

"Me too, little Olive," said Bessie, remembering the tiny child fourteen years ago, who desperately wanted to stay with Polly.

"Olive, do not push," Dr. Paulson growled. "Not yet. I'll tell you when it's time."

Finally, Sally returned. She handed the hot towels to the doctor.

"You hold onto these, Sally. I must make an incision to make room for the baby. Olive is too small for it to come out. As soon as I cut, the baby will try to move, so place the towels on the baby's bottom, immediately."

Olive wailed with the incision. She looked down and saw more blood; her eyes rolled back into her spinning head.

"Olive, push now, push hard!" Dr. Paulson's voice sounded fuzzy. Olive's ears rang. "Tabs, talk to her, keep her focused."

Paulson worked frantically to extract the baby.

"Olive, stay with me, Olive. You must help the doctor," Tabs whispered, directly into her ear.

"Now!" said Paulson.

"Olive, push now. Come, come, you can do it!" Tabs encouraged.

She pushed as the voices grew faint. Olive knew she was not alone, but she heard no one, not even Tabs. The buzzing of a thousand bees filled her ears. She looked up to see from whence they came. Instead of bees, she saw a tiny white light reflecting off the ceiling, peeking in from a crack in the draperies.

"Push, Olive."

"Olive, stay with us."

"Olive, focus."

"Olive."

"Olive!"

Olive concentrated on staring above.

The baby girl cried as she gulped her initial human breath. With overwhelming joy, Tabs viewed his child for the first time.

"Olive, darling! We have a beautiful baby daughter." Tabs clasped Olive's hand. "Olive, Olive!"

The illumination on the ceiling grew. Beams shot out from an intense, white-hot center and morphed into a circle of spots, resembling a necklace—a pearl necklace.

Olive focused on the pearl lights overhead and said with a smile, "Mama, it's me, Olive. Mama."

AUTHOR'S NOTES

- All characters and the town of Campbellsville in this novel are fictional. Any resemblance to places or persons living or otherwise is strictly coincidental.

- The National Society, Daughters of the American Revolution, was established in 1890. Any woman, age eighteen and above with ties to a direct ancestor that fought in the American Revolution, is eligible to apply for membership. The society verifies all lineage before granting membership.

- The author is a member in good standing of NSDAR. Her primary membership is with the Myakka chapter, Venice, Florida. She is an associate member of the Jacob Ferree chapter, Pittsburgh, PA.

- The cost of one strand of sixteen electric Christmas lights in the early 1900s is equivalent to over three hundred dollars per strand in today's money.

- Olive's wedding gift to Tildy of twenty dollars would be the equivalent of five hundred dollars today.

- Tommy and Tildy's loss of $5,200.00 was the loss of a small fortune, having the purchasing power equal to about $140,000.00 in today's economy.

- West Point's graduating class of 1915 was known as the "class the stars fell on." Dwight D. Eisenhower, Omar Bradley, Sydney Graves, Henry Pendleton, and Stafford Irwin were members of the class. Fifty-nine of the 164 graduates of the class of 1915 received the rank of General.

- John P. Mitchel was the second-youngest mayor of New York City, elected at age thirty-four.
- The description of the West Point graduation meal, parade ceremony and speakers are the creation of the author. However, both the mayor of NYC and the President of the US are examples of traditional speakers at West Point graduation ceremonies.
- William E. R. Covell graduated first in the class of 1915, followed by Edwin R. Kimble ranking a close second. Kimble died in WWI, Covell became a general during WWII. Kimble's brother's real name was Frederick, however, the author changed it to prevent confusion. The description of Kimble's mother was the creation of the author.
- The death of Aunt Clare from Philadelphia is loosely assumed to be from the Spanish flu. However, the pandemic of the previous century occurred between February 1918 and April 1920. The Spanish flu pandemic is attributed to the death of between seventeen million to fifty million people, worldwide. Some reports estimate the total death toll to be as high as one hundred million.

A FAMILY SAGA

Becoming Olive W.: The Women of Campbell County: Family Saga Book 1, is the first book in the series documenting the Westchester, Bailey, and Kepler families. Continue your adventure with Henderson, Tabs, and many new characters by reading *Under the Grapevine: The Women of Campbell County: Family Saga Book 2,* due the summer of 2021.

Do you want to duplicate the food mentioned in the book? Come join my newsletter and get some of Olive's favorite recipes.

https://www.subscribepage.com/q4y8x5

ACKNOWLEDGMENTS

With thanks to my darling husband Ralph and to my fabulous betas, Bridgett, Inghild, and Dar.

ABOUT THE AUTHOR

Becoming Olive W is **S. Lee Fisher's** second novel and the first book of her new *The Women of Campbell County: Family Saga* series. Book two in the series, *Under the Grapevine*, is expected to be published summer of 2021. Fisher began writing about emotionally charged relationships as a tool to channel her personal grief of losing her father. Happily married to her husband of thirty-six years, she and Ralph live on the gulf coast of Florida.

www.sleefisher.com

Facebook: @SherriLeeFisherProgar
Twitter: @ProgarSherri
Amazon: @author/sleefisher

WILL YOU HELP?

Thank You for Reading My Book!

I really appreciate your feedback, and I love hearing what you have to say.

I need your input to make the next version of this book and my future books better.

Please leave me an honest review on Amazon letting me know your thoughts.

With gratitude!
S. Lee Fisher